Don't Bug me
I'm Reading

Bill York

75 stories from a non-comformist's mind:
Educational-Contentious-Fictional-Adventurous-Inspirational
Levity-Reality

iUniverse, Inc.
Bloomington

Don't Bug Me; I'm Reading

iUniverse books may be ordered through booksellers or by contacting:

iUniverse
1663 Liberty Drive
Bloomington, IN 47403
www.iuniverse.com
1-800-Authors (1-800-288-4677)

ISBN: 978-1-4759-1387-3 (sc)
ISBN: 978-1-4759-1388-0 (e)

Printed in the United States of America

iUniverse rev. date: 8/8/2012

Other books

Fatal Encounters---Fatal Ambition---Reflection of the Great Spirit
Valley of Silent Drums---Episodes of Revenge---My Name is Cougar

The writer's conviction

WHEN GOD IS FORSAKEN
IDOLATRY WILL REIGN SUPREME

WHEN IDOLATRY REIGNS
SUPREME
EVIL WILL FLOURISH

WHEN EVIL FLOURISHES
THE END IS NEAR

Contents

Warning

The average lifespan of a society is 200 years. Nations wealthier and more powerful in their day than we are now have fragmented morally, been sabotaged from within, defeated by circumstances beyond their control and then disappeared into the annals of time.

Visigoths	Mayans
Saxons	Phoenicians
Wallachians	Polynesians
Celts	Goths
Franks	Abyssinians
Normans	Incas
Athenians	Mycenians
Trojans	Aztecs
Philistines	Macedonians
Hittites	Assyrians
Spartans	Persians
Babylonians	Estrucans
Carthegenians	Moors
Mesopotanians	Medes
Romans	Vandals
Vikings	Khmer Rough
Mongols	Canaanians
Huns	Ming
Byzantians	Shang
Ottomans	Xis
Olmecs	Yuan
Sumerians	Nazis
Maoris	Jomons
Clovis	Judahens

Toltecs

Zhou

Nubians

Minoans

Native Americans

IS AMERICA NEXT?

Jerusalem

History cannot be modified but people should be guided by the knowledge gleaned from that experience

During the time, from 800 BC to 400 B.C., spanning a 400 year chronicle, the world witnessed the destruction of Jerusalem because of corruption and wickedness in the city. The demise was assured when they became idolaters. If we do not learn from history, it is bound to repeat itself. This society is destructing with adulation of social fetishes and contrived sports idols. We grovel with supplication for an autograph. We blather in reverence at screaming entertainers on stage. We are being anesthetized by drugs and alcohol. We are mesmerized by pornography. We lust for gratification. We are drowning in materialism. We are obsessed with orgasms and lewd nakedness. We are brain-damaged by purveyors of decadence. We are trained like Pavlov's dogs and too many of us respond like herd animals. We are breeding a sub-human-culture of people including thugs, crooks, scammers, murderers, pedophiles and rapists. At our present rate of putrefaction we will replicate the cataclysmic end of Jerusalem in less than four-hundred years. Two hundred years have gone by since the beginning of our demise. Less that one hundred years remain for a nation that once was considered the beacon of hope in a troubled world.

Thoughts by the Author

While researching information for this book I was overwhelmed by the statistics I discovered involving criminality of every imaginable kind all the way from increased shoplifting to massive fraud.Those aberrations cover the gamut of criminal behavior. Earlier in this decade society was being traumatized with bank robberies, home break–ins, carjacking, and theft of anything that could be sold or exchanged for drugs. With the economy fragmenting thefts now involve desperate people who are preying on those more fortunate in order to feed their children, make house payments and survive. That need is being influenced by the increasing disparity between the exceedingly wealthy and the impoverished citizens.

Congress, by its members becoming ultra-rich after a short tenure in office, has created understandable hostility and resentment among the masses. Voters now feel that they have been conned by politicians who are intent on amassing their personal fortunes.

A tour golfer recently bought a $50,000,000 mansion. A retired basketball player purchased a $30,000,000 mansion while forty-nine million Americans exist below the poverty level, with many sleeping on the streets in cardboard boxes. A baseball player recently inked a $126,000,000 contract in spite of an unimpressive batting average and an equally unimpressive home run record. Sport players are now receiving multi-million contracts with many fans unable to afford tickets. Golfers, wearing designer's clothing, make thousands of dollars for winning one hole in a skins-game.

An idolized Hollywood star received $25,000,000 for making a movie about a whore.

BMW's, Mercedes, Jaguars, Cadillac's and Lincolns continue to sell in a lack-luster market. Auctioning of costly jewelry and paintings continues to flourish.

Astute theoreticians are beginning to compare this society to the final days of the Roman Empire. With the plunge in Presidential approval others are comparing America to the Titanic. We are moving across uncharted shoals without sufficient life jackets. At this rate of social decay anarchy will ultimately prevail. From the calamitous decline in morality the character of Al Adams evolved.

Prologue

"You may know me. We may have spoken while waiting in line at the grocery store. We may go to the same hairdresser, the same library. I may belong to your reading group or work out in the same gym. You could have served my lunch or dinner in one of my favorite restaurants or helped me select a dress in one of the small shops I frequent. We may even belong to the same church. I could be any of those hundreds of faces you encounter during your daily routine. However, reality is reality, along with an anonymous face, I can't be seen anymore anywhere because one year ago my husband murdered me."

"He is now in prison charged with 1st degree homicide and is awaiting trial."

"Hallelujah!"

My Husband Murdered Me

Chapter one

Al Adams took out his five-iron and fingered the face of the club. Wetting a finger and holding it in the breeze, Al's caddie recommended he hit the four-iron instead because of the wind that was blustering in their faces. Leaves swirled across the fairway.

"Look at the tops of the pines." Jack pointed. "It is blowing right at us," he said. "If you don't carry the green you are going to be way short of the pin. That's a tough green."

The gallery was strolling like snails across the fairway. Al wished they would get the hell out of his way. He glowered at the mob of teenagers who screamed just before the club head came into contact with the ball. They should be moved farther away from the fairway. The spectators were starting to piss Al off, clapping when he made a tremendous drive and clapping and screaming when he hit a hook or a slice.

"It makes no damned difference if we make an eagle or make a triple bogey they react the same," Al snapped. "They are like a bunch of damned organ-grinder monkeys, like marionettes, like Pavlov's dogs. They seem trained to applaud. We had one 68, a 69 plus two 70's in our foursome yesterday. That's 275 strokes. These morons clapped 275 times. I had four nuts run into me yesterday when they tried to get my autograph. Don't they have something better to do? The country has turned into a nation of spectators. Everybody is a brainwashed fan of sports of every kind, football, baseball, basketball, golf, racing, tennis and many more, and the reason for the lunacy is money, enormous salaries, signing bonuses, higher priced hot dogs and cokes. Television hustlers are marketing shit you don't need at crazy prices you can't afford. Shitty movies are promoting over-priced decadence. I remember when I could go to the baseball games for a couple bucks. Now watch the jerks. They'll clap if one of us farts."

"They sure clap at everything, don't they?" Jack said.

"They only know three words; oooohhhh, aaaahhhh, aaaawwww. I'm sick of the charade," he said.

"Jack said. "This foursome all had pars on the last hole and I listened.

Four fours is sixteen. The gallery applauded sixteen times like fuckin' clockwork."

"They are controlled and manipulated by the controllers of this sport," Al said. "They can't play worth a shit but out here they are in the glorified Kingdom of Golf. It elevates them from nothing to greatness."

Adam's tried to scratch the itching on his crotch without seeming to do so. The Doctor's report had indicated a probable venereal disease but the confirmation would come later. He was starting to worry about the shack-up-jobs he had been involved with lately. Neosporin hadn't helped.

They stood waiting for a player up ahead to find his ball.

"I'm really sick of golf," Al said.

"It has been good to you, man."

"I know but these damned screaming spectators are driving me nuts. I watched a tennis match last night. It's the same, fans yelling and clapping after every shot. Shaking cow bells. The match went for five sets. They must have applauded three hundred times. They even clapped when a player went to the crapper."

"It's the same in all sports," Jack said. "People went into a frenzy of applause one year when one driver went over the wall in a fireball in Indianapolis. They clap when a fighter gets decked or when a quarterback is carried from the field. A hockey player got zapped in his eye by puck and the spectators clapped like mad."

"I wish they'd speed it up," Al said. He pointed, "Look at those broads over there in yellow with half their tits hanging out. If I showed half of my dick I'd get my ass tossed in jail."

He slammed his iron down in the turf. "Tell him to hit another damned ball!" he yelled down the fairway.

Jack motioned. "They found it. You can hit now."

"Okay, Jack, it was your call," he said. He grabbed the four-iron. The screamers yelled just as the club head started down. The yelling distracted him. The ball arced too high and got caught in the wind, dropping short of the green.

"I'd like to stick a putter up their asses," Al snarled.

"They're a fact of life anymore. It's crazy," Jack said.

"We were both wrong, I should have hit the three." Al scowled.

"Your back swing was too fast. You let those jerks bother you too much," Jack said.

"I need to piss," Al said, "but I can't stomach those smelly out houses."

Al attempted to scratch his crotch while the gallery was looking across the fairway. A place on his penis had begun to sting. The doctor figured he might have gotten a venereal bug somewhere. Al guessed it was from one of the sluts he screwed. He worried about it though.

The ball had a good lie in the shorter grass but it was forty feet to the pin. Al kneeled on the green. He saw the undulations. He was having trouble lining up the putt. A birdie was vital for him to make the cut. A camera flashed. He glared in that direction, wishing the monitor would move the gallery farther back. He could hear the hushed murmuring. He suspended his putter, calculating the move the ball would take. His eyes were drawn beyond the green observing the girl again, spandex pants and meaty breasts, a flashy broad. She had been following him most of the tournament.

She smiled, giving him a thumbs-up.

It was hard to concentrate on golf when images of bulbous-tits kept intruding in his mind. He recalled the pink chameleon tattoo on her ass. He adored females that were interested in experimenting.

Followers were pains-in-the-ass but they kept his nights from being boring. She looked familiar. Then Al remembered the ménage a trios' session at the Famous Club last month. She was one of the girls that had come to his room afterward and spent the night. He felt stirrings in his crotch. Beads of sweat ran down into his eyes, burning like fury. He rubbed and squinted.

He noticed the referee standing at the edge at the fairway motioning to speed up the game. He looked pissed. Al had failed to make the play-off in San Francisco because of a penalty. He grimaced and walked up to the ball. Putting quickly he saw the ball roll over the second cut then gain momentum. Damn, he had misjudged the curve. Instead of going toward the hole it caught the carpet then slowed before rolling from the green back down onto the fairway. It settled on the sprinkler head. There went the damned tournament. Al glowered at the referee.

Shouldering his way past the gaping puppets Al ignored the golf crap held out for his autograph. He glanced toward the girl. She winked and rolled her eyes. Al went into the tent to record his score. She was waiting when he emerged. He recalled a robin tattoo near her navel. He smiled. He remembered nibbling around the tattoo while she was squirming.

"Where is your car?" Al said.

"A friend dropped me off."

"Jenna?"

"Yes."

"Is she going to pick you up?"

"Yes."

"I'll be at your apartment at 8:00 o'clock."

"We'll be there."

"Is it the same arrangement?"

"Sure."

"Will it be the same price?"

"Sure."

"See you."

"Sorry about you not making the cut." She smiled.

"Becoming a damned habit," Al snapped.

"You'll be able to forget later tonight," she said.

"You bet," he said. The excitement began to build.

Al got his cell phone from his golf bag. There was a three hour time difference between California and Atlanta. He flicked the switch on and checked every camera in his house. He cursed. It was afternoon in Stone Mountain, and the bitch was still in bed. He'd have to take care of her again when he got back home. The security technician had done a good job hiding the cameras. Of course Trina was so stupid she wouldn't know what they were for anyhow. He got into his rental and headed for Marin County.

Chapter Two

Al rested nude on his back. Through the open draperies he could see Belvedere Island across Richardson Bay. Out the side pane he could see Angel Island. A sailboat was maneuvering into a Sausalito pier. It had been a frustrating month. He had about decided to give up golf since his game was heading in the wrong direction. He lifted his flaccid penis and fingered the lesions under his foreskin. Al knew he had caught some disease from one of the broads he had been fucking. A couple of sore places on his forehead worried him. They looked like the same virus Al had noticed on another golfer in the shower who had developed full-blown AIDS and died.

He could hear background music. The scent of Elizabeth Taylor's Diamonds perfume wafted across the bedroom. Females sure loved that smell, Al decided. He wondered when the girls would show up.

The ceiling was mirrored with a kaleidoscope of subtle lighting emanating from the corners of the bedroom. There were oil paintings lining the walls, nudes of statuesque females posing with males in explicit sexual poses. Al suddenly realized that he was in a whore house of complete debauchery. It made him a little uneasy. He was accustomed to those under-fucked housewives and college coeds who were nymphomaniacs, intrigued by the world of sports. The bedroom looked like it was designed for the crotch and tit business.

Al strangely thought about Trina with her little tits and her antiquated ideas on morality.

He listened to the garage door going up and the front door opening. He heard womanly giggles coming down the hallway. Al's heart began to thud and he could feel warmth in his groin. For some reason, he thought of the one girl's tattoos. Possibly the other girl would have tattoos in interesting places for him to examine.

"Hello, big boy," the second girl smiled. She was over six feet tall and had wheat-tone hair. She was as black as polished obsidian. "You here for good time, honey?" she began disrobing, flipping each piece like a stripper on stage. Latin music began in the background. The lighting began to dim.

Both girls began to strip completely, twisting their bodies to rhythmic burlesque music. It reminded him of the burlesque house he had visited when he was a kid, and the Gold Club in Atlanta after he became wealthy. It got your blood stirring.

They were down to nothing but flesh. "You go down and I'll go up," one girl said. The lighting dimmed even more.

Al felt their movement on the cover as the women slithered onto the bed. He felt their hands beginning to search. Al could sense the enlargement of his erection. His hands explored.

Al could feel one of the girl's hands touching his thighs. He was not sure which one was where, but it made little difference. One of them was moving over his face. He clutched at her thighs and put his hands up, pulling her downward. He felt her pubic hairs touching his lips. He could feel hot breathing on his stomach.

Al suddenly smelled the odors of a dirty urinal as the girl positioned herself onto his mouth. The smell was putrid like she hadn't bathed in weeks. He could feel a tiny particle of something on his tongue. Oh, my God! His erection collapsed.

"You tired or something?" one girl said in the dark.

Al squirmed up from the bed and stood up. He felt sick to his stomach.

"I'm leaving right now," he said.

"That's okay, honey," one of them said. The lighting turned brighter. It had been the white woman sitting on his face, the one with the stinking crotch.

Al dressed hurriedly.

"Just leave the money on the quilt," one girl said.

"That'll be a cold day in hell," Al snapped.

The white one pulled an object from her robe. "This is a remote control device. When I punch this button," she pointed to a button on the object, "our friends, who are sitting in a white Escalade out front, will know we have a problem. One of them teaches martial arts and the other is an ex-marine. They both have crow bars and their 9 millimeter Berettas. So, unless you want to meet them tonight just leave the $1000 on the bed."

Al glanced in the direction of the Cadillac Escalade as he exited the apartment. He saw two men in the front seat and quickly averted his gaze. As he pulled into southbound traffic on Highway 101, heading into San Francisco, he wondered why he continued to fool around with whores. He screamed aloud as he paid the toll on the Golden Gate, "$1000 for nothing and my winnings in a damned tailspin." His fury increased.

Chapter Three

Trina moved the lighted mirror up closer. She parted her hair and gently fingered the fading discolorations. She needed her hair cut and colored but the timing had to be just right. If she waited too long, Brandy, her stylist, might not notice the fading bruises although the girl was really nosy and often questioned every little spot. Usually, Trina waited until the bruises were gone but now she wanted to be positive Brandy saw enough to arouse suspicions. Trina had changed hair stylists several times during her marriage, even driving to other cities where it was likely no one would recognize her. She checked her eyes with the blood vessels still visible, and rubbed on her cheek. It was still painful inside her lower lip. She opened the top of her gown, examining her stomach with the purplish bruising. She lathered cream on her hands and face, staring at her countenance in the mirror. The beatings had to stop, she decided.

She went to the kitchen, poured coffee, and turned on the television. The golf channel was still on. She glanced at the time. It would be 10 o'clock now at Pebble Beach. She wondered what time Al was scheduled to tee off. She had not noticed his position on the scoreboard. She didn't know if he was still in contention. The voluptuous brunette that had been following Al around the course was standing near the 18th green. She had on skimpy shorts. Farther away, she could see Al walking down the 18th fairway. He evidently had played earlier. The girl smiled and waved as if they knew each other. Trina was more positive Al was cheating on her while he was on tour.

Trina's former classmates wouldn't recognize her now. They would remember the girl that had been pretty enough to win four beauty pageants. When she and Al were married everybody thought they were a ideal pair, Trina, a dark brunette with smiling eyes, and Al, dark eyes and black hair and just as handsome as she was beautiful.

Her husband had been a great golfer during high school, leading his team to the state championship for two years in a row. He was President of the senior class and voted the most likely to succeed. And, indeed, he had won major tournaments after qualifying for the PGA tour.

She was walking on clouds when Al had asked her to the senior prom and was the envy of her friends. Funny, neither her parents nor her brother and sister liked Al at all. Her brother, Bill, had told her many times, "I don't trust the guy, Sis. He's as phony as a three dollar bill."

If only I had listened to Bill, Trina thought; but then she remembered how nice Al had been to her. He had often told her, "Nothing is too good for my woman." She had protested that he was spending way too much on her.

They had gotten married right out of college and of course, he had demanded a fabulous wedding, really more than her parents could afford.

"So I can show everyone how important my wife is," he had whispered to her. "It'll make them jealous."

Now two weeks had gone by since their last savage fight. Devilishly, she smiled at herself in the mirror, knowing that the reign of brutality was just about over. She heard the announcer commenting that Al had missed a crucial putt on the eighteenth hole that would keep him out of the last round. Al would be furious when he came home. She sensed the beginning of that uneasiness in her stomach again.

She grabbed her purse, threw on her slacks and a blouse, backed the Jeep from the garage and headed for a nearby phone booth. Trina knew that Al would not be back until the middle of next week, allowing her several more days to plan. She could keep track of her nemesis while he was playing in a tournament. Television had at least one good thing about it. Trina had stopped going to his tournaments yet she could still keep tabs on him. It was somewhat annoying to watch girls hitting on him as he smiled his way to the last green. She spotted one hussy whom she had seen once before walking with Al during the tournament. She couldn't help but wonder if he was paying for her room, or even sharing it.

The phone booth was empty. Trina checked her change and entered the booth. She hoped her sister was home and had time to talk.

"Hey, kiddo, I'm glad you called. How is it going?"

"I'm healing."

"Asshole home yet?"

"No, he's at Pebble Beach. He'll be home tomorrow. He missed the cut again. As usual, he'll be furious."

"When are you going to leave that nut, honey?"

"I've told you before. Al has repeatedly said that I will be dead within a week if I leave him. He's really crazy Trish."

"You talk to Bill recently?"

"Yes. He says the same as you. But listen, Sis, Al is getting worse, if that's possible. I'm embarrassed to tell you this but he is getting kinky. Every time he is home he has another demand for the way I dress at night. He is even bringing home bright colored Victoria Secrets underwear and demanding that I put flashy lipstick on my face, and look like some slutty whore. Then he wants me to perform kinky dancing. And I hate to tell you but he now forces me to accept oral and anal contact. I want to vomit. He makes me sick.

"I just wouldn't do it Trina," Trisha said.

"When I act like I don't want to do that stuff, you know, refuse, that is the trigger that sets him off."

"Girl, you're going to have to do something."

Chapter Four

After discovering a camera mounted behind one of Al's trophies Trina called the local security firm. When a man introduced himself as the owner she explained what she had discovered that concerned her.

"Could you come over and check this out," she said.

"What's your name, ma'am?" the man said.

"Trina Adams. 212 Longview Drive. That is Mrs. Al Adams. I didn't know about any camera," she said.

There was a noticeable pause. "Mrs. Adams, I think it might be a good idea if you came into the office and we can discuss what you discovered. I installed several cameras in your home a few months ago."

"You're kidding," Trina said.

"No. Really. There are eight cameras in all. Do you mean your husband didn't tell you?"

"No he didn't tell me. Why did you do that?" Trina said.

"I installed them at your husband's request, ma'am."

"Why on earth did he do that?"

"Perhaps you need to come on in and we'll talk."

"I've seen your building. I'll be right there."

Trina was ushered into Samuel Collin's office by his secretary.

Mr. Collins went to his file cabinet and took out a folder. He laid it on his desk and removed two sheets of paper. He laid the sheets on his desk.

"This is a layout plan of your home, Mrs. Adams. It shows where I installed eight cameras."

Trina studied the layout. She pointed to a wall in the library. "That is where I saw one of the cameras. It shocked me terribly. That's why I called you. What did my husband say was his purpose for installing cameras?" she asked.

There was another hesitation. "Mr. Adams said that your house had been burglarized twice and he wanted to catch the person who did it. He seemed to think it was some kids in your neighborhood."

"Our home has never been burglarized," Trina said.

"I asked him if he'd reported the break-ins to the police. I was surprised when he said he hadn't. That's usually the first thing victims do. The police respond a lot faster to a call when they know a residence had previously been burglarized."

"There must be another reason for eight cameras. I have an idea," she said. "But it's rather personal."

"Mrs. Adams, can we talk off the cuff?"

"Certainly. Why?"

"I don't know, but when your husband and I made the installation deal I didn't believe he was being honest with me."

"Why?" Trina said.

"Well, I thought it was rather strange when he said he could keep his eyes on you, implying that perhaps you were involved when he was out of town."

"That's disgusting," Trina said. "He is the one being unfaithful while he's out of town, which is a lot of the time." She averted her gaze. "I'm sorry, I shouldn't have said that," Trina said.

"I had one case in my family where a man cheated on his wife. But he always accused her of cheating. I guess when one partner does it they're convinced everyone else does, too."

"But you came in for information. Let me explain to you what I did"

"This is a state-of-the-art camera system. I put a computer in your attic that monitors this program. Your husband can open his laptop when he is out of town and see exactly what those cameras see."

"Do you mean he can watch my every move while he's away?"

"That's right, ma'am," Samuel said.

Trina continued to examine the layout. "Why on earth would he want a camera in my bathroom?" Trina said as she pointed to the location. "It seems like a strange place to hide a camera." She hesitated. "Unless you're a voyeur or something like that."

"Your husband said burglars sometime wash up before leaving a house," the security man explained. "He wanted to have every chance to get a clear image."

"Oh, I see," she replied, in a voice that clearly indicated she did not.

"I want you to explain this program to the police if we ever have a problem," she said.

"I don't know what you mean, ma'am," Collins said.

Turning away from him, she said, "Well, you did such a good job concealing the cameras, if we did have a break in, the police might never find them all. I would like to be sure they would see everything that happened. Would they have any way to know who had installed them?"

Collins looked at her a couple of seconds too long and then answered, "I'd be sure they found every one of them ma'am."

"So, if something odd ever happens to me will you inform the police about all the cameras?"

"Certainly, ma'am," the man said.

Trina stood up to leave but Collins stopped her with a question.

"Mrs. Adams, did you notice anything strange about the placement of the cameras?"

"Personally I think the entire thing is strange, especially in my bathroom. Actually, that's more than strange. It's sick." Trina answered.

"I agree with you completely, but, if your house had been burglarized and you decided to put in security cameras in an attempt to photograph the burglars, where would you want the cameras located?"

Trina thought for a moment and suddenly she knew exactly where Collins was going with his question and she answered, "Outside, of course!"

"Bingo," said Collins, "in all the years I've been in this business, this is the first time I have installed this many cameras inside a house and none outside." He added, "Do you mind if I call you Trina?"

"Please do," she responded. "I think we are well past formalities and I really appreciate you telling me all this."

"I was curious when you called, but I've had mixed emotions until I met you. You remind me of my daughter-in-law and I don't want anything ever to happen to you, Trina. I have no idea what your husband had in mind, but every room in your home, except your husband's bathroom, has a camera. As far as I can determine, your garage is where you are most vulnerable. Anyone could hide and be waiting for you there, or slip in while the garage door is opening. Be careful, lady, be careful and call me if you need me."

He walked her to the door and she gave him a hug as she left the office. "Thank you so much, Mr., uh, Sam. You may have just saved my life."

Trina was pleased with the way the visit had gone and knew without a doubt that Collins was now suspicious of Al's motives.

Chapter Five

Trisha answered the third ring. "How are you doing Sis?" Trisha said.

"I'm healing," Trina said.

"Is your lovable golfer out of town?"

"He's in Carmel and won't return until Friday."

"Great. Can you fly out for a few days so we can talk? I'm thinking up some more ideas. I think you'll approve."

"I have already made reservations. Will you meet me at the airport?"

"When are you due in?"

"Tomorrow at 2:15."

"You talk to Bill lately?"

"Yes, but we have a problem. Can you call him and ask him to meet us at your house?"

"What's going on?" Trisha wanted to know.

"It's a bit more complicated than we had thought and I definitely need to talk to both of you together, before Bill attempts to do some to Al. I'd feel better if the three of us could sit down and revise our plans somewhat."

"Oh no, don't you dare tell me you're getting cold feet! I thought you were ready to go through with this. You can't, you…you…just can't."

Trina interrupted her, "Whoa Sis, slow down. I am even more ready now than I have ever been. We just need a meeting with Bill before we can proceed."

"He's planning to open up Al's computer and check some files. I am so glad we have a computer geek in the family but I don't know if even he can solve this one," Trina said.

"If it can be done, our little brother can do it," Trisha said. "Do you remember when Dad first bought his computer and had trouble with the thing? It drove him up the wall. And when Bill, who had never seen a computer, started operating it without dad knowing, the child was fascinated, and within a week or two he was instructing our father on how to open it and develop files. Bill was what, six or seven? Remember?"

"I do. I still don't know enough about computers."

"Bill knows, so don't make him mad because he can send a bug to eat your hard drive from long distance."

"Does Al use the computer a lot?"

"I think so. Sometimes when I get up to go to the bathroom a light will be on in the den and occasionally I will sneak up to the door and listen and I can hear keys clicking, so I know when he is using the computer. Sometime he'll be in there for hours. At least he isn't pounding on me. That's something."

"Your problems are almost over. You can bet on it," Trisha assured her sister.

"I'll be so glad to see you and Bart. It has been over a year now. Twins should not stay apart that long. If we had been joined at birth we could have spent more time together."

"At least you still have a sense of humor."

"It comes and goes," Trina said

"Sis, we have two more llamas now. JuJu gave birth to twins last week. One of them is an albino. It's cute as a button. They are already up and scrambling around."

"Did you get the miniature ponies in yet?"

"Truck arrived yesterday. You are going to adore them, Sis. They follow us around like little puppies."

"I cannot wait. I will be really glad to get out of this hell-hole," Trina said.

"Bart has your cottage about completed, facing the lake. He gave you fourteen acres out on that point where a stream feeds into the lake. You can furnish the place the way you want to after you get here. You will almost be able to fish from your front porch. He has your pier nearly done, too. He bought you a kayak."

"I really can't wait, Trish. I am so very grateful to you and Bart."

"Trina, do you remember where the picnic table was located?"

"Yes."

"Your cottage will back up to that escarpment that you and I climbed the last time you were here."

"I love that spot. I really can't believe all you guys have done for me. How can I ever repay you?"

"Repaying us is the least of your problems. We're both just so excited about having you here. Bart also bought you an old Jeep. He had it painted a bright red. You can drive back to the cottage on that old logging road. The weeds are thick so no one will know there's somebody living back there. The Redwoods and Sequoias are enormous and deer are all over the place, also bears and a huge cougar. I saw it last week about to jump the fence into the corral where John raises his goats. Bart put four shots from his 3006 into the fencepost near its head. I don't think it'll be back. There's enough deer, it doesn't need to eat goats. He didn't try to kill the cougar. They gotta' eat too. Did you know that mountain lions eats one deer or an antelope or an elk every week? That keeps the wildlife population under control."

"Sounds like paradise," Trina said, "unless you are a deer or an antelope or an elk."

"Bart wired electrical lines out to the cottage so you won't need to have service in your name. We think it will be better than running a generator. You will have a stand-by generator, just in case a storm cuts power. We also have a generator. For some time you'll almost be a non-entity, Trina."

"Thank you. And thank Bart for me. I really do not know where I would've gone without you. And, of course, Bill too. I am looking forward to moving. It is getting close."

"You go to the hospital this time?"

"Yes, I did. There are records along with photos of my bruises, scratches, and my black eye. His temper is well documented. I made out another report with the Gwinnett County police, too. That's two more records."

"The more the better," Trisha said.

"Hey, Sis, I also have one more unit of my blood in storage. That makes three now. I figure that should make a bloody enough crime scene. The forensic people will have a blast with my DNA. Thank you for the syringes and for showing me how to use them. I found a vein in my leg so I won't have needle marks in my arm."

"Don't get anemic, kiddo. Once every two months is okay. Come to think of it we're twins so our DNA will be a match so I can give some blood, too. It will sure make the crime scene gory."

"That's great, hon."

"How soon are you planning the move?"

"That's one thing we need to discuss," Trina told her. I have a book on sedatives. I read about Rohypnol and something called CBH and Ketamine. Guys use that to put girls to sleep so they can have their way with them. I'll get some, probably Rohypnol. It really works and it is less dangerous than some of those others."

"I'm familiar with it. Remember I was a nurse?"

"Sound okay to you?"

"How will you get it?"

"I've got a friend who is a nurse. I can get some without anyone knowing. She knows Al and hates his guts. He tried bad stuff with her when she was young."

Trisha detected nervousness in her sister's voice. Trina's worries were becoming much more apparent.

"You don't have to worry about that. Remember I was a nurse, too. I'll have it when you get here."

"Where will you get it?"

"I have connections, kiddo."

"Good."

"Call me before you board your flight, okay?"

"I will, and thanks for your support. Incidentally, Al and I finished buying insurance policies last week, a million dollar policy on each of us."

"Lord! That's a lot of life insurance," Trish said.

"The bastard is devious," Trina said. "I suggested we buy insurance and I told the agent that it was Al's idea. Al sure agreed in a hurry. That fact gives me a sense of urgency to get out of here. I think he is making plans to get rid of me and I don't mean divorce. Do you think I'm worth a million dollars, Sis?"

"You are priceless, honey. You knew that I couldn't stand Al, but even in my wildest dream I never imagined him to turn out the way he has," Trisha said.

"I don't know what triggered his change. Maybe it's the fact that he has women all over him when he's on the tour. Some guys go brain-dead and forget about fidelity, I guess. It still bothers me a little. I don't know what those females in the gallery have that I do not have. I discovered bottles of Cialis and Viagra in one of Al's dresser drawers, hidden under his underwear. I know our love life became bad a year ago. Maybe he's becoming impotent. I see on television where millions of guys buy that stuff. I mean healthy looking men that look young enough to not need help. I don't know, Sis. Al began to lose interest in our physical relationship very shortly after we were married. I understand that is unusual but I just accepted it to keep harmony between us. It got worse as time went by. I didn't talk about it. It's really embarrassing, you know. It's not that important anymore, really."

"I'll pick you up tomorrow, okay?"

"I'll be there," Trina said.

Chapter Six

Trina seated herself in the chair as Mabel gathered the tools of her trade.

"How are you doing, Trina?" Mabel said. "Boy, your roots are sure gray. You haven't been in for some time. Is that a bruise?" she asked, pointing just at the edge of Trina's hairline.

"Where," Trina asked. "I don't feel anything."

"Girl, you know you can tell me anything and I will help you any way I can. Why, I have secrets I'll take to my grave. I've never asked before, but, are you having a problem with Al?"

"I don't know what you are talking about Mabel, Al and I are fine. I think I might like my color a little lighter this time. What do you think?" she asked, "and I really need to be out of here as soon as possible."

Trina could tell she had hurt Mabel's feelings but she also knew that the hairdresser didn't miss a single bruise, nor would she forget them, a perfect witness for the prosecution.

A beautician across the aisle from Trina raised a hair dryer. Trina's best friend and next door neighbor smiled a hello.

"Hi, Trina," Susie said.

"Hello Susie, long time, no see," Trina said.

"I know" Susie replied. "I've missed you. Do you have time to come over later this afternoon?"

"I'd love to," Trina told her.

"Mabel, did you get in any more of those wonderful fingernails, the ones that are wine colored?" she asked.

"Yes. You asked me to order them for you, but you know, no one wears that color anymore. It is so passé."

"Yes, you told me, but I like it. Can you put them on for me today?" Trina asked.

"I thought you were in a hurry, are you sure you have time?" Mabel was still a little miffed.

"Well, I am rushed this afternoon, but you are so good it won't take too long, will it?" Trina tried to placate her.

Chapter Seven

Susan Wells had lived next door to Trina Adams and her husband for seven years. They'd been bridge partners up until last summer. Susan answered her doorbell on the second ring.

"Come in, Trina," she said. "I'm glad we ran into each other at the beauty shop last week. It's been a while since we had lunch together."

"I know and I'm sorry, Susie. I've been kind of out of sorts lately."

"I have known for a long time that you and Al were having problems and they seem to be getting worse. Is there any way I can help?" she asked.

"Some of your sweet iced tea would help a lot right now," Trina said.

"Coming right up, but Trina, I hear the two of you fighting and I have come close to calling the police. I'm really afraid that one of these times he is going to kill you." She handed Trina her iced tea, and continued, "Tell me what to do. Don't you think he is a danger to you?"

Trina's eyes filled with tears. "Susan, truthfully I'm scared to death, but there's nothing I can do about it."

"Honey, why don't you divorce him? No one should have to live like that. Is it the money that's keeping you with him?" she asked.

Trina laughed. "There's not enough money in the world to keep me with him if I had a choice. Al has told me numerous times that he would kill me and my sister if I ever left him. I've thought about divorcing him anyway and taking my chances but I can't gamble with Trisha's life. Al knows where Trisha and Bart live."

"That's unbelievable. You and your sister could go to one of those underground organizations that assist abused women to relocate and change their identities," she suggested.

Trina enjoyed visiting with Susan, but she knew that no one could possibly understand what it was like to live with somebody like Al and to be in constant fear of being beaten, or even worse, depending on his moods, and his moods were becoming worse every time.

As they reclined lounge chairs side-by-side, Susan studied her friend. "Is life getting any better, Trina?" she said. "Does he allow you any breathing room at all?"

"No. I'm still not even allowed to come over here. If Al knew I was here the repercussions would be worse. He wants to control everything. I feel like a captive, a damned slave. Fix my dinner. Clean the stove. Sweep the floor. Then go to your room and leave me alone. Turn off the lights the electric bill is too high. That is all I ever hear. Then he screams about everything. You don't do anything right. He is always threatening me and when I say something in my defense that's when the fight starts. I feel like a caged animal. He tells me I make his life unbearable when he's home. Make his life miserable, can you believe that?"

"Well, friend, I know you've said you're afraid to leave him. We've gotta' figure out something."

"Susie, you know before my mother died how seldom I visited her, even after we knew she was dying." I have had friends I went to school with tell me that the few times he 'allowed' me to go; he was seen spying on me, I guess just to make sure I was there. He is insanely jealous of me. I never saw him there, but they told me he would park up on the hill behind mother's house and used binoculars to keep his eye on me. I have never given him the slightest reason to be jealous, and it's not as if he wants me; he is just that no one else will ever have me."

"You've said for a couple years now that you think Al's wacko. You'd better figure a way out of this crazy situation, girl."

"I am trying. I am really thinking. On the way to Mom's house last year I thought I saw him when I stopped for gas. He was in a different color car and drove right on by, if it was Al. I really don't know. I sleep a lot more now just to keep away from him. He really is mean and I'm afraid of him. Isn't that nuts? I know you've said to get away from him but I'll tell you, Susie, he has told me repeatedly that he will kill me if I leave him."

"You ought to think of something. You are looking kinda' haggard lately," Susan said. "Do you want to run down to McDonalds and get a hamburger?"

"I really can't. Someone might see us and it could get back to Al. Then I'm in real trouble. Unfortunately, it's that bad. Stupid, isn't it?"

"It looks to me like you're already in bad trouble, lady. Have you ever spoken to the police about Al?"

"I spoke to one officer a couple months ago. Twice. Al has played golf with some of the policemen when he's home. I stopped doing that because Al might find out. I worry about what I did. I honestly feel trapped, Susie."

"Your husband is a damned control freak, Trina."

"I know." Trina said.

"Come on inside. You can eat a hamburger here can't you?"

"I can as long as Al doesn't find out about it."

"So you're going to visit your sister?" Susie said.

"It's a quick trip."

"How long will you be gone?"

27

"Just two days. I told Al that Trisha was sick."

"He sure keeps a tight rein, doesn't he?"

"Too tight," Trina said, "He is playing in the Crosby Open at least until Friday, longer if he makes the cut. Last year he lost in a play off and he went nuts when he got home, yelling like he considered his losses my fault. He blames me for nearly everything. I really believe my husband is crazy."

Chapter Eight

The A 300 settled down into fleecy clouds. Trina felt a slight tap on her shoulder.

"We will be landing in fifteen minutes," the stewardess said.

Immediately the Captain came on. "We'll be in a holding pattern for a while. There is fog on the runway in Portland. Hopefully, it will clear soon. In the meanwhile we will go back up to 15,000 feet so you will be able to see a few mountains between Canada and California. You might even be able to see Mount Shasta in Northern California. The first peak out our portside is Mount Hood. To our starboard, as we make our turn, is Mount Rainier. We'll keep you apprised of progress."

Trina motioned to the stewardess. "I have a connection to Grants Pass. There's not much time."

"They know we're here. Your flight will wait," she said.

As Trina leaned back in her seat she felt the surge as the engines hummed louder and she knew she would soon be landing in Portland. She glanced at her watch. It was a half hour before her connecting flight, enough time.

The Saab twin engine prop-jet circled the Grants Pass airport. Below them lay a verdant carpeting mantling rugged canyons interlaced with the Rogue River tumbling its way to the Pacific. Toward the west, Trina could see the towering Siskiyou National Forest. She recalled the trip she had made overnight down the Rogue with Bart and Trisha. The Cascade Mountains appeared purplish. The plane touched down with a slight bounce then taxied down the runway. Trina could see Trisha in the window of the terminal as the airplane stopped at the ramp. Bart was standing beside her. The engine noise subsided. It was a good feeling. She loved her sister. Tears misted Trina's eyes knowing she would be with the people who loved her. She grabbed her overnight bag and hurried from the airplane.

Amid hugs and kisses they smiled and began to talk about her trip. "The fog was murder in Portland. We had to circle for almost an hour. They held up my flight to Grants Pass or I would still be in Portland."

"Glad you made it, kiddo," Bart said. "The Jeep is right outside." Bart took her bag. Trisha took her arm.

"How long can you stay?" Trisha said.

"Just three days. I told Al you were sick. Otherwise I would not have been able to come. Bill will be here later today. He's flying in from

Indianapolis. We can pick him up at the terminal. He'll call and give us his arrival time."

"I adore this place," Trina said as they headed out to the ranch.

"You're going to like it even more when you see the cottage Bart has built for you."

"Yeah, and I'm still searching for Sasquatch," Bart said. "I want to have Bigfoot hanging around your cottage in case that nut comes out here."

"Who's Sasquatch?" Trina said.

"He's a big old hairy guy, maybe an ape that folks have allegedly seen in the Siskiyou Mountains. You might like him. Be a lot better than that hot-shot you got."

"Bart. Stop kidding," Trisha said.

"How far out is the ranch?" Trina said.

"Fifteen miles. Trisha and I decided we didn't want to live in town anymore so we purchased this place five years ago. We bought two hundred acres. Zane Grey had a cabin on the Rogue right next to our place."

"Remember the rafting trip, Sis?" Trisha said.

"I sure do," Trina said.

"We'll do it often when you move out here."

"We have better than one hundred llamas, now," Bart said. "Lots of people are tired of fast food restaurants and strip joints. There's too damned many strange people living on top of each other in cities, even Grants Pass. Nuts are buggin' the hell out of each other. We decided that it was back to nature for us. We got in a truck load of miniature ponies. They are fun."

"Bart never stops talking," Trisha said.

"That's okay. It's kind of refreshing," Trina said. "I recall his subtle wit from when I first came out here. You guys had just bought the farm."

"I don't recall a cute cutie being here before," Bart said. "I suppose that was when I still had eyes only for my dictator cutie."

Trisha turned and looked into her sister's eyes. "You look tired, sweetheart."

"A little, I guess," Trina said.

"You got dark circles around your eyes."

"I know."

"Really getting you down, huh?"

"Ole' cougar got one of those newborns last month," Bart said. "Bring that jerk you're married to out here. I got a couple ranch hands that will square him away in a hurry. I think golf is a damned waste of time anyway, running around a big field hittin' a tiny white ball. It looks stupid to me."

"Bart, shut up," Trisha said.

"Just trying to get her mind off of the hot-shot. I got you a Winchester rifle, 30 caliber lever action, in case you need one," Bart said. "We are almost there. Hey Trina, look off to your right, up high," he pointed, "a bald eagle soaring. We have a lot of them now that they stopped using DDT."

Bart turned into a graveled lane. Trina could see a ranch house back toward the tree-line. Several llamas were trotting toward the Jeep.

"They come to greet us when we come home," Trisha said.

"If you ever get a bad cold, kiddo, I've heard that breast milk can make you feel lots better so Trisha lets me have some after the kid's through sucking."

"Lord, Bart, shut up!"

"What time we gotta' pick up Bill?"

"He'll call me here," Trina said.

"These creatures spit on you, too," Bart said.

"You're kidding," Trina said.

"No, really, you'll be talking to 'em and they'll spit right in your face."

Although Trina wasn't an animal devotee, she had to agree that the llamas were cute, but she didn't want any furry thing spitting on her.

Trisha said, "We will talk about girl stuff when we get inside." She winked at her husband.

"We had one girl llama broke both front legs. I had to shoot it. Trish wanted to give her a nice burial. I butchered it. She's out in the freezer. I had a steak from her already. It was like eatin' one of the family." Bart grinned.

"Bart, please!"

"Wantcha' to know everything." Bart winked.

"The man is hopeless," Trisha said.

"I like your husband, Sis. He's kinda' cute, too."

Chapter Nine

"So what is it you do with computers?" They were sitting out on the front porch overlooking the pasture full of llamas and miniature ponies.

"I work for a company that has a number of experts in the computer field. We do work for anybody who needs to find out what has been in someone's computer; Federal government, the military, divorce lawyers, prosecutors, FBI, DEA, defense attorneys, that sort of thing."

"You make a lot of money?"

"Bart, that is none your of your business," Trisha said.

"Yes it is, too. Bill Gates has a bunch of money but I don't know him. I know this fellow. He is family and if the llama business goes south I want to know where I can borrow enough money to keep afloat."

"Why don't we three go somewhere else and talk. My husband will drive you up a wall with what he thinks is wit."

"Naw, Bart's okay. He's just planning ahead. I make over a half million a year, for what it's worth, Bart. I am known as the nerd or a geek in computer lingo. The people who are knowledgeable about computers have weird names. Our company has three private jets. I came out here on one of ours."

"Do you want to purchase stock in this place? Can I get you something else, your Majesty?"

"Just ignore him," Trisha said.

"We paid two million for the ranch," Bart smiled. "Don't owe a damned dime on it either."

"Trish had already told me that," Bill grinned.

"A man can't have any secrets anymore," Bart said.

"That's enough now, Bart. Trina has a problem she wants to tell us about, right Trina?"

"Sweetie, don't you worry about one thing. With Bill's money, my brain, great looks and a super scope on the rifle, we can take care of every problem, especially one like old Romeo."

Trina had to chuckle; being around Bart was fun but time was short and she needed solutions, not humor.

"Bart, I wish it was simple, but I really have to make some changes in my plans and I need all three of you to get serious. I'm really concerned," she told him.

"What has happened Trina?" Bill asked. "Is Al on to our plans?"

"I'm not really sure but for some reason Al had cameras put in the house including one in my bathroom and I have been trying to think if there has been anything that would've made him suspicious."

Noticing the shocked expressions on their faces, Trina continued. "Bill, now there isn't any way you can come to the house and get in his computer, you know, for some reason, he is insanely jealous of you."

"That's not a problem, sweetheart. I can hack in to any computer in the world. I'll do it from long distance. I am considered a genius, Trina. I will get to it just as soon as I get back home. I have a couple of days off. Al will never know I've been in his computer. My know-how is why I am paid big bucks. There may be nothing there but, with him worrying you, it won't hurt to check him out. I know that visiting on websites is how some super-studs fool around without anybody knowing, particularly their wives. And most people believe if they delete something that it is deleted. It isn't. It's just sent to a secretive niche in the computer and remains hidden there unless that space is needed for other data and then it will be overridden and lost. And I get paid to find it if it is still there. Much of the time it is because a hard-drive like Al's has enormous capacity and as long as he does not deep-six his hard drive and the back-up system, I'll find stuff."

"When will you be ready?" Trisha asked.

"Al will be home in two days. The tournament ends Sunday. Al isn't playing well and he's going to be in a bad mood. We're probably going to have another battle the minute he walks in. It always happens that way and I'm tired of being beat up. I want this to be the last time that happens so I am ready to put the plan in place while I'm still alive."

"I am leaving the same time as you but in our jet. I'll be home long before you. I'll get right to finding what's on Al's computer system. So, when do you want me to pick you up and where exactly?"

"I'll give Al the knock-out drops at dinner. After I finish setting up the crime scene I'll drive my car to the Wal-Mart parking lot. It'll be dark by then. I'll go behind the store. You can pick me up after I wipe the fingerprints from my car. That will look odd since I drive the car all the time. There will be blood all over the garage. There will be his golf club with a broken shaft in the trunk of my car with dried blood and some of my hair stuck to it. That 7 iron will be missing from Al's golf bag. There will be a broken finger nail that I got recently from my hairdresser. The police will find spots and smears of blood inside the car. I will have on only what I will be wearing. Everything I own will be in the house. You might pick me up a jacket in case it gets a little cold on the trip. You can get me a toothbrush plus some other stuff you know I'll need."

"Does Al drive your car," Bill asked.

"Sometimes he does, why?"

"Then do not clean the car. You'll want his fingerprints found in the car. Why don't you wear some gloves just in case you accidentally touch blood? You can toss them away."

"Good idea."

"Better yet, after I pick you up, we will drive up to Indianapolis and I'll get one of the company jets to fly you to Grants Pass. We'll call and have Trisha pick you up at the airport. That'll save a long trip and I have big job to do at work so I can't be gone too long. We've got a football player financing drug smugglers and my job is to get him convicted."

"Why on earth would someone who makes millions want to do that?"

"It's the story of simple greed, sweetie."

"You guys should write a damned novel," Bart said.

Trisha suggested, "After Al is out cold you might want to put some blood under his fingernails and on the bottom of his shoes. And sling some spots on his shirt and pants, and the door into the garage. You can take a small amount of skin from somewhere on your body and put it under his fingernails. It will look like he scratched you while committing murder."

"Make sure you show footprints leading from the garage into his bedroom," Bill said. "Al weighs a couple hundred pounds. How are you going to get him into his bedroom in case he falls asleep at the table?"

"If that happens I'll show footprints to the table. And leave him there. God, this sounds gruesome!"

"You guys ought to write that stuff for television and the movies," Bart said. "If he's out cold you could put some scratches on his face and hands, too."

"You are pretty sharp for a llama rancher," Trina smiled." But I do appreciate your suggestion, anything for realism."

"We raise Shetland ponies and Angora goats, too." Bart smiled.

"Which day, precisely, will it be?"

"I'll call you. The day after tomorrow, probably," Trina said.

Trina suddenly developed a startled expression on her face, almost a look of terror. Then she grinned in a weird manner, her facial muscles twisting like she had no control over them. She raised her hands above her head, her fingers splayed, moving them like she was brushing spider webs from her hair, then she dropped her arms and stared intently off toward the mountains.

"You alright Trina?" Trisha rushed to her sister's side. She had never known Trina to act like that before. "Can I get you a coke, honey? What's wrong?"

Trina began crying, sobbing noisily, like her heart was breaking. She lowered her head onto the table.

"What's wrong, little sister," Bill moved closer to his sister's side. "Should we call you a doctor?"

"We use Doctor Thralls," Bart said. "I'll call him"

Trina's sobs stopped as suddenly as it had started. She looked solemnly at her family. She wiped the tears away with her hand, a sudden smile enveloping her face.

"You know it is ironic. This nightmare is going to be over and my super-great family has helped make it go away. I want to thank you all. It will happen in two or three days after I get back home. Enough is enough," she said. "Perhaps I'll walk away bruised but it'll be the last time, and worth every minute."

"Incidentally, Al had several cameras installed in the house without informing me. I found one behind a trophy while I was doing housework. I called the local security company to find out about those cameras. Guess what? They had installed security cameras in our house at Al's request. They figured I knew about it. We talked. The man said Al told him our house had been burglarized. I told him that we had never had a burglary. The man told me that he was kind of suspicious at the time because when a house is broken into, the homeowner usually has cameras mounted outside. It seemed strange to him. Al said he wanted to catch who ever broke in our house. I wonder now. The man said I should be careful when coming home at night. The garage is a vulnerable place at night."

"Be very careful, sugar," Bart said.

"Come outside, Bill. I want to show you a couple things."

Four Llamas came running in their direction as Bart and Bill ambled along the corral.

"Your sister has some emotional trouble," Bart said.

"Sure does," Bill said. "Looks like she has a plan to get out of what appears to be a bad marriage. I feel it will work, with your help."

"She needs to do it quick. She and Trisha had a lengthy conversation last night. She told Trisha that the first time they had sex after their marriage that Al demanded she put on cat house costumes, skimpy stuff, and do a strip-tease while he masturbated. I would have stuck his dick in an electrical socket. He is probably one of those psychos that send emails about how to make their prick big, and the guy sending it is probably jacking-off while he is sending emails. Trina also told Trisha he kicked her on her stomach while she was still pregnant, accusing her of getting pregnant with someone else and that was why she lost the baby. He's evidently a psycho son-of-a-bitch. I'd still like to get him out here and make sure he has an accident while we're hunting," Bart said.

"I guess it's logical that she would never discuss a problem like that with me," Bill said.

"Sure. It's bizarre. Trisha said Trina discussed it with her gynecologist and she had explained it as an odd physical abnormality, that guys who cum prematurely have to jack-off before having sexual intercourse so they are able to delay their climax."

Three llamas followed along inside the fence, snorting and prancing, demanding attention, as Bill and Bart stood outside the fence. They seemed friendly.

"So when are you going back to Atlanta?" Bart said.

"Tomorrow, I've decided to run for Congress. I have a meeting with the powers that be."

"Why would you want to be involved with crooks?"

"I know how to solve the high unemployment problem and apparently no one in Congress has a clew."

"How would you do it," Bart said.

"I recall when our economic shock waves began in the 40's, unions striking, intimidating management into agreeing to more pay and benefits. At first the benefits were good for unions but then greed took over; demands became too costly, executives began taking too much pay and too many perks that put industry into decline. Then politicians began sticking their finger into the cookie jar enacting high taxes. Expenses skyrocketed. Profits dropped. Appliances, apparel, steel, leather, porcelain, jewelry, electronics, replacement parts moved offshore. When union contracts were about to expire companies were threatened with strikes unless they agreed to greater hourly rates, more vacations, more sick leave and more benefits, more, more. Executives continued depleting operating capital and politicians piled on more taxes and regulations. With stockholders demanding more return on investment, costs became punitive. Business could not afford to modernize or to compete. This country lost 11,000,000 jobs during the past four decades. The analogy of the straw that broke the camel's back was true in American industry. In industry there were too many straws."

"Rising payroll expenses resulted in manufacturers resorting to automation which caused the loss of several million jobs but that still was not enough. The option for industry was to reduce quality, losing market share to foreign producers who made a better product, or move offshore in order to survive the ruinous costs. No industry can continue viable with the depletion of its operating capitol. The geese that laid the golden eggs were strangled, not by conspiracy but by a three-way onslaught of the greed factor.

"To escape the economic chokehold that unions held on business many companies moved from northern states, where unions were robust to southern states where the right-to-work laws helped keep costs lower. But that was only a partial cure. The other two thirds of the enigma, excess taxes and greedy executive compensation continued to reduce industry's ability to pay for modernizing that resulted in cheap products and further decline in market shares. Add government mandated regulations and it was no longer possible to make profit. With the implication that making profit was un-American, when a company was profitable and could have used profit to modernize their operation to stay competitive, the government passed a Windfall Profit tax, punishing industries for making money, further crippling incentive. Survival instincts in business resulted in their moving offshore where cost could be contained. Every time a business was forced to go overseas to prevent bankruptcy our workforce shrank."

"Politicians, who were too busy arranging their own financial future, allowed this calamity to happen We now have 10% plus unemployment due to destructive decisions and I don't hear anybody suggesting what to do about it. It will take the ingenuity of World War Two planning to reverse the trend. That demands starting over. There is no method for creating enough jobs to accommodate those currently unemployed, graduates and immigrants. Instead of wringing our hands in resignation we need to find a candidate with guts for President, someone smart enough to concede mistakes of the past, sufficiently persuasive to force cooperation and dedicated to removing gluttony from industry. The AFL-CIO, UAW and Teamsters grew even more avaricious. Executives became wealthy by depleting their operating capital. Politicians expedited the death knell. We need to get jobs back to America but enabling industry to manufacture products that can be marketed competitively; low taxes from cities, counties, states, and the federal government, smaller wages for workers, lower executive salaries, with tax breaks and subsidies for rebuilding factories, beginning in states with the highest unemployment rates. Full employment depends on recovering offshore jobs. At such time as profits are produced employee payroll can be increased. Our future depends on the recovery of jobs that moved overseas. Otherwise unemployment will remain at crisis levels."

"A commission of successful executives should be appointed to visit the industries that have sent jobs overseas to assure them that corrections will be made in the cost of doing business to create a fiscal climate so that businesses can once again be profitable here."

"We need a visionary who is not concerned about winning his next election but willing to get down into the trench and reopen abandoned factories across America so unemployed people can have jobs. The effort needs to be a relentless effort, otherwise we'll continue toward anarchy. Desperate people do desperate things. Desperate people are not interested in reality shows."

"No wonder you're rich." Bart said. "You are smart. You can likely win. You've got my vote. You'll piss away a lot of money running for an office. Are you really honest?"

"Of course," Bill said.

"Then you won't fit in with Congressional crooks."

"Someone has to do something. We're going to hell."

"Oregon had a crusader elected to congress. He was hell-bent on changing Washington. He made a few enemies with his acid mouth. Senator Byrd pulled him off to one side and gave him a message. Either play our game and become exceedingly rich or go drown yourself in the Potomac. Besides you probably don't have enough loot to be elected. They're talking about banning earmarks. It's bullshit. It won't happen. You can see it this year. The Republicans were elected with a promise to ban earmarks. The election is over and the first piece to be voted on is a major budget, on which the Republicans have loaded a massive amount of personal earmark money, those lying sons-of-bitches. They are giving voters a middle finger salute year after year."

"So?" Bill said. "You know about earmarks?"

"It's a corrupt way for politicians to steal money from taxpayers to pay for libraries, swimming pools and parks back home, so their constituents will love them and re-elect them again. They secretly put the earmarked funds on a defense bill, for example, so it will sail through. Congress They all do the same shit."

"We had a senator walking around with $100 bills in his pocket that supplicants had shoved there for favors. He and some other crooked politicians stopped the work on a highway project until they arranged to buy a farm where the highway would be routed. He bought the property from a dying widow for $500 per acre and sold it to the state for $15,000 per acre. The bastard never did go to jail."

A Georgia senator bought several farms in the boonies. He then went on a campaign to create jobs away from the big city by building roads out into the county. When the road to nowhere was finished he sold his property to a developer and made $2,000,000. Building that road was paid for by taxpayers, as usual, to enrich politician. It was a costly con-job."

"Be elected, buddy, you can get richer and then buy part of my farm," Bart said, grinning.

He pulled some bananas from a bag. Four llamas went nuts, stomping and surging against the fence.

"They love fruit," Bart said.

"You live a pretty good life here," Bill said.

"Trisha and I decided to back off that commercial merry-go-round shit when we bought the farm. My brother is in financial trouble up in Portland. Makes big bucks but spends bigger. Damned mansion on a bluff upriver on the Willamette, four cars, four jet skis, a sailboat, a 52 feet Carver, a Harley, a glitzy country club, a condo in Astoria, fuckin' zillion credit cards. Every time his neighbor was conned into purchasing something Ted had to buy something more costly. He is one of the stupid asses that are brain-washed by promoters into buying crap they cannot afford and do not need, getting in debt up to his eyeballs all in the name of keeping up with the Joneses. There is a big shot. I have had to bail him out twice. I told Ted to sell all that shit and get serious, I could not afford their extravagant lifestyle. I drive a faded jeep and he drives a Jaguar and she has a Mercedes. They purchased a Lexus for their kids. I didn't have a damned car until I was twenty-three. People are suckers. I told Ted to stop going to those glitzy restaurants where they pay for fuckin' atmosphere! It costs seventy-dollars for one order of Roast venison la Traviatta. I fix that same shit for less than ten bucks. Mine might be Roast llama la Traviatta. They see that Hollywood glitz, living too high on the hog, and get sucked into a quagmire, always in debt up to their asses."

"You're articulate Bart, vulgar, but articulate."

"Want to hear my bitching on another subject?"

"Why not?" Bill sounded resigned.

"Televised programming today with stupid shows and no plot with people screaming who haven't completed the evolutionary cycle, yelling stupid shit and acting like stupid simians. And that is enlightenment? Who watches poker games? Who watches automobiles being repossessed? Who watches jerks throwing pig shit all over each other? Who watches hamburgers being grilled? Who watches any of those senseless programs that are put on simply to fill up time slots? Jerks, that's who watches, jerks."

"We better get back inside." Bill said.

"By the way, and this information is about as sicko as anything could be, but Trina told Trisha that Al made her sit astraddle his neck and piss in a cup so he could watch her urinating."

"What ever happens to him he deserves," Bill said.

Chapter Ten

Bill sat in front of his computer and hacked into his brother-in-law's files. He opened to the Internet and began scanning records of where Al had visited lately. He went to favorites and scanned down a listing of perhaps a hundred stored files. He went to cookies and studied the details. Al apparently had never deleted cookies.

He picked up his cellphone and called his sister. "Do you use Al's computer, Sis?"

"A few times, to send an email to Trisha," Trina said. "I'm not technologically sophisticated. Why?"

"Just curious," he said.

"Find anything dirty yet?"

"No, just broke in," he said. "I'll let you know."

Al sure had a super computer, the latest Microsoft Vista Ultimate with enough Gigabytes to operate a battleship. The advances made by computer geniuses had been nothing short of miraculous.

He went into the computer and started searching in files that had been deleted. He recalled the advice of a Microsoft geek who said the only way to make sure a computer is clean is to remove the hard drive and throw the damned thing in a roaring furnace.

He discovered files needing Al's password to enter. Most people are numbskulls when it comes to passwords. Knowing the owner, a simple guess achieved entry. Bill was into material that shocked even him. A guy would have to be psycho to save pictures of nude females in compromising positions. He found an inordinate amount of foreign females posing in explicit positions, some in groups. Their poses sure took the magic out of females. It was crudity at its most disgusting. Some psychos find joy in being psychos. He could not reveal this crap to his sister, she might vomit. However he put in a DVD and downloaded some of the slimier images and marked the DVD with a Sharpie.

He went to Al's saved emails and read several exchanges. Apparently Al was carrying on a verbal love affair with women all over the country. From the revelatory words Al was having more than verbal contacts while he was away for tournaments. Bill guessed that womanizing was how golf professionals amuse themselves when they are out of town.

Bill hacked into Al's email addresses and composed some conversation and emailed them back to Al's address file. From Al's conversations in some of the emails his sister might be psychic in her assessment of danger from her psycho husband. The phraseology *so we can always be together* was his stock in trade offering to women.

One email stood out far above the others. It was a frank exchange between Al and what seemed to be some homosexuals in New York. There were accusations from Al accusing the queer guy of giving Al the AIDS virus. Man! Al is queer? No wonder he has problems. But Bill had played golf with Al. He seemed like a normal guy.

Deciding to look into the dilemma further he found where Al had used Google information about AIDS virus. This was a subject that he'd have to think long about before talking to Trina about it. It was one puzzler. Bill had read about guys experimenting with homosexuals for some kind of kick, unaware of the likelihood of contracting AIDS. He could only guess at the psychological reactions that must create. Al should have kept his zipper zipped. The reason for searches for multiple orgasms eluded Bill. Al's shenanigan with Bill's sister must stem from his psychological and emotional aberrations.

He wondered if it had been merely a simple drunken bout. Had Al become soused and jumped in bed in a ménage ET trio's situation, or a group? How long had it been going on? It was one subject Bill could not force himself to speak about with Trina. He might discuss with Trisha what he had found and let her talk about Al's aberrations with Trina. Living was filled with emotional complexities. Perhaps homo-sapiens should have remained tree climbers. Wild animals are not guilty of such disgusting conduct.

Bill visited some websites devoted to teaching how to kill someone without being discovered. Al had been a frequent researcher. It is astonishing how much explicit information is exchanged in the Ethernet today. Bill wondered why his brother-in-law would want to check out those websites. He looked eagerly at one particular website. It was Paladin Press. It was a place where you could order a book that would teach you how to hire a hit man to commit murder. "That's scary," Bill muttered. Maybe he should discuss that material with Trisha and with the police department. He determined to think about that for a while. He could not decide if Al had ordered the book online, maybe by telephone. One website sold information on how to improvise a silencer for firearms using packing material and duct tape. There were a few entries into websites on accidental drowning and arson to cover-up murder/ suicides and accidents at home.

Bill suddenly tensed. There was one website devoted to the science of poison. Al had apparently research the use of a poison to get rid of somebody, ethylene glycol, selenium, and arsenic. Bill was instantly

41

convinced that his brother-in-law was going to murder Trina. He had to do something very quickly.

He went to Al's hard drive and typed several ideas. Most novices have no idea that old entries can be recovered from the files of computer's incredible library. He found several disturbing files. Adding it all up he shut down the computer. He knew enough to convict that psycho nut. He also knew that investigators carted out computers at the beginning of their investigations involving even suspicions of murder.

Bill's first stop would be at the FBI headquarters in Atlanta where he had a personal friend. He could not report the data to the Gwinnett County police department because he knew Al had golf pals working there. He decided this posed a disturbing complexity. He needed to call Trisha. Meantime he felt a need to have a talk with his brother-in-law. Bart was observant and outspoken. From where he had been researching, Bill felt the need to take a hot bath.

Chapter Eleven

Trina stood at the window. She looked at her watch. Al had just called telling her he would be arriving before noon. She could tell that his attitude was surly. He had told her specifically what he wanted her to prepare for his lunch. Her pulse had already begun to increase. She wasn't positive she had bought the preparations he would like. She could feel her heart thud in her chest. It was already hurting. She hurried to the kitchen and opened the refrigerator to see if she had the items Al demanded. She choked, sweat forming on her brow. God, this had to stop. She heard the door open. She stared at her hands. Her palms were moist.

Al removed his coat and slouched down on the couch. "Did you see the Crosby finish this week?"

"No, honey," she said.

"You not interested in golf?"

"Yes. I am," she added quickly.

"Then why didn't you watch your husband play? That's how I make our damned living. That's what pays for this house and our groceries. That is what puts clothes on your body. Maybe you don't appreciate it, huh?"

"I didn't feel good. I was asleep most all day."

"You never feel good," he snapped.

"Is lunch ready?"

"Not quite, honey."

"I called and told you what time I would be home. Are you getting lazier?"

"I'll hurry, Al."

Trina busied herself in the kitchen. Al turned on the television to the Crosby final round.

"I suppose you know I missed the damned cut," he said.

Trina continued trying to put his lunch together.

"Are you listening?"

"I didn't hear you," she said.

"You must have some kind of hearing problem," he said.

"Al, honey, don't pick on me today. I really don't feel good. Can I go out to the delicatessen and get you something? I don't have what you asked for."

Al walked into the kitchen, glaring. He slapped Trina on her on her cheek. "Why the hell not, you knew I was going to be home today! You are a serious pain in the ass, a useless bitch." He struck her across her forehead. She fell to the floor screaming.

"Shut up dammit! The neighbors will hear you."

Trina screamed again, covering her head

*   *   *

Susan heard her neighbor's screams. "Enough is enough." She cursed. She hurried to the phone and called the Gwinnett Police department.

Sergeant Philip Pell answered the phone. "Yes?"

"I think you ought to come out here. I think a man is beating the hell out of his wife."

"Why do you think that, ma'am?"

"Because she's screaming and he just got home."

"What is your name, ma'am?"

"Susan Wells. I live next door."

What's your address?"

"212 Longview Drive."

"And what is the address of the screamer, ma'am?"

"Next door, 216 Longview Drive. Hurry, please. She just screamed again."

"We'll be there, ma'am."

Pell turned to Captain Gates. "I know that address. That's where Al Adams lives. I play golf with him. He is married to a bitch. He's the golf professional. You see him on television."

"So, what's the problem?"

"A neighbor just called and said she thought he was beating up on his wife."

"What made her report that?

"She said she heard her screaming."

"Well now that sounds reasonable. When wives scream it usually mean they're giving birth or their husband is beating up on them, wouldn't you say so? Go the hell out and find out! That's what you get paid for doing."

"But Adams is a friend of mine. He's a nice guy."

"Ted Bundy was a nice fellow. Jack the Ripper was a prince of a guy." The sarcasm in the Captain's voice was obvious. "Want me to do your job, Sergeant?"

*   *   *

Al opened the door. "Hello, Phil, what are you doing out here?"

44

"We got a report of someone screaming. Gates sent me out to investigate."

"My wife fell down and hurt her arm, that's all."

Pell hesitated. "Can I see her, Al? The Captain is sure to ask me if I spoke with her."

"She's in the bathroom. She's all right except for her arm. I may run her over to the hospital and have it x-rayed. She's okay, now. Trust me."

"Okay, Al. I'll tell the Captain."

"Want to play a round this week-end?"

"Sure," the Sergeant said. "Call me with tee time."

As Pell drove away he could see the neighbor woman at 212 looking out from her window. "Nosy broad," he said.

Gates was just coming back from lunch when Sergeant Pell entered the station.

"How'd it go?" Gates said

"Just as I thought, Al's wife fell down and injured her arm, that's all."

"You see the injury?"

"No, she was in the bathroom. Al was going to take her over to the hospital and have her x-rayed."

"You really did not see her?"

"No. I felt it wasn't necessary, Captain. Al says she is a bitch and eats sleeping pills like candy then falls down a lot."

"Sergeant, are you aware that Mrs. Adams has been in twice before reporting her husband for knocking her around a lot and is abusive in other ways?"

"No, I didn't know that, Sir." Phil could tell that the Captain was pissed.

"Also, are you aware that I saw your friend's wife last year at the hospital with two black eyes and being stitched up on her forehead? She had fractures on her arms, also."

"Al said that she falls down a lot, Sir."

"Did you ever in your life see anyone get black eyes from falling down, Sergeant Pell?" The emphasis was stinging.

"I guess not, Captain Gates."

"You got their phone number?"

Sergeant Pell fumbled for his notebook. "Yes, here it is. Do you want me to call them, Sir?"

"No," the Captain said, reaching for the note book.

He sat at his desk and dialed the number.

"This is the Adams residence."

"I would like to speak to Trina Adams, please. Is she in?"

"She's sleeping right now. Who's this?"

"I'm Captain Don Gates with the county police."

"Can I have her call you later? She's not feeling well right now," Adams said.

"Did you take her to the hospital for her injury?"

"My wife decided that she did not want to go," Al said.

"Will you have her call me as soon as she awakens?"

"Sure," Al said.

"If she is not able to call me I might check on her later," Captain Gates said.

⋆   ⋆   ⋆

Trina wandered out from her bedroom. "I have to go to the drugstore. I need something," she said.

Al looked up from the TV. "Don't be gone long," he said.

Trina backed her car from the garage and headed for the telephone booth.

"It has to be tonight, Bill. He has hurt me," she said.

"What's the matter, Sis?" Bill said.

"He's done it again. He beat up on me just about as soon as he got home. He's crazy. I have had enough. Pick me up behind Wal-Mart at eight o'clock tonight I'll park out in back. It'll be dark."

"How bad is it?"

"It's bad, Bill. He went nuts because I didn't have what he wanted to eat ready when he got home. I have several more bruises."

"I agree. It's time. Where are you now?"

"I'm at a phone booth downtown. I told him I needed to go to the drugstore. He's home watching television."

"Are you going to be okay going back home."

"Sure. The damned die is cast. Enough is enough. Do you agree Bill? If he hurts me again I am going to shoot the bastard,"

"I agree with your plan. Don't kill him. That will ruin all our plans."

"You really think it will work?"

"Yes."

"Please call Trisha. She'll want to know. Then meet me behind Wal-Mart at 8:00 tonight."

"I will be there, Trina. Be careful, sweetie."

Chapter Twelve

It was just before lunch. The Captain continued to be concerned about the call yesterday. Something was not quite right about Pell's report. Gates grabbed the file and picked up the record of the complaint. He read the details Sergeant Pell had notated. Something was not kosher. Why would a wife scream four times if she fell down once? His brow wrinkled in thought. He twirled the report around and around.

He dialed the telephone number of the complainant. "Mrs. Wells?"

"Yes."

"This is Captain Don Gates with the Gwinnett County Police Department. Are you the lady who called yesterday about a problem next door?"

"Yes, Captain,"

"Is there any problem today that you know of?"

"Well, I was about to call you. I saw a policeman over there yesterday morning. He didn't stay long which surprised me. My friend is usually out in the yard early each morning. I haven't seen her today. I can't call or go over there when her husband is home. He and I do not see eye to eye on marriage.

"What does that mean, Mrs. Wells?"

"Well, simply, he is damned mean to her. This crap has happened before."

"The report says she fell and hurt herself."

"Bullshit! Wives really do not scream for no reason now, do they?"

"Those are exactly my thoughts, lady. Are you going to be home for a while?"

"Yes Sir. All morning"

I'd like to come out and have a powwow with you."

"Coffee's ready now."

"I'll be there in maybe thirty minutes, okay?"

"I'll be here, Captain Gates."

*　　*　　*

"So tell me about next door, Mrs. Wells."

"Well, Trina, that's Mrs. Adams. She and I have been friends ever since they moved in."

"How long ago was that?"

47

"Almost seven years."

"Do you see each other a lot?"

"Occasionally but only when her husband is away. He's a professional golfer and is on the tour. A very good golfer, I must say. He has won many tournaments."

"So what happens when the husband is home?"

"They fight a lot. Bad fights too. She gets hurt. I have seen her black eyes and bruises. I think that's what happened yesterday. I've heard her screams before."

"He told me yesterday that she was asleep."

"Trina does sleep long hours but that's only to be away from his scathing denunciations of her."

"Wonder why she doesn't divorce him?"

"Trina has implied on occasion that her life could be in danger if she did that, perhaps her relatives, too. She has a sister and a brother"

"Has he ever threatened to do her in, maybe kill her?"

"Not really, in so many words, but the implications were always there."

"Guess I oughta' go over there and conduct a powwow with them. Maybe get 'em headed on the right track."

"I wish you would. I'm worried about her, Captain."

"I'll give you a report, ma'am." Gates said.

"I noticed you used the word powwow a couple times. Do you have Indian blood, Captain?"

The Captain laughed. "My great granddaddy got personal with a Cherokee gal many years ago before they got chased out of Georgia. Down the line, I resulted, I guess."

Chapter Thirteen

Don Gates strolled slowly around the Adams house just getting a feel for something. He didn't know what. Gates was more than a little concerned. He had investigated any number of cases of wives getting the shit kicked out of them by their husbands. Since becoming the second in command of the police department, he was coming to the conclusion maybe it would be best to stay single. Gates listened for any noises coming from inside the home. None. Maybe they had reconciled their differences. He hoped so but screams somehow bothered him. You simply don't scream for nothing. Screaming means you have a painful problem. He checked the time. People should be up by now, Gates decided. He peered into their garage. It was dark. He could see one car in the garage.

Don Gates stabbed the doorbell. He waited. He pushed on it again and heard a deep gong inside the house. He pushed it again. Maybe they had gone on a second honeymoon. But usually you don't honeymoon with your brutalizer. He jabbed the door bell once more.

Gates heard a deadbolt sliding in the door. It opened up slowly. Don Gates had never met a professional golfer before, so he wondered why this sleepy-eyed and disheveled golfer had scratches on his face. Golf shouldn't be that tough a game.

"I am Captain Don Gates with the Gwinnett County Police Department. I want to follow up on the phone call we received yesterday. May I come in?"

The door opened wider. The Captain entered. "How'd you get the scratches?" he said. "Are you Al Adams?"

"Yes I am." The man's hands went to his face. "I don't know. I must have done it in my sleep," he said.

"Looks like that would have awakened you."

"I drank a lot last night. I guess I was soused."

"You drink much?"

"Not really, but it relaxes me," Adams said.

"Is Mrs. Adams awake yet?"

Adams looked at the time. "Probably not, she sleeps late usually," he said.

"Mind if I wait?"

"Sometime she sleeps until noon," he said.

"Mind if I look around, except in your bedrooms, of course?"

"Grab yourself a magazine." Al motioned to a love seat. "I'll clean up meanwhile. I'll be upstairs for a while."

49

The Captain glanced into the kitchen. He opened a liquor cabinet in the den. He could see why the golfer liked booze; there was a dozen bottles of expensive marriage destroyers on the shelf. The ice had melted in a silver bucket. There was an empty quart of Brandy and Benedictine on the carpet. Gates had failed to ask the neighbor if Trina was a drunk, also. He wanted to check the bedrooms, but hesitated. He might walk in on an undressed wife.

The officer noticed a sizable smear of blood on the door jamb, leading into the garage. He opened the door and flipped on the overhead light.

Grabbing his phone, Gates called headquarters.

"Josh, send everyone available out to 216 Longview! Send Sweeney! Send our crime scene investigators! Send everyone in forensics. It looks like we have a murder here. Looks like the Saint Valentine Day massacre. This is one of the bloodiest damned crime scenes I have ever seen! Looks like a buncha' hogs have been slaughtered."

He swung open the doors to the bedrooms. There was no woman to be seen. He checked the bathrooms. He pulled his pistol and raced up the stairs expecting a man armed to the teeth. Adams was coming out from the bathroom, some bandages on his cheeks.

"Mr. Adams you are under arrest on suspicion of murder." Handcuffing Adams, the officer began to read him his Miranda Rights.

"Who the hell's been murdered," Al screamed.

"Mr. Al Adams, you have the right to remain silent. You have the right to an attorney, if you cannot afford a lawyer one will be appointed to represent you."

The Captain almost laughed when he said the word afford. He knew Adams was worth millions.

"Al Adams, do you understand your rights?"

"What the hell is going on," Al snarled.

"Where is you wife," Mr. Adams.

"I don't know."

"You said your wife was in bed. She isn't."

"Trina must have gotten up and gone to the grocery store or somewhere." Adams almost shrieked the words.

"Without any blood? I don't think so."

"What in the hell has blood got to do with it?" Adams demanded to know.

"When did you last see your wife?"

"Last night when she went to bed, shortly after we had dinner."

"Did you see her after that?"

"I can't remember."

Did you have an argument last night?"

"I can't remember."

"Did your wife fall down last night?"

"I can't remember."

"Are you saying that you can't remember anything?"

Al grabbed at his throat. His chest convulsed. He began gagging right where he stood. He wiped away some spittle from his lips. "I don't want to say anything. I want my attorney."

"Fine," Captain Gates said. "Grab what you need to wear. Call your attorney and tell him he can see you at the station in an hour."

"I need to bag your hands, Mr. Adams."

"What the hell for," Al snapped.

"You have blood on your hands. We need to know who the blood belongs to."

"It's my damned blood. I cut my cheek shaving. You can see that." Al's voice got louder.

Gates placed paper bags over Al's hands and secured them with tape.

He called the station. "Josh, are those people on the way?"

"They're probably near you right now, Captain."

"Did you report to the Chief?"

"Yessir-re-bob, Captain."

"Don't be a damned comic, Josh," Gates said.

"Sergeant Pell reported in sick."

"I'm not surprised. I would have too."

"What did the Chief say?"

"He went to lunch."

"I'll be down with a prisoner. Clean the crap out of a cell."

"Yessir-re-bob, Captain, Sir."

"Josh, if you weren't married to my sister I'd fire your ass."

Chapter Fourteen

"Pell, you mangled this case. If you had done your job a woman would probably be alive today. You have the brain of a slug. How the hell did you get promoted?"

"I'm sorry Captain, but Al and I were on the golf team in high school. I've known the guy for many years. I can't believe he would do anything like this. Are you sure he did it?"

"I guess you're as addled as my brother-in-law. I ought to take both of you out into the woods and shoot your asses. You violated every rule in investigating a crime. You've got blood all over the creation, a missing wife and her husband scratched all to hell then you can ask a moronic question like that? I may demote you to a turd. Why did you not demand to see her yesterday?"

"I believed him, Captain. We were friends"

"Did you know that Charley Manson had friends?"

"I get the point, Captain."

"Another screw up like this Phil and you are out of here."

"Tell Sweeney to come in here."

Beth Sweeney worked for the FBI until she tired of the agents fondling her woman parts. Sweeney was one of the top forensic experts in Washington. The department was lucky to have her come back home.

"How's it look, Beth? What's happened to humanity?"

"Too many have failed to complete the evolutionary cycle. We've got folks who should still be living up in trees. That was one of the worst crime scenes I've ever visited. That had to be pure rage."

"Wal-Mart security called and reported an abandoned car back of the store. It proved to be hers. How did he get back to the house?"

"It's only six miles. Remember Al's a tour golfer, and accustomed to walking hilly golf courses. It would have been a snap for him.

"Everything photographed and documented? Any prints in the car?"

"The team found some of his clothing in the washer and tiny traces of blood in the shower. I guess he took a shower and changed clothes. Probably was covered with blood from the savagery I saw in the garage. Spray drops of blood even up on the ceiling."

"What else?"

"He apparently hauled her away in the trunk of her car and dumped her somewhere, then dumped the car."

"Any guesses?"

"I don't guess, Captain; the guy's broken 7-iron in the garage, a sliver from the victim's fingernail in the trunk of her car. Hairs from her Australian opossum coat. I checked with a furrier and he says Australian opossum doesn't shed so I concluded the killer wrapped the body in her opossum coat to carry it out to the car and hairs were pulled loose and fell onto the carpet in the trunk in the process. What else would the prosecutor want? He murdered her. They do it all the time. When the spouse gets some stretch marks the bastard gets nooky some other place. That happened to me. Luckily, my man died before he got the guts to kill me."

"You can have all the evidence in the world but if the prosecutorial presentation is inept the result will be a not guilty verdict. Look at the O. J. Simpson case. There was irrefutable evidence; the murderer's blood found on the gate at the murder scene with blood droplets leading to his home, there was a glove with his blood on it, a shoe tread matching the one at the scene, a unique tread found only on four pair of shoes sold in California, one purchased by O. J. He had one of the most common reasons for murder; his jealous rage. Everything Simpson did prior to his arrest was indicative of his guilt. But you must have competent prosecution. The prosecution in his case was inept. They got so bogged down in their explanation about DNA, the jury went to sleep, except for the woman seen flirting with the defendant. When O.J. put on an act with the bloody glove, the prosecutor said nothing. Any moron knows wet leather shrinks when it dries. And when one of defense team blind-sided the prosecutor by asking if the witness had ever said the word nigger the case was lost. The defense convinced the brain-numbed jury that Simpson was innocent of murdering his ex-wife. I mentioned that case as an example of one that was handled badly. So we can't be too confident. Juries are unpredictable."

"I understand she has family in Grants Pass Oregon and Georgia. Brother and sister. Have they been notified?"

"They have. I expect her sister, a twin by the way, to be here tomorrow. Her brother is coming the next day. It'll be a bitch when they get here."

"You through with the crime scene?"

"I guess."

"Thought you didn't guess."

"I'm through."

"Captain, don't be too hard on Sergeant Pell. He's a good man. I made the same mistake one time, trusting a man I knew."

"I've already decided. When a patrol goes out next week Sergeant Pell will be dragged along behind the car until the patrol comes back."

"You're not serious?"

"No, I won't do that. We'll talk though."

"I think you are great, Captain."

"It's that Cherokee blood in me."

"Really. Captain? I am part Sioux. Chief Crazy Horse is a relative."

"Then we're Kindred Spirits."

"I knew there was something I liked about you."

"By the way, was there anything on those cameras?

"A wire was loose in the control box in the attic. Looks like he decommissioned the cameras."

Chapter Fifteen

"It's a slam-dunk Marlene, even without a body. He was born here and has hunted all over the state. Adams knew in advance where he was going to dump the body. He knows every pond, every cave, each ravine. That's why he was already home when I got there. He feigned being groggy and recovering from a bout with booze. I didn't detect an odor of alcohol on him. I found a half-empty Brandy bottle. So what? That was likely staged. According to a neighbor they fought constantly. Their fight turned into a savage confrontation and he lost control. It happens a lot."

"Grand Jury?"

"Piece of cake. They'll eat it up."

"Charge?"

"1st degree. He needs to be dead, too."

"Without a body?"

"I can give you four cases recently where the guy is on death row. Times have changed, Marlene. You know that. It's called overwhelming and irrefutable evidence. Let me have him for one day and he'll tell me precisely where he stashed her. DNA and forensics has replaced my preferred method of finding out the truth: brass knucks and a baseball bat. I used to get them squealing like pigs. In a way the good days are over. Judges have turned into wimps. And defense attorneys will tap-dance around the truth to save a child rapist."

"When do we want to talk to your boss?"

"We can see him tomorrow morning."

"Do I have to dress up?" Captain Gates smiled.

"Here in Georgia? Hell no. We're countrified."

"You read the newspaper yet, Beth?"

"I saw the front page when I walked by the newsstand. I have not had time to think since this murder happened. I was wondering where he dumped hid her body."

"Probably up in North Georgia."

"Really Captain? Why there?"

"He's smart. Along with hunting, Al's has fished for rainbows and brookies in the mountain streams between Dahlonega and the Tennessee line. That's wilderness in many spots. You can hide a body and if it is not found real soon it's gone. As soon as the body hits the dirt Mother Nature takes over and she sends in her cleaning crew. They are all meat eaters: bear, coyotes, raccoon, hawks, turkey vultures, rats, mice, chipmunks, weasels, minks, blow flies, maggots, foxes, and worms. It doesn't take long to reduce a carcass down to nothing but bones. If I was hiding a body I'd take it to one of the big clear-cut forests where they leave sickly trees piled in a heap. I would put her body back where she could not be seen, way back on one of the logging roads. I know that after land is cleared it takes some time for deer to return so no hunters will be in there. Mother Nature has ample time to really go to work and get rid of the mess of dead meat. If someone does see buzzards circling they'll just think an animal died. I gut-shot a deer one time, it ran into thick underbrush where I couldn't find it. One week later I went hunting again. Turkey buzzards were all over the place. I saw where they were descending and I found my deer. There wasn't much left. That's what's going to happen to her body if he tossed her out in the forest."

"God, Ron, that's gruesome" Beth said.

"In Duluth we had similar situation a few years ago with apparently a murdered wife, but no body. It looked like the husband was guilty but without a body he went free. We knew he killed her. It may be the same as Adams. The guy had property in North Georgia and we searched there. Evidently he had stashed her body somewhere temporarily. A few days after we stopped searching, a guy and his kid were riding their all terrain vehicle in that area. They saw buzzards spiraling down into a valley and they went to look. The vultures were feeding on a dead cow. They drove up close and saw what was left of a female's body. It was her. The guy had killed one of his cows and sewed his wife's body inside the bull. The news got out before we could arrest him. He apparently had heard about it on TV and he was dead when we went to his house. He had shot himself."

"There're some crazy folks around," Beth said.

"That's the way it happens sometime. You ever watch one of those hotdog eating contests? That is the way it is. A buncha' hungry critters, dartin' in and out bitin' off chunks of her carcass, consuming it and going in for more, until nothing is left. Even the marrow in the bones is tasty and because her bones have calcium they eventually disappear, too."

"You are so graphically descriptive, Captain. I've heard enough."

"So you have to build your case without her body. That should be easy having seen that carnage."

"It was terrible." Beth shuddered.

"I doubt we will ever find the poor woman. What you need to do is get the man convicted and sent to the gas chamber. If I had my way I'd shoot him tomorrow, even if he is a big-shot golfer."

The Atlanta Journal headline screamed about a pro-golfer arrested on suspicion of killing his wife, Trina. Al Adams, a touring golf professional was arrested at his home where the police found evidence of a murder. Captain Ron Gates said it was one of the most horrible scenes he had ever seen in his thirty years as a police officer. Adams had just returned home after missing the cut in the Crosby tournament at Pebble Beach in Carmel. Before leaving for home, Adams complained that a photographer took a picture as he started to putt on the 18th green. It was a makeable putt. However the flashes blinded him. Adams hurried off the course in a huff.

"I know that cameras are a pain in the ass on golf courses, players complaining about people in the gallery being inconsiderate, but that is no excuse for returning home and murdering your spouse," the Captain said. "What would trigger such rage is beyond comprehension."

"We probably have a winnable case but don't give me that slam-dunk crap. There are stupid jurors. All it takes is one fruitcake."

"But think what the blood experts said about the murder site, that they figured his wife lost at least seven pints of blood while he was killing her. Her body size was estimated at 120lbs. Bodies of that weight only hold about eight pints so she could not have been alive after the beating. She was definitely dead and he dumped her someplace so I would bet my pension that it's a slam dunk."

"Okay Captain. I give up."

"Let me tell you something else, if we did not have that Miranda Rights crapola, I would find out in a hurry where the son of a bitch dumped her body."

Chapter Sixteen

Ron Gates sat hunched in front of his computer when Beth entered the office.

"You look serious, Captain, bad night?

The officer continued searching the Internet.

"You're not talking today?" She grabbed a cup of coffee and a doughnut. "What's up?"

Gates clicked off the computer. "You're the first to know, Beth, he said.

"Know what?"

"Adams is dead."

"You're kidding."

"No, he was dead in his cell this morning."

"Well, no one deserved it more. What happened?"

"He must have had some pills with him we missed. The Coroner said he thinks it is cyanide. He says he died from poison. He's doing an autopsy right now."

"Saves the County a lot of money," Beth said. "Want a doughnut?"

"Sure."

"Beth, can you believe he beat his wife to death with a golf club? I wonder where he dumped her body. They need to kill that Miranda act. Before that stupid decision we could always find out what we needed to know."

I Still Go Fishing with Johnny

On December, 19, 1944, two weeks before General McAuliffe said "Nuts" to the Germans in Bastogne, a German Panzer killed my brother. I lost my fishing buddy, who was also my best friend. Johnny was a paratrooper in the 101st Airborne Division, two years older than I, but not yet 21 when he died. At that time I was on board an LCT in the Mediterranean. We had returned to Palermo after the invasion of Southern France. Communication then was by V-mail and letters was often as much as three months late, but his messages were uplifting at times when my spirit was being hammered. Johnny made fun of me for 'floating around in bathtubs'. I said it was dumb to jump from perfectly good airplanes. Often he would ask me if I had learned anything about China.

My brother

Johnny had a craze about Asia, with emphasis on China. He knew about the Boxer Rebellion and the Opium Wars. When we were kids he would get a world map and show me the Great Wall and the Yangtze and Yellow River. He knew there were more Chinese on earth than any other nationality. I knew Johnny was the smartest brother in the world.

I could find fishing worms by digging near the creek, where the cows grazed, and catch crawfish before the raccoons got to them. When we went fishing I always caught the biggest fish.

He used his knowledge against me all the time. When I shot the first squirrel he would invariably ask me some question about China to show me I was not so smart. When I held my breath under water longer than he, Johnny would ask me to explain what years the Yuan Dynasty ruled in China. He would smirk when I didn't know the answer.

There's a distinct advantage to being smart. You always get to decide things. Like wolves, my brother and I established our pecking order early. When Johnny was a Cowboy I had to be an Indian and be killed. When he was a General I had to be a private. That didn't bother me because I had the greatest General in the world. I understood that when we grew up he would be a Sheriff and I would be his Deputy, which was okay with me.

It seemed, when living was hardest during the Great Depression we could depend on each other. During the 30's, many fathers hitched rides on railroads heading to cities like Chicago and Indianapolis trying to find work. We felt sorry for our dad because he wasn't able to take us fishing.

Survival was hard for him. When the time came when we could have gone fishing my brother and I were in the war somewhere in Europe.

In spite of rugged times our future seemed assured until the smart half of our team went down in German panzer-tank fire in the Battle of the Bulge.

Resourceful

My brother and I made youthful plans during the mid-1930's, in a coal-mining town in Indiana, during the time when the union kept miners out on strike until there was little money for food. The Great Depression was in full swing. Johnny had a talent for innovation that emerged early in our life when it was needed most, which permitted us to survive even in tough times.

By the time I was eight and Johnny was ten we helped in our grandfather's garden and raided the woods for black walnuts and hickory nuts, with mushrooms in the spring and hazelnuts and blackberries in the fall. We'd set box traps that produced rabbits all year long. Frequently we cleaned a rabbit and sold it to a teacher who was one of the few people who had money. We could buy a box of rifle shells. We gigged frogs in a slough and seined for turtles and fish in creeks and ponds.

After the plowing was done we could saddle up two old horses and go into the woods and live off the land, day and night, for a couple of weeks. We took fishing-poles and 22 caliber rifles. We lived on fish and squirrel and occasionally we stole a watermelon and a couple ears of corn from a nearby farm. We cooked our meals in an old rusty galvanized bucket.

We climbed gnarled vines that tangled up high in the canopy and gave Tarzan's yell as we swung out over the creek and let go, plummeting buck-naked into the old swimming hole. We slept covered with leaves in the protective boughs of oak trees.

'Liberty' magazine was a major publication when we were young.

Johnny read where a leather dealer in Terre Haute wanted to buy furs and hides. We knew where muskrats and foxes could be caught. We knew about beaver dams. We knew where bobcats hunted. We stayed away from the swamp, said to be the home of a panther although only the town drunk had seen it. The rest of us heard scary screams sometime at night.

We hitchhiked to Terre Haute and talked to the skin merchant. He sold us traps and taught us how to set them. By the time I was nine, we were running our traps every morning before school. We got a quarter for a muskrat pelt and one dollar for a beaver. If we got a bobcat it was worth three dollars. Johnny took care of the money, explaining that he was our accountant, even though I wasn't sure what that meant.

Maybe our trapping and hunting together when we were young was the reason I devoted fifty years in the fur business. Over the years when cutting and sewing a fur garment I would pretend my brother was helping me. Invariably, I would create a work of art.

I guess Johnny teased me about floating around in bathtubs in the Navy to get even for the fact that I always caught the biggest crappie when we were young. He also got even by asking me a question about China that he knew I couldn't answer. I didn't think it was important. With his keen intellect and my luck with a rifle, the Great Depression was not that difficult.

Memories

Sometimes, late at night, when memories flood in unannounced, I get up and open the box from a shelf in my office and take out two Bronze Stars and two Purple Hearts. I polish them. I read the letter from President Roosevelt and I touch the Screaming Eagle patches. I study a picture of his youthful face and I wonder if he knew his death was imminent and if he felt lingering pain. With my eyes blurred I put his memorabilia back into the box. I go back to bed and stare at nothing with tears running down my cheeks and dawn still long hours away.

I still spent time fishing, with less enthusiasm. The pain was always there and sometimes I would feel a close presence and often an unexplained question would pop up in my mind, like what is the Capitol of Mongolia? I would think for a time and find myself saying that I didn't give a darn about Mongolia. Then it was hard to tie on my hooks with misted vision.

I retired in 1991 at the age of sixty-four. It occurred to me that my brother would have been sixty-six and perhaps President of the United States, although Johnny always seemed a lot smarter than that. More than likely he'd have headed up some University. I decided to take up fishing and write adventure stories about my experience. Instead of bass and catfish, I often spent weeks in the Canadian wilderness catching pike, trout, char and muskellunge.

On my vacation one year I went to an isolated river in Western Ontario. It is the home of muskies in sizes that will make you stare in disbelief. I caught several muskies, including three at over thirty pounds. I knew Johnny would have been proud of me.

A reunion of sorts

Sleep was elusive my last night there. I took out my canoe and paddled a few miles upriver. I lifted my oar and drifted. The silence was peaceful. I thought about how our plans had been altered and how reality was so different than our teenage dreams. I lay on my back gazing at the stars in the inky blackness, that my brother had explained to me fifty-some years ago.

The Big Dipper was still there. The moon was bright and looked the same. Even though I could not see it I remembered that Johnny had told me Haley's Comet would traverse back around about now. The spectrum was like a dome of precious jewels reaching from horizon to horizon and perhaps to infinity. I figured Johnny knew I was there, wishing he were with me.

Echoing across the tundra, I heard the howling of timber wolves possibly foretelling the death of an elk or another of wildlife's wonders. A snow owl on silent wings ghosted low between the moon and me. Loons exchanged haunting messages upriver. A swirling bank of mist suddenly enveloped my canoe.

I drifted off to sleep. In the darkness Johnny came out of the vapor and into the canoe with me. Our embrace was long. I wanted it to never end. I felt the love and respect I had for him from a long time ago. I held a hand that I had not held in fifty years. I saw the same grin and blue eyes I had looked into with awe as we became teenagers. He asked me if I knew anything about China.

I explained that China had a land mass of 3,691,500 square miles, including Taiwan and Tibet. I told Johnny that their population was well over a billion and that they were from Tungus, Chinese, Mongolian and Turkish ethnic origins. I said their capitol was Beijing, and that Shanghai had twelve million inhabitants. I wanted so desperately to impress my brother that details just kept gushing out.

He stopped me and said. "I'll be darned, my little brother finally got even with me, didn't you?" I told him I had attended college because I wanted to be as smart as him.

My finest muskie rod, with the tip bouncing, appeared in his hands. He was engaged with an enormous fish. I watched the scene unfold. He was a master angler, practicing the art of catching a trophy fish. He lifted the muskie into the boat. It had to be a record. He grinned the same crooked grin I recalled from our youth.

"You were right little brother," Johnny said. "China isn't that important. Catching the biggest fish is what counts."

I smiled, "I'll be darned. You just had to get even again didn't you?" He said he learned the technique so he could catch a fish bigger than mine.

I awakened with the sun coming over the top of the trees and felt a kink in my neck. I glanced across the river and realized I was alone. I couldn't explain the feeling that came over me but I knew, somehow, I had been fishing with Johnny again.

Vapor lingered around my canoe. I spoke aloud to a vaguely discernable figure and I thanked him for fishing with me. I said I wanted him to go with me again, very soon. Slowly, very slowly, my brother faded away into the morning mist.

For some moments I had to keep my eyes tightly closed to hold back fifty years of pent-up emotions. After a while I discovered it wasn't possible. The dike ruptured.

Later I returned to the lodge to the smell of bacon. I was hungrier than I had been in five decades.

Shadows

When I was a child I became fascinated with shadows. I could stay cool during hot summers in Indiana simply by staying in the shadow of trees. I could find out how tall an object was by measuring its shadow, then measuring the shadow of any subject with a known height, and then doing the comparative mathematics.

Shadows revealed the approximate time of day. A shadow can expose someone coming close. I learned that shapes and sizes of shadows were caused by the position of the sun, the moon and by different kinds of lights. Spooky shadows were created at night by kerosene lamps when wind caused the flame to flicker on the wick.

In the dim recesses of my collection of childhood memories, I remember a great horned owl swishing overhead allowing me a unique experience of being touched by its shadow. I marveled at the first airplane I ever saw. I attempted to jump on its shadow as it flew overhead.

As a kid I stood by a railroad track and tried to count the shadows of train cars as they rumbled by. I was mesmerized by the shadow of chickens and grazing cows. I chased the shadow of a kite as it did a dervish dance on a blustery day. I treasure the memories of a covey of quails crossing a lane followed by the same number of tiny shadows scurrying along.

One day I noticed that horses and mice had shadows. Ducks made indistinct shadows as they jostled for dominance on the pond. I followed endless shadows of telephone lines.

I recall my grandfather explaining that shadows had personalities. They were dependable and would always be there. He showed me how my shadow followed me, or went in front of me. Sometime it would be by my side. When storm clouds hid the moon I could make shadows with my flashlight.

When my grandfather walked with me in the fields our shadows were obliterated by the movement of windswept grasses, but they always returned. He said my shadows were my best friends and would stay with me when others might abandon me.

When the sun was slanting in the late evening he and I would stand next to the barn and compare our shadows. I noticed how big his shadow was and how tiny mine was by comparison. We stuck out our hands and wiggled the shadows of our fingers. When we hopped up and down our shadows were in harmony on the wall. Often he would set me on his shoulders. We made a towering shadow. I felt like I was on top of a mountain.

During the full moon my grandfather's shadow would hunt my shadow as I grinned from under the grape vines. When he found me my shadow would run wildly from his shadow until both of our shadows collapsed in hugs and laughter, followed by milk and crackers.

The height of my shadow was nearly the size of my grandfathers when the war came. He said for me to take care of my shadow. Our shadows hugged as I entered the Greyhound bus.

Years later, I returned from Europe. My grandfather was setting in the yard. He stood with a cane. I noticed his shoulders were stooped over. He smiled faintly. My grandfather had become withered and frail. I looked at his shadow on the sidewalk. It was also stooped. Tears flowed.

Three months later my shadow fell across the shadow of his casket as it was lowered into his grave. I had the feeling he knew I was there. I waited in the cemetery until the moon created millions of shadows moving mine up a knoll until it merged with the shadow of my grandfather's marker.

Last night I went for a walk with my grandson. He and I watched our shadows changing as we went under street lights. We carried sticks to defend against phantom grizzly bears when they came too close. We jumped, trying to touch the moon. We ran, trying to escape from our shadows, but it was impossible. We pointed to distant planets and our shadows pointed, too. I told my grandson his shadow would always be with him and would remain his friend forever.

I put the small boy on my shoulders and our shadow was as tall as a mountain, just like my grandfather and me, so long ago.

Years later I walked out in my yard. The moon cast shadows. I stared at my shadow and was astonished to see it was shorter. I could see roundness to my shoulder. They appeared the same as my grandfather's shoulders when I came home from the war. I remembered his birthday, a week after I came home, one week before he died. I realized my age was the same as his when he died. I hope my grandson will tell his grandson about shadowy friends when it's his time.

ALLIGATOR...AN OMEN!

The more I hear animal rights people screaming that they're no better than a warthog or a cockroach the more I'm ready to believe them. There is one store now that says animals are people. The lady who started PETA said that she is no better than a pig. Having looked into a mirror all of her life she is apt to know better than anyone but on my farm pigs were ugly, ate slop, grunted all the time, and smelled bad.

But that's not the point. No one that I know has asked animals if they want to be equal to humans, or would they rather be unique. I thought it might be a good idea to find out.

I was runnin' thirty knots up Spring Creek which flows into Lake Seminole in the southwest corner of Georgia. I was going to find a honey-hole to catch me a bigmouth bass for dinner.

A heron with a huge wingspan flew over my head and I yelled to the bird. "Hey, heron, how would you feel about being equal to us humans?"

I asked a beaver who was floating a load of limbs across the water. He slowed, lookin' at me as if I was looney. He raised his tail, mooned me, and disappeared underneath the water. I reconsidered the idea of trying to talk to animals. I saw fish on the surface a few feet from my boat close to some lily pads. About that time, an alligator, maybe 16 feet long, surfaced off my bow. He glared at me and I got the idea that he might have an appetite. My first inclination was to open up the throttle, take off fast, but I figured another inquiry wouldn't make me seem dumb, particularly since no one was around to hear

"Gator," I said. "Are we'uns equal?" He moved closer and began to vibrate the water. On television I had seen crocs do that same thing when they were thinking about making baby crocs. I figured since crocs and gators look alike maybe they did the same thing when a girl gator swam by. Beads of water bubbled on the gator's back and I could hear humming noises coming from its throat. I began to pull in my anchor.

"Can we talk?" the alligator said. Had I heard what I thought I'd heard? I leaned forward and peered down in the alligator's eyes.

"Did you speak to me gator?" I said.

"If only the two of us are out here on this lake and you heard someone say something, and you know it was not you then who do you think spoke to you, you dummy?" I know I looked perplexed. "I never figured alligators could talk," I said.

"Alligators, as well as other animals, can converse in several languages," the reptile said. "However, we don't speak when any of your kind is in our area. I'm not going to talk for long now because there is little value to words with humans. You know, out on this lake we hear lots considering that boatloads of red-necks run around the lake day and night throwin' out beer cans and screaming such stupid expressions as, it's a hog! oh, man! Haaweee! It's a biigg-un! Goooollleee! Thet thur fish just et thet thur bait Hank! One of them poor souls keeps yellin' at his son. I never saw his kid. That's about the only thing the guy knows. Some cuss about life generally. I know my mouth was open in amazement. "I can't believe this is happening," I said.

The alligator appeared to be warming to my presence. He moved a little bit closer. "We can continue our talk as long as someone does not show up. If they do, I'll submerge until they leave. Okay? If anybody else heard us talking it would not be long before some stupid newscaster would be out here askin' stupid questions. He would demand exclusive rights. Anyhow, enough criticism. How about the equality nonsense?" The alligator urged me on.

I explained the reasons for my question. "There are those who believe that if everyone would consider animals equal, and send in donations, so they can use that money to buy cars, airplanes, estates, take vacations and not have to work, then the world would be a much nicer place to live."

"Humans equal with animals?" That alligator laughed uproariously, sending out some ripples on the water.

"Who on earth would want to be equal with nuts whose obsession is sitting in bars uttering gibberish all night, and trying to pick up somebody with bunk-buddy mentality?"

I started to say something in defense of humans. That alligator would harbor no interruptions.

"Why would an animal with intelligence want to be the same as a human who will destroy their mind with booze and drugs, who mug old women and steal their Social Security checks, and who pay to listen to the raucous racket of Rap music?"

I interrupted the alligator's tirade. "Come on now," I said. "We humans have some redeeming value."

He slapped his scaly tail down on the surface, rocking my bassboat. "You wanna' talk? Then let me have my say!"

That gator seemed irritated. "How about a bunch of people sitting in front of a box watching sit-coms with plots so dumb that sound tracks are used to create laughter? That's to make humans think idiocy is funny." I raised my hand like the first grader needing to go to the bathroom.

"I am not finished." The alligator was mad. "Who would want to be equal to a bunch who spend more on deodorants than on vagrants that your society has fostered. We do not have homeless here." He hesitated. I tried again to protest.

"I want to cover another defect in your society, a trait that shows emotional insecurity. We make little gators and a few years later we make more little gators, just enough so the environment isn't totally destroyed. You folks are like bedbugs. There are way too many of you making too many more of you. That's not bright. With overpopulation plus increased social strife I project that within one hundred years you will be back living in caves wearing animal hides and killing each other with spears. Read your papers and see where you're headed." The gator seemed to be intentionally caustic.

I was curious about another thing, so I asked, "Are animals equal to each other, or are some different?"

The creature pondered for a moment. "We have a sub-culture who lie, cheat and steal eggs and grab more than they will ever need. We refer to them as lizards and vultures. You call them politicians."

I was getting tired of hearing an alligator criticizing us folks. "So what makes you so high and mighty?" I said.

"It is not that we're high and mighty but that you are crass and puny. I wasn't going to mention it but one redneck angler, maybe intentionally, dropped a book overboard. I don't know why he brought his dictionary aboard but he dropped it, and I got it. I read it and let me mention some of the superlatives you use to describe yourselves: Promiscuous, Malicious, Corrupt, Violent, Vindictive, Cruel, Selfish, Arrogant, Conniving, Barbaric, Vicious, Scurrilous, Sadistic, Slovenly, Psychotic, Covetous, Lawless, Pornographic, Murderous, Demonic, Alcoholic, Immoral, Glutinous, Lascivious, Heartless and Savage." He slowed. "I could go on but you get the picture. And animal rights radicals have the gall to compare us with them? No way friend!"

We glowered at each other for several seconds. We appeared to have established a kind of dialogue. I was no longer frightened of that gator. As a matter of fact I really appreciated his insight. It was refreshing.

"I like you," I said.

"I like you, too," the alligator said. "I'd like to make you a deal, okay?"

"Shoot."

"You fellows are always looking to catch a world record bass, right?"

"Right."

"I know where there are several large dudes that will weigh over twenty-three pounds each."

"You're kidding!"

"Yep, they're here. We don't eat them because, kind of like you raise chickens and hogs, we raise large bass, and we don't kill the breeders. I'll show you where the largest one is if you'll do me a favor. She'll likely weigh twenty-five pounds, even before spawning time."

"Man! That is a world record. I will be wealthy. It's a deal! What do you want me to do in return?"

"When you get back to Atlanta, I'd like for you to talk to everyone about contamination of the rivers and lakes. You are up-river on the Chattahoochee and I am in the last impoundment downstream. When you get sick I get some of it. Each time you vomit, I get some of it. Each time you flush a toilet I get bugs. You've got six million humans up river makin' downstream saline. Add chemicals, oil, acids, detergents; you people dump it, we get it. When you have a week, I'd like you to come back here and bring your scuba gear. I'll show you beer and coke cans six feet deep, tires, and mountains of rusting junk. You folks have trashed my home."

The gator appeared like he was resigned to the end of life in Lake Seminole, if things did not change quickly.

"We have frequent meetings now that our end is near. A bass came down from Lake Lanier with the last flood. That report he gave us is enough to make you worry. As a matter of fact that bass's scales were bad from the effect of acid rain. He says they are getting pustules and curvatures of their spines."

"In fifty years thousands of people have built houses around that lake," I explained.

"That's the problem." the gator said. "It's the heads in your boats and your don't-give-a-damn attitude. Some stripers went down the locks to the Apalachicola River, and out to the Gulf of Mexico. It is no different. It's a junkyard. They traveled the Seven Seas. While the stripers were feeding, garbage scows dumped rotting garbage on them. The barges were out of New Jersey, Boston, New York, and only God knows where else."

I was now starting to be ashamed of the human race and apprehensive about my grandkid's future. I know Mother Nature will only clean up so much.

"Let me tell you two other things buddy. When you people run out of fuel, you can scrape enough from the oceans' bottom in the world to last you for years. It's been seeping out from warships and transports you maniacs sank in your crazy wars. Armageddon will happen when those nuclear subs you morons sank, or scuttled, rust through their hulls, which a lot are doing, and nuclear waste spills out, these oceans will become flaming cauldrons and you humans will be cauterized in a ring of fire. We will be cooked like in one of your crock-pots. Mark my words."

The gator smiled up at me with a pitiful look of resignation.

I sat, dumfounded. I knew the alligator was right. "It is a terrifying fact that politicians do not want to discuss. We hear the overpopulation projections for humans, like ten billion in fifty years. Oh man! You people are nuts! I said hungry! Wait until the cauldron explodes! The fire will cover the planet and ignite everything. Earth will be one cinder floating in the universe. Only kudzu and cockroaches will survive."

"No," he said matter of fact. "We don't want to be equal with humans. We'd have to sink much too low. We are getting up a petition to have you stupid dolts give this place back to the Indians. We had no problems until milk-faces came here to steal virgin land and murder the natives who took good care of the earth for ten thousand years. You've polluted the place in just four hundred years. We can't get rid of you people fast enough! I would eat you now if I had any idea it would help."

Another bass boat rounded the point of land heading in our direction. I heard gurgling. I looked down. The gator was gone. I waited a couple hours. He didn't re-appear. I cranked my engine and headed home, slower this time. I got some cans that were floating in the water. I put them in a bag for recycling. My bladder was full but I decided to wait. It was a small favor to my friend.

OLLIE THE OCTOPUS

Ollie was born deep in the Marianna trench in the Western Pacific Ocean. He was one of twelve octopuses born within three minutes of each other. Ollie's mother was very busy with so many little mouths to feed. The world deep in the trench was very dark and food was hard to see. Along with their father the little octopuses crawled on the floor of the trench looking for something to eat.

Their plight became dangerous with the prospects of all of them starving so the Mother octopus and the Father octopus talked about the dilemma and decided that they should rise to the surface where the equatorial current was warmer and little sea creatures to eat would be more plentiful.

The trip upward was frightening with giant squid trying to capture some of Ollie's siblings. Off in the distance they could see enormous sharks and big Orka patrolling the ocean in search of octopuses to eat. By hiding under their parent's tentacles the little octopuses survived the ascent.

No sooner had the octopus family reached the surface than a raging hurricane roared in with towering waves that smashed the octopus family onto a reef. A school of tuna patrolling the reefs noticed Ollie with his brothers and sisters. They started eating the small octopuses and only because Ollie was able to hide from the tuna in a grotto did he avoid the fate of his brothers and sisters.

His father was not so fortunate. The reef held many perils. One of the fearsome dangers was two moray eels looking for something to eat for themselves and something extra to take back to their little morays. They discovered Ollie's father while he was too far from the protection of places to hide.

They attacked him with deadly savagery known only to moray eels. The two eels literally shredded Ollie's father while the little octopus looked on from his hiding place. It was the most heart-rending experiences of the little octopus's life to see his father being gulped down in different size chunks. Tentacle after tentacle was systematically severed and eaten, until only his father's torso remained. By then the hunger that had motivated the feeding frenzy was sated. Enough of the body remained to feed the baby eels back in their lair. The morays struggled but were able to drag the body back to their grotto where their baby eels could bite off pieces when they became hungry.

Ollie watched the horrible carnage and huge octopussy tears formed and dripped down his tentacles. He was so distraught that he screamed piteously for the only remaining member of his family.

From a distance, Ollie's mother heard her son's frantic cry and rushed to his side to console him. They both were bereft of feelings other than awful sorrow and longing. She suggested that for safety they should swim into an isolated quay where they would be safe.

While passing through the shallow narrows they were overrun by a fishing boat and Ollie's mother was caught in the pull of the propeller where she was chopped to pieces. Ollie was saved only because he was forced outward by the bow surge.

The last member of an octopussy family began floating in on the tide, along with bits and pieces of his mother. His guts recoiled to such pain when he watched pelicans and seagulls plummeting down into the water after tidbits of his mother. Under the surface were hungry schools of Spanish mackerel and barracuda that slashed through the soupy mixture eating the last of Ollie's mother except for one eye that sank down to the bottom. Ollie was able to grab his mother's eye from an aggressive sand crab. Her eye was the only memento of a strife-torn family of octopussies. He tucked it inside his mouth for protection.

The fishing boat began to retrieve their nets and Ollie was caught in the tight weave of a net. While being tugged onto the deck Ollie opened his mouth to scream and inadvertently swallowed his mother's eye.

The fisherman saw the tiny octopus in the net and picked it up for inspection. He had always wanted an octopus as a pet so he decided to take Ollie home with him. Ollie could live in the aquarium.

For the first time in his brief life, Ollie finally felt he was loved and a warm relationship developed between him and the fisherman's family. With a sense of security found in the loved atmosphere of a family Ollie grew into an octopus teenager. At night, Ollie would often slither out of the aquarium and explore the house. While rummaging in a closet Ollie discovered the reason for the fisherman's interest in octopuses. Inside a large leather case was another octopus. Ollie was perplexed by his find, and dragged the octopus into his room in order to get better acquainted. The new octopus was a brown tone rather creamy-white which was unusual. It was also a slightly different configuration, and its tentacles were rather stiff, a condition Ollie attributed to having been confined in the case. Still Ollie struggled mightily to establish a relationship with the unresponsive octopus.

Gently he intertwined his tentacles with the tentacles of the other octopus. He taunted it by pushing and prodding and trying to enter various orifices but the octopus would not respond. Ollie had no idea that different octopussies were emotionless. He didn't notice the family come into the room to find out what he was doing. After they left Ollie took the octopus and put it back into the case. After all it was unfriendly and obviously didn't wish to get acquainted.

When Christmas day arrived, Ollie decided to do something nice for the fisherman's family so he arose early. He went to kitchen and began to make breakfast. It wasn't hard for Ollie because he could sit in the middle of the floor and reach everything. With one tentacle he started the coffee. With another he popped slices of bread in the toaster. He began to fry sausage and eggs with another tentacle. When breakfast was ready he called to the family.

When they were ready to exchange presents Ollie volunteered to pass out the gifts. With one tentacle he gave a brightly colored gift to the fisherman's wife. With his tentacles he quickly gave out the gifts. When he was done Ollie saw that there were no gifts for him. Octopussie tears poured out of Ollie's eyes and ran down on the rug. The fisherman left the room and returned, carrying the leather case. He handed the case to Ollie. "This is yours, Ollie." The man grinned.

Ollie was so overcome with gratitude than he began to weep much harder. He grabbed his gift and ran to his room. After a second the people heard Ollie crying in frustration. They hurried to his room. In the middle of the floor, Ollie sat with his present open. It was the octopus he had found in the closet. The octopus was lying where Ollie had thrown it in irritation. That octopus still would not respond to him. Big octopussie tears were rolling down Ollie's face.

The fisherman patted Ollie on his head. "Don't you like the gift?" he asked.

Ollie continued to cry, totally dejected.

"Don't you like your bagpipe?" the fisherman asked.

Ollie looked intensely perplexed, his eyes flashing fire.

"Can't you play it?" the man asked.

Ollie's forehead furrowed in deep lines of bewilderment. He grabbed the gift and smashed it on the floor. "Play it," he screamed at the man, "I was trying to lay it!"

Isolation therapy

The bush pilot dropped the Cessna down through a swirling cloud cover into the Severn River gorge. The water looked smooth and placid from a few hundred feet up. Scanning up the river for boulders he picked a spot and set the floatplane down. Scudding to a stop he taxied to a rock jutting out into the stream, cut the engine and forced the pontoons onto a sandbar. I unlashed the 13 feet Old Town canoe and got equipment and supplies from the cabin. My mind brimming with memories of my last trip into the Canadian wilderness, I was to be isolated from the world for a month, my only connection a GPS, at which time the pilot would return to a pre-designated spot on the river and pick me up. I watched as the plane idled out to mid-stream. The pilot revved the engine, turned into the wind, roared down the river, giving me a thumbs-up as the plane lifted up from the canyon, disappearing over the escarpment. My umbilical cord was severed. I felt a surge of excitement.

At last I am alone, buffered from civilization by hundreds of miles of wilderness. From an overwhelming overpopulation of uncivilized creatures, I am now experiencing a simpler world of nature. I set up my tent, scrounged driftwood and prepared for the night.

The horizon fades as darkness creeps across the tundra. I see the Aurora Borealis begin to fire streamers of color across the cobalt sky. I hear the piercing cries of a Golden Eagle and watch massive wings in motion as the aerial predator swoops to capture its final salmon for the day.

Above, in the lingering vestige of twilight, Canadian snow geese, in a fragmented formation, wend their way to mysterious destinations, bending like gossamer, weaving, undulating with the vagaries of turbulent wind. I listen to their honking interplay.

A loon trills forlornly from downriver. Echoing and re-echoing across the river I hear the blood-chilling howling of wolves on a hunt, deciding finality for one of wildlife's wonders. A snow owl, on ghostly wings, is silhouetted between me and the moon. Faint wind-songs whisper from the tops of tamarack.

A phenomenon of heavenly bodies shine above like a dome of shimmering jewels, from horizon to horizon, and on out into the vastness of outer space, displaying celestial splendors created by the Master of All Artists. Fire flower petals flutter from above and drift on the surface like miniature yachts in a regatta. I crawl into my tent, snuggle in the sleeping bag, taste a tidbit of caramel, and settle down. I remember the Chippewa

Indian legend that advised that a frog in a well has a limited view of the limitless sky. I look toward the stars and wonder if infinity is there. I watch inquisitive eyes, iridescent ovals, reflecting from the glowing embers in my campfire. I will be under surveillance for the night. Tomorrow will begin a glorious week. I doze off and relish my wife smiling in a come and go dream.

I awaken to the sun coming up and as I crawl from my tent I feel its warmth. The eyes from the night are gone. A black bear ambles from a thicket of spruce followed by two robust cubs. She stares my way and growls a mother's warning to her young then disappears back into a thicket. A fox vixen barks annoyance at my being there.

I toss more wood on the fire and put on a pot of coffee. The river is seventy feet away. I see huge boulders, with water surging down the rapids. I know trophy fish are there. The coffee clears my mind and I head for the rapids.

I tie my #3 Mepp's Aglia on a twenty pound test line and cast it in a turbulent pool. The powerful strike is instantaneous. I see a flash of fire in the depths. The muskie fought like fury. I guess its length at 40 inches. I put the fish back into its realm. On my next cast, I hook a trophy Brook trout. Below a flume I catch two walleyes for lunch.

My surroundings are therapeutic. I feel a renewal of spirit. The air tastes sweet. Tranquility is all around me. I spot a moose with her calf frolicking in a shallow tributary. I see military aircraft playing war games high above. Peace prevails.

I bring water from the river and eliminate all evidence that I was here. I hear the drone of an airplane descending through the cloud cover. The bush pilot has returned. I lash my canoe onto the pontoons and climb aboard. I ask the pilot to call my home and tell my wife that she will see a restored man. I make arrangements for next year.

DID KILROY REALLY EXIST?

My wife and I were staying for a week in a motel in the village of Helen Georgia. A deck extended over the water of the Chattahoochee River. Oaks spread a dense canopy over the myriad flotation tubes taking tourists downstream. Mountain laurel and rhododendron bloomed in profusion along the banks.

About two miles above the village was a carving in the gnarled root of a hemlock bordering the river indicating that Kilroy had been there. The words seemed to have been carved many years ago, having nearly healed over with bark growth.

You might wonder who in the history of the world has traveled to more places on the globe. Billy Graham has taken crusades to many countries. Bob Hope's name comes to mind. Marco Polo is supposed to have traveled a lot. However, it made no difference, during World War Two, where American military personnel found themselves stationed. Kilroy had already been there.

From personal experiences, I discovered that Kilroy preceded me to the 8,600 feet level of Mount Rotondo on the Isle of Corsica. Kilroy had also ascended to the 6,000 feet level of Punta La Marmora on the island of Sardinia. He had visited on the Island of Elba that was Napoleon's home during his exile. There was little of Sicily where Kilroy hadn't left his signature mark. He had been to Anzio prior to invasion. He had visited the Piazza Del Cobra in Genoa. He must have walked the Apian Highway because his signature was noticed along the road. He had been to the Leaning Tower of Pisa and to Mount Etna. His name was in virtually every village in Africa, the Middle East and Europe, even scratched on the sun-baked entranceway to the Kasbah in Oran.

Possibly the most talked about individual among G. I's, during their absence from home, was Kilroy, but he also became well known in the United States and other regions of the world. He had been at the Great Lakes Naval Training Station and on Goat Island. Kilroy had visited Alcatraz plus the Golden Gate Bridge. For some unknown reason, he boarded a derelict barge up-river on the Amazon. He was reported across the world, in Thule, Dakar, Auckland, Katmandu, Yellowknife, Lisbon and the jungles of Indonesia were on Kilroy's itinerary. It's been reported that when Sir Edmund Hillary reached the summit of Mount Everest there was a sign sticking out from a snow mound indicating that Kilroy was first to climb the highest mountain in the world.

I haven't read many reports about Kilroy the past 50 years yet in my wanderings I'm constantly reminded that he probably did exist and I'm hopeful that we can meet and just talk. I think I came close to seeing him last August while fishing for Chinook salmon at Buoy 10 in the mouth of the Columbia River. As over 3,000 boats converged on Buoy 10 awaiting riptide and millions of salmon starting their spawning run up the Columbia, I noticed that the buoy had some writing on it. The waves were rocking the buoy and it was hard to read what was written. After the wave action settled and the salmon came rushing to spawn I did not have time to examine the buoy again, although that message appeared, oddly familiar. I scanned the faces of anglers, frantically maneuvering to avoid colliding with other vessels. The salmon surged to be first upstream to spawn. All the fishermen in the other boats were hunched over the gunnels grabbing at enormous fish. Then suddenly the frenzy was over and the boats were gone. I spun the wheel, circling the buoy a couple more times, moving in tighter. Sure enough, although corroded from the action of the salt water, was the message, Kilroy was here.

While living in a teepee for a month on the Nez Perce Indian reservation in Idaho, researching Indian lore and legends for Valley of Silent Drums, I decided to try the sweat bath. As steam rose from water dripping on heated rocks, I noticed an inscription carved in a hemlock log. I held the flaming torch close and sure enough, I could see that Kilroy was there, long before me.

The saga of Kilroy is likely the greatest phenomenon occurring in the Nineteenth Century and for that reason I would like very much to get in touch with Kilroy or anyone who has personal knowledge about him.

I would like to know if someone actually met Kilroy. It's possible that Kilroy was a girl. I'd like to know. To my knowledge, Kilroy's nationality hasn't been established. I would like to know. I would like to know where the reader of this story saw his signature. I am aware that 15,000,000 men and women that served in World War Two felt a kinship with Kilroy. He was like my friend, Ernie Pyle. He was with me to remind me that Stukas and German 88's wouldn't always be a part of my life. He was like a friend from home.

Kilroy, if by any chance you read my story, please communicate with me because I would like to finish writing the biography on your extraordinary and inspiring existence.

IRREFUTABLE EVIDENCE

"I know he offed her! I've been dealing with his kind of slime for over twenty years. I can smell the stench of a killer. There's an insolent sneer on their face that makes my skin crawl. I really despise murderers!

Dino Santino leaned back in his lounge, grimacing at his close friend and neighbor. "You know exactly what I'm talking about, Mike."

Dino put his feet up on the railing that encircled the deck where they were seated. He stared up in the trees on the hill sloping up behind his house. Chipmunks darted from their hiding place searching for food while watching for signs of danger. From a perch high up in the poplar a red-tailed hawk observed the furtive antics of the chipmunks.

Mike Hayden was twenty years Santino's senior, having retired from the Atlanta police department when he turned sixty. He had supervised the homicide division for over a decade. He was the reason Dino was in homicide. Mike had recognized that Dino had that instinctive 'nose for facts' capability while Dino was still a rookie on the force.

"I guess I've helped solve over four hundred homicides and interrogated thousands of suspects," Mike said. "After years away from police work, I still remember questioning criminals that I knew were guilty, and watching their eyes when they straight-faced lied to me. The memory still bugs me. I despise killers too, Dino, particularly those that get away with it."

Mike lowered his feet from the railing. The men had been talking about their police service for over an hour.

"I think premeditated murder is the most baffling kind," Mike said. "On the other hand I've always felt that killing a person who has committed atrocities against people like the rape of a child, gang rape, senseless murder, where you know it is fury against society, and other insane acts by two-legged creatures with the compassion of marauding pack animals, is justified by a need for retribution. Am I making any sense, Dino?"

Dino smiled at Mike. "I never knew you felt that strongly. But, yes, I know exactly what you mean. I think cover-up murders bother me most. Someone commits a crime and then murders to hide evidence. It's such a waste of life. I don't know how anyone can be so calloused to other human beings."

"My coffee's cold. You want another cup?" Mike asked.

"Sure, black. You can just feel it when killers lie," Dino said. "I get a strange churning in my gut. When it's going on, I kind of cock my head to one side and think that son-of-a-bitch really believes he has me conned."

Mike returned from the kitchen, placing hot cups of coffee on the railing.

"So what do you have?"

"I have a case involving a pretty wife who, according to her husband, simply walked out of the house saying she needed fresh air, and just disappeared. You read about it in the news a few weeks back. He did not report her missing until two days later. Says he figured she had gone to visit a girl friend and would be back the next day. She's been gone a month now."

"I would report my wife missing that same night," Santino said. "Was her walking out a frequent occurrence?"

"Apparently not. The family was argument prone, and there was a history of conflict, but nothing like a disappearance."

"That's the Melton case. Are you working it?"

"That's mine," Dino said. "I hate being conned by killers. You know wives don't just walk out at night. He expected me to believe his cockeyed tale. Baloney! He fits a murderer profile perfectly. My gut tells me he offed the woman."

"How come we have him on our records?"

"When he's been drinking, a couple of 911 phone calls from the house, several months before she disappeared, some earlier. Guess the man whipped up on her pretty often. According to one next door neighbor he was brutal."

"He looks mad. I saw a surly man. He's worked security for the past six years. He knows how the system works. Hunter. Elk head on the wall. He fishes. Trophies. A gun nut. Pick-up with a gun in the back window. Money trouble. A drinker. In the old days I would've thumped his head."

"How about kids?"

"Two. They say their parents fight and scream sometimes but not that night. Kids said they were asleep when the mother is supposed to have gone for a walk."

"Want more coffee Dino?"

"No, but I want to pick your brains a little more."

"How can I help?" Santino asked.

Santino slouched in the chair. He was a tall man with an Italian swarthiness. His ebony eyes were penetrating, capturing details and facts about cases and sending the information to a computer in his head from which he could retrieve instantaneous information. Dino was muscled, acid tongued, and would probably have been the Godfather had he chosen to be Mafia. Dino's voice during an interrogation could change the contents of a suspect's bowels into tepid soup, but now it showed indications of frustration.

"We're at a dead-dead end. We've been all over his truck looking for trace stuff. None. Nothing in their house. Nobody knows anything. Mike, you're experienced on killers. You have solved a big percent of cases. If you wanted to kill your wife and not get caught, how'd you do it? Think like my guy. I need innovative ideas."

Mike stood and stretched. "You got any plans for dinner?"

"No. Let me add one thing. Someone needs to teach this guy that for every action there's a reaction. For every cause there is an effect. There has gotta be some kind of retribution. You know, somebody needs to get even for the victims. It's revenge for misdeeds. I think it's our civic responsibility. I'm sick and tired of criminals getting off scot-free."

"Want a pizza?" Mike said.

"Sure. Make it small though." Dino pointed to his waist.

Mike grinned, reached for the phone, and dialed a number. "Whatdaya want on yours?" he asked Dino.

"Cover it with good Italian stuff," Dino said.

As the men devoured the pizza, more chipmunks appeared and were having a field-day with the pieces of pizza crusts the men tossed from the deck. The redtail hawk watched from concealment on a low branch. The more pizza the rodents ate the fatter they would become. The hawk was patient, and smart.

"Suppose I wanted to murder my wife without getting caught. What would I do?" Santino laced his fingers in the form of an elongated V, dropped his chin on his thumbs and rubbed his nose with his fingers. He unclasped his fingers and ran them through his thinning hair, pushing hard on his temples.

"You do want a perfect murder, right?"

"If you're not going to get caught, yes."

"There have been many perfect murders," Mike said. "There have been almost perfect murders, maybe one micro-mistake. What do I do first to keep suspicion away from me, and second, keep you from proving I did it, if in fact, I commit the killing."

"That's what I'm asking you," Dino said.

Mike leaned back on the chair, staring into a dark sky. He was silent for maybe five minutes.

"If I were an abusive man, as you say your guy is, I would declare a truce for a while. By doing that my family and friends would testify I was a devoted husband. I'd buy my wife gifts. I'd take her out often. I'd conduct myself in an extraordinarily compatible manner. On some of my hunting trips I would determine precisely where a body could be secreted with no probability of discovery." Mike continued staring into the darkening sky. The hawk had moved to a lower limb.

"It would be in a deep gully," he said, "filled with briars and old logs. I would put her body under the debris. I can even picture the precise spot. I gut shot a buck a couple years back. It ran into a deep ravine. Had a tough time dragging it out. Big buck. Dressed out over a hundred and fifty pounds. It's a tract of land that has since been clear cut. As you know, hunters wait until the undergrowth returns, which then attracts more deer, so there likely wouldn't be anyone traipsing around. That re-growth takes years. It's remote."

"I would plan the murder at the end of the hunting season. Few people roam the deep backwoods except during a deer or boar season. I would make sure my Bronco was finely tuned and I would buy a set of good used tires, discarding them after I was done. The tires are so that if I left tread marks they could not be traced to me. I would make sure my lights and turn signals were working. I would have my license and registration papers. I'd have buckets of slop and meat trimming I'd gotten from butcher shops, along with chunks of pork and beef. I'd keep the meat in sealed plastic bags several days in order for it to rot, and to keep the stink from escaping. I'd go to my farm and kill a bull, and gut it. Maybe a Guernsey. They're big. I would kill a pig and cut off its head. I'd stuff my wife's body in the stomach cavity of the Guernsey, and sew it up. I'd open the belly on one side so when I put it on the floor of the Bronco, the cuts couldn't be seen. The meat should be rotting at least a week."

"Sounds awfully weird," Santino said.

Mike hesitated. "One of the purposes is that in case I was stopped for some reason and asked to show what I had in the Bronco, I would pull the hog's head out of a bag. When they got a whiff of the stench and saw it was an animal's head, and saw the dead cow, and I told them where I was taking the meat, that would certainly stop a search. Besides, I'm not under suspicion for anything. I don't report her missing until the next week."

"Where are you taking the stuff?" Santino asked.

"Patience, Detective. Thorough murderers plan slowly."

Mike appeared to be in deep thought as his formula for a perfect murder developed in his mind. "I'd plan the murder for evening, shortly after the children were asleep," he said. "I'd give the kids one of my wife's sleeping pills to make sure they slept soundly. I'd put it in their hot chocolate."

"You think most murderers do this much planning?" Santino asked.

"Those that get caught don't," Mike explained "And I'm not finished yet because I'm planning a murder I intend to get away with."

"We know the reasons someone kills someone else. Except for a spur-of-the-moment passion killing, I suppose most murders are planned, although some not as well as others," Dino said. "Where is the meat in your plans?" He smiled. "A cute euphemism, huh?" They laughed. "All I've heard are preliminary preparations.

"The actual murder is the easier part. I would take my wife out to the back yard to see the stars. Remember, we are getting along now. I'd wear some hooded jacket to protect my face, and gloves to protect my hands. Those, just in case her fingernails got in the act. Remember it's after hunting season so the night would be cool or cold and my clothing wouldn't appear out of the ordinary for a January evening."

"Why in the yard?" Dino asked

"I'll hose it down afterward leaving nothing for forensics. Hosed lawns would reveal nothing."

"You're good, Mike. But you'll make a mistake."

"A piano wire looped around her neck with a quick twist of my back to her back, a strong lift upward while leaning forward, and the wire would cut into her larynx, crushing it as her body was lifted from the ground. She would be unable to make a sound. Her hands would be desperately trying to grab the wire."

"You're a mean man, Mike." Dino said. "What now?"

"Leaf bags. Three for strength. Each inside the other. Into the Bronco. Spill some of the slop in the back and put the cans near the door. The victim is in a bag, inside the Guernsey. The rotten scraps will go in other bags which will be strewn around the cow, leaking. The Bronco will stink to high heavens."

Santino frowned in confusion. "What's the smelly stuff for? I think I know where you're coming from, but I'm not sure."

"I have a friend in North Georgia who has a mink ranch. I often pick up old meat which I take to him to feed his mink. He also buys carcasses of horses, sheep and cattle that have died.

"God! You're going to feed your wife to minks?" Dino was aghast. "You actually take rotting meat to him?"

"Sometimes it's a little smelly, but I also take him scraps after we field dress a deer. The place I have chosen to dispose of the victim is several miles from the mink ranch in case of a problem with the Bronco while driving nobody will want to check inside the vehicle. A problem might be if a wreck occurred where the Bronco couldn't be driven away. I would call him to tell him I'd be there that night. It's maybe twenty miles up in the hills above Blairsville. That's my reason for being in North Georgia. I'd tell the police to call him to confirm why I had rotten meat in the Bronco.

Remember, I am not under suspicion for anything and all they'll see is rotten meat. Hiding the body inside the Guernsey is genius. I would tell them the cow died from anthrax. They certainly wouldn't touch an animal that had died from hoof-and-mouth disease."

"I thought I had experienced oddball cases," Santino said. "I'm beginning to think you're the screwiest killer I've met. Or maybe the most clever. How about someone stumbling on the carcass?"

"Even if that happened, it wouldn't be soon enough. There's a black bear population in the foothills. I've seen several sows with hungry cubs in that exact area. I've seen more. As you may know bears are omnivorous. They'll smell out the carrion. There are also wild mink. They're carnivorous. Raccoons that will eat anything, along with foxes, weasels, crows, buzzards, wild dogs, mice, wild boar, owls, hawks, blow flies, maggots, and zillions of ravenous bugs and worms. If you took high-speed pictures, you could see what a good housekeeper nature is. Also, if you had a recorder, you could even hear how the feast was relished. In short order the evidence would have been eaten. Anyone off in the distance who saw the buzzards honing in would think a deer or a wild pig had died."

"Bones last a long time," Dino said. "And dental records provide identification."

"The body's teeth would be pulled and hammered into dust," Mike told Dino. "And if, for some improbable reason, the body was found before nature had taken her full course carbolic acid would have been used to remove fingerprints and facial features before the victim was dumped."

"You're a smart killer," Dino said. "So if the authorities can't get a confession, you're home free, right? And you're not going to confess to murder because it's against the law for cops to beat confessions out of suspects? And if you keep your mouth shut the murder will go down as unsolved, right?"

"You betcha!"

"So you think maybe that's what I have with Melton?"

"The man has had a plan since he decided to do away with her. He knows he has you over a barrel because of the Miranda decision and other restrictions imposed on the police by dumb Judges to protect killers. Screw the victim. You can't whack a confession out of the suspect because you couldn't use it in a court of law as evidence."

"So what is the answer to my dilemma with Melton?"

"You don't need a confession. You need for him to tell you where he hid his wife's body. That's all."

"Great! How would you do that?"

"Psychological warfare. The same way the KGB and Gestapo got

83

confessions. The Gooks had some of our military saying stuff they wanted to hear. You will need to find out what scares him. Everyone has phobias, like snakes and spiders, or confined space like subs or caves. I could never be a spelunker. Some folks are scared of precipices. Some people won't fly in an airplane, for example. Get Melton engaged in conversation and find something. Let me have him one night and I'll get you evidence that'll put him where you want him. I'll need him quick though."

"What're you going to do?"

"If you want to be part of a conspiracy, I'll tell you."

"I'll do anything to get him."

"Then pick him up for some reason," Mike said. "We'll take him to the house out on my farm. It's remote. Nothing is in the home. I keep electricity on in case I spend a night fishing the lake. It's posted. No one is ever out there."

"But he'll know where he's going, won't he?"

"Not blindfolded at night."

"How can I get him to you?"

"Pick him up for more questions. We'll then meet someplace before going to the farm."

"You can't beat a confession out of him, Mike. And even if there are no bruises or other physical marks, he'll scream about coercion, intimidation, and other unlawful tactics being used to obtain a confession."

"There won't be a mark on him."

"And you'll still have a confession?"

"You don't need a confession, detective, you merely want to know where he hid his wife's body."

Dino sat thoughtfully, his face grimacing in concentration. "But what if he used your theoretical plot and used acid to take off his wife's facial features and fingerprints so she can't be identified?"

"Dino. You know most killers are stupid and make mistakes. The usual problem is that we can't find the mistakes. However, this one will be easy." Santino said.

"How so?"

"In the first place, the victim has only been missing four weeks. The body likely hasn't had time to decompose or be consumed.

"In your plot, the perpetrator poured acid on the victim's face and fingers. What if my guy did the same?"

"I told you, detective, murderers don't do everything right all the time. If you were a murderer disposing of a body and you removed identifiable features such as fingerprints, birthmarks, tattoos, and even facial visages, would you also remember that babies are foot-printed when they're born?"

"Probably not."

"All we need to know is where he put the victim. Footprints will identify the lady. If those are missing too, we'll convict him on DNA and an abundance of other evidence. We find out where he hid the body, and we'll accomplish that without bruises."

"How'll we do that? He's not going to admit a thing unless he's hurt."

"Psychological warfare, I told you, fear, terror, everybody has a breaking point. He will have his. You'll need to pick him up surreptitiously. Police can't be involved. After we plant enough evidence, like personal things, boot marks, a billfold under the body, and stuff like that, to get a conviction, we'll, covertly, see that it gets in the right hands."

"What you're suggesting is against the law, you know."

"Killing is against the law, Dino."

"How long will you need?"

"A day. Maybe two at the most. Pick him up at night. Let me know when. The sooner the better. Buy the man a beer. Put knock out drops in the drink, enough to keep him out for about three hours. Blindfold him after he's out. It'll take you an hour and a half to get to the farm. I'll be there. You'll leave and I'll call you when I've succeeded. As soon as we know exactly where he dumped her you'll get a warrant and go to his house and pick up enough irrefutable evidence to convict him, then we'll take it to where the body is and plant it. We'll take adequate stuff to convict him Dino, after confirming that the body is where he says it is."

"What do we do with Melton then?"

"Drop him off at his home and immediately have him picked up and charged with her murder. So see Dino, you don't need a confession when you have a body. I'll talk to you in a day or so, okay?"

"I need to use a little subterfuge when picking him up so no one around headquarters will know."

"Fine."

There was the sound of consternation in Mike's voice when he called Dino the next morning. "We have a serious problem old buddy," he said.

"Tell me about it," Santino said.

"I left Melton up on a table in the basement. I used your rattlesnake idea when you said he was petrified of them. He was completely nude, which is an important part of panic psychology. He began trembling when he saw the snakes on the concrete floor. He got a wild look in his eyes. He screamed he was terrified of snakes. I told him I would let him out when

85

he told me where he dumped his wife's body. He's a determined character. You'll have to give the guy credit. He was yelling his head off that he had no idea where his damned wife had gone, as I closed the door and turned the lights off. Through the door, I told him he would be ready to tell me precisely what I wanted to know by morning. He was hysterical, screaming that he didn't know where his wife went. You ready for a shocker Dino?"

"Wait a minute," Dino said. "I talked to a lawyer and the snake technique won't fly. It's against the damned law to even scare someone into an admission. A defense lawyer would get it thrown out as evidence. Even if it could be used when he began talking about snakes, he could cop an insanity plea. Everybody would think he was nuts."

"Too,late. Doesn't make any difference now anyhow. You still ready for a surprise?"

"Sure. And then I have one for you," Santino said.

"Dino, Melton's dead. He must have slipped from the table during the night. He had multiple fang marks all over his body. He evidently stumbled around after he fell. He was all swollen like that Michelin tire character. We have troubles Dino, even though there'd have been satisfaction in getting the suspect in an unusual way."

"Mike. Do you remember sitting up on your deck last month talking about that unique sixth sense we both have that enables us to recognize a killer just by their eyes?"

"Sure."

"Well, go look in your mirror, Mike. You'll see a killer. I'm looking into my mine. We're both so clairvoyant we caused an innocent man's death. He didn't kill her. His wife showed up at home last night."

"Oh my God! You gotta be kidding!" Mike said.

"Nope. She's home. What do we do?" Dino sounded distressed.

"Let me think." Mike said. "Did anyone know you got Melton the other night?"

"No. Nobody." Dino said.

Mike stared out toward the tree line, concentrating. The chipmunks were vying for their breakfast. The hawk's perseverance finally paid off as he watched it swoop down to capture a scurrying rodent. C'est la vie. He tapped a staccato rhythm on the phone with his fingernails. Sweat soaked his shirt. One of his legendary assets in his long career had been an ability to make quick decisions.

Mike carried the telephone back to the bathroom and studied his image in the mirror. Having worked forty years to earn his pension and social security, he rationalized that he was more than justified in being a survivor.

"You still on, Dino?" he said.

"Yeah, what do we do, Mike?" The policeman's voice caught.

"Santino, do you remember that gully in my fictional murder plot?"

"Do you mean the ravine north of Blairsville?"

"Right. Recent circumstance has forced a change in our ideology on right and wrong. Come on over. We are going out to the farm. We have ourselves a big Guernsey bull to kill."

If I must walk through the garden alone I will remember who touched the roses

I wasn't looking for anyone. I had avoided meeting women. I had ended my eighth year as a single parent with custody of four teenagers. One was now married and another was in the navy. That left two to go. It had been an arduous eight years but preferred to the pain of a fragmented marriage. I was determined to die single. But then an angel came into my life. That was thirty-nine years ago.

Now as I talk with widows and widowers in the course of my work I detect that their world has dramatically changed since losing their adored spouse. I see emotionally dispirited people, often shell-shocked, facing a lonely and unsure future. At the age of 85, and after many years with my wife I began to ponder about my own future in the event I am ever left alone and I wonder how my life will be different. I wonder if I will be traumatized, ambling around, not knowing what to do. I know my routine will be reshaped. Will the loss be disabling? In the past few years I have found myself awakening in the stillness of the night with worrisome apprehensions. Will I even want a future without her? The answer eludes me as I return fitfully to the sanctuary of Morpheus.

After she is gone I know there will be an unbearable silence in my home. I sometime wonder what I will miss most. Will it be her urging me to snuggle up closer to her for ten more minutes as dawn breaks? Will it be the coffee pot readied to turn on each morning? Will it be the excitement in her voice when she beckons me to see a tiny white sand crab coming from a hole on the beach at Destin? Will it be her adherence to her vegetarian diet while preparing me greasy pork chops? Will it be my awareness that she will never smile at me, ever again, except from tear-stained, vacation photographs? Will it be her asking me to put in a new light bulb? Will if be the fresh, laundered sheets each week with the top sheet upside–down? Will it be holding her hand on the upper deck, watching our hummingbirds do aerobatics? Will it be the enlightening repartee at breakfast? Will it be just being able to watch her while she reads her plethora of books? Will it be her advising me that my hair needs cutting? Will it be the morning and the evening hugs? Will it be no more chilled tapioca? Will it be the ardor that had diminished over the years, replaced by so satisfying predictability? Will it be seeing her catch snowflakes in winter? Will it be unloading the groceries together? Will it be her warm smile which was quick to come? Will it be her moral support when plans do not go quite right, her irreplaceable interaction with the children as they grew? Will it be the mind-numbing silence now that her friends no longer call? It assuredly will be the times when she patted me on the head and said I was a good boy when I handed her an extra $100 I didn't need. I will always remember her tear-pooled eyes when surprised with a bouquet of yellow daisies as a Thursday present, or a Monday present, or a Friday present. I will remember the joyous expressions as she watched porpoise surfing the incoming waves at Destin, the golden sunset. Will it be her mute computer that no longer sends words of encouragement to her friends in need? Will it be her Lexus parked, unused, next to my Buick. Will it be the absence of her quick wit? Will it be her watching the birds at the feeders? Will it be popcorn during the evening news? Will it be sharing the good prognosis after her visit to the doctor? Will it be that intensive listener as I explained my daily idiosyncrasies, the tiny twitching of her body when she dreams, her deep exhalations? Will it be cleaning her hair from the sink trap? Will it be the Christmas tree with the family hanging the personal ornaments she had made over the years? Will it be hiding the Easter eggs for the children, then the grandchildren and then the great grandchildren? Will it be signing the family birthday cards that she never forgot? Will it be helping her find her lost car keys? Will it be the mild scolding for tracking in a muddy leaf? Will it be that no one will ask or even care what I will be doing or where I will be going each day? Will it be her telling me that my fly is unzipped, that only old men are that forgetful? Will it be her smile, her spark, her zest, her smells, her exuberance, her intelligence, her touch, our unending honeymoon? Will it be that no one will tousle my hair, patting it down in back when I have a speaking engagement? Will it be her telling me to shave and that her oil needs changed and her brakes are making squeaking noises and would I clean her car windows on the inside and would I like tomato soup for lunch? Will I miss not having someone I love not there to return the loving words? Will I miss the smiling "Hi" each morning? Will I miss worrying about her when she drives off? Will it be the frantic calls for help when a bug crawls across the carpet? Will it be the clever emails that pass through our common wall? Will it be not being able to compliment her on the unique find of Hummel's at a garage sale? Will it be the absence of the one who was always there with moral support when I needed affirmation? Will it be those faint nasal sounds in the bedroom in the middle of the night, her sudden turn with an arm flopping across my waist, with warm breath on my shoulder? Maybe those Smiley Faces on informational notes, sometime downcast. Will it be that special hot chocolate mix in the cupboard, her numerous prayers for my recalcitrant being, our anticipation of every morning and night together? Will it be studying the silver in her hair as we continue cuddling on a frosty morning, with me aware I have indeed been fortunate? Will it be our moments together, sitting on the porch, watching chipmunks busily scurrying. Will it be her pleasant disposition? Will it be the ready twinkle in her eyes, her lilting voice and her lady-like poise? Will it be my always assuring her that angel wings have begun to grow on her shoulder blades. Will it be the back scratch where I can't reach? As we snuggle close for warmth I know it will be all of these memories, and so much more. I awaken each morning and I study her sleeping form and become concerned about how I will be able to walk through the garden again. I'm not sure I will want to.

The unwinnable war

In 1979, after building a road across the Hindu Kush Mountains, between Russia and Afghanistan, the Soviet Union attacked Afghanistan with massive ground forces and airpower.

Their stated purpose was to protect Afghanistan officials favorable to the Soviet Union. They initially committed 80,000 troops, helicopters, bombers and fighter planes. After several months, 50,000 additional personnel were sent into Afghanistan. When stinger missiles were introduced with the resultant loss of aircraft the incursion proved to be too costly to the Soviet Union in personnel killed and equipment lost. In ten years of warfare with guerilla fighters the Soviets lost 15,000 killed and 30,000 wounded. When Mikhail Gorbachev came into power he realized the war in Afghanistan was unwinnable and that they needed to escape the death trap. Saving face was not a consideration. Saving the Soviet Union's military force was foremost in Gorbachev's mind.

The United States hasn't learn from history; our catastrophe in Vietnam plus the Soviet's defeat in Afghanistan. If Washington had considered the Russian defeat in their unwinnable war we would not be involved in a fiasco in Afghanistan, Eventually, we will reach the death toll of Vietnam unless we learn a lesson from the Soviets. Russia's war in Afghanistan contributed to the ultimate collapse of the Soviet Union.

We are losing too many people; we now have 96,000 American military engaged against an unknown quantity of fanatics who are well armed in mountains where modern equipment will not operate effectively. If Russia, with 120,000 soldiers and hundreds of gunships, from right next door, could not conquer the Mujahidin we need to rethink how 96,000 of our military can succeed with incredibly longer supply lines.

I am devastated by listening to the nightly death counts announced on the news. Those announcements remind me of the nightly count back in the 60's, informing us we were winning because we had fewer people killed that day than the Viet Cong, a crazy rationale. One of really t traumatic scenes in memory was of desperate people clinging to the undercarriages of hovering helicopters in an attempt to escape the carnage.

Having served in the navy during WW II and having lost my only brother in the Battle of the Bulge, I am aware of how painful it is to lose loved ones. Watching Liberty Ships being sunk by U-Boats, knowing that we can't stop to pick up survivors, aware that the crew of the sinking vessel will die, I suggest we pull our personnel from Afghanistan. Not another son, father, sister or brother should be sacrificed in a war against crazies who can't wait to blow themselves up in some sacrificial mania.

Fanatics in the Mid-East have been murdering each other for thousands of years. We can't alter history but we should learn. Inevitably we will replicate the Soviet Union with their 15,000 caskets coming home to grieving families.

President Truman decided not to invade Japan based on his assessment that millions of Japanese civilians would be killed and thousands of our military would die. Military blood is too precious to be spilled unnecessarily. Enough is enough.

Our civilized treatment of captured Jihadists' must be changed. We can no longer be the good guys. I once encountered a grizzly up in the Canadian Northwest Territory racing down an incline toward where I was camped. Fortunately, I had a high-powered rifle with me. I could not hesitate to see if the beast was friendly. I knew about grizzlies. I killed it while it was 100 yards away.

Having strata-fortresses, satellites, cruise missiles, predators and drones we don't need to be supplying a meat-grinder in Afghanistan. Enough is really enough. No more dead Americans.

Postholes

When my grandfather decided to clear-cut seven acres of trees to provide more pasture, I still can't recall precisely why, at age 14, I was chosen to work with the post-hole digger.

That was before diggers were powered by gas engines. The diggers had two half-round handles and two metal scoops which were sharp on the bottom. It was hinged so I could jab it down to fill the scoop with dirt. I had to jab it deeper into the holes, then push the handles apart so I could lift the digger up filled with dirt.

With the weight of the digger and the weight of the dirt often my last iota of strength was drained. I had to pull the handles together to release the dirt. Several of the holes had to be dug in swampy areas. The muck weighed more so lifting that load was naturally more tiring, especially when I could hear the sucking noise the glop made.

I still can't remember just why my grandfather insisted that the hole be 36 inches deep, always 36 inches deep. I also could not figure out why it was necessary for the holes to be 12 feet apart. When the summer sun burned down like an acetylene torch I wondered why the holes couldn't be 18 feet apart. When the Indiana sun hit high-noon I wondered why the holes couldn't be put a mile apart.

As I sweated day after day I tried to figure out just how many holes would be needed to fence in seven acres.

My grandfather was a brutish man yet he had compassion and when he saw me crying he took me to where cross-cut saws were being used to cut up 33 inch diameter oak trees. If there is one thing that will inspire a 14 year old boy to dig post-holes it is the idea of using a cross-cut saw to cut up 60 downed hardwood trees into logs. I looked at the trees and began to doubt his compassion. Maybe it was some kind of lesson on reality.

The summer sun in Indiana can broil vegetables on their vine. It seemed as though there was no end. I got blisters on my cheeks. I asked if I could do something else. He stated the stalls needed cleaned. I hadn't given thought to how much cows eat until I started cleaning the stalls. I was sure I was going to die from the furnace-like heat in the barn.

I stood in the yard and watched my brother, father and grandfather doing their job. I sold my rifle, hitchhiked to the bus station, and caught the Greyhound bus for Chicago.

Years later I came back from Europe. My brother had been killed in

Bastogne. My father had died from cancer and my grandfather had died from old age. I walked down into woods and stood staring at the fence, which was not finished. I had shirked my part of the work. Maybe if I had remained and worked with them I would not have thought about my laziness so often during the war. Maybe one of them would still be here. Tears formed.

I would finish the fence. I went to the barn and found the post-hole digger. I went back to the pasture and began to dig post-holes. I dug post-holes until the sun went down. I got a lantern and continued digging.

DESTINY

Millions of little sperm were on vacation in a tropical climate. Unfortunately, there were no recreational facilities and the sperm were bored. They wanted to do anything to cut the monotony. They knew that their lives would be over soon.

Late one evening they suddenly sensed an approaching cyclone. Their home started to shake from the leading edge of the tempest. The fury of the storm was at first only scary. As the storm got worse they were scared by having never experienced such vibrations. They remembered that it was the season for storms and they needed to run before it arrived. Time was short.

When they could find no door from which to escape they became terrified and began to rush, falling over each other in their desperate attempt to leave while there was time. They were in despair, not knowing what was ahead.

One channel opened up the moment the hurricane force struck the vacation spa. The sperm raced for the opening knowing it would lead to safety. The channel was long and suddenly they began dancing and yodeling as they raced through the opening, knowing that their problem would soon be finished. "Hi ho, hi ho and off to work we go!" They chortled with gusto.

They were still worried somewhat about their future. The future for the sperm was dark until they were all inspired by the visions of a superb fallopian tube. Suddenly, they understood their destiny and raced much faster to reach that opening at the farthest end of the tunnel.

Somehow, sensing that there would be a decided advantage to being first to get to the fallopian tube, they raced pell-mell toward an orifice at the far end of the tunnel where they spilled out into a moist and scented cavern. Wanting to be first to find the magic tube they began a frantic search, looking under the tongue, a bicuspid, around some gold inlays and other recesses. They probed under molars. One anxious sperm spotted what he thought must be a fallopian tube at the back of the grotto. The rest of the sperm saw the one sperm hurrying for the tube. They tried to overtake the speeding sperm. They avoided tonsils and tap-danced around a stalactite that interfered with their passage. As they rocketed en masse down the hole, they realized that it was not the tube for which they had been searching. But, what the hell! It had been a macho trip. Since they knew there would only be one vacation like this in their life, what a better way to go.

Nez Perce Reservation

I stared out from my teepee on the Ne Perce reservation in Idaho. The time was four o'clock in the morning on the first day of October 2008, Overnight, the weather had turned colder. In spite of the chillier weather, I was anticipating a week of revisiting a unique time in history. It would be the time of pride and independence maintained by people who nurtured this land for thousands of years before the arrival of the Europeans. Cruel marauders crossed the ocean from distant countries intent on conquering the native people by any means including the eradication of their simplistic way of life.

Down the boulder-strewn embankment I heard the sound of water lapping on the shore. The river was cloaked in mist, mysterious, and secreting a treasure trove of migrating salmon. From up the valley the howls of timbre wolves foretold the death of one of nature's wonders. They were not far away.

The moon bathed the night in a silver patina. The tawny image of a cougar leaped across a ravine leading to the river. The silence was complete. When I was positive the panther had moved away I walked outside the teepee. The sky was filled with celestial splendor, spreading from the bluffs to the mountain peaks on the horizon. Everywhere I looked had an aura of familiarity. Nothing was changed since my brother and I lay on a mound of straw studying the same phenomena years ago as wide-eyed kids. The harvest moon was brilliant and seemed close enough to grasp.

I remembered that my brother and I often camped out in the woods back home, slept in the boughs of ancient oak trees, and lived off the land. We had .22 caliber Springfields and weathered fishing poles. We pretended to be intrepid travelers of the universe looking for galaxies to explore. We climbed hickory trees and shook the nuts down. Mulberries were succulent treats.

We studied Indian burial mounds, wondering who they were, where did they go and what were they like.

I wondered how long I had been meditating when the first glimmer of dawn began appearing slowly over the bluff. I looked to the west and saw jagged crests of mountains jutting up through the early fog like the serrated scutes of some primordial dinosaur. Traces of snow had eluded the sun. To the south and east towering peaks, garlanded with forested slopes formed the barrier of the Bitterroot Mountains. Heather in bloom began to appear as the sun rose, Sage cloaked the village. Smoke rose from flue holes and the aroma of cooking venison floated on the breeze. Thundering down the ravine across the valley was a waterfall. Appaloosa horses on the hillside were silhouetted against the morning sun rays. I heard awakening grouse in the underbrush. A flight of Mallard ducks skimmed low over the river, dropping toward the water. Life had been plentiful in the valley where the Nez Perce lived peacefully.

Remaining outside my teepee, I reflected to earlier times. I envisioned myself a Nez Perce Chief, living with my wife and children. My brother lived in a teepee next to me. Sixty teepees in the village comprised three hundred industrious Nez Perce. Our ancestors were buried in the sacred burial grounds across the river.

My parents lived in the village. We bred Appaloosa horses. The river was filled with Chinook and Coho salmon. Elk and deer wandered in the deep valley and out on the prairie buffalo roamed unimpeded by fences. Kouse and Cama roots were bountiful. Nature provided an abundance of nourishing things to eat. There were cherries, huckleberries and chokeberries, that when mixed with various meats, made succulent pemmican. We had ducks and geese, and wildfowl eggs.

We could hunt beyond the horizon and no man told us where we must go and when we must return. The people were in control of their destiny and life was arduous, but richly rewarding.

To defend our villages against the occasional renegade that attempted to steal our horses or take food from our larder, we had bows and arrows, war-clubs and spears.

Our ancestors were proud and had lived productively and peacefully for thousands of years in the Clearwater River Valley.

Aware of the atrocities perpetrated on Indians by United States soldiers east of the mountains the past three centuries, I wondered what I would have decided when confronted by soldiers sent to relocate my people to some desolate reservation void of water and of wildlife, all because they coveted our fertile land. They wanted our rich forests. They lusted for the gold in our rivers.

Our presence interfered with their plans to conquer the land and possess the fruits of our mountains. Aware that we were too few, and outgunned by relentless barbarians void of compassion, the decision would have been made instantaneously. I would defend my people and our land, and die, as did many Nez Perce.

Greed--Job killer

I detect increasing pessimism where I live in Stone Mountain. I recall when our economic shock waves began in the 40's, unions striking, intimidating management into agreeing to higher wages and benefits. At first the benefits were good for unions but then greed took over; demands became too costly, executives began taking too much pay and too many perks. That put industry in decline. Politicians began sticking their finger in the cookie jar, enacting high taxes. Expenses skyrocketed. Profit plunged. Appliances, apparel, steel, leather, porcelain, jewelry, electronics, replacement parts moved offshore. When union contracts were about to expire, industries were threatened with strikes unless they agreed to higher hourly rates, more vacations, more sick leave and greater benefits, more, more. Executives continued looting capital and politicians assessed greater taxes. With stockholders demanding more return on investment, costs became punitive. Businesses could not afford to modernize or compete. The analogy of the straw that broke the camel's back was true in American industry. In industry there were too many straws.

Rising payroll expenses resulted in manufacturers resorting to automation which caused a loss of several million jobs, but that still wasn't sufficient. The only option for industries was to reduce quality, losing market share to foreign manufacturers who made a better product, or move overseas in order to survive the destructive costs. No industry can continue with the depletion of its operating capitol. The geese that laid the golden eggs were strangled, not by conspiracy but by a three-way onslaught of greedy gluttons.

To escape the economic stranglehold that unions held on businesses many companies moved from northern states, where unions were dominant to southern states where right-to-work laws helped to keep costs lower. But that was only a partial remedy. The other two-thirds of the dilemma , too much taxes and excessive executive compensation, continued to reduce industry's ability to pay for modernizing, resulting in cheap products and a further decline in market share. Add government mandated regulations and it was no longer possible to produce a profit with the implication that making profit was somehow un-American. When a company was profitable and could have used profits to modernize their operation to remain competitive, the gluttons enacted a Windfall Profits tax punishing business for making money, further crippling incentive. Survival instincts in businesses resulted in their moving over seas where costs would be lower. Every time a business was forced to go overseas to prevent bankruptcy America's workforce shrank.

Politicians, who were busy arranging their own financial security, let this crisis happen. We now have plus-10% unemployment due to destructive decisions and I do not hear anybody recommending what to do about it. It will take the mastermind of World War Two planning to reverse the trend. That demands beginning over. There is no method for creating enough jobs to accommodate the growth in population added to the influx of immigrants, and graduates Rather than wringing our hands in resignation let's find a candidate with guts for President. Somebody smart enough to apologize for the errors of the past, sufficiently persuasive to force cooperation, and dedicated to removing gluttony from industry. The AFL-CIO, UAW and Teamsters unions grew even more avaricious. Executives became richer by depleting operating capital. Politicians expedited the death knell. We need to regain lost jobs back to America, but enabling industry to manufacture goods that can be sold competitively; lower taxes from cities, counties, states, and the federal government, lower wages for workers, lower executive salaries, with tax breaks and subsidies for retooling factories, beginning in those areas with higher unemployment rates. Full employment depends on recovering offshore jobs. At such time as profit is produced employee benefits can be higher. Our future depends on the recovery of jobs that went overseas. Otherwise our unemployment will remain at crisis levels

A group of patriotic executives must be appointed to visit those industries that sent jobs overseas to assure them that changes will be made in the cost of doing business to create a fiscal climate so that businesses can again be profitable here.

We need a visionary who isn't worried about winning the next elections but willing to get down into the trench and re-open abandoned factories across this country so people can find jobs. The campaign must be relentless otherwise we will continue drifting toward anarchy. Desperate people do desperate things. Unemployed workers are not interested in dancing with stars

Economy Trips

It is 600 miles from Georgia to Indiana where I was heading to my 63rd high school reunion. I kept looking in my mirror concerned that I looked my 83 years. Reading signs kept me from worrying about my age.

I began reading advertisements on billboards and watching for an egress from the highway in case I needed gas or became hungry. About the time hunger pangs hit, I saw some messages on some billboards telling about a free breakfast. Many of them served continental breakfasts. Trees hid some of the words but I realized that at none of the motels was there the requirement for people to have stayed in those motels serving the free breakfasts. The menus looked tasty so I decided to check one out.

I pulled in Holiday Inn. I drove in back, entering the restaurant from the adjacent courtyard along with several guests. I walked in the restaurant, yawning sleepily as I said to the hostess. "You have superb accommodations. I'm going to recommend your motel to my friends. What's for breakfast?"

"I'm glad you like it." With a flourish of her hand the waitress showed me to a table where there was fruit, hot rolls, juices, biscuits and jelly, with chocolate or coffee and as I watched another waitress bring in biscuits and link sausages, my taste buds went crazy.

As I enjoyed the hospitality I saw that lunch would be served from 11AM to 1PM. I looked at my watch. It was nearly 11AM.

I asked the waitress, "I'm sure you're going to throw the rest of this food away so is it okay if I take some of those cinnamon rolls?"

"Of course, help yourself."

"I know milk should not be put back in the refrigerator, so is it okay for me to have a couple of the cartons?"

"Sure. Go ahead."

"And could I have an apple?"

She glared, then gave me two apples. She was curt. "Anything else?"

"I would like two sausages and biscuits if it's no bother." I got two sausages and biscuits, wrapping them in a napkin. "This is a great motel" I smiled. "I'm going to write notes of commendation to the home office. What's your name?"

"My name is Melody Perkins. Please come again." She had become a little unfriendly. Maybe she thought I was El Cheapo. I handed her a dollar tip.

"Is that spelled with a y or with ie?"

"It's spelled with a y."

As I pulled back onto Interstate #24 my mind reflected back to my free breakfast visit. So that my God-fearing grandmother wouldn't roll over in her grave, I remembered I had not misrepresented one thing nor told one falsehood about how nice it was for them to provide me a free breakfast. My conscience was not burdened. I had not told them that I was a registered guest and the billboard didn't say that people had to stay there. I ate a cinnamon roll and drank milk under an oak tree on Mount Eagle Pass. Life is so abundant. I ate an apple a day for the next two days. I froze the sausage and biscuit just in case I was late for work some morning.

My wife doesn't understand my frugality. Of course she wasn't around in the Great Depression. However I'll stop by Holiday Inn next year when heading to my reunion and on a budget. I might begin stopping at each motel along the way because I'm aware that their breakfasts are free. Mother's Day I am going to take my family. Isn't America great?

Trauma in the Fur Industry

The first sale of beaver skins from the New World was held in Garraway's Coffee House on January 24, 1672 by "The Honorable, the Governor and the Company of Merchants, Adventurers Trading into Hudson Bay" in honor of which Dryden wrote:

"Friend, once 'twas Fame that held three forth, to brave the Tropic Heat, the Frozen North; Late it was Gold, then Beauty was the Spur; but now our gallants venture forth but for fur."

Despite the satirical remarks of Dryden, the world it appeared had more respect for furs than for gold. To the inhabitants of the New World, the beaver was literally an emblem of wealth. It was so important to frontiersmen that an emblem of beaver was embossed in the first shield of New Amsterdam's seal. After the revolution, the eagle supplanted the crown but two beavers remained on the shield.

The story of fur trading in early America is the actuality of our expansion. Valiant fur trappers led the way into remote areas of America and Canada. Commerce naturally followed with John Jacob Astor amassing a fortune and was virtually the first man on the continent to be the employer of thousands of gainfully employed people in the various aspects of the fur trade under the name of the American Fur Company. America exported millions of dollars in furs to y European and Asian markets with the incomes amply funding America's initial development. We can thank the fur business for jump starting American emergence as a world financial power.

Along with being absolutely necessary in frigid climates as a protection against humans freezing to death, fur has also gained importance as one of the world's greatest fashion images. Fur is long wearing and fortunately for the environment, biodegradable. Synthetics, on the other hand, are made from petroleum products which, as we saw in the Bay of Valdez, can pollute the world for all eternity. Additionally, synthetics must be burned for disposal, further polluting the environment, or piled on already overfilled landfills with long range destructive impact on the land which has little area remaining on which to hide garbage.

Fur has remained a strong segment of our economy with the United States' fur industry providing good jobs for over a million of our fellow citizens. A peak $2 billion sales volume provided city, state, county, and federal government's annual taxes and licensing fees exceeding $500,000,000. Another $300,000,000 was spent by the industry for advertising benefiting newspapers, magazines and the electronic media. Additional millions of dollars contributed heavily to the prosperity of insurance companies, equipment suppliers, shipping companies, security businesses and many more.

A dramatic downturn in business began immediately after Congress passed the tax reform of 1986 with big ticket items taking a big hit. Real estate, small aircraft, pleasure boats, furs and jewelry got hammered when interest on charge accounts and sales taxes on purchases could no longer be used as tax deductible expenses. The free fall in business precipitated the stock market plunge of 1987 where investors lost a huge percentage of their stock value. Confidence in the intellectual capabilities of politicians charged with handling our fiscal affairs disintegrated.

A psychological shock wave drove business volume downward and contributed to an accelerated loss of jobs across the country. The cause and effect scenario created financial terror among taxpayers causing a strict curtailment of most purchases other than necessities. Simply, consumers were reluctant to spend when their own personal financial future was in apparent jeopardy.

Governments with voracious appetites loaded more taxes on an already staggering economy. Residential and commercial real estate taxes shot skyward. Fuel taxes increased. Sales taxes at both city and state levels, increased by as much as 20%. Confiscatory taxes on business reached new plateaus. At that precise moment when taxpayers were screaming revolt Congress strong-armed George Bush into signing into law the biggest tax increase in history proving that "read my lips" was nothing more than a political lie. It looked like a blueprint for the ultimate destruction of the economy of the United States.

Thousands more businesses folded with hundreds of thousands of people thrown out of work. Sales of all big ticket merchandise plummeted. At that exact moment a gluttonous Congress passed a 10% excise tax on expensive items where retailers and manufacturers were already floundering from business losses attributable directly to burgeoning tax burdens.

Manufacturers of small aircraft bankrupted. Boat builders failed under the heavy load. Over 50% of the fur business was destroyed throwing thousands of artisans out of work. Jewelry firms laid off hundreds of employees to permanent career loss.

To prove that political idiocy is incurable, the job killing taxes are still law, except for the 10% excise tax. The biggest barrier to job growth and business expansion is the overload of oppressive taxation and fees heaped on the backs of consumers and business. The back of the camel is already broken. Unless changes are made expeditiously it is only a matter of time when a final breath will be drawn.

On top of many problems over which furriers had no control many members of the industry aided and abetted in their own downfall. When business soared in the middle-80's, promotional stores resorted to scam tactics in selling their product. Simply, mink coats worth $7,000 according to the amounts of pelts used in the coats construction multiplied by auction prices of those pelts were inflated to absurdly high prices in order to scam the consumer into believing they were making huge savings on the purchase. That scheming was possible because famous name stores had their furs overpriced supposedly justified by designer labels affixed to the garments. Many of the designers whose names were on the fur had nothing at all to do with the creation of the coat and many of them were dead.

The promoters had only to use the high prices of the high priced fashion stores as a comparison in order to provide the phony discounts. A $7,000 garment would be priced maybe $17,000 with a 50% discount advertised. The coat would then be sold for $8,500 when it was only worth $7,000 in the first place. Inflated appraisals were provided to the gullible buyers to further convince them that great saving was a part of the transaction when in fact there was no saving. Customers eventually discovered they were being suckered and simply quit buying.

Mother Nature further traumatized the fur industry and most other outerwear enterprises by providing five consecutive warm winters across the entire country lessening the need and desire for the product. Memory of long, bitterly frigid winters, lends impetus to the following selling season. Conversely, a mild wearing season reduces outerwear sales the next year. A comment made most often by customers was that they did not have sufficient wear to warrant the expense of purchase.

Nationwide, the fur business has dropped approximately 50%. Nearly 50% of retail fur stores and fur manufacturers have closed or merged. Several major retail organizations, such as Macy's, have either closed out furs or resorted to only a fur service operation. In the 80's, Atlanta boasted over 25 fur businesses which now has been reduced to less than 8.

Fur prices have stabilized during the most recent auctions in the United States, Canada, and Scandinavia with wholesale prices moving upward at the manufacturing levels. Inventories in stores are at an all time low with manufacturers prepared for a strong upturn as stores replenish depleted stocks.

Evan's Fur Company, which operated leased departments across the country, including Marshall Fields in Chicago reported a 7% increase in 1993 over 1992 with profits on the plus side for the first time since 1985.

The American public has finally been turned off by recent antics and sometimes criminal behavior by radical animal activists' organizations. Donations to these groups have understandably dried up because of a declining economy and the fact that people sending in donations have found there is no accountability as to how their money is being squandered.

There has always been and will always be a viable fur business in America. There are enough people who appreciate the ultimate magnificence fur brings in the pride of ownership to assure the industry's survival. Cyclically, the fur industry has ridden the rises and falls of the economy since the birth of the nation and as the purchasing power of consumers increase so will the fur business in direct proportion to the economic resurgence.

The fur industry will survive the convulsions of the 1980's as it has persevered through other troubles at other times and will doubtlessly emerge smaller but stronger depending once again on integrity with furriers holding themselves to the high ethical stands and prestige it once enjoyed.

Brainwashed

At the turn of the last century Russian physiologist and psychologist Ivan Pavlov, experimenting with canines, discovered the phenomenon he described as conditioned reflex. He found that when responding to directed stimuli dogs could be trained to react in controlled ways.

After the capture of the Pueblo, by North Koreans, in 1967, men aboard the craft were exposed to intensive questioning by their captors, resulting in some of the crew responding to questions with dictated answers.

During Desert Storm Americans who had been taken prisoner by Iraqis, and after lengthy interrogation by the Iraqi military, were put in front of television cameras and forced to expose specific inaccurate remarks intended to condemn the actions of the United States in Iraq.

Today, Americans are being trained to respond to promotional stimulus the same way. One has only to stand up during the seventh inning during a baseball game and become a participant in a stadium-wide stretch to understand that you have been trained to accept baseball as the national sport so owners can exact higher prices for tickets, hot dogs, drinks, plus sports paraphernalia and receive favorable tax exemption to build palatial edifices to themselves.

Watch a crowd of spectators during golf matches applauding every player, when they score an eagle on a hole, birdie a hole, par a hole, bogie a hole, double-bogie a hole or set a new record for the worst scores on a hole. Without being aware of the Pavlov influence, people are trained to scream and applaud en masse.

Television is a prime example of media brainwashing of the viewer. Sit-coms and talk shows that have nothing cultural or humorous to offer receive rave review from promoters to convince advertisers to spend enormous sums of money to be the sponsor of those shows. That is accomplished by paying the actors and actress's sizeable salaries, intended to create an aura of talent, at its best is illusionary. Another part of the con is the off-camera prompter who holds up an applause card reminding the compensated audience that it's time to applaud, exchange looks of celebration, and animatedly utter oohs and ahs. Those who applaud squeezing fruit juice and cooking hot-dogs are examples of compensated shills.

Machines that have recorded applause in earlier live shows, where there really was humorous dialogue, are used to give viewers the impression that shoddy sit-coms are humorously entertaining. Those techniques can be detected by noticing that faked applause is used after exchanges of dialogue by people in the sit-coms and is of pre-programmed length and intensity.

Pills and diets that have marginal values are promoted with the participation of compensated advocates who testify that the product works. The photographers of those paid endorser participants are the same photographers used by politicians to portray their opponent in an unfavorable light: simply use poor quality lighting first and good lighting in the comparative view. Visual spin is effective and even if many people aren't aware of the swindle they, like Ivan Pavlov's dogs, are being methodically brainwashed to spend money.

When producing a newer drug, manufacturers spend enormous sums of money promoting their product as a cure-all for illnesses ranging from toenail discolorations, to acid reflux, to embarrassing body odors. Compensated actors testify repeatedly as to how effective the product is. Over a long period of time, pictures of suffering people on T.V. who have been miraculously cured is effective in convincing susceptible viewers that they suffer the identical sickness thus; a virgin market is created for that drug.

One of the most unique marketing techniques was conceived for corporations by such as Nike, Tommy Hilfiger, Nautica and more where fawning minions are induced to buy tennis shoes and wearing apparel with logos allowing the companies free advertising wherever people wear their shirts, apparel and sport shoes. The Pavlov Dog society has become little more than billboards. Our Civilization is in decline when it's glorifies name-brand merchandise.

Watch the servile worshippers at the Oscar, Grammy, Golden Globe, Emmy and other Awards Banquets groveling around to get an autograph from contrived idols with splashy jewelry, bulging wallets, painted faces, driven in limousines and flaunting their custom designer apparel, so costly that millions of impoverished citizens could be fed for one year with the same money.

The usage of subliminal technology has become a fact of living. That technique involves the projection of images on a screen below the threshold of conscious perception. The images are micro-seconds in time and inadequate to effect any awareness but able to produce a response. Promoters use the technique to surreptitiously create a desire or a psychological need, which did not otherwise exist, for a product or service. It is manipulative brainwashing at its technological best.

You have only to see weird body-piercing, caps on backward, tattoos, bare navels, drooping pants with cuffs dragging on the floor, hear boom boxes, and be aware of youngsters on drugs at RAP festivals to recognize the Pavlov's Dog Syndrome at work.

You Gotta' Love Those Telemarketers

10:30 PM. Exhausted after a hard day. Had just dozed off. Telephone jangles.

Sleepily. "Hello."

Syrupy voice. "Hello, is this Mr. William York?"

"Yes."

"May I call you Bill?"

"Sure," I said, wondering.

"Bill, Congratulations. Your name has been selected to receive 4 free dance lessons from Arthur Murray Studios."

Hesitating, and because of the late hour verging on a vitriolic outburst, I said, "So?"

"Bill, Arthur Murray is the premier dance studio in America." She oozed sensuality.

"What's your name, honey?"

"My name is Ann." She oozed some more, low sultry voice.

"So what's this great freebie?"

"Bill, you'll want to come in to our studio and meet our lovely dance instructors."

"Are they real purty?" I did my Indiana Redneck imitation.

"They certainly are, Bill. You'll see for yourself when you come in."

"I've been thinking about purty girls ever since my wife left me," I said.

"I'm sorry to hear about your wife." Ann is now a shoulder on which I can lament my plight, a confidant."

"It's funny but I've been thinking about learning to dance since my wife left."

"You might want to sign up for a series of dance lessons."

"I've dreamed about the Conga with a bevy of beautiful babes," I said. "How much will it cost me?" I plugged in the coffee pot.

"Oh we have a great selection of options, perhaps 10 lessons."

"How much does that cost, Ann? Can I dance with you?" I am getting chummily personal now.

"Of course, Bill. Eight lessons will only be $100 because the first four are free."

"Money's no object, Ann. My wife and I were well off and split three million dollars right down the middle."

I could envision the gleam in her eyes. She wiggled her bait again.

"You'll enjoy our exquisite girls so much you might want a longer series."

I poured a cup of coffee and grabbed a doughnut. "What else goes with that service?"

She giggled. "You can never tell." She was implying nice goodies. Teasing, tantalizing.

"When can I start" I wiggled my hook, too.

"Any time, how many lessons will you want?"

"I think I'd like to take two lessons each week for a year." I nibbled another doughnut.

"Oh that'll be marvelous, Bill. You can join our girls on world cruises and parties at local hotels. You can learn new dances."

"Can I learn to jitterbug? I've always wanted to jitterbug."

"I see you like the oldies, right? Sure you can, plus the Samba, Tango, Cha-Cha, and the Charleston. Maybe the Bunny Hop. Think of being in a long line of beautiful girls weaving in and out, having a great time."

I could imagine my hands on some gorgeous gal's hips. I giggled.

"Oldies, except my women." I giggled again. "Can I learn to tap-dance? I've always admired Fred Astaire."

"Absolutely, you must be an interesting man, Bill." She was vamping me like Lorelei.

I poured another cup of coffee and downed the last doughnut. I scanned the clock. 11:30. One hour of glib telemarketing.

"For someone special like you Bill, I suggest the 1 year plan."

"How much will that cost?" I warmed my coffee.

"With the parties and cruises we have scheduled, and our voluptuous instructors, that'll only be $8,000.

"What's that word voluptuous mean?" I never stopped wanting to learn.

She hesitated. "You know, kind of chesty, Bill." She giggled some more.

I said OHHHH!!! "When will I have to pay it?"

"You can bring a cashier's check when you come in for your free lessons."

It was almost midnight. I poured out the remainder of the coffee. It was cold.

"Bill. Did you hear me?"

"Yes, Ma'am, I was just thinking about how nice it will be to dance with all of them purty girls.

"When can you come in, Bill?" Ann was a good marketer, persistent, patient. She was now closing the deal, setting the hook.

"You'll have to pick me up."

"Why?" she responded.

"I guess I forgot to tell you. I was in a bad wreck last year and was injured. That's why my wife left me. The insurance settlement was where we got the three million dollars."

"I'm so sorry," she said. "How badly were you injured?"

"I lost both arms and both legs. In orthopedic vernacular I'm designated a quadruple amputee."

Maybe ten-fifteen seconds went by.

I figured I should play Taps on our relationship. "I'm also blind." I said. "I lost my eyesight in the accident. When do you want to pick me up, Ann?"

Another couple second passed.

"Ann?"

I heard a click and Ann hung up the phone. I'd lost a new friend. I went back to bed. I had a hard time going to sleep. Too much sugar in the doughnuts.

I ADORE THOSE TELEMARKETERS.

Drug War Fiasco

I read the reports of illegal drug interdictions along our coastlines. Travelers are searched in airports where Federal agents discover caches of mind-altering substances secreted in traveling bags, bars of soap, cameras, body cavities and a host of innovative places expected to pass customs. Smugglers hire people called mules, to ingest capsules of drugs in the hope that customs will be duped. Those mules frequently die when the capsules containing illegal drugs ruptures in their stomachs while en route to deliver their cache. From many reports it has been determined that less than two percent of illegal drugs are being intercepted. The balance of the drugs ends up in drug addicts. In between the origin of drugs and those addicted are billions of dollars in profit. Therein is the reason the drug program in the United States is a failure.

A comparison has been made between drug enforcement and the 1920 law that prohibited the sale of alcoholic beverages. After the Prohibition law was enacted people who wanted to drink continued to drink. The cost of enforcement spiraled. Smugglers and agents died. The drinkers prevailed and Prohibition was rescinded. That rescission did not cause more drinkers. Drugs legalized and controlled, will not cause a dramatic increase in drug users. With the profit motive removed, drugs, like methadone, should be dispensed by the agencies whose purpose is to reduce the craving of addicts. A benefit will be the cessation of gangs competing for turf in deadly battles where thousands have been killed in the insane fiasco.

The certainty learned from the experience is that alcoholics will continue to be alcoholics until they decide not to drink. Masses will be exploited as long as the masses allow themselves to be exploited. Addicts will be addicts until they decide not to use drugs. Billions of dollars has not altered aberrant compulsions.

The United States needs an immediate rapprochement to the problems of drugs. Illegal drugs should be legalized and imported or manufactured under government supervision. The profit of smugglers and pushers would disappear and prices can be controlled at a low rate, with taxes levied on drugs at the same level as alcoholic beverages.

Addiction will increase only among the people with a proclivity to deaden their brain in the first place. Prisons and jails could be virtually emptied of those whose infractions were simply as users, or those that were found to have small amounts of illegal drugs in their possession. Pushers would not be able to control neighborhoods. Crime, related to drugs would stop and the enforcement agencies that have spent years failing to control drug smuggling could be assigned to other areas of criminal behavior. Pusher would to longer have the reasons to get children hooked on drugs. That concept is a win-win approach to an obvious failure. The only people who will scream at this innovative concept are the smugglers, pushers and the behind-the-scene financiers of trafficking who have made millions of dollars from the miseries of mentally and emotionally belabored people.

Massive amounts of the money saved should then be devoted to a nationwide campaign to teach teenagers that self-destructing in a quagmire of deadly drugs is not an astute decision.

There will certainly be those snivelers with opposing viewpoint but if intelligence should prevail then the billions of dollars currently being poured into the bottomless pit could be used in needed places. Then, allow drunkards to be drunks and addicts to be addicts and stop that costly and futile attempt to control human behavior.

Doctor Livingstone, I presume

Doctor David Livingstone, a Scottish missionary, while exploring Africa traveled through Botswana. In 1841 he came into contact with a large colony of baboons that apparently had been ostracized from the primary group and had been banned to a region in the jungle where it was more difficult to exist lacking sufficient water and certain vegetation that formed a major part of baboon diet.

Doctor Livingstone was curious as to why baboons were not allowed to stay with the main society so he watched the societal actions and noticed a number of oddities such as exposing their private parts as though the conduct was comporting itself with acceptable behavior in most baboon groups.

Such behavior was repugnant to the general society who would have chosen a less intensive display and the unusual demonstrations were the reason for forcibly segregating certain baboons of loathsome moral persuasions.

Another bizarre antic Dr. Livingston noticed in that small group consisted of movements best described as crotch grabbing accompanied by loud cries. The gyrations lasted for several minutes then ebbed away to total silence. The freakish activity would begin again with a ferociousness involving the entire community and after several hours of genitalia flagellation, accompanied by screams of agony from bruising on their genitalia the baboons would collapse, moaning and jerking until silence settled over the colony.

When Doctor Livingstone returned to Africa some fourteen years later the small colony had rejoined the primary society and after obvious assimilation the cryptic behavioral oddity had become a part of the daily practices among the entire society. It was noted by the Doctor that in privacy baboons still continued to cup their genitalia in their hands, while shrieking screams reminiscent of the keening sound of widows when throwing themselves on the funeral pyres of their husbands.

Doctor Livingstone also noticed outlandish conduct that was unique to the male baboons had become ritualistic with female baboons, with an added act of squeezing their mammary appendages while at the same moments shrieking in agony or ecstasy. Dr. Livingstone was unable to determine which of the reactions was applicable.

While visiting London during an absence from Africa, Dr. Livingstone talk about what he had witnessed in 1841 with acquaintances that were experts in the field of medicine and psychology. Their opinions were that baboons cross-breeding with chimpanzees had precipitated that behavior seen years earlier and was now a dormant trait, having disappeared, but was destined to re-appear sometime in the future.

After discussions and assessing the possible evolution projected for baboon populations, those specialists concurred that the most probable re-appearance of the abnormality best described as crotch-grabbing, would be in the 21st century and would be demonstrated by the animals that had descended from the original baboons. They also theorized that the crotch grabbing would re-appear among their descendants who would, by then, have become sweat-stained singers, and bulbous comediennes. The disgusting habit of crotch-grabbing had obviously passed down through evolutionary generations.

Descendants of Dr. Livingstone went back to Africa and retraced his journey. The site where the doctor had discovered the peculiar baboons was overgrown and showed no sign that life had ever existed there. After excavating where baboons might have been they uncovered buried skeletons. The archeologists were sure they had discovered the site of the group Doctor Livingstone had seen back in 1841. Condition of the pubic bones, leading to a certainty they were right, was the fact that the bones of the skeletons were fragmented apparently from the frequency of mistreating their crotches.

Water War

I can't drink water from the Chattahoochee? Someone is obviously pulling my leg. I've been drinking water from the Chattahoochee ever since I arrived in Atlanta in 1962. How some Judge can decide he is so imperialistically ensconced in office that he can decide to kill everyone in Atlanta defies my imagination. He must be ticked off at the South for some reason. Maybe he is from the South and is mad about something and intends moving and this is to get even.

The guy must be uniformed about Grandfather Clauses and Riparian Rights. The law says I can drink water from this side of the river and the other side is for folks living over there. And I can visit over there and drink some of their water. As I see it, that's the law.

Although I'm not a dyed-in-the-wool southerner, at least my wife has convinced me that grits is to eat rather than being used to patch the driveway. A little milk and sugar and grits are somewhat tasty. So I get a little burnt up when I get pushed around. Taking away my drinking rights riles me.

But I have digressed. My great granddaddy stood stolidly with his Winchester in Indiana to defend his right to some water flowing in a stream. I hope it doesn't come to that.

Someone needs to take a switch to that guy. Then find out how a decision as big as that, affecting almost six million Southerners, can be made by a Yankee.

He must really be upset. Maybe a Delta stewardess slapped his exploring hands. Maybe he's getting old and crotchety and wants to be remembered by doing something memorable, kinda' like Charley Manson or Jeffrey Dahmer or Bernie Madoff, something that would cause people to remember him after he's croaked. Some folks get desperate about their future as they get closer to the old guy with the scythe.

Maybe he really is from the North and his granddaddy lost a foot at Shiloh. That's a heavy load to carry around for a hundred and fifty years.

Perhaps traffic got to him as it does to me, but I'm not a reactionary to that extent. He might have developed a vengeful personality from middle-finger-salutes and had to go back up North to figure out why people middle-finger saluted him.

But he's faceless and I'm not fond of people I can't see. My computer is filled with faceless people aggravating me as much as this Judge.

We might have to gets several volunteers with 5 gallon cans and at night set up a water brigade from Buford Dam to Atlanta and steal enough water to bathe and water my Angel Trumpets.

But then I wondered what would happen to all that water if Alantans can't use it. My Angel Trumpets would die. And I'm sure not going to pour bottled water into a galvanized tub just to take a bath. I did that during that last Depression out on the farm. I got to bathe after my Grandfather, my Grandmother and my Aunt. By then I could almost plant potatoes in the muck. Not again.

CREDIT CARD CRISIS

I lost count at about thirty solicitations from credit card companies and businesses that extend charge account privileges in their names. I'm not collateralized for a $250,000 credit line yet some offers emphasize that I'm pre-qualified for up to $250,000. Sounds good.

At one time, their card was simply an unembellished credit card. Later, it became a Gold Card, then a Platinum Card, then a Titanium Card and more recently their offers were for me to possess the most prestigious credit card in the world, and they will actually pay me to use their credit card to make purchases: the more I charge, the more they will reimburse me, plus they will allow me the right to do that for an annual fee of $150. I am also assured that many restaurants, hotels and Spa Maitre De's around the world will bow to me in respect when I present them my prestigious card. And I get free Sky-Miles too!

Their accompanying letters explained that I was selected for this unique offer because I am a creditworthy person who's respected in my community and one who historically has made his payments on time. Their letter contains checks that I can spend immediately for taking a long vacation I've always wanted, buying a new car, remodeling my kitchen, transfer balances from the high-interest cards in my wallet, or any number of reasons to quickly charge purchases on their credit card. And behold! I can accept it for the introductory rate that is the lowest in the industry. They really want me to have their card.

As I shred the waste of good trees, I wonder why they did not take time to find out that I never accept credit card offers. That key to my decision can be found after putting on my glasses and reading the fine print and discovering the potential fees and interest rates. The temptation to spend money that I can't afford has not changed.

I drive a 1994 Buick Park Avenue with 131,000 miles. My wife drives a 1994 Lexus. My car is serviced regularly, and can keep pace with the costly SUVS on the highways. Occasionally replacement parts are needed and when that happens my son tells me to buy a new car. I tell him the repairs cost less than the depreciation on his new car. I tell him that the license and tax is $36.45. I also inform him that the sales-tax on his Toyota was $1,200, and that I can drive just as comfortably as he. That stops the ineffective advice.

People have allowed themselves to be ensnared in a quagmire of commercialism keeping up with the Joneses. Having been born during the Great Depression, I was repeatedly advised by my grandfather that I could only sleep in one bed at a time. Frugality was absolutely necessary for survival. I have found myself influenced by his admonitions for seven decades: I do not buy anything I cannot pay for in a month. After some years of careful budgeting, I've discovered that if the dishwasher breaks down we can wash the dishes by hand until enough is saved for a new dishwasher.

Credit Card companies encourage people to buy more than they can afford and then those astronomical interest rates kick-in, which produces enormous profits. How important is a wide-screen television or a sporty bass boat when you lay awake all night wondering how you'll make the payment? We live in a world hyping immediate gratification and until people learn to control their lust for everything, right now, bankruptcies will increase. The credit card companies are not concerned if credit-card-holders file bankruptcy. Loss companies sustains by way of bankruptcies are written off as a cost of doing business and the write-off reduces the tax burden proportionately.

When the credit card promoters decided that their offer was not succeeding with me their technique changed. I received an embellished, multi-colored, cardboard replica of their credit card with the stern warning that my time for deciding was limited or I would lose out on so much of life's goodies. It's like fishing. They alter the color of the lure but the angling continues.

Memories of my youth

I was recently invited to a wedding that was to be held on a farm up in Jackson County. Having been born on a farm in Indiana I looked forward to the event.

For some years I had mentioned to my wife that upon retirement I would like 10 acres of farmland with a pond in the middle. I would have a horse and a couple llamas. I would purchase a miniature pony. I'd own a Malamute. And I would fish. Replaying my childhood, I would milk the cows, slop the hogs, and sit wide-eyed during barn dances, hayrides and wiener roasts.

Unfortunately, my plans didn't quite work out so when I heard the wedding would be on a farm and the bride was my fishing buddy when she was 14, the affair had appeal.

My wife and I drove back a narrow lane winding through undulating hills with pines and hardwoods everywhere. We passed an occasional house. Eventually, we emerged out in an open field. A barn sat on a hillside with an eight acre pond down below. It was a replica of what I had indelibly imprinted on my brain for years.

Grabbing my wife's hand, I said, "You bought this place for me, didn't you?"

"Dream on," she said.

We were directed to a parking place by a young woman. As I exited my car I asked who owned the place. She said that her sister did, and pointed to another attendant. Knowing my nutty proclivities my wife quickly headed for the barn.

I asked the second woman if she had sympathy for a wounded veteran from WW II. She kind of stared at me a little then said yes. I asked if that sympathy included permission to fish in the pond. I then, smilingly, admitted that I really hadn't been wounded in war, just scared.

I stared at the pond during the ceremony. My wife told me the ceremony was beautiful. I didn't really care. I wondered how heavy the biggest fish was in the pond.

Three days later the father of the bride and I launched a Bass Tracker in the pond. The bet was a dollar for the first fish and a dollar for the biggest one. I lost both bets. My plastic worms failed me but a tiny spinner hooked four yearling bass. The water is spring fed and so clear you can see huge catfish cruising two or three feet down on the bottom. I needed my Bear bow and arrows.

From a deck which extended into the pond we fished for catfish. The girl had told me her father tossed dog food pellets to the fish when she was small. She loved to see the fish swirling.

Using pieces of hot dogs to chum in front of the deck we caught 5 blue channel cats with the biggest weighing in at a hefty 20 pounds.

The farm has been in the family for over 150 years, appearing in a 1936 land deed and is now a special events facility; weddings, receptions, family reunions, and private parties are held there. The visit to the farm brought back fond memories of my childhood. I hope I am invited to another affair soon. The owners' father still lives on the place.

An ancient Indian shrine

I am intrigued by unique, one-of-a-kind places and things; Eiffel Tower, Hope Diamond, the Great Wall of China. Another location fits the unique one-of-a-kind concept and that is Stone Mountain in Georgia. It is like no other rock formation on earth. the Ayres Rock in Australia is a close second but it is smaller and does not have the aesthetic appeal of Stone Mountain.

Formed over 3,000,000,000 years ago during a violent upheaval in the earth the mountain was visited by Spaniards soldiers 550 years ago when explorer Hernando Desoto marched from the Atlantic Ocean expecting to find precious jewels, silver and gold around the mountain. He left when he realized that the legend was not true.

The proposal for the monolithic carving was conceived in the 1920's but because of WW II, disagreements about the carving and budget problems the effort was not completed until 1972. When completed it rivaled Mount Rushmore but will be smaller that the Crazy Horse monument currently underway in South Dakota.

When we moved to Atlanta from the flatlands of Indiana one of my kid's favorite places to go was to Stone Mountain where we climbed to the top many week-ends going up the steep eastern end. I wondered why quarrying was destroying the mountain. I complained to people in the park. I guess my voice had some effect because soon after my complaint about desecrating an Indian shrine, the quarry closed. The eastern slope is now off limit.

The Creek Indians, who inhabited the area, revered Stone Mountain, practicing religious rites on top. Native American artifacts were unknowingly destroyed by pushing them off the sides before workers began carving. Encyclopedia Britannica estimates a half-million natives lived in what is now the state of Georgia.

After retiring from business I decided it would be fun to work around the park so I filled out an application with the Silver Dollar Corporation. Since I was in the navy during WW II, I expressed my preference for operating the river boat. However that job had been filled. They offered me the job riding the cable car and talking about local interests. I was to be nice to the visitors and answer questions. They did not inform me I would need to speak other languages. So, I smiled and nodded a lot, trying to look like a visitor.

When the lift reaches the upper level there is a noticeable bump and the lift sways a little. At that time a child from somewhere got sick to his stomach.. Arriving back at the bottom I was told that part of the job was to keep the lift cleaned. Looking at the mess on the carpet I decided cleaning it up was below my pay grade. I returned to the office and handed in my resignation. I was paid $54.80 for working at Stone Mountain. However, the mountain is an interesting resort. There is much to enjoy. And it is one-of-a-kind.

Entitlements.

During World War II most everyone gave up something. The sacrifice was for the benefit of the country. There was one motivational ideology that applied; _use it up, wear it out, make it do or do without_. Everyone was equal. When I became fifteen jobs in industry were increasing. Emerging from a Depression America was becoming a manufacturing giant because of WW II.

I washed dishes at a drive-in theater, parked cars, and worked in a grocery putting away stock. When rationing began I seemed to acquire new friends and I soon discovered the reason. They were convinced I could get them extra rationed goods like coffee, sugar and milk without ration coupons. I was sometimes offered money but that was before bribing became popular. I worked in a filling station for a time and bribes were offered for extra gas. Times were rugged but except for John Dillinger, Pretty Boy Floyd, Bonnie and Clyde, and a few other villains. No one stole from their neighbors. Times haves changed.

Because I had welded on the farm I applied for a welding job in a defense plant. Insley Manufacturing Company, in Indianapolis, had been building draglines for years but had begun producing tanks for the army. The money was great but red-hot slag rolling down my back was the turn-off as a career. When I turned 17, I enlisted in the navy.

The thing I recall most about those times was that there were no unemployment funds or food stamps. Yet no people marched in protest because the government was not supporting them. Men worked on the WPA and CCC, which were not give-away programs, they were designed to provide work during the Depression but required working, instead of entitlements. There was no unemployment compensation yet no one complained because the government wasn't handing out freebies. Today many people seem to think government should be supporting them. Some people insist that they are entitled by birth to entitlements from birth.

A mother in a grocery in Marietta complained while she was checking out. She said, "I live conservatively and I buy cheap cuts of meat in order to feed my children. I drive an older car. That woman who just checked out purchased expensive steaks and paid for them with food stamps and she is driving a new Cadillac. Don't you think there is something wrong with that picture?" The cashier smiled. "I see it everyday," she said.

Sadly, it's a sign of the times, dependency on freebies instead of work. Lyndon Johnson activated the Great Society programs that encouraged voters to depend on governments; _vote for us and we will take care of you_. Dependency breeds more dependency.

I believe older people are tougher than the younger generations because we grew up not having everything. We didn't complain because the library was not open every day. We used it when it was open. We shopped when stores were open which seldom was nights or on Sunday. Stores in most small towns were closed Wednesday afternoon. The demand now is for personal convenience 24 hours a day, instant satisfaction. When we didn't get our way as kids we pouted and sulked. Now, as adults, we protest, march and riot.

Around Atlanta voters recently approved having alcoholic beverages sold on Sunday. It proves my contention that we have too many drunks drinking.

Loof Lirpa

Mayors from several communities in Central Georgia will be meeting in Atlanta next month to discuss a problem that may occur again this year.

Officials from the Department of Parks and Recreation in Macon, Athens, Columbus and Atlanta will meet in the Ritz Carlton in Buckhead to develop plans to control the grackle migrations into cities during the summer months.

The phenomenon began two years ago when swarms of the birds would fly into the areas of the cities and roost for the night. Piedmont Park was particularly hard hit with people wanting to go for a walk finding deposits from the birds making a mess. With so many limbs extending over the sidewalks the birds became particularly objectionable. After rain the sidewalks became slippery and somewhat dangerous. Occasionally, birds would become overly aggressive, dive-bombing passers-by, with droppings hitting the people and dogs that were in the park.

The problem began in cities to our north but recently came southward. One ornithologist said that is a condition affecting many regions of the world, birds flying out into fields each day to feed and then returning every evening to roost in trees in parks and populated areas.

A city in Indiana decided to remove the trees where the birds roosted. The birds moved out to the residential areas. Understandably the homeowners complained about the raucous noise the birds made when settling down for the night. Setting off fire crackers and zooming rockets the Indiana officials attempted to scare the birds from the neighborhoods. It worked, but drove the birds to the downtown streets where they roosted over the streets in crevasses in old buildings. The sidewalks, where people walked to stores for shopping, became unsightly. Merchants protested that the program was unworkable and the birds should be shot or poisoned.

World renowned Finnish ornithologist, Loof Lirpa was asked by city officials in Indiana to use a technique he had patented that was successful in Helsinki, Copenhagen and Oslo, where the birds had become a serious health problem.

Coincidentally, Loof Lirpa will be visiting relatives in Atlanta at the time of the meeting and he has agreed to speak to the assembly and explain his successful program.

Before the grackles come to roost, Loof Lirpa attaches pine cones to the branches of the trees. The cones are covered with peanut butter. In the peanut butter are embedded lead shotgun pellets, painted to look like grains of wheat. Before the grackles settle down for the night they find there is a good meal and begin to feed on the pellets.

Since lead is not digestible the buckshot accumulates in the bird's stomach causing them to become top heavy. They start hanging upside down and begin to soil themselves, eventually losing their grip on the branches and falling to the ground where they are in danger of being eaten by animals.

An Animal Rights spokesperson protested that the treatment of the birds is inhumane. They protested that the birds are humiliated by soiling themselves but it is also unsanitary. They offered to pick up the birds and take them for surgery to remove the buckshot before the creatures develop lead poisoning.

Because the Professor was already visiting in Atlanta, he declined to accept his customary fee of $50,000.

Based on his efforts having been successful in Scandinavia officials here see no reason for it not to be a workable technique in the United States.

Loof Lirpa (April Fool)

The wilderness

Morning on an isolated river. Fog low to the water. My canoe is repacked. Depending on the current, maybe fifteen or so miles downriver before dusk. I examine my map and mark a few rapids that will require scrutiny before shooting. A bowl of Red River will hold me until lunch. I push the canoe out into the dark water. A chill is in the air.

The Canadian wilderness holds me in a hypnotic spell. I have been advised that that it is foolhardy to canoe alone on a rogue river. I respond that it is more perilous driving on America's expressways. The idiocy rate is much higher.

On a hillside I see a bear with two cubs coming down to the water. I raise my paddle and drift quietly along. A loon dives for fish. The river is veiled in vapor. Bulrushes line the margin. Boulders keep an eternal vigil. Off to my left a flight of Mallards skim the surface with a show of watery crystals, form a V, and honk their way to some unknown destination. The sun climbs over a stand of spruce. I slip off my vest.

I pass a village of Cree Indians. They wave a greeting. I'm tempted to stop and powwow but the GPS tells me that I have a lot of paddling to do if I am to rendezvous with the bush pilot who dropped me off upriver five days ago. Children on a pier are playing cowboys and Indians. Amazingly the Indians are winning the battle. I dip a cup of water and drink deeply. Back home if I did that my guts would begin cramping and my inlays would glow. It is satisfying being out of civilization. Parent swans, shepherding three cygnets, eye me warily, while maintaining their protective distance.

A canoe with two Indians comes alongside. They're from the village I passed a few miles back. I lift my paddle and put out my hand. Tying our canoes together, we drift downstream with the current. They fish in an eddy, below the rapids, where walleye spawn. They say if I stop I can have fish for lunch, in fact, they offer to cook one for me. I see in their smile they have forgotten that my ancestors killed their ancestors. I haven't forgotten. I accept their offer. I see fishing nets and bows and arrows in the canoe. I ask if they use the old ways. They say the old ways gives all animals a better chance. I agree with nurturing nature.

In late morning, the vapor lifts. I see turbulence far ahead and hear the sounds of a rapid.

I secure my canoe to a ledge and climb the escarpment for a look-see. It's a good one. I take out my binoculars for a look see. It looks like maybe a portage. My Old town weighs eighty pounds, a big load for an ancient man. Then there are supplies. Four trips maybe. Dying when shooting a rapid would be all right. Dying incrementally in a nursing home is not the way I want to exit my life. I prefer being in control of my destiny. I opted for the dangerous route. My pulse rate rises off the chart.

The sun slants toward the horizon. I beach the canoe between two large boulders and make camp for the night. I gather driftwood and start a fire. The Cree gave me an extra walleye Cooking a fish on a spit excites my taste buds. My supplies seem to be dwindling. I look at the time and realize that I have one more day until my pilot will drop out of the sky to pick me up. Twilight comes and mosquitoes begin taking blood samples. A tundra fly gets frisky as I pitch my tent. I will sleep well this night. I look through the mesh and watch the Aurora Borealis fire streamers of color across the cobalt sky. Wind music begins to sound in a stand of tamarack. As night descends, eyes, reflected by the flames in my fire, appear on the perimeter of my camp. I will have company as I sleep. I snuggle in my sleeping bag. I suck on a chunk of caramel.

When I awaken I crawl from my bag to find my friends cooking over a roaring fire. They say they killed a deer on the way to another village and thought I would enjoy some venison. We eat breakfast together, strips of venison plus scrambled goose eggs, breakfast on a boulder in the middle of nowhere…now that's real atmosphere.

I get out my GPS and see that I am near our rendezvous point. I explain the function of a GPS and present it to my friends as a gift. I inform them I will return next year and that I'd like to visit their village and find out more about their old ways. They say I'll like hunting seals from a dogsled. I tell them, "You betcha," that I will definitely be back.

Above the escarpment we hear the sound of an airplane as it sweeps onto the river and skids to a stop. My friends watch as I lash my canoe to a pontoon, and climb aboard. They wave as we lift from the surface and head south. I make reservations for next year. I wish things were the same as it was four hundred years ago. As we reach cloud level, I stare down into the canyon one more time. The Indians are not in sight. I call Winnipeg and ask then to call my wife and tell her the trip was incredibly satisfying and that I'll soon be home, completely renewed.

Consequences

"Consider the consequences' is one of the most significant messages in the English language.

People should consider the possible results of their actions. Unfortunately, many fail to consider the potential consequences of thoughtless decisions.

I don't go to parties or clubs where alcohol and drugs are consumed. I am aware that if decisions are made by addled minds they are often unpredictable and if someone commits a felony I might be a victim or be considered guilty by association.

Decisions made without considering repercussions result from mental insufficiency. During my youth I was exposed to unpredictable results of alcohol, a father, who became angry and abusive when drunk. His personality underwent change from sociable to argumentative to combative the more he consumed. His conduct when drinking forced me to leave home and cut our relationship at age 14 to avoid being subjected to his infuriating behavior.

Experiencing the destructive effects of inebriation caused me to become a confirmed teetotaler. That negates the premise that alcoholic children come from alcoholic parents, or that wayward children necessarily evolve from dysfunctional homes.

Because of inadequate attention and low income, children from many single parent homes don't get the advice necessary to understand the possible repercussion of fatherless homes; behavioral abnormalities, psychological dilemmas and cultural aberrations. We find many of those children with attitudinal aberrations at an early age come under the jurisdiction of the courts.

Too many males, with more hormones than conscience, demonstrate their macho-masculinity by producing babies whom they have no intention of supporting often committing their offspring to vandalism, gangs, graffiti, robberies and prison. Even primates nurture their young.

I've read where women, seeking friends in the wrong places, were gang-raped, as a consequence of becoming alcohol impaired while associating with similarly alcohol impaired strangers.

Driving under the influence of mind-altering substances will inevitably cause problems: injury, financial ruin, imprisonment, psychological impairment, death, so drivers must be demented to drive when drunk or under the influence of drugs even some prescription drugs. Being drunk is not against the law but driving while drunk is not only against the law but totally stupid.

Tobacco companies have been warning of the damaging effects of smoking and yet I see people, knowing the danger, committing themselves to lung, throat, mouth and heart deficiency without regard for the fact that they will become burdens to society and often die early from smoking.

When my dental hygienist advised me that there was a discoloration on the roof of my mouth as the result of smoking I quit, no craving; no patches, no artificial cigarettes, no Nicorettes and no gimmicks. I simply quit. Anything else would have been senseless.

Boating without a life jacket can have lethal consequences. Hunting without an orange vest can be dangerous. Reckless driving can ruin career plans. Playing with guns is a mindless activity.

There is speeding, tail-gaiting, drag racing. I see mutilated bodies on the highways, prisoners in jail and corpses in morgues and I wonder what happened to cause such insanity, and why. They are the consequence of imprudent decisions.

My grandfather said that if you put your hand on a hot stove you will be burned, or if you walk too closely behind a horse you can be kicked, both simplistic truths.

Everything we do has consequences, but if possible results are considered in advance, tragedies can be avoided.

You never know who is driving on the road.

A car pulled alongside at a stop light. I was meditating on my life, wondering how I could have done better, if I had enough money to last me until I die. At age 85, I had begun to contemplate the inevitability of death. I was doing some serious pondering.

A car stopped in the adjacent lane, vibrating heavy brass. The windows were open. I could hear garbled words. In my peripheral vision I could see a man keeping time on the steering wheel. I recognized the car. He had cut me off a few miles back when I was entering a ramp.

I was tempted to flip the driver off or turn up my CD player to max-volume with Lenny Dee on the organ and Dick Contino on an accordion blasting the Beer Barrel Polka. It's so loud I expect my windows to shatter.

But I restrained myself. I never know how nutty some nut might be. But he might not know that I have a short fuse sometimes. Maybe confrontations ignite me.

I waited a micro-second as the light turned green. I wondered about the man as he pulled away; if his mind had been damaged by methamphetamines, was he practicing for an audition for one of the stupid TV shows or was he intentionally being a nuisance.

But then he didn't know that I had a 380 Beretta within six inches of my hand, thirteen killers in the clip and one in the breech, and a permit to carry.

But then maybe he had an Uzi under his dash, could be. I wouldn't know.

We did not know each other.

My mind might be mangled. I may have just found my wife cheating and had shot her.

I might be deranged, burdened, irrational, and dangerous.

Maybe my partner had stolen our operating capital and I was bankrupt.

I might be returning from my physical where the doctor said I had incurable cancer.

Or my son had been arrested for drug trafficking.

Perhaps I had just lost my home in foreclosure proceedings.

It's possible the FBI had confiscated my computer looking for evidence of murder.

We do not know the temperament of someone in the adjacent car.

We don't always know the triggering mechanism for violence.

Jealousy can be a trigger. Hate can be a trigger. Drugs can be a trigger. Terror can be a trigger.

There are hundreds of reasons confrontational behavior is triggered.

It's possible I hate boom boxes hammering my brain.

It could be that I had just been fired from my job.

Maybe I had just found out my neighbor's daughter had accused me of molestation.

Maybe I was late for an appointment for a job interview and was furious about slow traffic

Maybe I had robbed my grandmother and stolen her car.

Maybe I was brain-damaged from alcohol, or drugs, or from birth.

It could be that I was ticked-off at the world.

And then I may simply be one of the crazies driving around looking for trouble.

There are many kinds of firearms....you won't know which until the gun comes out.

Then one of those triggers could have applied to the boom-box guy. I was prudent.

Some people are not.

—Bad dreams—

I was lost once north of San Francisco. When driving Highway 101, I came upon a construction site. A sign pointed to a detour. There was a drizzle and the sky was leaden. Night was close. I followed an arrow and made a turn-off to the detour then made several sharp turns. Maybe two miles later I didn't see any more direction signs and realized I had missed a turn. I tried to turn around but became mired in mud. At daylight I walked out to a busy road for help.

I often dream about being lost in unfamiliar places. I have had bad dreams since I was a kid but being lost is scary.

For a time last May I was lost in Gwinnett County. Leaving a son's house in Dacula, I followed his directions to another son's house two miles away. Evidently I turned left when I should have turned right. It was overcast so I couldn't see the sun for my bearing. I purchased a GPS the next day and programmed in my home address. I believe in the Boy Scout motto.

Last night may have been my worst dream ever.

I walked out of a strange hotel somewhere, intending to meet my wife for lunch. The buildings were adobe with faded pastel colors. None were built in conventional configuration. Some had broken windows and several had no windows.

I had no idea where my wife would be so I began walking down a zigzagging alleyway strewn with debris. Realizing I was lost, I asked a vagrant for directions. He pointed in some direction and I walked away. After a time, I was completely lost and tried to return to the hotel, but then realized I didn't know the way back.

From apprehension I had become frightened. I knew my wife was waiting and possibly in some kind of danger but I was unable to remember where we were to meet.

Asking a stranger where I needed to go and not understanding what he said, I became terrified, knowing I could not find my wife. I could feel myself trying to awaken with my heart thudding. I flung my comforter onto the floor, struggling frantically to wake up.

Suddenly I was in a canoe about to capsize in a swirling rapid with water rushing down the road amid uprooted trees and scattered buildings. I looked for my wife and saw a piece of cloth under the surface, caught on a limb. I remembered she was wearing a yellow jacket. A reached for her and the material ripped, with the flood carrying her away. A horse was caught in a tree. A snake slithered across my face. My canoe capsized and I struggled to remove my coat. A building fell into the maelstrom and sent a wave gushing over my nose. I gagged and spit out water.

I remember screaming. The sound of my voice awakened me and I sat upright in bed trembling in the night looking for anything familiar. My armpits were sweaty. Then I was awake, gasping and shaking with relief.

I got up and sneaked over to my wife's bed, crawled in and snuggled up to her warmth. She was like my security blanket. Man-o-man! I was safe again.

Beware of wolves in sheep clothing!

There are thousands of predators searching for ways to get to your money. The victimization is directed at your savings and credit cards. They are clever, ruthless, relentless and often friendly. They don't always look like bad people, but they are.

They appear at your front door. They call you on the telephone. They are hidden on the internet. They read the obituary column. They case your home. They know you are a widow. They know you live alone. They know about your husband's occupation. They know you have something in your house that is valuable. They know where you buy your groceries. They know the bank you use. These people plan effective campaigns.

They come in many sizes, ages, colors, and genders. Their intention is to get your money or steal something from you that they can sell. They swindle you with friendly personalities, nice smiles and convincing double-talk. Their obsession is to take your money!

They don't care if you are left destitute, flat broke, and homeless!

They work alone or roam in gangs. When someone offers you something that looks to good to be true you can be positive today that it is too good to be true. Con-artists offered investments paying interest rates far above the rest of the market, yet people are fooled and hand over large amounts of money when they should have questioned how it is possible to earn interest much higher than all of the other investment markets.

Swindlers do not produce those percentages they rig the figures to scam investors. Replace trust with common sense.

Your defense against being a victim is simple: never give nor send money, open your front door or provide personal information to anyone that you do not know. Don't even be tempted without calling your banker or your police chief about the wisdom of what you are considering.

Your money is your security. Do not give it to strangers.

When you're working in your back yard and some friendly person appears asking for yard work, make sure your front door is secured because while you are engaged in a lengthy conversation in the back yard the person's partner will open your front door and steal jewelry, silverware, laptop, coin collection, guns and anything that can easily be carried out and sold.

There are individuals and gangs of thieves testing how defenseless or gullible you are. In today's environment, unfortunately, there are fewer people whom you can trust.

With the economy in convulsions and the unemployment rate unacceptable some of those people out of work will resort to criminal activity just to feed their kids, pay their bills and survive. That is a fact of life today.

Because of impotence in government the problems are increasing. Only when we decide enough is enough and get the stumbling blocks out of office will there be the chance of improvement. All anyone need do is listen to the vacuity of some politicians and you become aware of which ones are adversely impacting our lives.

The unemployment rate in Congress is zero. That reveals we a being mishandled by self-serving politicians.

Pandora's Box

1961. I watched crowds in the Haight Asbury District in San Francisco. The first signs of social change were the unusual hair styles and weird garb, purple braids and Mohawk cuts, green with multicolored tufts and ribbons.

The odor of marijuana permeated the area, people sucking on homemade cigarettes, eyes glazed, dreaming of places far off in some other world. The drug culture was being born.

Woodstock came with the incredible scenes of decadence and debauchery followed by the Bryon Festival in Georgia where hospitals in Macon, and surrounding towns, were busy saving the first-time drug experimenters, overdosing with chemicals not intended for ingestion.

Murders made the novel Helter Skelter a New York Times bestseller. Otis Redding played while America began a transformation. The Beatles came to America pounding thunderously on guitars and quickly became a significant influence in America's psyche.

Timothy Leary became the man to emulate. He advocated the use of LSD which altered peoples' brains. Leary spent his last year chasing blue elephants and trying to convert trashcans and alley cats to Judaism. Sniffing paint spray became a strange rage.

A fashion model in San Francisco experimented with LSD. She did an Olympian swan dive from a 2nd floor balcony, splattering onto the apron adjacent to the pool, her runway days were over.

The son of an attorney, heading for a successful career in banking, experimented with cocaine. It altered his career plans and he spent his last days as a missionary in Katmandu communing with Nepalese Gurus.

It was like some like some strange phenomenon was doing irreparable damage to our culture.

I began drinking while in the navy during WW II. After coming back from overseas our ship was decommissioned on the St. Johns River, in Florida. Ocala was close. A roadhouse on the edge of Ocala was the site of my misfortune. After many down-the-hatches I decided it would be okay to challenge someone to fight the Civil War all over again.

Three sailors, much bigger than me, figured the idea was great. For me it proved to be a mistake. While recovering in sick bay I decided that conduct contributing to my disfigurement was stupid. That conviction still exists. I do not intend to have my brain destroyed, caused by substances not intended for human consumption.

I've read about the chemically induced behavior of people racing to self-destruction and killing others in car accidents. It only benefits car repair shops, doctors, hospitals and morticians.

Cocaine, Heroin, Marijuana, Ecstasy, OxyContin, Hydrocodone, Methamphetamine, Inhalants, Steroids, LSD, then add prescription drugs which are abused and it is easy to see why the user's judgment is impaired. I have not used illegal drugs but seeing my neighbor hallucinating during withdrawal made a believer out of me.

The psychology of addiction to alcohol and drugs astonishes me. Watch a swarm of anchovies or a flock of sheep; where one goes the others follow. When personalities in Hollywood snort drugs many of their supplicants begin the same abuses. When a baseball player injects chemicals it has an effect on youngsters who believe that doing the same will lead to fame and fortune.

In the 17th century England subjugated China, primarily an agrarian society back then, by getting Chinese people hooked on opium. Drug cartels and pushers apply the same principle in America. It seems to be accomplishing their purpose. The solution is simple; don't experiment with drugs to benefit the promoters of human misery.

Self protection in troubled times.

The mother with the shotgun, who called 911 for advice on shooting the man she was convinced   was breaking into her home, was prepared. She was evidently aware of the Scout's motto.

She was sure he was the same person she believed was stalking her because of seeing him watch her too closely when she shopped. After the death of her husband to cancer one week before, the protection of her infant and herself had become her sole responsibility.

With home invasions occurring on an unprecedented scale, people are buying more firearms than ever before, particularly females who feel vulnerable.

Having a gun in the home is an absolute necessity in today's environment. Without the safeguard of a firearm people are defenseless against armed criminals looking for drugs, or something they steal and can sell.

However, a firearm is dangerous to use in your defense unless you are thoroughly trained in how to use one; where to keep it in the home, quick access, and a complete understanding of guns. If you are downstairs watching television and your gun is upstairs you might as well not have one.

A jeweler was held up in his store. Working alone he was suspicious of a person in the store who did not act like a typical customer. The jeweler was armed with an automatic. When the criminal turned with a gun in his hand the jeweler pulled an automatic but could not remember how to use the safety. He was shot three times in his midsection. He survived but learned a lesson; when you have a gun become an expert in its use.

Discretion is the better part of valor. Peril is greater today. Criminals are more desperate because of drug addictions or the lack of money to feed their children or pay their bills. Desperate people do desperate things and are therefore more dangerous.

In a confrontation the decision to pull the trigger must be instantaneous because if you ask a thug to put down his gun, you will have made a fatal mistake. When you have a firearm for protection you have to be emotionally and psychologically prepared beforehand to shoot a person because if you hesitate at the time of confrontation your actions will be too late. Thugs have no hesitancy to shoot you first.

Most men like owning guns. I have had guns since I was young. I don't have guns for aggression but I like cleaning them and practicing at ranges. I also keep a revolver close by. I worried about my automatics; would I remember how the safety works when I need it. Rather than worry I sold them and now rely on revolvers.

Having a permit to carry a concealed weapon reduces possible problems. Read the laws on gun ownership and your responsibilities. Speak to a local policeman about its use.

It would be a good idea to understand the law regarding your use of a gun for protection. The use of a gun will pose legal problems unless you know under what circumstance you are permitted to shoot. State laws vary, but the generalized understanding of the law is; if you or your family is in danger you are entitled by law to protect yourself.

If an intruder in breaking in my home or is already inside even though he is facing away from me I can shoot. The key is if your life is in danger. With an intruder in my home my life is obviously in danger and by Georgia law I can protect myself.

Three bananas.

I stood in a check out line at Kroger in Stone Mountain. I watched an elderly lady in front of me fumbling in her purse. I heard her tell the cashier that she had the amount in a bag where she kept her change.

After a lengthy delay the lady told the cashier she would have to leave the bananas explaining that she didn't have enough change. I stepped forward.

"How much is she short?" I guessed the woman's age at maybe 85.

"$1.10," the cashier said, smiling, embarrassed for the customer.

"Put the bananas in the cart," I said. I handed the cashier $1.10.

"Oh, no Sir," the woman said. "You don't have to do that. I'm just a little short this month. I can get bananas next week when my social security check comes."

Her smile was weak. You should be able to afford three bananas.

I smiled and said, "I think we dated when we were young."

"Oh no, I'm not from here," she said, looking down.

"Neither am I. Where're you from?"

"I grew up in Hopkinsville, Kentucky."

"I knew it," I said. "I'm from Evansville. I remember walking across the river. The bridge allowed us to be together."

"You're funny." She smiled a little.

"I'll bet twenty-six cents I'm older than you," I said.

"I don't bet," she said. "Besides you already know I don't have change."

Her eyes looked tired. I guess if you can't afford bananas you can feel bad.

"Want to get a cup of coffee?" I said. I had a feeling the lady was all alone.

The market had coffee. There were chairs. We sat down. I got the coffee.

She looked downcast. She needed some perking up. I consider myself a pretty good perker-upper.

"So, could we have dated?" I said.

"You were much too young." The aging lines in her face eased some.

"So I would have lost the bet, huh?"

"I think so, I'm 88."

"I'm 85. I adored mature girls in high school," I said. She perked up a little.

"My husband was much like you, amusing." Her chin trembled. "He died last year." Her lips quivered. I saw tears forming. One trickled down her cheek.

I handed her a napkin. "Got any relatives, ma'am?"

"My daughter's in California but I don't see her very often," she said. "I try to keep my home up but we had a lot of expense his last year. I worry a lot. Living alone it's hard to find someone to cut my yard and clean my gutters. My husband handled that."

One social security check gone, CD rates down, anemic 401K's, prescription prices skyrocketing, County Commissioners contemplating tax hikes, politicians talking penalty for not having health insurance, house break-ins increasing, gas prices going through the roof, scams, rapes, murders. It's no wonder she worries.

It's scary when you're 88, and alone. It's even frightening at 85.

I carried her groceries out to her car. I checked her license number. I figured I could cut her lawn and clean the gutters. It's good to have a friend. That is what life is about. Acquaintances are plentiful. Real friends are a rarity.

Aging

I sat on my porch having my morning cup of coffee with a brisk breeze tousling with my hair. I was thinking about getting old. It's scary but it's happening. I can feel it. I can see it.

Appreciating little things, I have begun to recognize some symptoms of aging, sometimes a little wobble, some aches from too much tennis, forgetting something important.

I asked the pharmacist in Kroger if he had something to retard or reverse aging. He commented, "If I had something like that do think I would look like this?"

As I approach the end there are some things yet to be done, things I'd like to do again.

I'd like to skate on the frozen pond again with my friends. I'd like to play mumblety-peg. I'd like to sleep on my grandfather's front porch with my brother with our coon hounds curled up against our backs.

I would like to put another stink bomb behind the radiator so the school would have to close the first day of deer season and I could go hunting. I want to spiral fifty yard passes to my sons. I'd like to discuss boys again with my daughters.

I recognize the symptoms of aging, the occasional stumble going upstairs, strange clicking noises in my shoulders when I shower, tee shots that are shorter and off line, less zip, the tendency to sit down more often, and for longer time.

While going to the food court at Northlake shopping center I observed, in a window, an old man keeping pace with me. He had rounded shoulders with his head bent forward, looking down with steps a little unsteady. I felt sad for him wondering if he might also be a WW II veteran and if he was alone in life; hair thinning, almost white, maybe homeless. I wondered if he was going to the same place for lunch and maybe we could eat together and talk about our war experiences.

He looked ancient, tired, shop-worn; older than me. I wondered when he was born. The old man appeared to be older than me. He looked a little dejected.

I glanced again and stopped to study the man. I moved close to the plate-glass window. The man moved toward me simultaneously. The closer I got the more bedraggled he looked, Then, it took me a few moments to realize the aging man in the plate glass window was my reflection. It was a real shocker. I stood, riveted. That can't be me. But it was. Man-o-man!

I thought about navy boot camp; 'Stand up straight, sailor, chin in! Chest out! Tuck in your gut! Shape up, sailor!'

I straightened up. "Yes, Sir," I said aloud.

My reflection and I smiled at each other We saluted. We instantly looked younger, more erect with some snap in our cadence, added energy. We grinned. I could hear John Philip Sousa's rousing marching music; 'Hup two three four!'

On the good-side of after-life I will see no more mangled mailboxes or middle finger salutes. I will hear no more screaming commentators on television. I might ascend to sit on a fleecy cloud with an ample supply of Haagen Dazs, or I could descend into the fiery chasm and be with those politicians who promised me filet mignon in exchange for my vote then tossed me some fatback. There is certain to be a lot of them there. They'll hear a vitriolic tirade.

Dependency

Living on a farm during the Depression benefitted me many ways. When something was needed I saw my grandfather delay the purchase until he could pay for it. With limited income he began saving to buy something. As the result he never owed for anything and we still had most of what we needed.

And there was always some extra tucked away somewhere for emergencies.

Long hours and hard labor served us well. We milked ten cows each morning before dawn. We had a milk route and often worked in a strip mine, digging coal. We tended to bee hives, made sorghum and butchered hogs and beef. My grandmother canned fruit, vegetables and meat. My brother and I ran a trap line every morning before school. We mowed yards and shoveled snow from sidewalks in the winter. We seined for turtles and caught fish.

As produce ripened we worked on nearby farms, picking peaches, apples, tomatoes, beans, and we dug potatoes. In the fall we shucked corn, mowed and baled hay. We gathered hickory nuts, hazelnuts and walnuts. Mushrooms were abundant in the spring, with blackberries, raspberries and mulberries in the fall.

Our understanding was basic; either work or do without. There were no entitlements. Churches provided flour, streak-o-lean, potatoes, margarine mix and lard and opened soup-lines in cities.

At the ages of 12 and 10 my brother and I bought 22 caliber, single shot, Springfield rifles for $2.95 from the Montgomery Ward catalogue. After shooting squirrels and trapping rabbits we cleaned and sold them to school teachers who were the few people who had jobs.

Politicians continue raiding the cookie jar. We have elected a cadre of long-tenure opportunists. There are officials in Congress dedicated to re-interpreting the constitution: reducing freedoms, banning guns, confiscatory taxation, and gaining voter loyalty by providing mega-entitlements.

There are ways to become wealthy; con others into paying for your political campaign, play the earmarks game, promise filet mignon and deliver fatback, receive a federal pension then become a paid lobbyist or consultant for one of your previous donors. That's how the con-game works.

The spread between wealth and poverty is widening at an alarming rate. The difference is driving a wedge between haves and have-nots and generating discord. Protesters express their concept of wealth re-distribution by demanding more entitlements.

The same scenario played out in France and Russia with both governments overthrown in violent revolution. We can look upon protest marches with disdain but the root causes, lack of education, and the possibility of reduced entitlements, continues to simmer.

When babies are not fed, nor their needs satisfied, they scream. When dependent citizens are not given that to which they have become accustomed, they protest with rioting. Dependency breeds dependency. A country of beggars ferments a climate of unrest. Coveting the successes of others contributes to the downfall of nations. We are seeing that corrosion weakening America.

Historically, great societies have disappeared as the result of overpopulation, indolence, gluttony immorality, corruption and enfeebling inequality. The average lifespan of historical civilizations was 200 years. We have been here for 236 years. The pot is boiling and could become a seething cauldron. I'm concerned. From what I hear, most everyone is worried.

Brain Stimulation

One of the greatest treasures we have is our brain. Our mind will let us go on journeys via books and photographs created by others. Because of time limitation and other involvements we cannot experience everything in this vast universe but because of the adventurous spirit of others we can become aware of sights in the world to which others have thrilled and revealed to us with camera and word.

I have a friend who sends me photographs from many places across the planet. I have been able to run the Iditarod in Alaska and walk the Great Wall in China. My eyes have feasted on Monte Picchu in the Andes Mountains. I have pondered the last days of the Incas.

I have explored the Amazon jungle, and canoed the largest river in the world, where I have seen the biggest otters on earth and giant Anacondas engorge large prey.

I have watched vampire bats drinking blood from live animals without them suffering pain. That is a marvel of nature.

I have travelled by camel caravan over the remote sand dunes of arid deserts and sensed the same relief when an oasis appeared in the distance.

I can almost feel frostbite on Mount Everest or experience claustrophobic terror in the wondrous chambers of underground caverns.

While hosting a wilderness canoeing documentary for Georgia Public Television my Cree Indian guide told me a tribal truth; 'a frog in a well has a limited view of a limitless sky'. Based on that adage there is always one more horizon beyond the next horizon, a concept I have nurtured since I was a kid. I never want to stop experiencing something new. Knowledge is glorious.

When I was six years old I pounded a keg of rusting nails into an apple tree in my grandfather's orchard to see what would happen. What happened was, the tree died and I then learned about a leather strap hanging in a shed. Learning from my grandfather was wonderfully educational.

I was fascinated with English literature when in high school. I read all of the famous writings of Chaucer and Lord Bryon. I was so intrigued by Canterbury Tales that I memorized the prologue in archaic English and can still recite it.

Along with those treasures from strangers I have been privileged to canoe with Beluga whales in Churchill, Canada, watch caribou fiord a wild river, see Canadian snow geese honk their way to some mysterious destination and watch a mother moose frolic with her calf in a turbulent river in Manitoba. I have lain for hours, spellbound away from civilization with the aurora borealis firing streamers of color in a cobalt sky.

Where nature prevails emotional and psychological regeneration is assured. Isolation is instantly therapeutic. The ills of contemporary society dematerialize into nothingness.

With other crewmen we sank a Nazi submarine in Mid-Atlantic in 1943. I killed a grizzly while camped on the Mackenzie River in Canada's Northwest Territory. I have hunted seals and bear with a Cree Indian using harpoons and bow and arrows.

Living in this world has been a fabulous experience and as long as I live I will continue bowing to Mother Nature. In July our hummingbirds will assemble in their coats of mauve and emerald and perform amazing feats of aerobatics intended, I'm sure, to refurbish our lives. Last year one hummingbird hovered in front of me and saw its reflection in my glasses. It perched on my arm for a moment, chirping a message of gratitude for our nectar filled feeders. That was an event I will never forget.

Reflections of the Great Spirit

From the cold Atlantic Ocean
to the might of the Pacific
stretched a land of wondrous bounty,
filled with deer and ponderous bison,
rich with fur and open prairies,
tinged with wild flowers in profusion,
painted green with towering forests,
crowned with snow-capped fortress mountains,
laved with pristine rushing rivers.

Nights were cooled by gentle breezes
days were long amid the wonders,
fiery gusts swept clean the deserts,
stars like diamonds glowed in heaven,
rainfall soaked the fertile valleys,
caressed by seasons ever changing,
abundant fishes teemed in waters,
maize and berries filled each harvest.

In this place so full in bounty
lived the Indian, tall and stalwart,
lived in peace with all their spirits,
took the bison just when needed,
took the wild-fowl for their larder,
raised their young with wise contentment,
loved their land and to their bosoms
held natures treasures for the future.

Around the night fires fabled stories
passed among them rife with wisdom,
tales of glorious hunt adventures,
tales of things beyond horizons,
things experienced in other seasons,
facts of truth and yarns of fiction.
Late into the night narrations
filled the children's minds with wonder.

Tawny men bedecked in deerskins
smoked a peace pipe filled with birch bark,
chanted songs of bygone ages,
danced the dance of generations,
ate the bear meat from the fire pit,
bragged and boasted of their prowess,
flaunted dress with flowing feathers
from the loon and golden eagle.

Younger ones in robes of beaver
snuggled warm inside their wigwams,
teased and taunted in the darkness,
laughed in mirth at senseless prattle,
pinched and frolicked with each other,
told of dragons in the swampland,
talked of ghosts in hidden places,
whispered secrets not for others,
until sleep removed the mischief
replaced by dreams of new tomorrows.

In long and warmer days of sunshine
children romped and chased each other,
climbed into the tallest aspen,
tried to imitate the marten
darting through the lofty branches,
gathered pebbles from the beaches,
threw them at the great horned owl,
scared him deep into the forest.
Shot their arrows at the rabbits,
chased them into deep dug burrows.

They watched the otters in the river,
skipped flat stones across the surface,
watched them sink in moving currents,
saw the hummingbirds assemble,
to partake of flowering sweetness
in their coats of mauve and emerald.
They gathered nuts and hazelberries,
cracked them with the larger pebbles,
ate the fruits and fed the ponies,
swam in brooks of cool fresh water,
lived as the Great Spirit wanted.

As the season changed from summer
cold winds blew in from the Northlands,
whipped the waters to a lather,
carried spits of snow and hailstones,
from the sounds of far off thunder.

Squirrels took nuts from giant oak trees,
stored them in each nook and cranny.
Warriors hunted for more deerskins,
took the coyote from deep canyons,
captured beaver from the marshes,
scraped and tanned the skins for lap robes.
Women dried the meat from bison,
made more clothing for the village
and moccasins to thwart the coldness.
Living things prepared for winter.

The blizzard came with blasts of fury,
swirled the falling leaves of autumn,
trampled memories of summer,
froze the surface of the waters,
drove the birds away for winter,
drove the marmot into hiding,
forced the bear to hibernation,
piled snow deep inside the forest,
filled the trees with glistening hoarfrost,
painted scenes of frigid splendor,
banked snow high upon the wigwams,
chilled the people with its frenzy.
It made the ponies stamp and shiver
with their tails turned to the North Winds,
suffering long into the winter.

In the early days of spring time
all the warriors took the young men
out across the open meadow,
taught them use of bows and arrows,
showed them water in the cactus,
showed them how to catch the groundhog,
taught them how to shoot the pheasant,
showed them how to race the ponies
riding fast on lathered bare backs.

They taught them how to track each other,
showed them things to eat from nature,
let them hear the piercing war cries
echo from the barren canyons,
let them skin the mighty bison,
made them race for far horizons,
told them to beware of wolf packs,
told them not to challenge panthers,
made them climb the steepest hillside,
let them feel the haunting stillness,
let them sleep all bathed in moonlight,
helped them learn for their survival.
All the women took the maidens
to the center of the village,
taught them how to shell the maize seeds,
taught them how to bake the corn-pone,
taught them how to flint the firewood,
showed them how to chew the deerskin,
how to cut it thin for bow strings,
how to make it strong and supple,
how to sew the robes for sleeping,
how to cook the meats and berries,
how to make them last the winter,
how to mind the new papooses,
how to set the broken leg bones,
showed them how to be a midwife,
helped them learn for their survival.

The Great Spirit loved his people
lived beside them, moved among them,
gave them life and inspiration,
told them how to solve their problems,
showed them rules of limitation,
taught them how to fill their larders,
kept them from life's bad beguilements,
gave them knowledge of the seasons,
told them when to plant the maize seeds,
showed them how to trap the beaver,
helped them learn for their survival.

When the Indian faced temptation,
succumbed to lust and provocation,
caused for others agitation,
broke the bonds of long duration,
committed sin among his people,
the Great Spirit chose the judgment.
It was firm, uncompromising,
meant to warn the misbehavers,
revealed his will with great vexation.
The Great Spirit took strong measures
to influence the errant parties.

Sent our visions from the heaven,
meteors and bolts of lightning,
searing hot volcanic ashes,
earthquake tumult in the mountains,
monsoon rains across the valley,
turned the streams to raging rivers,
turned the day to cavern blackness,
sent down floods on errant people,
fiery maelstroms on the prairie,
swirling dust storms in the village
gave them drought and burning tempests,
white hot heat and plagues of locust,
brought seething anguish to the sinners,
made them suffer chills and fever,
quelled aggression, made them humble.
Such was the power of the Great Spirit.

When the sun dropped from the heaven
and the day had turned to darkness,
and the village was all sleeping,
there were some with eyes wide open,
thinking of loved ones departed
who remain so clear in memory.
Thoughts alone late in the nighttime
feeling how their heart is aching,
knew that there was no relieving,
that the pain was now eternal,
knew that never prayer or signing,
could erase this great affliction,
and the mind would always wander,
when it was the time for sleeping,
longing, craving, yearning, grieving,
for ones who now are only vapor,
and the tears rolled down in silence
in a private world of loved ones.

One remembered always laughing
had a face so young and tender,
one that loved the whole creation,
one that smiled at tiny pleasures,
spread her goodness to all others,
gave to all who needed solace.

Now is left just minute traces
noticed still as time is passing.
Like blue beads and ermine sandals
words still seen high in the aspen,
carved are words of adoration,
words of hope and expectation,
fainter foot prints on the beaches,
scent of jasmine on her lap robe,
leather dress with sea shell necklace,
dried wild roses from her tresses,
touched to lips that still remember.

One recalled so reckless daring
tawny face with dark eyes flashing,
strong and agile like the puma,
wise and clever like the snow owl,
tall and stalwart now a warrior,
wore a neckband made from talons,
wore a loincloth made of wolf hides,
and moccasins from rugged bison,
wore a head band made from feathers
taken from the highest aerie
while facing danger from the eagle.

He swam across the mighty rivers,
took the pike with bow and arrow,,
captured wolverine and badger,
chased the foxes into burrows,
caught the eyes of all the maidens,
thinking far into the future.
But it was not bound to happen.
Lurking in some dismal darkness
that came in silence on the east winds
was a strange and unknown illness.
It spread its tendrils filled with toxin,
found the young and daring warrior,
took his power and made it weakness,
forced his manhood into frailty,
thrust his flawed and failing body,
to the other side of shadows
to the land of the hereafter.

One young maiden most affected,
walked in silent meditation
where they strolled before as lovers
thinking of the missed tomorrows,
thoughts benumbed by flaming sorrow,
exists each day with muted ardor
until the time to be together.

At a time when all were sleeping
came the sounds of violent thrashing,
came the noise of grunts and snarling,
came the ponies' neighs of terror.
Men and women grabbed their torches,
dipped them in the slumbering fire pit
filled with still hot glowing embers.
Lighted torches with their deer fat,
ran to see the loud disturbance.
Found a grizzly raging fury,
standing high upon his hind legs
twice as tall as any warrior
rending logs to bits and pieces.
Savagely it smote the ponies,
raking, biting, slamming, charging,
breaking down the wood enclosure,
dealing death and wanton slaughter.

Determined men with burning passion
attacked the bruin with their spear points,
darted at him throwing torches,
shot him full of flint stone arrows,
hit it with the broken timbers
as he ravaged other ponies.
When its red blood began pouring
from the eyes and mouth and spear holes,
glistening in the flickering firelight,
then the bear rose up in panic,
tried to scramble through a thicket,
ran into a stone outcropping,
crushed his head which sent him reeling.
When the giant omnivore
fell with breath and heartbeat failing,
then the people started dancing,
yelled with joy their jubilation,
gave up thanks to their Great Spirit.

All the people in the village
gathered round their mighty Chieftain,
waited for his words of wisdom,
watched the smoke drift from his peace pipe,
patient while he meditated
listened to his incantations,
Then he stood tall like the fir tree,
spread his arms with one great motion,
formed a moon and spread arms outward,
then he spoke, his words like thunder.

"We are the people, the supreme nation,
spread across the northern woodlands.
Many are our lakes and rivers,
many are our plains and mountains,
from the land of the Ojibwa,
to the home of the Apache
we share our crops in times of hardship,
share our fish with loon and osprey,
share our fur in coldest winters,
share our wigwams with the traveler."

He told them of old deeds and daring,
told them of loved ones departed,
extolled the joy of past adventures,
rekindled visions of their legends.
They listened to his truest wisdom.
All the chiefs from all the nations
must abide the Mighty Spirit.

Came a time when all the warriors
took up spears and bows and arrows,
burnished knives and wooden war clubs,
did a war dance to the Spirits,
plotted vengeful retribution,
on a sudden raiding party,
who had kidnapped one young maiden,
that had stolen from their larder,
and had burned too many wigwams,
causing hardship for the people.
Out across the darkening prairie
rode the warriors, faces painted,
gleaming in the dimming sunlight,
minds intent upon one purpose,
seek revenge upon the raiders,
save the maiden from tormentors,
burn the village of the robbers,
display the might that all should witness.

Furiously they rode their ponies,
black eyes glowering in the sunset,
evoking yells of righteous anger,
attacked with vicious indignation,
stormed the village, killed the Chieftain,
made the bandits flee in terror,
left nothing standing for the outlaws.
Killed enough to leave a message,
leave in peace this mighty nation.
Rode back to their safe encampment
with the young and smiling maiden,
divided things among the people,
held a night long celebration
until from the east horizon
rose the bright sun from its resting.
Gave fervent thanks to their Great Spirit.

Into this land of wondrous bounty
came a people pale in skin tone,
came from great potato famines,
came from tyrant persecutions,
came from poor and arid countries,
came from lands of yellow faces,
came from places of great hardship,
came from toil and virtual slavery,
came from tropical diseases,
came from virulent oppression,
escaping from demonic terror,
came at first in tiny trickles,
came at last in teeming masses
to a melting pot of races.

Came to find a land of respite
where to rest their weary bodies
Came to find a better future
praying for a place to prosper.
Came to find religious freedom
where to love their own Great Spirit.

Came with threadbare coats and trousers
came with knapsacks filled with trinkets,
found a land of simple people
who shared their larder with the strangers.
They traded beads for lands and forests,
forced the natives from their homelands,
set up forts and strong defenses,
fired with vengeance on objectors,
slaughtered proud and peaceful natives,
murdered women and their children
in the name of their Great Spirit.

Pushed them from the fertile valleys
forced them from the mountain forests,
chased them from the Mohawk basin,
hounded them like so much cattle,
razed and burned their rightful village,
lowered them to destitution,
tore apart their family unions,
shot and lynched the strong protestors,
robbed and plundered all possessions,
raped and maimed the fairest maidens,
assassinated once proud Chieftains,
subverted laws among the people.

The Eastlands saw the forced migrations.
The Northlands witnessed mutilations.
The Southlands pulsed with depredations.
The Westlands suffered subjugations.

During thoughts in watchful silence
The Great Spirit saw new changes,
larger wigwams full of wonders,
people living longer life spans
because of medicine and science,
telephones and transportation,
leisure hours for all the workers,
added time for rest and pleasure,
abundant hours for meditation,
for the paleface and his offspring.
All these things should make them happy.
Why then are they not contented?

Drove them from the coastal lowlands,
pursued them through the Smokie Mountains,
pushed them westward, ever westward,
tracked them down like beasts of burden,
herded them with calloused venom,
spit and hurled insults upon them,
changed the robust native people
into beaten serfs and vassals.
Crushed them all in reservations
void of trees and vegetation,
gave them land both dry and fallow,
doled out food not fit for eating.
Swathed in rags and tattered clothing
Natives stood with spirits broken,
voices low in lamentations
without hope or expectation,
fading like a blurry sunset,
waiting for the time of darkness
to be with their own Great Spirit.

The Great Spirit now will ponder
how to aid his faltering people
to regain their one time greatness.
Just by watching modern progress
he believes the time is coming
that will see a great uplifting
to the olden times of greatness
those who suffer scorn and hatred
just existing on the pittance
rationed out to reservations.

There are harbingers and omens
that refute a healthy image,
of a land so full of promise.

The Great Spirit senses reasons
why a place with much abundance,
shows increasing social discord.
People stacked on one another
much like firewood used for warming,
much like boulders on the levee.
Sees division in the families
over half of them divorcing.
Sees contempt for law and order,
sees the fear that comes with darkness,
lust and rape and dreadful beatings.
He sees the turmoil overpowering,
hears the constant din of noises.
Sees pollution ever growing,
acid rains denuding forests.
Hears the clusters in rebellion.
Sees the drugs and wild defiance.
Sees revolting sin with children
sees the unrelenting violence,
sees the wild salacious dancing.
Sees the rampant fornication
with its virulent diseases.
Sees the wigwams, old, decaying
filled with frightened huddled people
preyed upon by savage hoodlums.
Sees the glaring looks of hatred.
Sees the riots and the looters
victimize defenseless people.
Sees a world so full of madness
sin and mind defying sadness.

Sees avid greed and strange perversions,
lurking peril in cities dying,
intolerance and child abusing,
sees a world beset by terror,
neighbors killing one another.
Sees the millions of abortions,
sees the death row executions,
countless lost and wayward children.
Sees the hungry looks of people,
feels the pain of those despairing,
feels sympathy for old and feeble.

Sees corrosive radiation
with its lethal power for killing
hidden in the land and waters.
Sees suffocating tax oppression
piled upon a weakened people.
Sees men divided based on races,
Sees vast marauding armies
slaughter people by the millions
at the will of men demented,
heard a term called ethnic cleansing,
knows it as an act of murder,
just to steal the land and wigwams
of the ones exterminated.

Sees the mansions for the rulers
safe in fortress like enclosures,
use of dogs and stockade fences,
chains and bolts to thwart intrusions,
to ward off the poor and hungry.

All these things spell ruination
for a land seen as a beacon.
These are frightful contributions
adding to a new prediction
of a world so much in peril
that there may be no tomorrow.

What the Spirit sees will happen
as it did among the Mayans,
as it did among the Aztecs,
as it did among the Romans,
as it did among the Mongols,
as it did among the Incas,
as it did for the Phoenicians,
as it did for the Mycenians,
too, the Carthagenians,
as it did for other people,
decaying from internal weakness,
seen throughout the darkest ages.
So will other dwindling cultures,
who have lost the real direction
fail and falter in the twilight
of their zenith, now declining.

Just as flames reduce to embers
embers then reduce to ashes.
Such will be the destination
of those lacking civil graces.

Then restored will be the Natives
rising to the great occasion,
back upon the open prairie,
deep inside the darkest forest,
riding fast across the meadows
with their ponies in full gallop,
building up a land of wigwams
for an ever grateful people,
taking back the land of plenty
that belonged to those departed,
taking bison just when needed,
taking wild fowl for their larders,
restoring pride amid the people.

Finding needs for restoration
mighty Chiefs from all the nations
sent out word to every village,
saw the need for one great Powwow,
sent out word with swiftest runners,
sent messengers on fastest ponies,
sent smoke signals from the hilltops,
gave notice with the deerskin tom-toms,
sent birch canoes along each river.
Emissaries traveled widely
to announce important meetings.

Came powerful leaders from each homeland,
towering men so dark with sunshine,
robust men with forceful voices,
fervent men with dark eyes burning,
dressed in flowing feathered bonnets,
riding ponies swift and eager,
sure hoofs pounding, thick manes shining,
bringing more important Chieftains,
meant to save their plundered nation.

All the Chiefs now came together
came to hear the wisest message,
came to give their sage opinions,
brought with them sagacious counsel,
carried gifts for other Chieftains,
brought their peace pipes for the Powwow.

Came together, gave the peace signs,
sat on deer mats in a circle,
pondered long and smoked their peace pipes.
Cherokees from southern mountains,
Seminoles from distant swamplands,
Senecas from eastward forests,
Arapahos from western deserts.
Came Dakotas from the north plains,
came Mohicans and Algonquins,
came the Crow, the Ute and Cheyenne,
came the Delawares and Blackfeet,
came the Ottawas and Hurons,
came the Choctaws and the Shawnee.

Came the Mandans and Snohomish,
came the Erie, Cree and Piaute,
came the Mohawk and Apache,
gathered all in one great union,
with the Sioux and with the Pawnee,
with the Creek and the Shoshoni.
Spoke of things that had to happen,
talked 'til sunlight lit the heavens,
made plans for a brighter future.

Found there was no opposition
unified for endless effort,
spreading out across the prairie,
traveling to each distant valley,
every lake and every river,
all the forests, every mountain,
every place with hope for dwelling.

Cast new seed on barren hilltops,
seedlings to renew the forests,
try to save the giant Sequoias,
aid the failing coastal Redwoods,
build new herds of mighty bison,
clean up all the lakes and rivers,
cleansing all the air for breathing,
blowing smog from off the mountains,
give the land a chance for healing
so that in the promised future
with firm resolve and dedication
they will witness as they labor
from horizon to horizon
again a land of wondrous bounty.
All convinced that this will happen.
Such are the plans of the Great Spirit.

Sleepless in Stone Mountain.

Sometime around 1:30 and 2:30, after midnight, my brain begins to awaken with an awareness that something is creeping into my psyche, vague, undistinguishable, maybe worrisome dreams. To my knowledge there is nothing significant about that particular time but I glance at the clock before I get up and am amazed that the time often is exactly the same as it had been on previous nights. It's like a pre-set alarm clock in my head, night after night.

When going to bed as a very young child, I was always told to sleep tight and not let the bedbugs bite. After the kerosene lamp was extinguished my miniature brain worried about bedbugs biting me and I sometime found it difficult to go to sleep.

As I grew to be a teenager I continued to be a light sleeper. I would think of how many things I could accomplish if sleep was not necessary. I kept a flashlight at bedside and often would read comic books or draw pictures or write some simple story.

After being awake for two or three hours I would become sleepy and doze off again until dawn.

I never seemed to be tired because of the loss of sleep.

That quirk followed me into the navy during WW II. Upon awakening I would go up topside and stand by the aft rail and watch the phosphorescent sparkle created by the churning wake. After a couple hours of meditating I could go back to the sack and sleep well until reveille.

I read where Thomas Edison needed only four hours sleep and because of the thousands of extra hour he had to think and invent we have artificial illumination among many other inventions.

With out the noise of the day, telephone ringing, the roar of trucks picking up garbage, the whine of jets descending toward Atlanta's airport, I am able to concentrate on my writing. Occasionally I hear a train off in the distance, but that is nostalgically pleasant, remembering the trains hauling coal from the mine when I was a child. Then it was magic wondering where they were going and who was in the engine compartment. It's preferable to the artificiality of contemporary television and movies.

Because of the silence of night I have been able to write six books with another ready for editing and proofreading. That satisfies a lifelong dream. Unless something worthwhile occupies the day I can be much more creative during late night.

Are we better off today than yester-years?

1963 seems like a hundred years ago when I arrived in Atlanta. A sign on the old Darlington apartments on Peachtree indicated the population was less than 700,000. I-285 wasn't completed in Dekalb County between Chamblee Tucker and I-20. The road from Sandy Springs to Roswell was two lanes separating pastures full of grazing cattle.

My job was merchandising the fur departments in the Davison Paxon stores. Nieman Marcus was not here nor was Saks. Furs were purchased at Riches, Davison Paxon, Regensteins, J. P. Allen and Leon Froshin. My office was in the downtown store on Peachtree Street. I thought about opening York Furs in Buckhead. There were no Mega-Malls except Lenox Square which had just opened. The tallest building had a revolving restaurant on top. Two high-rise apartment buildings were just north of downtown. I hunted deer on a farm where Gwinnett Mall now exists. Winder was somewhere east. International Boulevard was Cain Street. Delta flew French Caravelles, DC3's, Lockheed Constellations, Boeing 707's and 727's. There were only six apartment complexes on Buford highway east of Druid Hills. Rent for a 3 bedroom apartment was $225 per month. Walmart had a store in Arkansas. Gwinnett County was country. Courtesy was common. It took more than one call to sue someone. John Portman was an entrepreneur in commercial development. Ernest Vandiver was Governor. Mills Lane held sway at the C&S Bank. Phipps Plaza was trees. There were three TV stations. I walked around downtown Atlanta at night without fear. There were no Toyotas. Strip joints were secretive. Marijuana was smoked in the Haight Asbury district in San Francisco. Lake Lanier was five years old without residential glut. It cost nothing to visit Stone Mountain. If you became sick, you could afford a doctor. Navels were on oranges. Except for Duluth, Suwannee and Buford, the Chattahoochee basin between Atlanta and Buford Dam was farmland. I could afford to play golf at Bobbie Jones and Chastain Park. My woods were actually wood. Jack Nicklaus won his first Masters. Ted Turner was marketing billboard advertising. Martin Luther King was marching in Alabama with his cadre of people. Ivan Allen was Mayor. Sam Massell sold travel tickets. A joint was a bar. Krispie Kreme was a novelty. Underground Atlanta was forsaken. Jails were mostly empty. Aunt Fannie's Cabin was the place for fried chicken. Gasoline was 31cts.You could sure eat in Atlanta, the

Magnolia Room was a must. Old Hickory House ribs stuck to your ribs. The Varsity was a magnet. The Francis Virginia Tearoom was elegant. Truett Cathy was dreaming of an Empire. York's poolroom on Pryor had tasty hotdogs. There was Paschal's, Colonade, Mary Mac's, Catfish King. Boom boxes were unknown. Tattoos were for sailors. Earrings were for women. You could blacken your lungs with the Marlboro Man without a lawsuit. Plaza Drugs was open all night. No one shot you without reason. Underwear wasn't exposed publicly. America wasn't at war. Spam was food. Car-jacking was unknown. Graffiti didn't exist. Girls had not gone wild. Cigarettes were 26ct. Neverland was a valley. Educators could punish students, parents understood. Swimsuits covered everything. The divorce rate was 17%. There was no sales tax. Russia was rattling sabers. Jonas Salk was a genius. Timothy Leary introduced LSD. Infidelity was rare. As a confident society are we better off today? I don't think so. Nostalgia helps me cope with reality.

Synopsis

Cougar is the story of a Nez Perce Indian boy who witnesses the destruction of his village by the United States 7th Cavalry, in 1819. Returning from hunting in the mountains he watches in horror from a bluff as soldiers on horseback charge back and forth through his village hurling torches into teepees and indiscriminately firing at old men, women and children trying to escape the attack. He watches his father decapitated by the slash of a saber. He sees his brother killed. He sees his mother shot through her back. Given the name Cougar by his grandfather because of his interest in wildcats when he was young, the boy escapes the carnage by hiding in the forest. After the soldiers leave Cougar walks around the compound and picks up a long knife and an Osage bow from his father's bloodied hands. He studies the faces of his dead family. Tears flood. His horse nudges his elbow. Cougar spends two days burying the bodies of the villagers in the sacred burial grounds. When he is finished he stands in the middle of the compound, lifts his arms to form a circle, then begins chanting to the Great Spirit, his cries carrying into the trees on the hillside, up across the boulder strewn escarpment, up into the snow-covered mountain peaks, echoing and re-echoing the agony of his torment. The Great Spirit hears the funereal lamentation of the Indian. Cougar constructs a travois and piles it with furs. He gathers a supply of arrows. He mounts his Appaloosa. All that remains of a once vibrant native people quickly rides away to commence a new life in a remote valley in the mountains. Cougar beckons to the cougar that he had saved from being killed by wolves. It growls then follows. Practicing Moon and Sun Dances taught to him by his grandfather the boy becomes a conjurer, provided great power by the Great Spirit, finding that he can assume any visage, including making himself invisible, and able to traverse in time, so that he can observe the paleface civilization and see changes brought about by the conquerors. He discovers exhibitionism and rampant immorality with millions of aborted fetuses. He finds the relentless pursuit of materialism, alcoholism, voyeurism, gang violence, ostentatious lifestyles, unfettered sin, impoverished vagrants, squalor, pompous millionaires, political corruption, sex orgies, corporate embezzlement, Hollywood debauchery, glorification of human idols, child molesters, decadent pornography, home invasions, the pursuit of immediate gratification, infidelity, the evolution of males and females into an enfeebled unisex engaged in anal penetration and insalubrious mouth-to-crotch copulation, incestuous sexuality, nakedness, environmental pollution, looks of hatred and the gluttonous depletion of natural resources. Most astonishing is to see millions of people with infantile brains being de-humanized in an avalanche of mind-killing drugs. He finds fork-tongued attorneys through the gibberish of hyperbole and a deliberate distortion of truth; protect criminals from justice they deserve. Cougar sees into the ailing soul of a decaying society. He decries the murder of millions of Indians to make room for people that a few hundred years later are destined for extinction as the result of unwholesome priorities and the flood of wickedness he sees sweeping across the land.

Just as firewood turns to embers,
Embers then become ashes.
There will be just minute traces,
Of those bereft of civil graces.

Sinful

Chapter One

After two hundred years of existing in seclusion, secure from the palefaces who had torched his village and killed his family, Cougar decided to leave the valley and visit the homes palefaces to see how they had fared since the murderous attack so many moons ago. He also wished to visit those sacred burial grounds of his ancestors and find where he had lived as a youth.

After riding the Appaloosa up to the plateau where it could roam until they returned Cougar and the cougar left the valley, ascending above a covering of gossamer clouds. A storm cloud loomed in the distance with brilliant flashes of lightning. A chilling breeze blew down the side of the mountain. A condor spiraled above searching along the edges of bluffs, eyes focused, seeking a carcass. Two Golden Eagles soared alongside in concert with the pair yet maintaining a cautious eye on the cougar but feeling safe since the predator was now in their domain.

Traveling invisibly, Cougar and the cougar followed a valley to its confluence with a stream that had a strangely familiar look to Cougar. He recognized rugged arroyos that led to a meadow. Everything was different though. He saw no evidence that a village had existed where the two rivers merged together. Instead of trees Cougar remembered having covered the earth; he saw big buildings rising to the sky and roadways of concrete running in all directions. People scurried amidst the sprawl. Automobiles belching noxious vapors, roamed the asphalt trails. Where were the horses? The river was filled with ships spewing smoke. Where were their dugout canoes? It was difficult to remember the exact location of his compound, but he studied one point of land where his village was probably situated when the soldiers began hurling torches into teepees while the people were sleeping and shooting them as they tried to escape. Now there was concrete and asphalt covering the entire area. He could not find their sacred burial grounds where he had buried his family.

He patted the cougar's rump. The feline twined itself around Cougar's leg. It growled. They rose above the jumble of concrete. A surge of sadness swept over the Indian when he stared down, realizing that he had no past. Evidence of his childhood was buried under man-made clutter. It was as if the Nez Perce Indians had never existed. Yet the memories were acute.

Observing from above the jumble Cougar was astonished by the barren scars on the mountains where verdant forest once grew. Buffalo and other wildlife no longer wandered the lands. The city was covered with clouds of pungent smoke indicating the palefaces were ruining the atmosphere by the over-consumption of natural resources. He could see mountains of garbage littering the hillsides and valleys. Cougar recalled the sagacious words of his grandfather when he had said that a man can only ride one horse at a time. Palefaces were living as if nature's resources were without limit. The words 'wasteful' and 'greed' came to Cougar's mind.

Moving slowly across the city he was astounded by the congestion of people existing on top of each other like maggots on a carcass. He wondered why palefaces lived in teepees so much bigger than they needed. Again the word 'wasteful' came to mind. He recalled how frugal his people lived and with respect for nature when he was young. He also recalled one more astute counsel his grandfather always emphasized; that you never take from nature more than nature can replace. Palefaces were using up the earth by the over-consumption of natural resources.

Cougar and the mountain lion found themselves above a golf course where a tournament was being played. On the few occasions Cougar had left the valley he had watched other golf tournaments and was intrigued by the outdoor activities. He was curious about the throngs of people that followed golfers around the course like trained sheep. They applauded when a golfer made a good shot. They applauded when the player made a lousy shot. They oohed and aahed when players adjusted their balls or scratched their butt. They followed the golfers like Pavlov's dogs, sticking their faces in front of cameras attempting to get just one golfer to smile their way so they could smile knowingly to him. When more golfers smiled their way their spirit was lifted even though the smiles were not intended for them. They pretended the smiles were just for them anyhow and they were emotionally and spiritually fulfilled.

The spectacular sickened Cougar a little. Why were palefaces so emotionally dependent on the activity of others? Cougar and the puma wandered invisibly in and out amid the fawning worshippers. Cougar smiled, knowing that those spectators would be stricken if they were aware a 200 pound mountain lion was near them. Cougar noticed one downcast golfer ambling slowly along the final fairway. The Indian decided to become that golfer to learn why the man was so despondent. Cougar became Jack Gresham.

Chapter Two

It was the fourteenth time Jack Gresham had missed the cut in one season. During his extraordinary career Jack had won several tournaments including the Masters but he knew his game had begun going to hell the past season. Frequently the last year while he ambled along to the final green he wondered why he was becoming tired so fast. His normally easy repartee with the gallery had slowed. His friendly banter was gone replaced by pre-occupation. His legendary shot placements were gone, with his longer irons causing the balls to stray into sand traps and shorter irons missing the green or leaving him with impossible putts. He hadn't eagled one hole in the last four tournaments.

Jack Gresham was known for destroying the myth of course invincibility with a display that had elicited screams of adulation for a decade. His scores were now soaring above par and his earnings were plunging. He would be happy to get the last hole over with and go back to the resort. His embarrassment had increased until finishing the final hole was humiliating. He had become annoyed with spectators clapping when he made good shots, but also applauding noisily whenever he made a triple bogey. Spectators were puppet-minded-idol-worshipping pains-in-the-ass.

That night, in his resort room, Gresham again felt that itch coming. With such a heavy schedule and prize money reaching asinine amounts, creating more pressure to perform, milling minions of sucker-uppers looked for golfers to perform sensational shots then, between holes, they would shove pens in his face for his autograph. He had begun to feel like he was playing for cultists.

A seeping lesion underneath his tongue was sore and it seemed to be getting larger. His tongue explored the lesion. Make-up hid the open abrasion on his lower lip. There was a sore place under the foreskin on his penis. Neosporin had not eased that discomfort. He decided to see a doctor when he returned home. He pulled down his pants and checked the lesion. He was aware that he had gotten something from one of those sluts.

Sleep would not come that night. Lying restlessly in bed he glowered at the clock. It was early evening. Jack put in a phone call to his wife. She wasn't home. He missed his wife. He turned on the TV and watched a stupid sit-com with a machine creating laughter. After failing to pound his pillow into submission he decided he couldn't endure the tossing and turning. His sheets were damp and he couldn't find a comfortable position.

His flight out was not until the following morning. He took out the notepad from a zippered pocket in his golf bag and looked up a number. Dialing, Jack waited impatiently, tapping his finger on the phone. She was home. Yes, he could come over but wait a couple hours. As a matter of fact, she would come over and pick him up in her new convertible. She said that Arthur was on location on a shoot in Mexico. She purred she had seen him on TV, hoping he would phone. She said she wanted to show him the Oscar she had gotten last week for The Uprising. She asked why he had not called early in the week. She sounded annoyed.

Not only was Jack Gresham recognized as a world-class golfer while he was in high school but within two years after graduation Jack was the father of adorable twin cherubs, Tina and Tana. The girls were the result of the union of teenagers who dated during high school. From the sixth grade friends assumed that Jack Gresham and Gini Molinara would be paired forever. Jack, a star athlete, and Gini, winner of two Miss Georgia pageants, fulfilled a marital union designed in heaven. Tina and Tana were approaching their puberty years and Jack had begun to find himself strangely aroused when the girls snuggled on his lap. Sometimes he noticed one of their budding nipples and his heart would pound. Sometime he would rub their belly under their pajamas and his heart would thud even harder and he would have to adjust his erection. Tana would laugh and move her body to enable him to touch her down there. Tina kept her legs closed tightly together.

Jack glanced again at the notepad filled with phone numbers. He had Lydia listed as Lydia_Nymph. There was no other identity. There were the initials of ten other tour golfers who had used Lydia at one time or another. Phone numbers passed among good friends. Lydia had been married when he first met her at a pro-am tournament in the valley. With the tour in California, it was amazing to know how many Hollywood starlets were ready to screw professional golfers. The fact that they had wives made no difference. To hell with morality, this is today.

Jack lay nude on his back, with moonlight streaming in the window. He could hear sounds of the ocean in the distance. Gossamer threads of lightning illuminated the bedroom.

Like a hovering wraith she positioned herself above his body, clutching him with nails like stilettos.

Jack had had sex with Lydia four times prior, after meeting her during a golf tournament. She'd been in the gallery. Now, he was once again exposed to the magic of her naked artistry. He would not think of Gini and the twins. Jack would not worry about his failing game. He would be taken to a plateau of orgiastic ecstasy found only in the phone numbers listed on his notepad.

He watched as she raised the gown up over her head, throwing it casually on the rug. Her breasts swayed as she arched her back lowering her scented vagina to his lips, gyrating like a dancer. His tongue probed upward, seeking then penetrating the deep recesses of her body as he pulled down on her thighs. Pubic hairs moistened by the application of FDS, and the ejaculations of the basketball player she'd been fucking when Jack called, gently wetted his face and neck. Lydia was a master of feminine talent. The FDS masked her need for a douche. There wasn't time. An application of Vagisil protected the abrasion on her anus left by the basketball star's penetration and his roughhouse antics.

Along with her movie contract, Lydia's income was well above a million dollars providing her service to the visiting football, baseball and basketball teams. She thought of the funny story told to her by one of the Atlanta Braves players, about the little Georgia woodpecker that was visited by a friend from northern California. The California bird derided the tiny pine trees in Georgia, telling the Georgia woodpecker that he should visit him in California, that he would find giant redwood and sequoia trees where pecking was pure delight. The Georgia woodpecker flew to Eureka and his friend pointed out a 200 feet tall redwood, suggesting that the Georgia bird fly up to the top and peck to his heart's content. While pecking the redwood a storm came over the coastal range with lightning hitting the tree, splitting it, and knocking the bird to the ground. The California woodpecker flew over, asking what happened. The little Georgia woodpecker explained that he was up in the tree pecking away when all of a sudden he split the tree right down the middle. "It's amazing how much harder your pecker gets when you get out of town."

Gresham's heart started pounding, while his tongue began a flicking exploration. She was releasing a musk scent which cart-wheeled his brain into an incredible world of fantasy. He could sense the moisture flowing from her. It ran down his face as his lips synced with the slamming of her thighs and his tongue explored her yeast infection and vaginal warts. Lydia swiveled in a frenzied undulation as she reached behind, taking his hardness in her hand. A particle of feces, expelled by her stuttering release of bowel gas generated when the basketball player had probed in her anus lodged behind a molar. A chancre in the vestibule of her vagina oozed infectious pus.

For some reason, his reflections went back to Gini. Every time Jack had interludes he felt guilty, knowing that Gini was waiting. After some years of disagreement on sex experimentation he knew that it was her religion that had kept her from approving of oral copulation and other deviances. Jack loved Gini but his propensity for variety was something over which he had little control. That was Jack's rationale for hiding the notebook with the phone numbers in the cities where he was scheduled to play.

Lydia's fingernails dug torturously into his penis as she slithered lower on his hips, inserting him into her vagina. There was some burning sensation where his foreskin curled back. He relished that feeling knowing that they would soon have an orgasm so satisfying that she would scream, "Oh God! God!" as their sweat-soaked bodies writhed in unison slamming flesh against flesh, lusting creatures seeking release, surrendering to the battering cadence as old as the sea.

"I will be playing at Pebble Beach one month from now," he said as he exited her convertible in front of his motel. "I'm in the Crosby"

"I have a cottage in Carmel," Lydia said. "Phone me in advance and I'll plan on driving up for a couple of days."

"I'll let you know,"

"You won the Crosby a few years ago, I recall," she said.

"No. I was ahead by three going to 18. I hooked my second shot down onto that dammed beach."

His forehead twisted into a scowl as he recalled. "I lost in a playoff. It was about the time my whole game started going to hell."

"I will encourage you good next time," she smiled, reaching, walking her fingers down to his zipper.

They parted, having generated magic. Undetected on his tongue was that particle of feces. Moving into the opening under his foreskin was the HIV virus which had been deposited by the basketball player. Searching for open lesions was the spirochete Treponema Pallidum which was transferred from her vagina onto his tongue. The virus found the soreness under his tongue, and entered his blood stream. He had infected her with herpes simplex. With Lydia's exposure to sexually-transmitted-diseases, by the time they would tryst again, in one month, the pair would have transmitted their viruses to more sex-crazed people, acquiring other diseases in return.

Cougar quickly left from what had been a disgusting experience. He figured that people were enroute to hell with such immorality. He wondered if the girl's husband had knowledge of her sexual indiscretions. Cougar decided he would go see the woman's husband and determine if he knew about his wife's out-of-town meetings. He remembered the comment about her husband making a movie in Mexico. He willed himself above the restaurant where Lydia's husband was enjoying lunch with another man. He hovered nearby listening to the enlightening conversation between two men.

Chapter Three

Arthur Model ordered two more tequilas with another basket of tortilla chips with salsa. He couldn't recall how many drinks he had consumed since he and Ed entered the Rio Bravo lounge. He was aware his tongue was thick and his concentration fuzzy.

Ted Ketterman took out a legal pad from his attaché case and positioned it on the table. "I hope you're not a jealous man, Arthur," he said.

Arthur Model rubbed his unshaven face. "I used to be insanely jealous of her. It does not mean crap anymore," he stated emphatically "This is money. What do you have?"

Ted Ketterman was a close friend of Art Model. He had retired from the San Diego police department after nine years running the homicide department. Four years into retirement a mutual fund, in which his retirement account was invested, went belly-up. Ed's instinct was to locate the bastards who had embezzled the money and kill them. Instead, aware of dangers inside a jail and needing to supplement his social security, he became a private detective. One of his first fees came from Art Model with his cheating wife, Lydia.

"She's a busy woman." Ted scanned his notes.

"I know that," Arthur said. He sipped his tequila. "How busy is she?"

"Busy. Averaging three each day since you came down on the shoot three weeks ago. She was with a golfer and a basketball player in Portland yesterday."

"Two tricks at the same time?"

"No, a couple hours apart."

"Jesus Christ!" Art frowned. "That is a helluva-lot of screwin'. You get graphic shots?"

"A gold mine. You won't have a problem with her."

Arthur took another drink and exhaled noisily. "The power of pussy, can you believe it? They spread vaginal juice everywhere and believe they can control the world with what's between their legs. I found that broad just in from Boise. She was about twenty and set on being a star. She had been married one time. I took the slut and made her a star. They come here from Cincinnati and Indianapolis, fondle a few dicks, get some bit-parts in B-movies, use their mouth expertly and fame is assured. My daddy used to call that being pussy-whipped."

"You're not fond of females, huh?" Ted said.

"Not much," Art said.

"I shot her on telephoto. I have a friend who owns a helicopter. We flew his chopper up a couple thousand feet away; mansion under construction.

It looked like we were checking a home site. I aimed the camera over your wall, and shot into the enclosure and I got some super outside footage. You will see great resolution. I filmed it with the brand new gyro-stabilized camera, the same equipment used by producers when shooting movies from a helicopter."

"How explicit?"

"You don't want to know, Art," Ted said.

"I'm paying you good money, damn it, and little you can reveal will upset me. What happened?"

"I'll show you. I cut a few shots out of the film." He placed a number of pictures on the table. They were ultra pornographic. It was Lydia with friends.

Arthur's face took on a scowl while he scanned the photos. There was one picture of Lydia going down on a muscular stud, while another muscleman lay flat on his back licking her crotch. The bizarre picture had been shot around Arthur's pool.

Art put the photographs in his lap. The photos were disturbing. He gazed out over the incoming rollers. Far out to sea a convoy of navy ships was heading somewhere, maybe to San Diego or Seattle. The sun was a sliver of orange near the horizon. Art thought of Sonja, wishing she was with him. He began to feel despondent.

"See the guy on the ground?" Arthur pointed.

"Sure."

"He is one of those Hollywood super-studs you see all the time with a different broad. He worked a racing accident for me a couple years back. He has the reputation for rooting around in crotches like a pig rooting for acorns. What germs that son-of-a-bitch gets he deserves. I hope his tongue rots off."

"Your boys know about your problem, Art?"

"Sure. Both of them left home after jokes started buzzing around about their beautiful stepmother. Jake is crabbing in Alaska. Art, Jr. flies a bush plane in British Columbia. I rarely hear from them. They both were pissed when I left their mother for that bitch." Art scratched his forehead. "I wouldn't tell anybody else but you this, Ed, but I think both of them were bangin' Lydia after we were married."

"You're kidding."

"No. They were teenagers chasing around with hard-ons all the time. I saw Arthur naked in the pool with her one night when I came home early. I drove back to the office. Sonja yelled I was a schmuck for becoming involved with a broad young enough to be my daughter. Sonja was right. One time I got up to piss. Jake was being hand-stroked out by the pool."

"You did nothing?"

"No. By then I knew it would stop sometime soon. I had to find out about property laws. Enough porno pics and she'll lay off the big money demand. Patience will save me a few million bucks. I've kept her much longer than I should have. Men get pussy-cowed when they are young. Don't want their broads to find out that there are bigger dicks around"

"You're sure down on women, aren't you?"

"I've found there is nothing special about females. Errol Flynn opined, 'If you turn them all upside down they will all look the same'. Imagine the smiling manikins hunched down on the crapper straining to eject a brick instead of a banana. The aftermath is swirling stink whether it comes from Roast Venison Loin Trattoria from La Bodeguita de Pico's or soup beans and hog jowls from Bennie's hamburger joint. Their toilet paper has the same stains as everyone else."

They ordered another tequila.

"You ever get your pecker in trouble, Ted?

"Yep. Once in Palermo, while I was in the navy. I got a dose of clap. Back in those days you washed up, got a syringe of burning gunk from sick-bay, squeezed it in your dick, and then worried your ass off for a month that your dick might fall off. I wanted no more of that so I keep my pecker in its nest. Screwin's overrated."

"Promiscuity is out of hand," Art said. "I'm in a business where I see it, watch the broads in their designer's gowns, swivel-hipping down the carpet during the Academy Awards banquet, expecting to be anointed for their B-rated performance. Hollywood is little more than society's self-lionized crème de la crème staring into cameras with that attitude of superiority. Everyone is screwing everyone else, posing, demure, kittenish, with exaggerated smiles, showing their capped-teeth to their wide-eyed minions."

"You are pretty vehement on the subject," Ted said. "Knowing you, I guess I'm not surprised."

"Damned vocal. I'm sickened by what is happening in Hollywood. I knew everybody at the Screen Actors Guild Awards. Many of them have had kids out of wedlock. Many of the sluts have phony tits. Hollywood is an unending orgy; ménage ET beaucoup. They gape in the camera with smiles of piety convinced that if they drop their Kotex on Sunset Strip in the middle of July it will not begin to stink. I see Hollywood couples breaking up after having been shacked up for years."

"I have pretty much stopped watching television, a lot of crapola, not worth seeing. I see programming with some guy hammering nails or sawing a 2X4, or some broad covering up her pimples with face paint.

Watching a tomato being sliced is not too scintillating either. How often do we need to see our ancestors swinging from trees, or the numbskulls we work with everyday who haven't completed the evolutionary cycle?"

Arthur grimaced. "The ones that sicken me are the nearly naked broads swiveling their fat asses in front of the camera with the lens focused up in their crotches. Lenny Bruce wrote a book several years ago titled Fuck. Every word in his novel was Fuck. He would get a Pulitzer Prize today."

"When I began detective work my initial client had a problem like yours, perhaps worse, but he handled it real smart. She was a starlet when he married her. She had the goods on him screwin' around and was going to take him to the cleaners. But he was sharp. He got her soused one night and was in the sack with her, then got up to take a leak and left the light off. He had hired some dude to hide outside his house when it was dark. He let the stud in. He zapped him with Old Spice, the same perfume he used. I was inside, too. Instead of hubby back in bed, the hotshot went in, crawled in with her and started screwin' her brains out. No covers, thrashing bodies with good ole' doggie-style connecting. Using infrared equipment I shot some fantastic, full-face, bare-butt award winners. You should've seen the look on her face when she saw them. I recorded her moanin' and groanin' on tape, also."

"Jesus, Ted. Where's your ethics?

"Ethics-schmethics. I got fifteen grand for the shots. Ethics will improve with improved payments. That's the way democracy works. She went away quietly."

"I'll admit it was a good idea." Art said.

"I have to get going, Art. My flight is in an hour. I'd like to spend a month here but duty calls. When'll the movie be finished?"

"Another couple weeks. Get me some more pics of the tramp. How much do I owe you now?"

"Don't worry about it," Ted grinned. "I'll bill you when I'm done. What kind of movie you doing? "

"Movies suck today. Writers continue writing after they have run out of talent. Actresses and actors are snotty and overpaid. I'm making crappy, short, B-flicks. You know, dark-tanned cowboy chasin' wetbacks across the border trying to get back the virginal girl and a wagonload of stolen gold bars. Not my best work, but low budget."

Ted studied Art's eyes for a moment. "Because we're friends I have got to ask you, Art, and I don't want you to get pissed." He hesitated.

"What?"

"Have you caught anything from Lydia?"

"Maybe. But after I discovered she was screwin' the clowns in town, I visited my doctor and got some doses of antibiotics. From then on I stopped dippin' my tool in her pool. I am too old for that bunk-buddy crap anyhow. It's too sweaty. I've had to restructure my priorities."

"You're lucky."

"I suppose. Some of that crap is incurable and will kill you. I have a friend who believes he is Jesus. It's syphilis. The crap destroyed his mind. He used to have a business back east. Now he walks around mumbling to himself, smelling of stale urine."

"Wouldn't you think people would be concerned?"

"Apparently not. It's insipid. I am convinced this country is headed the same way as the Roman Empire. When they began getting laid in the Coliseum while gladiators killed each other and then decided that strange lifestyles were was preferable it was not too long before they were extinct. I believe we are headed the same way. It seems like people's brains have been relocated between their legs. Just listen to the bleeped shit on television now."

"I'll see you in Beverly Hills."

"Yeah, Ted, I want to talk to you when I get back home."

"You want me to just bring the bill over to your house?"

"I'll call you."

"What's it about?"

"I know we're being swindled by politicians, and by bureaucrats. Attorneys double-talk juries and let murderers back on the street. Scammers are hustling the public, selling overpriced gimmicks on television. Getting drunk and acting stupid is cool. Kids are being brainwashed that there's safe sex. The public is so stupid that they're not aware that wrestling is a first class scam. We have cage brawls where Neanderthals try to seriously injure each other. Sit-coms are idiotic. Entertainers scream filth while grabbing their crotches. America has its priorities backward. We gawk at females with silicone tits, insipid movies and television crap. We have carnival barkers selling God. With many around us living in poverty we idolize the purveyors of smut instead of admiring those people who have benefited society."

"I agree."

"Do you know Johnny Fellino, Ted?"

"A small-time hood?"

"Yeah, he wanted to be the head Mafioso a few years back. Wanted to take over when Bugsy Siegel got it. New York told him to tone it down or die. He took up making flesh flicks, and hustling drugs to pushers.

"You interested in him?"

"Yes. He is why Lydia is the way she is. Just after she and I met she was struggling for bit-parts. Fellino conned her into doing pornography flicks. Drugs were part of his tactics. She got caught up in the local cocaine merry-go-round. By the time I knew what was happening she was a lost cause. I owe the bastard, big time."

"How'd she get the Oscar?"

"Good typecasting. She played the part of a drugged whore."

"I gotta' run. See you in L.A."

Listening to their scurrilous revelations Cougar confirmed what he already knew to be a fact from his previous visitations to California. For some yet unknown reason the residents of Hollywood, and most of the major communities in the state, were the fore-runners of a climate of decadence that was beginning to contaminate everybody. With the unending publicity that the movie colony receives from the networks it was not difficult to understand that Hollywood had evolved into Sin City. He could no wait to get back to the sanity of his wilderness home. He was disgusted by the filthy language he had heard from the men. The same crap was being spoken on the networks and on television, but bleeped out as if that was an acceptable method for speaking cesspool language on the public's airways. Cougar realized what he had just heard was further evidence that the paleface society was descending into purgatory.

Unique species

We were sipping warm sassafras tea laced with honey from a fruit tree. Its taste was a virgin experience for me. I complimented Cougar on his cougar. I began. "One of the enigmas in our society is the rejection of integration by major ethnicities," I said. "Nobody seems to be interested in establishing a bond between them and it is remaining in stasis. In 1964, President Johnson passed the grand revolution and announced that his great society would be the hallmark of his Presidency, and citizens in the future would live and work together in harmony. It hasn't happened that way."

"It'll never work, Cougar said. "Mother Nature does not allow it simply because every unique species wants to maintain its own identity. That is why polar bears do not co-habitate with the grizzly. Deer don't cross-breed with elk. Ducks don't migrate with geese. Cougar don't breed with wild cats of any kind, only their own. Nature is aware it doesn't work. The Great Spirit believes in Mother Nature. I recall a tragedy that occurred in New York years ago. A girl in Alabama was born in a black family. For some unknown reason, her coloration was pale and her features Caucasian. Being unhappy at home she decided to leave home at an early age. She went to New York and became a top fashion model. When a renowned physician, the member of a prominent family, attended a fashion show, he became enamored with her beauty. They dated. A relationship developed. They were married and she became pregnant. The girl did not tell her husband of her ethnic background. Wanting to witness the birth of his baby and while serving on the teaching staff at a maternity hospital he invited one student to witness the birth of his baby as a part of the study. When the child was born it was black. The doctor hurried from the room convinced that his wife had been unfaithful. The day she arrived home he filed for divorce. That's the reason Mother Nature does not condone any cross-breeding. Those relationships are cultural anomalies from which many unpredictable consequences will transcend. Nature is determined the zebra keep its wonderful stripes. It's an undeniable fact that if you mix black and white the result is a shade of gray. Individuality will be gone. I would be called a racist by Afro Americans or those politicians wishing to con the voters to assure their tenure in office. In speaking with cultured Afro Americans though, I know that they choose to keep their unique ways, too. With my people I'd be known as a realist."

"I recall when the fur industry began trying to develop new colors of minks. We only had brown mink and they did not sell well. Some furriers and ranchers formed a Breeding Association with the idea of breeding specific colors to get other newer colors. It was hit or miss. Eventually, with keeping records of certain colorations bred with other strains we produced predictable mutation colors. It required a great amount of record keeping. And yet, mistakes were made with undesirable results. To perfect colors took years. We got a lot of peculiar shades in the process. I agree with Mother Nature that uniqueness must be maintained. You do not want to dilute the gene pool of unique species and have unusual appearing results. The aberration will transcend through succeeding generations of mutants, and by the reason of continued breeding between the descendants' appearance will be unforeseen and maybe undesirable. The worst part is that the children evolving from those unions have no say in the tribulations related to cross-breeding."

"Mother Nature is always right," Cougar said.

Reality

'I cried because I had no shoes until I met the man who had no feet'. (anonymous)

I was sitting in an antique store in Stone Mountain village waiting for my wife to examine everything in the store. The coffee was good. It was freezing outside.

A man walking in the front door caught my attention. He needed a haircut and shave. His clothing was raggedy. He was very thin and needed dental attention. He had an old soft drink bottle.. He approached the front desk. Owner Nan Nash greeted him by name.

"My truck ran out of gas," he said.

"I can only pay $4.00. These don't sell well now," Nan said, taking the bottle.

"That's okay. At least, I can get some gas."

She handed him $4.00.

I went to the counter and asked about the man.

"He picks up cans and bottles, and anything else he can sell. I can only get $5.00 for the bottle."

The increasing disparity between ultra-rich and ultra-poor strikes me as ominous for this country.

I went to my car and got my billfold. I had $26.00. I took the twenty and went back inside.

"How often does he come in?" I said.

Nan said, "Every couple days."

"Give this to the guy when he comes back in." I said.

I thought of the Great Depression when I was young. I thought of baseball players making millions for hitting a stupid ball. Something really is lop-sided in our country.

* * * * *

They were having lunch when I arrived. I guessed 35 people above 18 years old, with differing degrees of brain-damage. The menu was turkey chili. I was invited to lunch. It was delicious.

I was introduced to several of them as I spoke with Virginia Vaughan, Resource Coordinator. I was told that an ex-sailor made good barbecue. Standing close by, he corrected her by saying, "I make excellent barbecue."

I said I would come to his house for barbecue. He said his momma wouldn't like that.

I said I'd bring a whole deer for him to barbecue.

He grinned broadly and said, "Forget momma, I'll let you have my sister's room."

I told him I had been in the navy, too. He saluted and said, "Anchors aweigh."

He had been coming there regularly for more than five years and he showed a remarkable sense of wit.

SIDE BY SIDE BRAIN INJURY CLUBHOUSE was founded by Cindi Johnson 10 years ago in Decatur. 7 years ago she moved to Stone Mountain Village. They mentor people with brain damage so they will be able to rejoin families, and with some being ready for independent living. That is the goal to which the staff is dedicated. I sensed their dedication to the objectives.

'No man could make a greater mistake than he who did nothing because he could only do a little'. (Edmund Burke)

Swindled

Attending Butler University after serving in the navy during WW II I had a chance to date a girl from an affluent family in Indianapolis. I figured if I could make some points with her I might be considered for an executive position with her father's company.

My navy separation bonus was $200. The veteran's administration was sending me to college for as many months as I had served. They bought my books and paid my tuition then paid me $106 a month allowance.

She wanted to go to the fair out in Broadripple. I couldn't afford a car so I suggested we ride the streetcar. I took $20 which would short me the rest of the month. I was embarrassed not having a car.

Upon entering the front gate at the fairground, the first tent was a palmist whose sign stated she read palms for $1. My date wanted to have her palm read and asked me to do the same. Although I was not sold on palmists, I thought about the good job. She was ushered into one tent. I was put in another.

No sooner had the palmist started twirling her fingers around on my hand my tent flap was raised and my friend's palmist said she wanted a $30 reading. I showed her I only had $18. The woman grabbed it, saying she would give the $30 reading for $18. I did not have time to complain. After that I was ushered outside.

I stood outside, ticked off. There had gone the Ferris-Wheel, and the Merry-Go-Round. I was flat broke and embarrassed.

My date soon came out, red-faced.

"Why on earth did you want me to have the $30 reading?"

I explained what happened to me. We had been swindled.

Furious, I started to go back inside to get my money back. Carnival roustabouts are huge, too big for one 180 pound ex-sailor. My date had to pay our bus fare back home. There went the big job. But I was determined to never be scammed again.

Two eyes for an eye

We are living in perilous times. The Mid-East can explode with a single incident. Pre-emptive actions are justifiable. Being prepared is mandatory because of constant threats by radicals.

When canoeing the Mackenzie River in Canada's Northwest Territory in 1948 my buddy and I set up camp for the night on a rocky promontory. The following morning we saw a grizzly with two cubs bounding downhill toward our campsite. We evidently had made camp where the bear fished. We were intruders and our lives were in serious danger.

I did not have time to call PETA or the Humane Society about animal rights. When planning the trip we understood the danger to which we might be exposed in such rogue country. Fortunately we took high-powered rifles. My Ruger 3006 was loaded and ready. When the grizzly was still some distance away we shot it, and when it stood up, we shot it two more times.

Of course there was collateral damage because we couldn't take the cubs with us and they could not survive with out their mother. Mother Nature handles natural emergencies.

I'm uneasy when I see government officials failing to respond to threats to eradicate Israel from the face of the planet, and destroy American infidels.

The point of those threats is that when your life is in danger all means must be taken immediately to protect yourself, even pre-emptive actions.

Some societies in the world are now under constant threat of genocide, including our own. Iran is threatening to annihilate Israel and the United States. North Korea acts threatening. Venezuela is buying large amounts of war materials from Russia. Syria poses a serious danger to Israel. Israel is surrounded by 100,000,000 avowed enemies.

Being diplomatic is good up to a point. After an attack is launched, it is too late for niceties.

Trying to be civilized in a hostile world we have a law against assassinations. President Teddy Theodore Roosevelt said speak softly and carry a big stick. A stick would be to rescind the law against assassination and make certain that any person threatening death to Americans is aware that being assassinated, even incinerated, is part of our protective veneer.

There must be a limit to political correctness. Those individuals advocating the destruction of the United States must be met with the same capabilities as when the navy seals took out Osama bin Laden. To remain the nice guy with threats of extermination is a flawed policy.

In 1981, with Saddam Hussein spewing anti-Israelis venom and simultaneously purchasing the Osirak nuclear reactor from France, the Israelis determined the potential dangers and destroyed the reactor with a well planned attack from the air.

With the Iranian President vowing to eradicate the Israelis from the face of the planet and destroy America, a pre-emptive strike is justified to assure his threats don't happen. There'll be collateral damages but that is their price to pay for allowing a radical to become so powerful.

If someone had assassinated Adolf Hitler in 1936 fifty million people worldwide would not have been killed. I wonder why Emperor Hirohito was allowed to live after the defeat of the Japanese. 2402 Americans died at Pearl Harbor and more on the Bataan Death March. The total American military killed in the war with Japan is estimated to be 200,000.

When a person utters repeated threats it should be assumed that they have that intention on their mind. It can also be assumed that the person expressing those intentions is an imminent menace. Remember the grizzly.

Iran is probably aware that Israel has a massive nuclear capability and the trigger will be when Netanyahu determines that a pre-emptive strike will be necessary for the Israelis to survive.

The Sting Operation

The man came in to my fur shop in Buckhead. He looked like a cowboy, with scruffy boots, a hat from the old west. A beat-up pickup truck was parked out front.

"I have a problem," he said. A toothpick dangled from his mouth.

"What's your problem?"

"I've got to get back to Texas. I need some gas. I killed a jaguar last month and I need to sell the hide, real cheap." He emphasized the words 'real cheap'.

"How much?" I said, following him out to his truck. I was curious. I had a suspicion the guy was not being truthful. In forty-some years in the industry this was a first.

"It's worth a lot of money but if I could get a hundred dollars I can get home," he said, smiling.

I examined the pelt. It was much too stiff for a recent kill.

"Which government agency are you with?" I asked, also smiling..

He looked quizzical. "What do you mean?"

"You're trying to sell the hide from an animal which was listed on the 1973 Endangered Species Act. A license to buy raw hides and fur is $5000 in Georgia and I don't have it. Buying a skin on the endangered specie list can mean jail time. So you're in a sting operation for the DNR, or you are stupidly violating the law." I smiled again "I think I'll report you."

He grinned. "I was told downtown you were legit.

I unrolled the pelt and examined the leather. "Also, get a fresh pelt. Your cat's been dead way too long. There's no bullet hole. This jaguar died from old age. You get it in a zoo?"

"Where'd I go wrong?" he grinned broadly.

"Picked the wrong pigeon," I said, grinning back

"You do any hunting?"

"I hunted and trapped before I was ten. I also operated a mink and fox ranch."

"It figures."

Depravity

They sit, sometime for hours, in the dark of night, while their family is asleep, hunched in front of their computer, mouths drooling, eyes glazed, brain twisted, searching for child pornography to build up their cache of lurid nakedness, lewd files secreted behind personal code numbers.

Who are these people seeking victims? Strangely it is fathers, truck drivers, lawyers, politicians, physicians, baseball players, pastors, cab drivers, garbage collectors, salesmen, coaches; the list goes on ad infinitum.

Why have they become so incredibly depraved?

What has happened in this country to corrupt men's morals?

One is my neighbor? That's not possible. He is a nice person. I played golf with him. He attends our church. He is the friendly guy who was so entertaining at the neighborhood party.

But when the little girl disappeared from her nearby home the police came and confiscated his computer and a box of CD's hidden in the back of his clothes closet. Despite the fact that after downloading thousands of pictures and deleting evidence that he had a crazed mentality the FBI confiscated his files. Unknown to him the filth he thought he had deleted hadn't been over-ridden by other files and the FBI was able to collect ample evidence of his rotting mind.

They took my golf buddy from his house in manacles. Neighbors, friends, looked on in shocked disbelief. His wife stared from their doorway as the police car drove away. Fortunately his three children were still in school.

The mother tried to hide the situation from their kids but Facebook and texting told it all. Daddy was arrested as a child molester, being investigated on suspicion of murder.

How could he have known that one of his cherished websites was a FBI sting operation, looking for psychotic creatures strung-out on disgusting child pornography?

Shame-faced, Susie whispered to her brother, "Daddy tried to touch me down there several times so I was uncomfortable around him when mommy was gone."

Another tainted man destroyed the sanctity of an All American family.

Sadists exist among us; fathers, uncles, judges, preachers and neighbors with dwindling morals and as evil flourishes effete brains react with fewer barriers between survival and Armageddon. Female nakedness is causing a battle between the forces of good and evil, with evil flourishing.

There are wicked opportunists roaming the highways at night seeking unfortunate females whose cars have broken down, disguised as saviors, psychotic men, evil men with defective brains.

The more naked Hollywood's elite pose on camera the skimpier the clothing of their supplicants.

Movie colony couples display babies born out of wedlock as if they had created something great.   Fleas and bedbugs and lice do the same.

School break at the beach expose the extent to which civilization has deteriorated; naked fertility dances, drunkenness, brawling, debauchery, trashed virginity.

On a wager, an intoxicated female student, studying to be a lawyer, attempted to swan-dive from an upper floor balcony and missed the pool.

I don't know the man who first said 'going to hell in a hand basket' but I'm becoming aware of the thought. I often lie awake at night wondering how to reverse the tsunami of wickedness I see sweeping across the nation.

There are lunatics among us, despicable humans in our midst, soulless creatures that apparently didn't finish the evolutionary cycle; Charles Manson, Gary Leon Ridgeway, John Wayne Gacy, Ted Bundy, Jeffrey Dahmer and hundreds more still unknown enacting their deadly deeds.

There was Eddie Gein whose farmhouse was a scene of horror where authorities found pieces of female bodies, saved like trophies, so inconceivable that the images inspired the movie, 'Silence of the Lambs', a movie about a killer who dressed in clothing made from pieces from the bodies of his female victims in some bizarre transvestite ritual.

There are humans who lust to kill, like Serengeti male lions that takes over a new pride then kill all the cubs so only his genes will be passed along to the future.

Insanity is insanity only there are varying degrees of the sickness. There are the date-rapists that use Rohypnol to render a female unconscious so the insane man can violate the body in fiendish ways while photographing his depraved acts for his library of madness, to view again and again.

Sadists are among us; fathers, uncles, judges, preachers and neighbors with failing morality and as evil flourishes, twisted minds react with fewer restraints against our complete moral collapse.

With the advent of birth control pills promiscuity skyrocketed as women unleashed their pent up curiosity. The divorce rate doubled quickly as fidelity 'went to hell in a hand basket'.

Sperm donors are busy, the recipients giving birth to more sperm donors and more depositories, with the morally corrupt cycle contributing to the end of civilization.

Living frugally

Solvent means you have more than you owe. Insolvent means you owe more than you have.

My 1994 Buick has 125, 000 miles on it. It runs fine. My wife's 1994 model has 179, 000 miles and also runs great. The combined expense of license plates and taxes is less than $90.00. Repairs are needed occasionally but are less than the depreciation on new cars.

We bought our home from a bankrupt builder in 1975, and while larger houses are being built near us our ceilings are high enough for us to move around so we decided we didn't need added debt and higher taxes. Being old fashioned I see no logic for excess space.

I see dinner advertised around town for $14.99 for two and even recently $29.99 for two. There is a Chinese restaurant nearby where you can buy lunch for $6.99 when you go in and sit down. I get carry-out for about $2.00 then add salad when I get home. Iced tea is cheaper at home. I like living low-on-the-hog. There are fewer uneasy nights.

There is an old motivational concept about keeping up with the Joneses. Those Joneses left us far behind years ago but some of them are now having negative cash flow.

I have one credit card. I don't use it often but for the many years I have kept it no one has ever denied me its use. Because I flew Delta for years, I continue to get solicitations from American Express to sign up for their card. They have romanced me like Lorelei sang to Jason. I haven't figured out why I would pay $150 annually for an American Express card when those benefits are available with my BB&T card and it costs me nothing. They're both made from plastic.

President Eisenhower advocated investing 10% of my income, preparing for retirement, and the inevitable rainy day. I did that for several years; endowment policies, CD's and a conservative stock portfolio.

Then I listened to George Walker Bush's 'Read my lips, no new taxes' and then I got slammed with the elimination of interest paid on credit cards as a taxable deduction and other adjustments that benefitted government. It had the same effect on business as Novocain in dentistry. Insipid modifications to the tax code caused more businesses to flee out of the country in the 1980's.

Congress then enacted the excise tax on big ticket items; fur, boats, jewelry and aircraft. That caused the loss of millions of jobs. Intellectuals would not pay more and quit buying. Congress rescinded the irrational tax but only after many businesses went belly-up.

County commissioners built an edifice to themselves. They had a building. Then, with some odd rationale, they put an expensive sculpture out front. They did not ask me if I wanted to waste my money. I retired early to escape the confiscatory evisceration of my financial security.

When the buy-one-get-one-free promotions are here my wife loads up on great stuff. She went to lunch with a friend today. She appeared classy, her blouse and skirt looked like Rodeo Drive, $1.00 each, at Lilburn co-op. That's frugal.

Magic in Stone Mountain

The time of magic is here. The colorful bundles of beauty have finally arrived en masse and set up camp on my top deck, probably 12 in all, hungry little critters, but how better to spend time preparing nectar by the half gallon and then experiencing the aerial antics that goes on from dawn until dusk. It's mesmerizing.

This year by mid-summer, I had become concerned that the hummingbirds had forgotten to come. Normally, by mid-July, I have three or four zipping from the front porch feeder to feeders on my upper deck. This season I had noticed only the occasional aerodynamic entertainer until one morning. Suddenly there were five. The next moment was hypnotic.

I glanced through the slats in our blinds and low and behold three hummingbirds were on the feeder at the same time. That usually indicates a family. I got so excited that I opened the door without shutting off the alarm. Fortunately, I still have quick hands and was able to intercept the signal without awakening the neighborhood.

One bird flew up to my storm door and hovered back and forth looking directly at me. I got the impression it was thanking me for putting out fresh nectar. Like flecks of emerald and mauve, they paused, hovering first in the lantana then stopping by the fluted hibiscus then the morning glories then to the feeders. Seeing hummingbirds doing aerobatics gives me a great outlook on life.

I sometime see one male fly up into a tree and perch on a bare branch where it can keep watch over its chosen territory, zipping down to chase off those attempting to sip at the feeders it apparently considers its private domain.

I stood, fascinated with the exquisiteness of nature. The anticipation of hummingbirds in my life begins with the arrival of warmer weather. For a predictable hour each morning I am spellbound by their antics as they rise up in tandem, lock their tiny claws, then spiral down tumbling, noisily chirping, disentangling just above the lawn and rising again to perform the same incredible feats.

They put on a spectacle, speeding off like colorful bullets to some mysterious destination only to reappear minutes later. A bird will frequently sit on the feeders preening, stretching its legs and cleaning its feathers, its pink tongue darting in and out. If I remain quiet for a few moments the birds will begin to feed near me.

On one occasion last July an emerald bird noticed its reflection in my glasses, hovered in front of my face for a moment, then sat on my shoulder for maybe ten seconds. It was a precious moment in my life. I sat motionless wishing it would stay forever.

My aunt lived on a farm in Indiana and attached hummingbird feeders on maple tree branches. She sat outside. My wife and I visited her one summer and watched a spectacle few people are privileged to see; hummingbirds entangled in her hair and preening on her hand. My aunt is no longer there but my cousin had taken up the task.

Even though Indiana is farther north, for some phenomenon of nature her hummingbirds arrive earlier than in Georgia. She used to bug me by telling me how much time she spends preparing nectar. She estimates that 10 to 12 hummingbirds perform aerobatics all summer long, until cold weather.

My feathered friends will soon leave but for one moment in time I was the luckiest man on earth, one of the few people to have a hummingbird sitting on my shoulder.

War is hell

I sat in the lobby of the veteran's hospital on Clairmont Road in Atlanta awaiting my turn to fill out some registration forms. The documents would entitle me to veteran's benefits. So far, in 85 years, I've been lucky. My health has remained excellent attributable to proper diet and exercise. The avoidance of intoxicants, cigarettes, drugs and all-you-can-eat buffets made it possible

The room was crowded with the din of muted conversations, calling out names of those next in line for some kind of help.

People were in a hurry, wearing white uniforms with aprons, the scull caps indicated they were probably doctors or nurses. They looked serious.

It seemed there was a steady stream of tired looking men searching for somewhere. Others were sitting or standing passively with their individual agony hidden inside. I noticed their eyes rarely made contact with other eyes. I figured many of them had ghosts of past battles haunting them. I have a couple that sneak in unexpected sometimes

I sat watching, curious about those passing by; grizzled men from wars over the years; one with a leg missing, frostbitten on Attu, gangrene, with an amputation on a boat that wasn't equipped for amputations.

A motorized wheelchair, the eyes of the occupant fixated ahead, maybe having seen horrors eyes were never meant to see. Memories hang on.

Tall, broad shouldered with stuttering footsteps, remembered battles better forgotten; but he can't forget. The images are always there, and in the stillness of nights unwanted dreams relive the day it happened; marines wading ashore on Peleliu, Japanese machine guns chattering from the dense foliage. Six steps and the war ended for him, and life changed instantly, never to be the same.

Thank God for the Veteran's Administration.

I spoke to a black man sitting next to me, gray beard, Alabama born, who carried a football 102 yards on two kick-off returns in the same game. Big time football was in his plan. But Vietnam came. Not questioning the logic for being there, he volunteered instead of talking to Notre Dame.

"Did you speak with Notre Dame when you got back"?

"Parseghian didn't want me without legs, didn't think I could get to the goal line," he said.

I hadn't noticed. Seated, it didn't show.

"What happened?"

"Vietcong mortar outside Saigon, during the Tet offensive."

I noticed he never smiled. His eyes looked tired. Sacks of rocks can be heavy.

I talked with a P-51 pilot whose riddled plane crashed on approach, a 101st Airborne paratrooper who landed badly on D-Day, a chauffeur for a Colonel whose jeep crashed in a gully in Belgium when Stukas strafed the column. I saw tears form in his eyes. "The Colonel was killed instantly," he said. "He was my friend."

Memories linger; an army nurse who spent time in a Japanese prisoner-of-war camp. "I relive the time once in a while," she said, unsmiling. I thought about the Bataan Death March. I wondered if she was taken at Corregidor. I wondered if she saw MacArthur.

I saw an occasional wave of recognition between two veterans who had evidently met, the rare eye contact, each with their personal burdens.

I began thinking about my brother who was killed in the Battle of the Bulge. He wasn't quite 21 when he died. Tears burned, but the dike held this time. Not always. Late at night, in the silence of darkness, there is often a rupture.

I left the hospital aware I was part of a family of combat veterans. I was a lucky one.

The beauty of nature

After the invasion of Southern France was completed in 1944 with the Germans escaping north my ship was directed to Marseilles to see what we could do to assist the people in the city. They had been under Nazi rule since being occupied.

We entered a narrow channel that led a quarter-mile into Vieux Port harbor in the middle of Marseilles. The channel was lined with towering medieval fortresses that had been built when the Moors conquered the Romans who had conquered the Visigoths who had invaded France centuries before. As we idled through the channel we kept a lookout expecting to be attacked by Arabs with broad axes, swords, cross bows, lances and with red-hot pitch cascading down from cauldrons high on the ramparts.

The short trip actually proved uneventful until we entered the harbor and headed for the wharf. Throngs of people lined the harbor waving and screaming with exultation. We'd just liberated them from three years of serfdom under the German's Gestapo. What was especially interesting was the bright clothes they were wearing. Equally amazing after years of Nazi rule the buildings were freshly painted, with flowers blooming everywhere. I was told that even with suffering the buildings were spruced up regularly. It was considered a subtle show of defiance.

Traveling around the country I often see pride in small towns, shrubs trimmed, and with homes well maintained with flowers blooming where ever a plot of dirt exists.

Thomasville, Georgia is known as a city of roses. Portland, Oregon has the same name. Before coming to Atlanta, my job often took me to the Pacific Northwest. After spending hours at work I enjoyed driving along the Willamette and Columbia rivers and seeing the artistry of Japanese landscapers. On the slopes above Puget Sound and Lake Washington was the same dedication to keeping a city colorfully fascinating.

Communities neglecting to maintain flowering landscaping are missing a golden opportunity to add aesthetic value to living. It is easy if people maintain their own property and if a neighbor is disabled, assist with that clean-up. The effort adds community value to what otherwise could be time-worn.

You could look around your area and remove dead trees and shrubbery, litter, vines, rusty cans and discarded sandwich wrappers and where there is a plot of dirt plant flowers. The result will reinvigorate the community.

Many cities on the West Coast have flowers lining the downtown streets. In Portland and Seattle flowers and flowering shrubs are all around the city to be enjoyed by the residents and tourists. On the Monorail out to the Space Needle riders, from up above, can see the devotion to natural beauty.

Carmel California is bright with color. The town of Key West, Florida, built trellises on major streets for Bougainvillea and Mandeville vines. Hummingbirds are attracted to the flowers and tourism abounds accordingly.

On a recent cruise up the West Coast to Alaska my wife and I went ashore in Victoria Canada. We were spellbound by the abundance of flowers and flowering shrubs in the city. I wonder why so many communities in Georgia remain covered with patches of weeds.

Fantasyland

"I look at the fantasy in Hollywood and I wonder why people allow themselves to be taken in by super-hyping unless they are born just to be adulators of pretense. Those people pass gas and leave skid marks the same as we common folks except their gas escapes through Victoria Secret panties and Rodeo Drive Designer shorts. They are no different than we common people. I wonder, as they swivel into the Academy Awards, which ones have venereal infections. For generations women remained chaste because of fear of unwanted pregnancies. Birth control pills unlatched Pandora's Box and females began hanging out in clubs and becoming flirtatious in their search for a relationship. That contributed to the spread of sexually transmitted diseases. People who are involved with multiple sexual partners, will sooner or later be the carrier of crotch disease. I see immoral behavior glorified in Hollywood. They produce kids out-of-wedlock and pretend something wonderful has happened. We need to go back to fidelity or we are going to hell in a hurry."

"You're a perceptive man. Mike. You are unusual for a paleface. You could qualify as a Shaman with the Nez Perce." Cougar smiled, reaching for his pipe once again.

"Remember I'm four times your visual age." I said. "I've developed a lot of insight in eighty-two years."

"But you are really different," he said.

"In what way?"

"As you know, I can read the mind of anyone. I was in a paleface church a few years ago and was curious as to what palefaces ask for in their prayers. I was surprised. Some older men were on their knees praying and I was curious so I intercepted a prayer from one of them. I expected him to be praying for the world's salvation and food and health for the people. Instead I was astounded. His prayer was avid; *God, I have been a dutiful adherent to your teachings. I have tithed abundantly, and have never taken your name in vain. I have practiced the Old Golden Rule and I might have sullied a commandant or two, for which I am humbly repentant. Please, dear Lord, I beseech you, please grant me one more fantasy, and that final orgasm, and I will remain your faithful follower, forever. Amen.*

"That is sorrowfully indicative of the direction your people have taken," Cougar said.

"Is it okay if I'm a little agnostic?"

"I like people who are who they are," he said

"My cathedral is on a rogue river, away from the fakery of this make-believe world."

"You're a lot better off out in the wilderness than being involved in contemporary society. You're better off right here. Sanity prevails here. Some time ago I considered associating with palefaces without them aware of my history. I read extensively so I would be more knowledgeable about the problems with which you contend. One fact I fortunately discovered was that intimate relationships between women and men are fraught with deadly danger. So much, that it caused me to quickly reconsider."

"What happened," I said. "What fact?"

"In wildlife Mother Nature allows association among animals of different genders. Animals do not become intimately involved however until it's time to reproduce. So that happens for example with the grizzly about every two years. Among humans that intimate involvement is incredibly excessive and as a direct result sexually transmitted diseases are killing billions of people all over the world."

"I have read the figures on AIDS. And syphilis used to be a real destroyer of humans. I knew one wealthy banker from back home who would leave our town and go to Florida on vacation several times a year. He would acquire the services of hookers, often three or four at the same time. His Florida vacation was devoted to disgusting debauchery. He died at fifty years of age ravaged by syphilis. His mind failed and his physical appearance was appalling, sores, pustules, eyes rheumy, mouth drooling, hands shaky. I saw him a week before he died. I didn't recognize the man. Can you imagine how many other men those hookers have infected? And syphilis is on the increase again with unhealthy sexual practices."

"That's awful but there are even worse conditions. Sexual relations today is like playing Russian roulette," Cougar said. "There are over a dozen sexually transmitted diseases and with promiscuity on the rise, and with your liberal, 'I have to get laid now' lifestyles the future of your society is precarious."

"AIDS and syphilis. What others that I don't know about?"

"I'll just give you a run down of what I learned. Plagues of syphilis alone have been responsible for million of the world's crippled, blind, insane and dead. Obviously, your banker included. AIDS will surpass the devastation of syphilis. Gonorrhea infection in the blood associated with birth canals causes blindness in babies being born. Chancroids are painful lesions and are spread by unhygienic sex practice.

Genital herpes is incurable and sexually transmitted. Hepatitis B causes jaundice and liver enlargement. Protozoan Trichmoniasis is a frothy, odorous greenish-yellow discharge, causing itching of the genitals. Symptoms are usually absent in males yet they can transmit that disease to their sexual partners. Fungal candidiasis causes intense genital itching, a thick curd-like, whitish discharge, inflamed and dry vagina and inflammation of the vulva genital area."

"I think you should stop. I've never heard of those diseases. It sure kills the idea of fun-time."

"Monogamy prohibits the advance of sexually transmitted diseases. Promiscuity advances the diseases. That's why it's like Russian Roulette. Keep pulling that trigger and you will definitely catch something, probably fatal."

"I knew some guys in the navy that caught the clap in cathouses overseas."

"There are many more venereal problems; pubic lice, genital scabies, Chlamydia trachomatis, granuloma inguinale, yeast infection, Gardnerella vaginitis, lymphogran uloma venereum, shigellosis..."

"Will you stop? Please."

"Sure. But some advice, Mike. Condoms don't protect you from venereal diseases. Fool around long enough and you'll have it. Sexual diseases are transmitted by both males and females. Women just have a more secretive cavity in which to grow the little bugs."

"If I were single I damn-well would be celibate. I've had the same wife for forty years."

"You should keep it that way," Cougar said. "One other thing. You should tell your friends who have uncontrollable hormones that I saw a doctor's report indicating that he is seeing a huge increase in men patients who have pustule chancres and lesions in their mouths. That's from what's called oral sex. And that can be the beginning of dying. Men have to be totally retarded to do that."

"Why does society accept promiscuity as healthy, when it is so damned unhealthy?"

"Homosexuals are most at risk but some of them also engage in heterosexual behavior and so the diseases spread like a raging wildfire. When people have one-night stands, no one knows who is infected so it's kinda' like shooting craps. The likelihood of boxcars or snake-eyes is always there."

"It's either that they are stupid or just don't give a damn," I said. "Screw now, worry later."

"So, I take it you aren't impressed by Hollywood's imprudent practices," Cougar said.

"Right on."

"So, I guess you're really a true individualist. Welcome to my world," Cougar said.

"One other question," he said. "Who's going to win the World Series this year?"

"I have no idea who's playing," I said.

Cougar grinned. "And neither do I."

We clasped hands, smiling, in a show of mutual admiration.

The wilderness

As kids camped out at night in the woods near my grandfather's farm, my brother and I would study a couple of Indian mounds and wonder who they were, where did they go, why did they leave, and how many lived there. It still remains a mystery. I discovered that at one time there were many Indians in Indiana; Kickapoo, Potawatomi, Shawnee, Chippewa, Wea, and Wabash.

My interest in Early Americans began at an early age and continues today and I have found that most of the history of the indigenous people who nurtured the land for ten thousand years before the arrival of Europeans is not taught in schools.

After retiring I have written six books including, Valley of Silent Drums and Reflections of the Great Spirit, My Name is Cougar due this summer, chronicling eras of Indian existence on this continent. To glean information on Native Americans I have lived for several weeks on Indian reservations in Canada, the Dakotas and the Pacific Northwest.

Eighteen years ago a floatplane dropped me off on a Canadian wilderness river with a 15 feet Old Town canoe and a GPS. The pilot agreed to pick me up in ten days downriver. I had a supply of Trail Mix, a 3006 Ruger rifle, a supply bag containing a tent, a water purifier, a sleeping bag, mosquito repellent and fishing tackle. I intended to live off the land. I ate fish, turtle, beaver, and some ducks. Wild raspberries and blueberries were abundant.

Several days into the trip I passed a Cree Indian village. Kids were playing cowboy and Indians, Surprisingly, the Indians were winning. Two braves came alongside my canoe and offered to take me to a nearby flume to catch some walleye. We ate fish on a rocky island in midstream. A golden eagle and a black bear cleaned up the scraps. We became kindred spirits. We talked about old days. The Indians seem to harbor no resentment for what my ancestors did to their ancestors, not too long ago. I remember.

The next morning I awoke to find my fire flaming. I crawled from my tent to find the Indians fixing breakfast. They had killed a deer and were cooking chunks of venison in bear fat, which was sure to raise my cholesterol level. We ate venison and goose eggs on an island, 400 miles from civilization. Now that is true atmosphere.

After determining the pick-up point on my map I showed the Cree the functions of a GPS and I gave it to them. I promised to return and visit their village. They promised to take me seal and bear hunting in a dogsled using harpoons and bow and arrow. The offer that was sure to get me back.

There is something satisfying about the old ways, without the superficiality of contemporary glitz. While dozing off to sleep, the Aurora Borealis held me spellbound. Opal eyes reflecting from the dying embers in the campfire kept me under surveillance. By morning they were gone.

I crawled from my tent to a brilliant sun rising. I prepared to leave the isolation. I carried water from the river to erase evidence of my having been there. I packed up and strolled down to the water. Above the mist cover I heard the drone of the plane returning for me.

I reflected on the wondrous tranquility I found in the wilderness as the pilot tied the floatplane to a boulder on the bank. I climbed aboard and made reservations for next year. As we ascended up from the canyon I glanced in the distance and spotted a herd of migrating caribou. On their trail were wolves loping along. Patience would pay off when calves became careless. Mother Nature provides well for her wards.

"Good trip?" Eddie said.

"Great."

The marvels of golf.

At age 12, I began hitching rides with the milkman every morning, who was heading to the milk plant in Terre Haute to load up for the day's delivery. He would drop me off at Allendale where a lane led in to the Terre Haute Country Club. If I was lucky, I would get to carry doubles for 18 holes for which I would make $1.50 and tips. Monday was caddy's day for play. I learned to play golf while quite young.

Becoming rather good I would sometime take my earnings and go into the city and play a round on the public course. If I had some extra I would get a caddy and feel important as I played. The cost of golf balls wasn't a problem because The Terre Haute Country Club course was hilly and we could find balls in the valleys after caddying.

One summer later I lucked out when Tony Hulman, a Terre Haute manufacturer, needed a caddy for a tournament and I was the only one available. I instantly liked Tony and he liked me, plus he paid me $5.00. His foursome won that tournament. We became friends to the point that when he purchased the Indianapolis Speedway he invited me to ride in the pace car one year. There was a public golf course inside the speedway oval.

When I was discharged from the navy in 1946 I listed on my discharge papers my career choice as a golf professional. I worked a year at the Jewish Country Club in Indianapolis. Not doing so well in the golf business I decided to become an author. The fur industry gave me the chance for a wonderful career, while writing.

Arriving in Atlanta in the early 1960's I immediately met three other avid golfers and we began playing every golf course we could afford, Bobby Jones, Chastain Park and others.

One of the rare jewels in golf is the Smoke Rise Country Club in DeKalb County. When it was excavated by a friend I was asked to tag the wild azaleas and dogwood trees so they would not be harmed. You can see them blooming each summer.

I have been lucky to have played the Augusta National course four times, thanks to my friend Brice Newman. I have never made a hole-in-one but came within one inch on the 12th hole at Augusta.

I recall paying $12.00, including a cart, in the 60's. Today's prices are reasonable, considering the costs to build and maintain a great golf course.

Customer service

I walked into the bank to cash a personal check. I had been a customer of the bank for maybe 20 years. It was not the branch where I normally go. Where I bank the cashiers usually give me eye contact and greet me in a cordial manner. I counted five employees behind the counter.

There were five people waiting in line for a cashier. There was one cashier assisting a customer. The others were standing near a computer and seem to be having an animated discussion. I heard murmuring among those waiting. They were complaining about the bank having only one person cashiering and others apparently trying to solve a problem.

I wondered why someone didn't look up and acknowledge that we were waiting. I also wondered why some employee did not apologize for the wait and explain to those in line how much longer it might be. I glanced at my watch. I had an appointment. I had time, so I waited. No one was smiling.

Eighteen minutes later the one cashier motioned me to her opening. There was still no smile.

I said to the cashier, "Have you called a doctor?"

"For what?" she said.

"Everyone seems to be feeling bad."

"What do you mean?"

"No one is smiling," I said.

"Yes they are," she said. She still hadn't smiled.

"I didn't see anyone smile," I said, now irked even more.

"You just didn't notice," she kind of snapped at me.

"I guess my eyesight is bad, old age is tough," I said.

We finished the transaction.

"Have a good one," she said. A vague smile curled her lips.

"It'll be better outside," I snapped a little, too.

A line was queuing up again.

The other employees were still huddled together at the console.

Having spent fifty years nurturing customers in the retail business I am perhaps more conscious of customer service. I also know how easy it is the send clients to competition. It's not like there is only one bank in town.

I remember the ten years spent with Sears and the completeness of their initial training program.

It was an educational experience; first apologize and then solve the customer's problem. I could have written the policy. The knowledge was beneficial when I opened York Furs at Regenstein's and later York Furs in Buckhead; don't ever irritate a consumer, the flawed judgment will come back to haunt you. A happy customer will suggest you to friends. An annoyed customer will tell everyone about their bad experience.

And always smile, even when you have a headache. If you cannot smile then take the day off.

If that location had been the bank's only branch, I would have immediately changed banks.

Several years ago I was subjected to an imperfect customer satisfaction policy at a pharmacy. I have not been in that store since. My family agreed and they now trade with another pharmacy. Customer satisfaction is vital to business. A flawed customer satisfaction policy guarantees the customer will start going to other stores. I calculate that with my family no longer shopping at that drugstore they have lost well over $28,000 in business. They can multiply that amount by how many other customers were treated with disdain.

I applaud parents

Speeding is foolish considering the possible consequences. Becoming intoxicated is fraught with danger. Illegal drugs can impair your brain. Succumbing to specific peer pressures can ruin your life. Being charged with felonies results in a record impacting your future. Pierced eyebrows will assure you will not be considered for many jobs. A prison record permanently stigmatizes.

I applaud parents who are involved in the development and conduct of their kids, guiding them in the right direction, advising them on how to be successful, inspiring them as obstacles occur, encouraging them to avoid the temptation of drugs and alcohol, teaching them morality and the importance of stability and predictability.

I know a mother who said early in her sons' teenage lives, "You can have an affordable car and an excellent education or you can have a costly car and a minimal education. I can't afford both." Both boys drive used cars. The advice was good. One will be in the medical profession the other will compete with Bill Gates.

Their father was equally prudent, "You can have a blast in the back seat of your ford or you can avoid parental responsibilities until you are mature and have enough income. Foolishness in the back seat also increases the chance of contracting a disease. Contrary to liberal opinion youthful sex is not a safe practice," he said. "Passing out condoms in schools is a monumental blunder. It gives the idea that early sex is acceptable. Children should be preparing for the future instead of having premature financial, psychological and emotional responsibilities."

I sat and listened to the wisdom of devoted parents. They talked about the fork in the Y of early   decisions; one choice assures low paying jobs and periodic unemployment, the other guarantees achievement. Priorities must be set early. They emphasized the importance of setting goals.

Spending time with your children is vital to their maturing with confidence; golf, fishing, soccer, hunting, vacations, school work plus family discussions. Solving emerging dilemmas gives your kids the assurance of continuing parental support. Without sound advice they often fall victim to peer pressures that gets them in trouble.

I advised my kids early that they could do anything they wanted to do in life as long as they did not encroach on the rights of others, including mine. I explained that during their life they would be confronted with many temptations and unless they were strong willed they could destroy their future by mistakes in judgment.

Too many people suffering today didn't get that advice. Prisons are overflowing with those who had no fathers from whom they could learn common sense during a critical time in their lives.

A huge problem is that there are many children who are unsupervised because of having a single working parent and who have never known masculine influence. With the absence of male input we see hostility, graffiti, smashed mail boxes, gang violence and other anti-social behavior. Kids desperately need involved parental guidance during their formative years.

Everyday time is perfect for nurturing family relations, by touch and voice instead of glitzy cars and credit cards. I appreciated the scout knife and mittens when I was a kid. Everything was real.   Wood feels nicer than plastic. Wood has a good smell. Wood has unique grains. I can whittle on wood. I can make something useful or just make shavings. The therapeutic value is the same.

Dirty Water

I thought about coming to Atlanta in 1962 from the City by the Bay where clouds of marijuana smoke drifted over the area while seminal fluids were being exchanged in the Tenderloin bathhouses. A sign on a hotel on Peachtree Street showed fewer than a million people the metropolitan area. Now it is over five million stressed out folks stacked atop each other like boulders on a levee. And water from the major river contains a disturbing amount of chemicals.

Being an avid fisherman I backed my bass boat in the Chattahoochee River below Roswell when I first came to Atlanta. I ran wide-open to Bull Sluice where I had been told yellow perch abounded. My depth finder indicated over fifteen feet deep in the channel. Inside a metropolitan city the area reminded me of wilderness scenarios I had visited in my wanderings. Bull Sluice really was a honey-hole for perch. Tossing number 6 gold hooks with minnows into water adjacent to submerged grass beds produced forty yellow perch with over half keepers. I wondered about contamination of the river in a major city. Could I eat them? I decided since they were caught before the water swirled through the toilet bowls of thousands of homes that they were likely safe for human consumption. Some years later I was asked by the producer of a wildlife program on Georgia Public Television to participate a documentary showing yellow perch in the Chattahoochee River.

To my surprise my propeller got stuck in mud flats several times on our route downstream. The depth finder indicated that the river channel was only a few feet deep, filled with muck from the out-of-control residential and commercial construction boom. I called the director of the Department of Natural Resources, and bitched. I asked why they did not dredge the channel so that it would be a lot deeper. He said it was impossible because dredging would stir up mixtures of pesticides, mercury, arsenic, cadmium, PCB's, DDT, lead, chromium, dioxins and herbicides, creating a lethal potion that would poison half of the people below Atlanta. He asked me to forget what we had discussed.

I recalled finding three-legged frogs in Minnesota ponds and curved-spine bass in Lake Lanier, caused by acid rain drifting down from industrial plants up north. I wondered how long people can live being deluged with deadly chemicals. I remember oil spills off the California coast. I had devoted days cleaning gunk from seals, sea otters, pelicans and cormorants.

I tried to calculate how many people could occupy this continent before quality of life began to deteriorate and was suddenly shocked to realize we were probably already there. I wondered how many people could be piled on top of each other in Atlanta before unexpected repercussions would commence. Upon reading the daily killings in the newspaper and watching anti-social conduct on television I knew we were already encountering problems stemming from overpopulation. When I arrived in Atlanta you could walk downtown at midnight without being mugged. Today people can get shot seemingly just for being around, like it is joyous entertainment for some social misfits. When asked by a passenger seated next to me if I was afraid of bears, wolves and wolverines in the wilderness I explained that if I did not encroach on their domain or threaten their young they were predictable., unlike the two-legged animals roaming Atlanta looking for victims. She stated that she would be afraid of animals in the wilderness. I suggested that we make a bet. I would spend a month out in the wilderness where wolverines, grizzlies, and wolf packs live and she would spend a couple nights camped-out on Peachtree Road in downtown Atlanta and we would see who lasted the longest. She wouldn't make the bet.

The urge

My wife, Pat, and I sat out on the deck enjoying iced tea, relaxing in the sun. A cool wind had begun blustering down the slope signaling the likelihood of rain. I lay in the hammock watching a red-tailed hawk that was perched in the poplar up on the hill. It was eyeing one of the remaining chipmunks that scurried around underneath our deck. Over the past few weeks the hawk had about cleaned out the small rodents. Such is nature.

Pat was engrossed in one of her novels. She is an avid reader.

"I want to go to Idaho," I blurted.

She closed her book to stare at me. "You want to go where?"

"I want to go to Idaho again."

"Go for what?"

"You remember when I went there a few years ago. It's beautiful country, particularly when you get up in the mountains. I love it there."

"You showed me some pictures of Indians," Pat said.

"When I spent a month on the Nez Perce reservation four or five years ago, doing research on Thundering Drums, I heard about an old Nez Perce Indian who lives in the wilderness of the Bitterroot Mountains. People who live there talk about an Indian that has been seen on several occasions for over two hundred years living somewhere up in the mountains. I want to interview him. I wanna' speak with him. I need more material for my book. I am stymied. I need inspiration."

"How do you know an Indian is there?" Pat said.

"People who live in the Pacific Northwest say they have seen him over the years. Loggers, who stripped the mountains of trees, claimed to have spotted the Indian just watching them near their logging operations. They say he has a large mountain lion with him. When one guy tried to go near him, he and the cougar just disappeared. There used to be millions of Indians all over the Pacific Northwest perhaps three hundred years ago, and for over twelve thousands years. No reason one isn't still there."

"But two hundred years old? No way. It's probably a myth, like Bigfoot, or that Yeti creature in the Himalayas, or that Loch Ness thing." Pat grinned, devilishly.

"Perhaps not, the Nez Perce Elders I talked with on the Nez Perce reservation are convinced he exists. Maybe he's a Shaman with unusual powers."

"It'll probably be a wild goose chase."

"I don't know. Their Great Spirit did cool stuff. Wouldn't it be a coup if I'm able to communicate with an Indian who's lived for two hundred years? Anyway, I haven't been in Idaho for years. I need to go. I want to go. The old wilderness bug has bitten me again."

"Aren't you a little too old for that stuff," Pat said, a look of concern spreading across her face.

"Eighty-two is not that old. It's all in the head. I'm in great shape, kiddo."

"Hey, if your life insurance premiums are paid up, then sure you can go," she chided.

"Honey, since I have been doing research on Native Americans I have often thought about how terrifying their lives must have been when their villages were attacked by heavily armed cavalrymen and all they had to defend themselves were bows and arrows and spears."

"The truth is sometime sad," she said.

"My ancestors committed murder on seventeen million people. Today no one wants to talk about it. I get some people pissed when I try to discuss genocide. They say Indians fought among themselves. I agreed, but not the virtual extermination of a culture. It was the most ruthless genocide in history until Josef Stalin and Adolf Hitler. And the sad part is that the genocide was endorsed by the highest office in our government. When Andrew Jackson approved his removal order he noted: if those savages refuse to leave their villages willingly, they are to be shot. 'The only good Indian is a dead Indian.'"

"That is sad," Pat said. "So when are you going?"

"I'm checking Google for weather conditions in the Bitterroots. I can fly into Lewiston. I've been there before. I'll rent a car. I will take highway 173 to a place called Lowell, a small town. I'll leave the car with someone and head up a logging road to the Selway-Bitterroot Wilderness. The Indian has been reported in the foothills, and into the Nez Perce National Forest. It's a huge wilderness. I'll get a horse."

"You got everything you'll need?"

"I think so. Last night I checked my survival kit. I have quinine pills, trail mix, venison jerky, nasal spray, fire sticks, mosquito netting, matches and a GPS. I'm taking the bow so I can hunt quietly. I also have a foil blanket in case it's real cold, fishing tackle, a sleeping bag rated at 20 degrees, some plastic garbage bags and my survival kit."

"Why take garbage bags?"

"I learned in survival class that I can make lean-to shelters, make a hole in the bottom, and put it on like a nightshirt, stuff it with leaves and grass to keep me warm, make boots, not for walking, but to keep me from getting frostbite by stuffing them with dead grass and leaves. And then if

I hollow out a concavity in the dirt and cover the hole with a garbage bag, pushed down into the hole, I get some pure water from dew falling during the night. It collects in the bottom."

"That's nice."

I detected some sarcasm. "Wanna' go?"

"No!"

"We can both get into my sleeping bag."

"For what? You're 85." She grinned.

"So, you're no spring chicken," I said.

"How about a grizzly bear chewing on you?"

"I'll take my Ruger 30-06. It won't be a problem. I'll need some topography maps. Mountains go up to 9000 feet."

"How long will you be gone?"

"However long it takes to find him — two, possibly three weeks."

"Seriously, what if you don't find the Indian?"

"Then my story will be mostly fiction."

Clearwater village

I hate long flights on airplanes. Because of congestion on the highway I arrived late at the airport and hurried through the concourse in order to catch my flight. Boarding, I was one of the last to locate a seat. It was a Boeing 727 with a heavy load. The last remaining seat was between a Sumo-wrestler and a Texas cowboy with the rancid smell of cow shit on his boots. Tex wanted to discuss his recent conquests of females but I wasn't interested. I don't know why people want to talk all the time.

Jets fly so high you cannot see anything. I should soup-up my tri-pacer and pretend to be a crop-duster. As we cleared SEA-TAC, I could see Mount Hood over near Portland. The prop-jet out of Seattle to Lewiston allowed me to see the scenario down below until I got a kink in my neck. The peanuts were too salty.

Lewiston Idaho is a sun baked town on the Clearwater River across from Clarkston, Washington, which is also unimpressive. Named after Lewis & Clark, of the famous Lewis & Clark expedition, it lays stricken in the heat waves of the Northwest. A couple trees. A drab hue of brown, located before climbing up into the wilderness elevations of the Bitterroot Mountains.

On my way out highway 173 I stopped to see Jim Cook who operates the Clearwater Camp on the Nez Perce reservation where I had spent four weeks, two years ago. I wouldn't forget the 20 lb. steelhead that I hooked when canoeing the river near the rapids where Lewis & Clark crossed to meet the Nez Perce in 1805. It proved to be a fatal meeting for the people in the Pacific Northwest. During those next seventy years of lop-sided battles the natives were almost exterminated.

As usual Jim was out front with his guests. Some Nez Perce Indians, who work for Jim, were showing the art of bow making. Others were chipping on obsidian for arrowheads.

Jim saw me and hurried over to my car.

"Why didn't you call me before coming," Cook said. "Why are you here?"

"I didn't intend to stop. I just remembered as I was making the bend and saw your sign."

"Where are you heading."

"Up in the National Forest."

"What on earth for?" Jim said.

"I'm going to look for an ancient Indian that I hear lives all by himself in an isolated valley up in the mountains. You heard of him, or ever seen him?"

"Everyone says they've encountered some native in the wilderness between here and Missoula. Some say it's a hoax, like Bigfoot. That story has been around for many years. It's a fable that a lot of folks keep alive because it's good for business, like having you out here spending money."

"Maybe so. I'm still gonna' search a little."

"Some of the Nez Perce on the reservation believe that story. One of them that work here told me he had seen an Indian with a cougar, crossing the Clearwater River last summer. Floating in the air then disappearing. He said it looked like a young brave. Not old, dressed up like he was headed to a powwow."

"I hope I find out. I gotta' meet him."

"You recall that professor you pissed off when you were here the last time?"

"It's a vague memory. Why?"

"He was here last year. I have two of your books. He began reading Reflections of the Great Spirit. He handed it back. He is still upset because you write complimentary stuff about Indians. He hates them."

"I remember he provoked me to the point where I was about to kick his ass. If it hadn't been for you in the way, I might have. He was an arrogant prick. He is also irritated because Indians can seine for salmon and he's not allowed too. They have a casino, too. I recall him moaning about the Indians having everything. I told him that they owned the whole fuckin' continent before his ancestors come over here and stole the place."

"We've got a lot of his kind. How long will you be gone?"

"A month, maybe. Until I decide he's not there, that maybe he really is a mythical vision."

"Aren't you a little old for such strenuous activity?"

"Maybe. I'll know when I get back from out there. In the meantime I'll see beyond the horizon again. It has been a while since I escaped from our fantasyland with all that crapola that goes on today. Memories of my wilderness trips often keep me from sleeping at night with great images in my head, satisfying memories, as compared to the reality of today."

"Want anything to take with you?"

"I'm an old Boy Scout. I'm prepared," I said. "I have a cellphone. Where's the closest tower?"

"Orofino. Deeper in there you will likely have to climb a mountain to use it. Of course, you are gonna' be in high elevations most of the time anyway. If you find who you're looking for be wary of his puma. Those that reported they have seen the Indian say the cougar is a huge, mean bastard. Protects his pal. You gonna' stop by on the way out?"

"Sure. See you, Jim."

"Mike, you may run into something awful strange if the story proves to be true. I heard that four loggers were looking directly at an Indian with a cougar lying near him, real close. One logger wanted to move closer to speak with him but as he started walking down the hill toward them, the Indian, who was riding an Appaloosa, and the mountain lion, just disappeared. All three vanished."

"You mean they went back into the trees?"

"No. Just kinda' dematerialized, kinda' faded away. The logger said it was eerie. Up northeast of Wieppe."

"I didn't intend going into that area but the Indian has been reported seen in a number of spots. I plan on going due east from Lowell. Maybe I'll have luck, we'll see. It will be an interesting experience. I have never been in Lowell."

"You cannot miss it. Take 173 on out, then cut off on 12. A quaint village. Little place. A resort called Three Rivers Resort. Nice people, good food. You can get something in there to eat. Maybe forty residents. Good trout fishing in the rapids."

"I'll hunt. Nature's been good to me in my life."

"Want some coffee to take along?"

"Sure. Plain."

"I'll get some for you. You got a GPS?"

"Sure."

"That'll help you. They positioned a satellite up above the Rockies. You'll know exactly where you are all the time. I'll send your coffee out. Stop by when you're heading back home. Good luck."

The Bitterroots

I've been through many tiny towns in my life. As a matter of fact I was born in a crappy town in the coal mining region of South Central Indiana. My town was so tiny that when folks suggested building a one way road to get out of town they realized if they did nobody would be able to get back into town.

Lowell, Idaho is kinda' like that. A little glitch on Highway 12, between Kooskia and Missoula. Perhaps forty residents living there. On the confluence where the Selway and Lochsa Rivers become the Clearwater River. Near to where Lewis and Clark explored westward in 1805 to the sorrow of the Native Americans who had lived there for thousands of years. Part of the Lolo Pass.

From Lowell the mountains go upward toward heaven. After a big breakfast at the Three Rivers Resort, I went over to see about renting a horse. Suzette Nigard showed me an Appaloosa stallion that I felt like I had known my entire life. We made a deal after she determined I was experienced with horses. "We had a swayback mare which my grandfather let me ride after my chores were done on the farm," I told her. "I still have great memories of her. We had a lot of good times together. "

I got my gear from the car and checked the supplies I would need. I mounted the stallion and cantered around a ring on the property. Two circles around was enough, we meshed perfectly.

The eastern sky was afire with a tiny sliver of the early sun silhouetted by jagged peaks of the Bitterroot Mountains, appearing like the scutes of some primordial dinosaur. We moved out.

Crossing over the river through a shallower section we began riding up into the cedar forest. The Appaloosa felt easy between my legs. Even though I had not ridden a horse for many years, it's kinda' like a bicycle, you never forget. He had unusual tufts of brownish hairs on the tips of his ears. Pink palm prints had been painted on the stallion's rumps. I had made a friend out of the animal in the corral when I handed him a clump of crisp redtop clover, then two apples and two carrots. We were already buddies.

A silver salmon, perhaps a six pounder, leaped from the water and sucked up a gadfly that had ventured much too near the surface. A Golden Eagle soared across the sky, undulating, and spiraling, seeking prey.

I stopped the stallion just inside the trees. I sat perfectly still in the saddle and listened to the quiet of nature broken only by winds cruising through the tops of the cedars. Below, the river gurgled. In the distance a woodpecker pounded his rhythm, extracting grubs. Some squirrels cavorted up in the trees. I was in a place of mystical beauty, like a natural cathedral. Through the branches I could see the vaporous contrails of military aircraft lacing the sky. The silence was awesome. There was an aura of tranquility. The stallion snorted.

I suddenly sensed an uneasy feeling like I was being watched. I scanned a 360 degree circle. Nothing. Perhaps my nerves were acting up after all; I had not been in the wilderness for a few years. Maybe I needed time to adjust. I kneed the Appaloosa. We moved deeper into the trees. It would be a glorious week. My mind inventoried the items of survival gear in my saddlebag. I was prepared. The feeling of being watched went away.

I studied my topography map and decided to explore the area between the Lochsa and the Selway rivers, the original Nez Perce homeland, hundreds of years ago. It was a big wilderness. To my south was the Salmon River. I figured I would not be able to find a crossing so my best bet was to continue climbing eastward, working my way up to the higher elevations of the Bitterroots. The Indian had been reported seen a number of times in that section of the wilderness.

We climbed upward for maybe an hour. I spoke to my horse and patted his shoulder. The saddle creaked. Two reddish foxes with fur the color of flames fled across our path. The Appaloosa frequently lowered its head to munch something succulent. I chewed on a strip of venison jerky. I was in awe of the beauty around me.

After a few hours the trees began thinning out and I could see obscure evidence of logging trails from long ago when a gluttonous population began scalping nature. I'd read where a hundred years was necessary for the planet to renew itself. Animals had been following the trail keeping it from becoming overgrown. I brought my Appaloosa to a halt, climbed down from the saddle, and dropped the reins. I bent over to study the tracks left by passing animals. I saw the fresh tracks of a cougar. Again I had a disquieting sense we were being watched. I slowly scanned the woods again. Nothing.

The air chilled with a promise of rain. I wondered if I had been too impetuous in coming at this time of the year. Mother Nature displayed her eccentricities at higher elevations. The stallion felt warm between my legs as I re-mounted.

The terrain was becoming steeper with craggy knolls breaking the sloping hillside. My horse was getting skittish on occasion. I could feel his shoulders tense, and then relax. He shook his mane, snorting. I thought of my old swayback mare when I was a kid in Indiana doing the same thing when a bear was in the forest. I became more watchful. We stopped beside a giant boulder where water trickled out from a crevasse. I untied my pack and used a bottle to catch some water for me and the stallion. The taste was incredible. If I drank ground water back in Georgia my guts would develop cramps and my teeth would glow in the dark.

I topped a rise and looked down into a tiny valley. I brought the horse to a halt and dismounted, dropping the reins. The valley in the distance was narrow with thick trees mantling the slopes rising to a backdrop of barren, snow-covered mountains. I was spell-bound. I breathed deeply. My sea-level lungs were not accustomed to the thinner air at this elevation.

This is nature's cathedral, I decided. I stood with my thoughts for a long time. I wished my wife were with me. I listened to the wonderful silence. Here and there wildflowers swayed in profusion. I saw a worn path used by elk and deer when migrating to their different grazing fields as seasons changed. A gentle mist began. I flicked a horsefly off of the ear of my horse.

Periodically, I dismounted and cut a Y in the bark of a tree along the trail. In case of an accident, a good tracker could follow my marks. I cut one fork of the Y a little longer to indicate the direction I was headed. As we crossed a plateau, I carved a Y ever so often in the cedars along the trail. When following a ravine to a higher elevation I continued to carve the Y.

The stallion suddenly reared, snorting loudly as a bear appeared coming out from the tree line. The beast stood up, and stared at us. It apparently decided that the Appaloosa's slashing hooves were too dangerous. It turned and disappeared back down the slope. I gentled the horse.

My mind went back to Atlanta. I thought about the people packed into smoky cocktail lounges bullshitting each other with stupid conversation, the men ogling female breasts, the females becoming more inebriated so that they could later blame their sexual escapade on being intoxicated. Night Clubs have become flesh markets. I wondered why people had nothing better to do.

A Great Horned owl, on silent wings, drifted down from the tree line, disappearing over a rise in the terrain. Grouse chattered noisily in the underbrush. Wind played melodies far out among the cedars then flirted with my unkempt beard.

Wilderness Idaho

I filled two canteens from the trickle. I knew it came by way of a hundred miles of filtering and purification before seeping out from the boulder. The stallion and I drank again, deeply. I filled another canteen.

From far up the mountain I heard the howling of wolves on a hunt. I wondered if they were the packs recently re-introduced into the homeland of the Nez Perce.

When following a bubbling stream coming down from a bluff we came upon a small lake created by industrious beaver. As the sun began sinking below the cedar forest I figured it was a good time to set up our camp for the night. I searched for an outcropping, where it would be simple to make my lean-to. I tethered the horse near the bank were rich grasses grew. He began to graze. Up the lake I saw some ducks splashing in the water, scuffling and making quacking noises, perhaps mating. I put on moccasins and my camouflaged outfit. I took my Bear bow, attached the retrieval reel, and slipped back into the trees. After crawling abreast of the birds I mounted a broad head with blades that open on hitting the target. I waited for the right moment.

On down farther, a mother elk with her frisky calf was mincing across the stream. They stopped, glanced around and stooped to drink, wonderful nature, thrilling.

The ducks were keeping their eyes on the elk while feeding. I was able to crawl somewhat closer. Having won seven medals back home in the Gwinnett Olympics, I was ready. I drew back on my recurve then waited until one of the fowl turned butt-up to feed on weeds on the bottom of the stream. The arrow swished into the duck. Eureka! With the bird impaled, I reeled it in.

Building a fire the old way is fun. Using shavings from a dead branch and spinning a dried stick into the pile of tinder causes the tip to become hot eventually glowing reddish and by blowing on the liter a fire is soon ignited. A magnifying glass would be easier. I had brought one just in case shavings would be wet.

I cleaned the duck on the bank. Minnows gulped the scraps as I threw them in the water. Brightly colored feathers floated downstream. Across the stream I saw a bobcat leaping up onto a boulder. I heard wolves howling further up the valley. From somewhere up on the plateau I heard replies. I wished I could understand the magic of their mournful calls.

The bird was a tasty treat even without my wife's seasoning. I tossed the remaining scraps in the underbrush and heard rustling noises. Dessert was a square of caramel

I gave the horse a ration of oats and walked him to the stream for a drink.

A huge bear ambled from a cedar thicket followed by two rowdy cubs. She stopped and stared in my direction then growled a warning. Heeding maternal admonitions the cubs followed her back into the undergrowth. I had experienced one encounter with a grizzly in Canada. I listened until the sound faded. Bears with cubs can be mean. A chance encounter with a mother grizzly bear with two cubs while I was canoeing the Mackenzie River in the Northwest Territory caused me to have to shoot the mother bear to keep from being killed. Unfortunately, the young cubs were collateral damage.

Remembering that gold had been discovered, downstream at Orofino, on the Clearwater River, I began to think I might find a mother lode. I got a pan from my back pack and found a small, rocky rill. I began panning for gold my mind excited by the possibility that I might strike it rich, like at Sutter's Mill. I wondered if I had been born much earlier if I would have had the guts to give up everything and traipse over mountains to seek gold. After one hour I had a few specks of fools-gold and one piece that might be 24 carat but a tiny fleck wasn't going to make me rich. My back was aching. Two river otters rippled the surface a few feet away and eyed me curiously. One was munching on a sizable brook trout. They stared at me I guess because I was the intruder. I asked if they knew where a huge nugget was located. I stared back. The pair submerged and apparently left to area. I didn't see them again

By the time twilight drew near I had my lean-to made of heavy-duty garbage bags secured on the slanted edge of an outcropping. I anchored the bottom part with rocks. I cut off some branches from a cedar and piled them inside my make-shift bedroom. The aroma of nature would cause magical dreams. I wondered if my wife was worried about me.

Once again I had an unusual feeling that something, or someone, was close by. I made certain the rifle was loaded with the safety off. I stared into the darkness and saw gleaming ovals. I knew I would be under surveillance through the night. I was in their domain. I prayed that they were tiny and not hungry. A breeze picked up in the treetops playing a super-sweet song. I thought of my wife and I began to doze off. Something scurried close to my lean-to. Blackness kept me from seeing. I had a chilling premonition of danger and wondered why any 85 year old, supposedly intelligent person, would explore this wilderness when the comforts of home were back home.

I was consoled by the realization that in a few weeks I could go home. My muscles hurt from the saddle. I sucked on one more nougat. Wind whispered to me from the treetops. My hands remained on the rifle as I tried to sleep.

My brain kept reflecting on things from my past. I thought about my only brother, killed in the Battle of the Bulge. Not quite 21. I would like to have gotten to Hitler before that insane son-of-a-bitch shot himself. I could have killed him in increments. I thought about my first wife with her eccentricities. . I felt a sigh of relief knowing that I didn't have to put up with her foibles. I wondered why more people were not up here in these lush mountains pigging-out on nature.

I heard doves cooing off in the distance.

Even though tired, I found it hard to go to sleep.

I heard unfamiliar noises up and down the valley. I felt strangely uneasy.

I grabbed another caramel and just held it in my mouth, like a baby with a pacifier.

I heard something moving near my shelter. I flipped on the flashlight. Nothing.

I reflected about Harry Truman and the decision which he made that saved thousands of military lives when he ordered bombs dropped with many Japanese being killed. But they started the fuckin' war. I remembered Pearl Harbor and the Bataan Death March. I read about the raping of Nanking. I recalled the arm-wrenching fight after I hooked a trophy northern pike on the Wolverine River in Nunavut. It was still pulling me across the river when I finally dozed off to sleep. Strange woodsy sounds kept waking me up to a half-doze. If I was at home I could turn on the television and watch elephantine broads attempting to dump manatee pounds and dysfunctional people revealing their odd-ball transgressions in life.

I went out and got the Appaloosa and brought it to my shelter. It lay down with its head inside my lean-to. I thought of my wife working the cross-word puzzle knowing she needed my help.

I began thinking about the Indian. Would I find him? Would he be a simple native person? Would he be aware of the enormous change that had occurred throughout the world during his two hundred years of living? Would I learn something I could use in my book, to impart something educational to readers?

Would he know, for instance, about the potential death of the world when the nuclear submarines that had been scuttled off Murmansk finally imploded releasing nuclear materials into the oceans? Would he be aware of the inevitable maelstrom, with earth turning into a gigantic cinder floating around in outer space devoid of life? I wondered if he would know how to control retarded teenagers who were showing indications of the killer mentality.

A zillion questions flooded my brain. I hoped he really existed. It would be an extraordinary coup if I could actually interview someone who had lived for two centuries. No other writer had ever done that. And then maybe he would be a savage like Hollywood portrays and I would be scalped in my sleep.

The stallion was snoring. I didn't know that horses actually snored, but why not? Stranger things happen in life.

Sometime later I finally dropped off to a fitful sleep.

Sometime during the night, I awakened with a start. I had been having scary little vignettes of a nightmare. I was a caveman during the era of dinosaurs cowering in a cave with a huge lizard attempting to claw its way into the back where I was hiding. I could see its claws digging closer then I realized that I had backed in as far as I could go and I was doomed to be consumed by some prehistoric carnivore. My bladder got me fully awakened. I sighed with relief. Then I heard a low growling just outside my lean-to. I grabbed my flashlight and aimed it through the mesh toward the sound. The light revealed the blackest eyes of the biggest wolverine I had ever seen. Its lips were drawn back. I could see razor-sharp teeth. I cleared my throat loudly and screamed, Boo! The king of weasels turned tail. I heard it crashing through the underbrush. I raised the flap and crawled from under the outcropping. The horse whinnied. A breeze whipped through the branches up above as I relieved myself. I shuddered with the chill. My stallion took a piss then turned and wandered down to the river. I started to crawl back inside my lean-to for one more hour catnapping, waiting for dawn's light, rapidly appearing over the mountain.

I heard the Appaloosa near the stream. It shook its mane, its head in my direction. A movement to my left caught my eye. I cringed. From the forest, three forms like whitish, spidery wraiths, like gossamer fog started taking form. There were three clusters of vapor moving up close to my campsite. I reached for the rifle.

"That's not necessary," a resonant voice said.

The forms were now visible. There was a huge cougar and another Appaloosa horse. Between the animals walked the most impressive Indian I had ever seen. He was over six feet tall with wide shoulders. He was wearing a sleeved white ermine mantelet that covered him to his moccasined feet. He wore mink moccasins. His jet black hair cascaded down over his shoulders to his waist. Two colorful feathers were in his pony-tail. Over one shoulder was slung an Osage bow. A quiver of arrows lay across his back. A gold ringlet pierced his nose. The Indian's deep-set eyes were ebony toned.

The Indian looked at me with an intensity I had not experienced before. I felt like I was visiting with royalty.

He said, "My name is Cougar."

The end of an era

In my peripheral vision, I studied the individual I had come to respect like no other human I had known since Johnny. He appeared to be a youthful, educated man, and yet he was reputed to have lived ever since his family was killed two centuries ago. I decided that his Great Spirit did possess amazing power.

"There's a lot to write about the ones who nurtured this land for centuries. I could take you to the plateau at Bear's Paw Idaho where the dispirited Nez Perce Chief Joseph finally surrendered his starving, rag-tag tribe of old men, women and children, to the 7th cavalry after they were attacked, again and again, with most of them killed. After one final attempt to save his people by fleeing into Canada during a frigid winter, failed, Chief Joseph spoke these tragic words."

Tell General Howard I know his heart. What he told me before I have in my heart. I am tired of fighting. Looking Glass is dead. Too-hool-hool-sote is dead. The old men are all dead. It is the young men who say yes or no. He who led on the young men is dead. It is cold and we have no blankets. The little children are freezing to death. My people, some of them have run away to the hills, and have no blankets, no food; no one knows where they are--perhaps freezing to death. I want to have time to look for my children and see how many I can find. Maybe I shall find them among the dead. Hear me, my Chiefs. I am tired; my heart is sick and sad. From where the sun now stands I will fight no more forever.

Cougar and I stared at each other for maybe five minutes. "Sad, isn't it," I said. "Just imagine the horror of an inescapable death of your people unless you surrender your way of life, giving up everything. And even then, thousands of them were murdered just because they were Indians. Those killers were my ancestors."

"Yes, it was filled with great sorrow, but only one of hundreds of like travesties in the Pacific Northwest where several million of my people were murdered after Lewis & Clark's Expedition in 1805 opened a floodgate to immigrants pouring over the mountains seeking land they were told was theirs, free for their taking. The place had been the homelands for the

Nez Perce, Coeur D'Alene, Blackfeet, Lemhi, Lapwai, Spokane, Yakama, Colville, Jocko, Crow, Kalispel, Shoshone, Walla Walla, Kalapuya, Cayuse, Modoc, Blackfoot, Umatilla, Bannock, Columbia, Tillamook, Nisqually, Kootenai, Wenachee, Palouse, Flathead, Cascade, Colville, Yakima, Molalla, Wenatchee, Salish, Paiute and so many more I can't recall them all. That genocide occurred across this land during the past three hundred years. My village was set aflame by American cavalrymen as they shot unarmed villagers who were frantically attempting to avoid being shot. My mother, father and brother were killed by ruthless barbarians."

"You sound embittered," I said.

"A little, at one time. It passed years ago," Cougar said.

Again we looked at each other, mutually understanding how incredibly cruel some people can be to others just to steal their possessions. Genocide is a worldwide evil.

Chief Joseph was never allowed to visit his homeland in Wallowa Valley in Oregon His last years were spent on a reservation in Colville Washington where he refused to live in a house but chose to spend his final years living in a teepee, a last symbol of the great Indian Chief's freedom. The Nez Perce nation was ultimately reduced from hundreds of thousands of acres, extending into Washington and Oregon to a small reservation along the Clearwater River in western Idaho.

Friends

We moved down the mountain, to where the town of Lowell was in sight. "I won't go any farther because people become nervous when I'm around." He smiled.

"It's been a good visit," I said.

"Yes it has. Thank you for listening."

"Thank you for such enlightening information."

"Earlier you said you had two more questions. There is still one unanswered."

I pondered for a moment. My brain raced back to my book. What beneficial suggestion would I like to convey to my readers? It was a momentary dilemma.

"What do we do to survive?" I said.

His response was instantaneous. "Your barbarians spent hundreds of years laying waste to the continent which we had nurtured for many centuries. It won't be easy. There are monumental barriers you've raised. I would start with the fact that no person in your society is ready to accept responsibility for their actions. A woman had a deadly wreck because she never inflated her tires. The front tire on the left was down to 15 pounds pressure. On the Interstate, where the speed limit was 65 MPH, the woman was driving 85 MPH a deer bounded onto the highway. She tried to avoid the animal by swerving to her right. The left tire, because of under-inflation, succumbed to the stress. It exploded when it rolled from the wheel. When she tried to recover her car catapulted in front of a semi-trailer, which wrecked. As a result several people died. Whose fault? An attorney sued Ford and Firestone for defective tires. If she had her tires inflated properly and driven at the legal speed limit the wreck wouldn't have occurred."

"When a man died from lung cancer, after smoking two packs of cigarettes each day for thirty years, a lawyer showed the jury a photograph of his blackened lungs. It took a brain-fractured jury just three hours to award his wife a 30 million dollar settlement. Of course, her lawyers got a whopping 15 million of that amount, which brings up another subject about the necessity of tort reform. Lawyers are becoming very wealthy via frivolous litigation."

"When a curious teenage girl gets pregnant, it is the boy's fault. When a drunk falls and breaks his toe it's the fault of the bartender who served him."

"When people become fat and die from clogged arteries, it's the fast-food industries fault."

"When a kid plays Russian Roulette with the pistol he found in his dad's clothes closet it's the fault of the dealer who sold the gun, the manufacturer who made it, and the National Rifle Association that advocates private ownership of firearms."

A couple was climbing up the hill.

"Can I ask you a couple of quick questions?"

"Shoot," Cougar said.

"How about the disposal of spent nuclear fuel rods?"

"Some day it may cause the end of life on earth."

"How about water pollution?"

"Some day it may cause the end of life on earth."

"How about the massive burden of accumulated garbage?"

"Someday it may cause the end of life on earth."

"How about sexually transmitted diseases?"

"It may cause the end of life on earth."

"How about global warming?"

"It may cause the end of life on earth."

"How about the depletion of natural resources?"

"It may cause the end of life on earth."

"How about the build up of caustic chemicals?"

"It may cause the end of life on earth."

"How about air pollution?"

"It may cause the end of life on earth."

"I have read where the world's population will increase to ten billion by the year 3000. What will be the results of having that many people on earth?"

"Simple. Earth can hardly provide enough food and sustenance for the present population. With an increase of 66%, with people already starving in many regions around the globe, more will starve and those that do not will be the ones who will have become predators, migrating to countries where food and water is available. I think we discussed this earlier. You'll see genocide similar to what Indians suffered long ago. I remember the study you mentioned about a school subject involving rodents. Over-population is the same problem whether it's human or animal. Nature can only support so many species. After that it will be necessary to start over with fewer people on earth. Probably eight billion humans will die."

"How do we change so that incredible tragedy never happens?"

"As I explained before, humans will have to stop breeding like bedbugs."

"How about a world-wide nuclear war?"

"It will cause the end of life on earth."

"I think I'm depressed," I said.

"We are kindred spirits. You're safe," The Indian said.

"Thankfully. My wife, too?"

"Com'on, Mike. You said a couple questions."

"More opinions for my book," I said, smiling.

The climbers were getting closer.

"I must go, my brother," Cougar said.

"Me, too, brother," I said.

The cougar purred. Both Appaloosas whinnied.

"Quickly, when you get back home if you ever need counsel or wish to talk, simply think. From now, and forever, I will know and I will come." He extended his hands.

I took his hands in mine. "Because we are kindred spirits I'll have extra sensory perception? All I will need to do is to concentrate and you will know? You will think and I will know?"

"Yes," Cougar said.

We really are one. I'll visit you again, soon," I said.

"Peace," Cougar said. He gave me the victory sign.

"Peace," I said. I gave him a vigorous thumbs up.

Before my eyes my friends began disappearing, like thinning vapor that disperses into nothing.

I sat astride the Appaloosa, studying the people climbing closer. A diminishing outline of my brother continued to fade up into the overcast. Then they were gone.

"Peace," I said. After sixty-two years of longing. I felt like I had been with Johnny again. Once more I repeated, "Peace," as wetness dimmed my eyes. Lifting my reins I kneed my Appaloosa and said, "Giddyup."

"Beautiful country," I said to the people who were climbing.

Kindred Spirits

I sat in the SEA-TAC airport awaiting the flight. I thought of my experiences over the past four weeks. I thought of the nuggets in Cougar's mountain. All of a sudden I realized that I had been in total agreement with every opinion offered by the Native American. We really must be brothers considering our mutual understanding of the natural order was almost identical. With a few hours before flight time I decided to visit the Space Needle again. I hadn't been there for several years.

I ambled around the catwalk outside the Needle, stopping to view spectacular sights. To the north lay Mt. St. Helens in all its remaining glory. Of course, all that remained to be seen of the crown was hidden by the cloud formation that encircled its peak like a spectral mantel.

Beyond Puget Sound, lay the snow-capped Olympic Mountains.

Looking over Puget Sound my mind went back three hundred years to when the shoreline was the home for Indian societies who lived gently on the land; Snake, Snohomish, Suquamish, Tillamook, Osettes, Nisqually, Makah, Umatilla, Kootenai, Molalla, Kalispell, Crow, Bannock and Duwamish, before the incursions by the Conquistadores searching for gold bringing with them breast-plates, brass helmets, cutlasses, cross-bows, smallpox, syphilis, and death for the native people. Over half of the people were dead within ten years, until the Conquistadores found there was no gold and left to plunder, murder and ravage other people. It seemed as if all of the Europeans marauders reveled in murdering, an insatiable lust obvious throughout their history.

I thought about a paragraph from one of my early books on Indians. It was a poignant speech delivered by Chief Seattle, Chief of the great Duwamish Nation, who spoke these words to an assemblage of troops and councilmen in the newly founded city of Seattle;

"The Indians' night promises to be black. No bright stars hover about the horizon. Sad-voiced winds moan in the distance. Some nemesis of our race is on the red man's trail, and wherever he wanders he will still hear the approaching footsteps of the great destroyer of people and will prepare to meet his doom, as does a wounded deer that hears the approach of the hunter. A few more moons, a few more winters, and not one of the mighty hosts that once filled this land, or that now roam in fragmented bands through these vast solitudes will remain to weep over the tombs of a people once as powerful and hopeful as your own. But why should we complain? Why should I murmur words of the fate of my people? Societies are made up of unique individuals who are no better than others. Men come and go like waves in the ocean. A tear, a moment in time, a funereal dirge and they are forever gone from these longing eyes. Even the white man, whose God walked and talked with him as friend to friend is not exempt from a common destiny. We, upon our deaths, may be brothers after all. Our dead never forgot the beautiful world that gave them being. They still love the unspoiled canyons, its murmuring rivers, the magnificent mountains, its sequestered vales and forest-lined lakes and bays, and ever yearn in tender fond affection over the lonely hearted living, and often return from their Happy Hunting Grounds to visit, guide, comfort and console them. And when the last Red Man shall have perished and the memory of my tribe shall have become a myth among the White Men, these shores will swarm with the invisible dead of my people."

My eyes were burning. In my ear I heard a voice. "I've read it, also, brother. I cried, too." I recognized Cougar's voice.

I continued to stare out over the city with its overcrowded streets and edifices, where people were stacked atop of each other like logs in the fire pit. My eyes swept 360 degrees as I walked on around the Needle my mind calculating just how many natives had loved this land since the time a boat first arrived from the West with people seeking animals, followed by more migrants traversing the land bridge over the frozen Bering Sea. Recalling the history that I knew when the first people arrived on these shores I came to an incredible conclusion that tens of millions of Indians had lived and died since the migration of the first travelers, fourteen thousand years ago when the earth was not polluted, water pristine, air pure, and mountains unspoiled, and with trackless firs mantling the mountains and valleys, where animals wandered and great herds of buffalo roamed and grazed unimpeded by fences. In three centuries these natives were well on their way to oblivion. I thought of the terror of the Indians as they encountered a more powerful army than they could repel. My mind went back sixty years when I was heading for Bizerte and our convoy was attacked by Stukas screaming out of the dark sky, with tracers lacing the night and with bullets ricocheting down on the deck. I was strapped in a 20 millimeter gun mount wondering why in hell I'd enlisted. I had just turned eighteen. I was terrified when slivers of metal meant to hurt my body slammed down on the deck. I cried out in the night when a shard of shrapnel struck me below the knee and I could feel blood on my calf. My loader went down shrieking in agony. I continued shooting up at the flaming tail pipes as the bombers made another run on our ship. Off my starboard stern an ammunition ship exploded, sending a blazing fireball up into the night, illuminating our ship like day. Damn! I turned off my memory machine.

I watched a diesel below on the streets, belching a black toxic mixture of lung-destroying death.

I thought of Cougar's remote valley.

My mind wandered back to my grandfather's farm in Indiana when as a youth my brother and I explored the forest below the farm. After chores were finished we could take our swayback plow horses and go in the woods and live off the land. Often we sat by old Indian mounds, wondering who they were, where did they go and why did they depart. When the war was over I went home to visit Grandfather's farm. I sat by the mounds. My brother had been killed in 1944, during the Battle of the Bulge, so I sat alone feeling the agony of losing a loved one. Indians had lost most of their loved ones. The Cherokees suffered the Trail of Tears. The Potawatomi's suffered the Trail of Death when they were sent marching in the middle of winter to a vast waste-land over the Mississippi River and told it was to be their home. The same fate was ordered for the Wabash, Wea, Shawnee, Kickapoo and the Chippewa. I wondered what fear Cougar had felt when returning from a hunt only to find his family being shot and his village plundered. For what reasoning I asked myself? I decided it was an inborn lust for conquests among my ancestors, a defect caused by inbreeding with family members that went back to the times of the Vikings, Crusaders, Mongols, Huns, and Alexander the Great when killing people was the sign of gallantry to be acclaimed as that noble deed. I wondered just why Alexander the Great was considered so great because what he really accomplished was to murder millions of people on his campaigns of death.

I felt a hand on my arm. "We're closing now," an attendant said.

At home

I sat in front of my computer reading the evening newspaper and wondering where in hell the nation was heading. Child molesters flooded the news, sick kooks coming out of the woodwork. I wondered what made men so evil as to prey on young girls and boys. Was it a recent phenomena caused by the exploitation of women by media? Was it publishers of Playgirl and Playboy filth which reveals such graphic nudity that prurient instincts take control of psychotic brains? Perhaps the sickness is inherited from their parents. Maybe pedophiles are a result of being sexually abused as a child. I remembered talking with Cougar about that aberration during one conversation, with emphasis on pedophiles. Cougar was not one to evade answering. I remembered what he believed. I wasn't surprised when his opinion flashed instantly in my brain.

Cougar acknowledged that morals are disappearing. His knowledge seems inexhaustible. I'm convinced that he's one of the smartest humans I have ever met. With me, it is reality that, unless cured, pedophilia will increase. With current trends, what will the world be like for my grandkids and their children? With all of the chaos and mayhem in the world I wondered what had become of common sense. Obviously Cougar was tuned in to my mind because my fingers began to type.

Common sense has become a forgotten value. People drive too fast seemingly unconcerned that speeding is the primary cause of highway deaths. During the Great Depression my grandfather was a farmer with pearls of wisdom. He told me that if you put your hand on a hot stove it would be burned. He also told me to not walk too close behind his horse. People drink too much and are apparently oblivious to the fact their mentality is diminished exposing them to errors in judgment and unknown consequence. Practicing common sense prevents reckless misadventures. Use of mind-altering drugs is senseless. I prefer controlling my own destiny. Jails are filled with people that failed to practice common sense. Common sense compels a person to check weapons before use to see if they are loaded. Playing with a gun without checking the weapon is a complete lack of common sense. Becoming pregnant when not yet married shows a total lack of common sense. For preservation, common sense is the guide line people need.

There are two truisms: for very cause there is an effect: for every action there is a reaction. Morgues overflow with cadavers of people that failed to learn about those truisms.

I pointed to bold type on the monitor. "Those are that Indian's opinions," I said. "Cougar communicates with me telepathically. He can operate this computer. I have made a really intelligent friend."

I noticed a look of disbelief on my wife's face. "Go ahead and doubt the truth," I said.

As we ate lunch, I explained to my doubting wife some of the material the Indian and I had discussed.

She said, "I still don't believe an Indian is two hundred years old. I don't believe you talked with a live Indian. You're pulling my leg, aren't you?" She squinted up her brow.

"I really did," I said.

"Prove it."

"Hold out your hand, palm up," I said.

She opened her hand, palm up, still dubious.

"An obsidian arrow will pierce your skin."

"Is this one of your stupid pranks?"

"You'll see," I said.

"Yeah, sure, Mike," she grinned, still skeptical.

"Ouch!" She flinched as blood began to ooze from a tiny laceration on her palm.

A massive, tawny, mountain lion intertwined itself around her legs, purring. She screamed. An Appaloosa horse nuzzled her shoulder.

She yelled. "Hey, I believe! I believe! I believe! Mike! Get them out of here!"

From the doorway, a handsome Nez Perce Indian said something to the puma and to the horse, motioning.

"I am glad to have met you, Pat," Cougar said, as the trio began to disappear, drifting up, fading slowly upward, cloud-like, into the ceiling, hazy, like gossamer. A wave, a whinny, a guttural growl, and then they were gone.

My wife stood with a look of total disbelief. Not known to use profanity, she blurted out, "I'll be damned. I would have sworn you were full of manure. He is a hunk! I'll go with you the next time." She batted her eyes, flirtatiously.

"You're pretty old to be acting so frisky," I said.

"You used the words, pretty old. That's pretty, and old," Pat said smiling broadly. "Little do you know what goes on while you are away. That Indian and I may already be Kindred Spirits." She winked.

Geetar Minnie

Someone said if yah build a better mouse trap the world will beat uh path to your door. Now ahm kinda stand-offish un ah doan cotton much tuh weird folks so ahm gonna leave thet mouse thing be, cause ah doan want strange folks hangin' round mah place pesterin' me un messin' with mah mind.

Fishin' is a whole lot different. Yah doan need artificial stuff tuh fish. All's yuh need is uh good natured minny. Yuh jest throw thet minny ennywhar in thu water un hits supposed tuh draw fish lak bears tuh honey. Based on the funny kind uv folks doin' them tellyvision fishin' shows, yuh doan even have tuh be edjicated.

Ah had been on thu pond nigh on ter six hours, jest me un uh onery allygater thet kept nosin' up close. Ah hadn't caught nairy a fish. Ah begun tuh figger thu gater had et all uv em un lakly wuz jest layin' out thar laughin' ut me. Ah wuz down almost tuh thu last inch in mah moonshine jug un mah eyes wuz gitten uh mite crossed, so ah didn't much care iffen ah hooked one or not.

Ah pulled thet minny out fer maybe the umpteenth time. Ah said tuh hit, "Minny, yer fer-sure a sorry 'scuse fer a minny." Thet poor thing wuz rat tattered un beat up with some uv hits scales missin' un looked purty sorry, with jest uh little wiggle left in hits tail, so ah stuck hit intuh thu shine un sloshed hit around uh coupla times. I tossed thu line back in thu water un leaned back tuh finish off mah shine.

All's a sudden, ah heered uh Gawd-awful splashin' un thrashin' un ah looked up tuh see mah bobber wuz gone un thu pole bendin' lak mad. Ah raired back un started windin' lak mad. Hit took me nigh on ter un hour but when ah got hit tuh thu boat mah minny hed thet gater by thu nape uv hits neck un jest wooden' let go. Mah misses now has purty gater shoes un a handbag. Ah let thu minny swim in mah still til' hit died. Hit wuz so pickled hit wooden rot or nuthin' so ah tossed hit in uh drawer un forgot about hit fer maybe a month. Ah figgered hit wuz so good ketchin' thu gater ah decided ta use hit as a mould un make a fishin' lure, kinda' lak thet flyin' thing or thet perpeller thing what they show on tellyvision. Course, ah hain't never caught uh fish on neither one uv them, but they's names shur do sound purty fancy.

Ah came from a piture show one night. hit kinda' hit they had them two banjos goin' at hit, kinda fightin' lak. Hit gave me uh idea. But, then on mah tellyvision ah seed someone already invented uh thing called thu banjo minny.

Now thu sound of them banjos wuz kinda' gratin' on muh nerves, so ah figgered maybe a nuther music thing-uh-muh-jig might be good. They seemed to be ketchin' sum fish on thet banjo thing, at least them folks they pay tu say how good somethin' is wuz earnin' they's keep. They showed pitures uv thet thing pouncin' on big ole' muskies, un pike. They didn't say how many weeks hit took tuh ketch one. They made hit look lak all's yuh hafta do do his throw hit in thu procksimity, proxicmity, proksimy, pro-dag-nab-hit, near whur thu fish his un it clobbers thet fish before yuh can say rottin' dirty jackrabbit.

Ah thought about inventin' a ukulele minny or uh harmonica minny, or uh zylaphone minny or maybe uh zither minny. None thet come tuh mind sounded lak they'd sell. Bout thet time, thet woman thet wus sired by uh coal miner up in thu hills uv Kaintuck came on muh tellyvision un wuz playin' uh geetar un hit jest sort uv hit me. Ah would invent uh geetar minny.

Ah took mah minny out ter thu garage un sprayed hit with four coats uv shellac, so's hit would shine above mah farplace un folks thet wanted tuh could come by un say them ooh's un aah's at thu geetar minny thet took on thu banjo minny whuppin' hit rat good. At least thet banjo minny never caught uh gater.

Mah geetar minny's goin down in history as thu goldangest fishin' thing as wuz ever invented. Now yuh got thet there blond feller who's all's yellen' fer his son. Iffen he doan spray thu juice frum rottin' goose guts on thu banjo minny hit probly wouldn't ketch nothin'. Hit didn't ketch nairy a one fer me anyhow, what with all thet goose stuff sprayed on. An then yuh got thet feller frum Georgia all's told folks Stren wuz thu onliest fishin' line ats worth it's weight in salt. Them folks what pulls thet stuff frum out uv spiders offered thet guy frum Georgia more money tuh say Spider Wire wuz thu onliest fishin' line worth its weight in salt. There's lot'sa flipfloppin' goin' on there, I'd say. I bet thet poor spider is mighty hurtful in one place, havin' all thet wire pulled out frum hits body.

The other day on tellyvision them folks what invented thu banjo minny said yuh only needed one tuh ketch all thu fish yuh kin eat. I called them up tuh buy one un they wouldn't sell me jest one. Ah couldn't believe hit. They's a real talky girl answers thu tellyphone that says I gotta' buy uh package uv fifty un it wuz gonna' cost me maybe thutty dollars. What ah couldn't figger out wuz why I hadda buy fifty if yuh kin ketch all's yuh kin eat with jest one minny unless they's minny doan work. An iffen yuh kin ketch all's yuh kin eat with jest one minny then why cain't yuh use hit agin un ketch all's yuh kin eat agin. An iffen hits as good as they say, then why'd they invent uh frog un uh lizard un other banjo stuff. I git thu impresshun mah legs bein' tugged on uh little.

Thet's why ah invented thu geetar minny. Y'all call me un ahl sell yuh jest one. Ah hain't gonna' lie tuh yuh. Thet's all yer gonna' need. Ah got these huntin' buddies at'll git on tellyvision un tell folks how good muh geetar minny his. All's I gotta pay them tuh swear tuh thu absolute truth his uh hind quarter uv a deer un some possum meat. Fer thet, they'll tell yuh thu truth. Uh little swig uv whaat latning helps nudge along they's memories on how great mah minny his.

After ah make all they money frum sellin' mah geeter minny, ahm goin' back tuh school, at least tuh thu third grade, un git edjucated lak them fellers on tellyvision, so's ah kin git a good job lak they's got, un have all them fancy folks fishin' on mah boat, sayin' all thet sintinlatin, seinliatin, cinterlatin, shucks, edjicated stuff. Then ahm gonna' invent a orchestra minny un then uh string-quartet minny un then uh philharmica minny. Gawd mah mind jest explodes! Thar hain't no way uv knowin'jest how fer yuh kin go once yuh sets yur mind tuh somethin'. Thu skys thu limit.

Eternal Memory

Glory One Star was sixteen years old. Already the pretty maiden was the center of attention for the young men in the village. Her jet-black hair cascaded to her waist. Her eyes were like pools of onyx. Glory One Star and Little Star, her mother, strolled hand in hand up onto the meadow where goldenrod, buttercups and sunflowers blossomed in a profusion of yellow color. Mother and daughter listened to the humming as industrious bees collected pollen.

A soft wind moved the flowers in a spectacular choreography of rhythm. Doves settled on the meadow and quickly pecked their way under the bright golden canopy.

Little Star lovingly squeezed her daughter's hand. "I was but a young child when these beautiful flowers sprang from the earth and blossomed in this place," she said.

"Who planted them?" Glory One Star asked her mother.

"Her name was White Raven. Her father was Chief before Twisted Hair. Her mother's name was Hummingbird."

"Why did she plant so many, mother?"

"White Raven's mother adored flowers and there were many growing wild up in the mountains, but not as many as here."

"Why not?"

"Let's sit among the flowers and listen to the honey bees and I will tell you what I was told as a child."

"The bees will sting me, won't they?"

"No, not if we don't disturb them. They are our friends."

They gathered tufts of grass and dried leaves and made thick cushions at the edge of field of radiant flowers, then sat and made themselves comfortable.

"White Raven was a lovely child, a lot like you. When she was your age she told her mother that she wanted to go out in the world and learn more about living than she was able to learn in the village. Her mother told her that the world was a dangerous place for young girls to travel alone."

"White Raven believed their Guiding Spirit would protect her and against her mother's bidding she departed the village. The child told her mother she would come back with wonderful treasures. Her mother said that her life was already overflowing with treasure and that she would rather have White Raven at home than possess all the wealth in the world.

White Raven left the valley and travelled many days eastward across the snow-capped mountains toward where the sun rises."

"She discovered that away from her village was a very frightening world. She witnessed terrible inhumanity of one people against another people. From a distance she saw savage wars waged pitting people that looked like her against pale-colored men wearing strange uniforms and metal breastplates and helmets. She saw men, women and children killed and many buffalo shot for no reason. White Raven walked across vast tracts of land where millions of trees had been cut leaving only the stumps. Monstrous engines rumbled across the prairie belching clouds of black smoke that burned her lungs. Fences had been erected. She saw multitudes of people with white- faces concentrated in small areas. She saw them gathered in buildings, drinking something called whisky that made them act crazy, stumbling around and falling down. They would begin arguing and fighting and frequently take out guns and shoot each other. White Raven now understood her mother's wise admonitions. The world really was dangerous."

"However, not wanting to be proven wrong, White Raven stayed away for many moons, but finally decided to return to the village. She wanted desperately to see her mother and father. She wanted to touch her mother hands and feel the warmth and affection of her father, the Great Chief."

"During her wandering she had accumulated a rabbit pouch filled with tiny slivers of gold metal that she had discovered in the shallows of the streams she had forded. White Raven opened the bag and looked at the golden treasures she would give her mother, as promised. She removed two tiny nuggets and let the rays of the sun shine on them. Her mother would be pleased with her gifts."

"Autumn was in the air and as White Raven crossed the last mountain into the village she immediately noticed that the beautiful flowers in the meadow were withered and had fallen to the ground. The doves and honey bees were no longer there. She became alarmed."

"She hurried down to the village, calling for her mother. There was no answer. She raced to the tepee of her father. She raised the buffalo-hide flap. Thunder Man bade her to enter."

"Where is Hummingbird," she cried. "Where, please tell me. Why is my father not here in his lodge?"

"Thunder Man beckoned White Raven to him."

"Come to me my child," he said. "Sit with me and I will tell you what you wish to know. It is not something you will like to hear," he said, as he patted her affectionately on her shoulder. "You must be a brave girl."

"Your father died while canoeing down the river to attend a powwow.

A storm came over the mountains, flooding the valley. He was drowned. Several months later your mother died from a broken heart. She confided in me, saying that without her daughter and her Great Chief she was without reasons to live."

"With tears streaming down her face White Raven hurried from Thunder Man's teepee and raced to the meadow where she opened the rabbit pouch and flung the gold slivers randomly across the meadow. They were not treasures anymore. What had been wondrous had turned ugly. Her mother was gone. The Great Chief was gone. White Raven knew that her life would become barren, like her mother's. She threw herself on the dried up flowers wailing her desolation. White Raven was lost forever."

"Suddenly small green shoots began to rise from the meadow. White Raven watched with surprised awareness as goldenrod, black-eyed Susan, buttercup, daisies, and sunflowers began to emerge from where each nugget of gold had fallen. The meadow became a magnificent carpet of beautiful yellow blossoms, spreading out to the forest. Tears flowed unashamedly from the girl's eyes as she realized that her mother would never see the exquisite treasures that she had gathered just for her. The doves began to return and White Raven saw swarms bees humming, distributing pollen onto the blossoms. She spoke with her Guiding Spirit, praying that she would someday be reunited with her family."

"White Raven's eyes were drawn upward and she noticed a dense cloud descending into the valley above the meadow filled with yellow flowers. The gossamer vapor drifted toward her and was transformed into ethereal shapes of her mother and father. Strolling together they looked at the spectacular landscape of yellow. The girl watched her mother stroll into the meadow, stand and touch each petal, stooping to catch the scent. Her father picked several flowers and fashioned a bouquet that he intertwined in Hummingbird's tresses."

"Her parents looked at their daughter and began smiling. They beckoned her to join them. They held each other's hands as they ascended above the carpet of yellow and rose up to heaven, becoming twinkling stars in the distant galaxy, to be together forever."

"At night when the clouds part, White Raven, with her mother and father, smile down on the precious gift she brought to her mother."

Little Star sensed her daughter's hand exploring for hers. The small child looked into her mother's eyes. Tepid tears pooled, leaving tiny tracks down her cheeks.

"White Raven's gifts for her mother are now for our people to love forever," Little Star said, as they found the path and, hand in hand, returned to the valley.

Overpopulation

Before the Europeans came to this part of the world an estimated sixteen to nineteen million indigenous people nurtured their land with respect for Mother Nature. After the Indians were nearly eradicated in four centuries of genocide, the invaders began a campaign that continues to the present to denude the land of its natural resources, pollute the water and create a situation where people are stacked on top of each other like boulders on a levee. Humans lack the intelligence to limit population. Emerging are the indications of too many people living in too close proximity to other people: deprivation, conflict, social tension and hostility. Wildlife is more intelligent than humans because they urinate a scent around their domain and from that scent others know not to encroach.

When Indians became aware that resources were being depleted they held a powwow, discussed the situation then decided that some of the families should move farther away and begin a new village to stop overpopulation and the depletion of natural resources. People now build megalopolises where they exist in sardine-like proximity that augers trouble. To keep their minds from dire situations people drink alcohol and use drugs with conflict in direct proportion to the social degradation.

Years ago a study was conducted in classrooms with mice as a subject to learn how problems are created by overpopulation. A community was built with adequate food and water to provide for 150 mice. Additional food and water supply was not programmed for the study. Cubicles, wheels, ropes, and other items were added for recreation and privacy.

Four female mice plus two male mice were placed in the environment with observations of their behavioral habits started immediately.

They played and cavorted around the compound. It was a scene of complete tranquility. The mice began to reproduce. While the population remained below 150 they were sociable with each other but as the population increased, with food and water insufficient to meet needs, problems developed.

With a huge increase in the mice population peace was replaced by gangs of mice marauding in search of food and water. The supply was soon depleted. When that happened they began to prey on each other, even engaging in cannibalism.

They developed a nervous disorder, indicated by habitually chewing their skin until they bled. The mice stopped breeding and within six months of the beginning of the study the mice were dead. The study is an example of conditions developing over the world. The population of the planet is projected to increase to ten billion inhabitants within fifty years. Predation will become a fact of life when desperate people without sustenance begin migrating to regions where food and water is available.

As the fissure between the rich and the poor widens desperation will increase and impoverished people will not just sit idly and starve but will begin predation on the wealthy and a replica of the study on mice will occur. The problems can be seen today in many regions in the world and will unfortunately end the same as that social study on rodents. A societal collapse is happening at this moment in America as those with little education or job skills prey on others as their method for survival. With the onslaught our law and order agencies will be under greater stress as lawlessness becomes increasingly prevalent.

A nation of glut.

I avoid promoters of distractions as attempts are made to empty my pocket. When I complained about an overcharge AT&T upgraded my channels from 69 to several hundred. I did not request the upgrade and when scanning the additional channels I discovered my television had become a sewer for paying for sexually explicit slime and a lengthy menu of pornography. If my mind was sick I would have loved the choices.

I see channels of fakery, promotions for cures for everything from renewed erections to reversed aging. For easy payments I can learn to do the same things I did as a kid, step forward, then step backward, then jump up and down, with arms flailing, smiling, then stepping backward grinning en masse with other joyous puppets, purported to rejuvenate youthful capabilities.

When I was a kid we did the same things without cost. Television companies now promote even more channels of hustlers, selling tubes of instant energy to products that will cure every ailment and guaranteed to eliminate bowel gas and urinary tract leakage.

And to mesmerize the intended victims, female participants are becoming nakeder and nakeder, to where commercials are virtually pornographic in content with scantily clad females writhing and twisting like wanton nymphomaniacs in the throes of primitive fertility dances.

I watch masses crowd stadiums and golf courses thunderously applauding each play or golf shot. I listen to the organist order me to stand and stretch in the 7th inning. I would prefer to stand and stretch in the 4th inning, or the 16th, not when some faceless person plays deafening music. Even better yet, I stay away from screaming crowds slopping beer on my neck

In order to not have my strings manipulated like a wooden puppet I avoid screaming crowds of people and have learned which buttons to push on my channel selector to thwart the charlatans.

I have never been a spectator. I consider myself unique in that isolation is appealing and Mother Nature offers more memorable delights than being a screaming spectator.

In the silence of my home I can watch the portion of all sports I wish to see without the abrasive presence of noisy booze swilling crowds and the mind-stultifying dialogue of commentators.

Luckily, I can tune out the comments of announcers who feel their remarks are more significant than the sport. I don't have to listen to statisticians telling me which quarterback had the record for interceptions over the past eighty years. I really don't care.

The remote control is a great device because when I know something idiotic is going to happen; tennis players glowering at their opponent and spraying spittle when they win a point; people begging for autographs, Madonna appearing at the super bowl; I watched her sing once, and I decided never again. We are worshipping contrived idols; baseball players in dugouts, spitting and scratching, and spitting seed hulls isn't educational, entertaining or enlightening.

Watching scarred fighters injuring each other in a cage defies imagination, the same as muscle-bound wrestlers glaring at each other then faking lethal blows and body slams. As astonishing is the audience applauding the obvious deception.

And the greatest invention of all is the remote used to turn off the television set allowing me to go on my upper deck and thrill to the aerobatic maneuvering of a dozen colorful hummingbirds.

We have become a nation of glut; too many baseball stadiums, too many golf courses, too many race tracks, too many psychiatrists, too many shopping malls, too many cars, too many resorts, too many pickpockets, too many mansions, too many TV channels, too many boom-boxes, too many rock concerts, too many yachts, too many tennis courts, too many out-of-wedlock babies, too many charlatans, too many pornographers, too many philanderers, too many politicians, too many spectators, too many scam-artists, too many rapists, too many pills, too many commercials, too many everything. We're drowning in a tsunami of regressive social progress.

I have won my share of tennis sets but I have never flopped on the court after winning nor have I danced some dumb jig to endear myself to the spectators. We now have too many players jigging around the tennis court squirming and wiggling after winning that it seems to be the monkey-see-monkey-do syndrome.

In this world of manipulated superficiality Mother Nature is preferable.

Observations of the author

America would erupt into anarchy if it were not for the thin blue line of law enforcement

I attended the 12th Annual Citizen's Police Academy in Gwinnett County, Georgia where I was privileged to go out on live emergency calls with patrolmen during the most dangerous time of the night. I experienced first-hand the terror-engendering dangers that confront police officers when assigned to investigate actual shoot-outs after dark between rival gangs, (gangs being defined as three or more people banding together to commit a felony.) Gwinnett County has documented one hundred twenty three gangs, a phenomenon that has increased in the past ten years. If it were not for our first line of defense, the police departments across the country, people would be even more at the mercy of killers, pedophiles, corruptors, merchants of filth, scam-artists, swindlers, rapists, looters, and brutal thugs. America is suffering a growing social meltdown.

When I was a youth growing up in Indiana I slept with my doors unlocked. During WW II, I witnessed maniacal acts of inhumanity. Similar behavior is infesting our society on an increasing scale. At four o'clock in the morning I sit before my computer writing with a 38 revolver on my desk. When driving I have a 32 automatic in my car. America is not the same as it was four decades ago. The Boy Scouts have a motto every American should remember; Be Prepared.

Over 17,000 people are murdered annually in the United States. Every year one and one half million people are victims of violent crimes. Prisons burgeon with killers and rapists. Home invasions, robberies, drug related crimes are pandemic. Senior citizens are targeted for crime on a level unparallel in history. We see increasing psychosis infecting the nation during spring break when young people flaunt similar decadence of the Roman Empire just prior to its collapse. We watch looters and crooked contractors prey on the victims of natural calamities. Guns are the weapons for hoodlums preying on people without protection. A weakness in our criminal justice system is highlighted in Atlanta where one murderer has remained alive for three years, at the expense of taxpayers, while the people he shot have been dead that same period. We know he shot them. There were witnesses to two of the killings. An indication of exactly how fractured this system has become? The man is not guilty? How? Why? He did it. Witnesses saw him kill the Judge and the recorder. The murderer stood with the lawyers assigned to represent him and with a straight face one of his lawyers declared him to be not guilty. How can a lawyer state that a killer is not guilty when dozens of people witnessed him shoot two of his victims? His trial was finally held and he was convicted in spite of an insanity defense. Three jurors failed to remember the awful devastation of the families of his victims and sentenced him to life in prison, where he will have food, a place to sleep, be able to use the library, and other freebies, while the victims have decomposed. Three years later, the killer will still be alive. Meanwhile his victims are dead! A review court will probably find some technical violation of the trial procedure and will reverse the decision and we will have another trial. With a plea bargain to avoid expenses the killer will be sent to an over-crowded prison to live out his life at our expense. Meanwhile four people who would rather be alive are dead.

Another flaw in the criminal justice system is the use of testimony by expert witnesses. Lawyers will use hired-guns who get paid to testify for the defense or the prosecution, whoever gets to them first or offers the largest reward. They will sit and spiel what the lawyers want them to spiel. They will take a fact and make it a non-fact. A fact is interpreted two ways until the fact is no longer a fact but opposing theories. Those experts are skilled but are compensated to have opinions favorable to the side that paid their fee; mauve is not mauve, but claret, burgundy is not burgundy but maroon. Justice has been bastardized until criminals who can afford the most glib-tongued attorney and slick-tongued experts are able to usurp the system. Lawyers develop their reputation by winning cases, whether the culprits are guilty or not. The more cases they win the more will be their future opportunities and fees.

The normally achievable middle-class dream is becoming a myth at the present rate of collapse. The wealthy class purchase private jets, yachts, exclusive country club memberships, mansions and live extravagant lifestyles while the middle class survive by working extra jobs, maxing their credit cards, closing their savings account, and obtaining home equity loans that lead to their inevitable economic ruination. An example of the income inequity is the flood of scandals on Wall Street, the banking industry and throughout the business world where the rich become wealthier by way of intricately complex financial manipulation while the poor become poorer. The American dream has become an illusion for millions of citizens. We are seeing the disruption of families as the economy falters because fewer people are prepared for the fact that their established way of life is under attack and there is the terrible reality that more productive people will be forced to join the ranks of the helpless homeless.

As the disparity between the wealthy and the poor widens the deepening abyss will reach cataclysmic proportion, and is showing evidence of violence and discord and as we collapse into anarchy our homes will need to be barricaded like medieval fortresses to guard against desperate people who are already reacting in desperate ways in order to survive in this inhospitable world.

Why I tend to be a loner

Adolf Hitler	Sergo Hennard
Josef Stalin	Baruch Goldstein
Pol Pot	Toi Mutsuo
Idi Amin	Lizzy Borden
Admiral Yamomota	Campo Elias Delgado
Ted Bundy	Cho Seung-hoi
John Wayne Gacy	Myra Hindley
Charles Taylor	Ahmed Ibragimon
Genghis Kahn	William Unek
Alexander the Great	Martin Bryant
Nicolae Ceausescu	Woo Bum-Kon
Nebuchadnesser	Nero
Arminus	Anders Behring Breivik
Atilla the Hun	Luis Garavito
Charles Taylor	Jean-Bedel Bokassa
Tamerlane	Oliver Cromwell
Charlemagne	Shiro Ishii
Pharoah Thutmuseill	Osama Bin Laden
Ashoka	Kim Jong Il
Cyrus	Beverly Allitt
Ch'in shih Huang	Caligua
Augusta Caesar	Belle Gunness
Mao Zedong	Mary Ann Cotton
Adolf Jodl	Illse Koch
Heinrich Himmler	Bob Jones
Hidoki Tojo	Ted Kaczynski
Chuichi Naguma	Irma Grese
Timothy McVeigh	Eric Rudolph
Terry Nichol	Wayne Williams
Carlos the Jackal	Dylan Kiebold
Gary Leon Ridgeway	Eric Harris
Napoleon Bonaparte	Katherine Knight
Robert Dale Segee	Elizabeth Bathorg
Alexander Keith	Andrei Chikatilo
Joachm Kroll	Albert Fish
Dennis Rader	Jack the Ripper
Charles Manson	Richard Trenton Chase
John George Haigh	Gilles de Rais
Jared Igbal	Jeffrey Dahmer
Josef Mengele	Herta Oberhauser
Eddie Gein	Albert DeSalvo

Lucifer

If I were Lucifer, having the ability to assume any visage, I would roam among you in disguise. I would have unlimited power and would sow seeds of discontent, immorality, gluttony, hatred and racism. I would convince average citizens to prey on others who did not accede to my edict.

I would create dissension in the family and avarice in the workplace. I would stimulate distaste of government and spread fear in the neighborhood. I would demean achievement and advocate   mediocrity.

Many with consciences would become devoid of compassion. Many of you would succumb to the ravages of prurient temptation and become a nation of revelers and debauchees, devotees of hypocrisy and, revilers of normalcy.

Win or lose I would incite riots after sporting events by burning and trashing the downtown areas of cities. After devastating natural disasters I would traumatize the victims even more by stealing   their possessions when they were hospitalized or otherwise rendered vulnerable.

I would infiltrate political offices and ply officials with money and sex, nullifying the integrity of governments, and destroying the confidence of voters.

I would staff inner-city schools with incompetent educators making the studies so boring that the drop-out rate would skyrocket. I would begin teaching elementary school children about the joy of sex and distribute condoms to them without parental permission or awareness so that children can engage in mature activity long before they are mentally and emotionally prepared.

I would turn your television into a sewer for the promotion of evil with charlatans using devious techniques to destroy the purity of your culture. I would accomplish my purpose with irresistible enticements; programs glorifying intoxication, lurid behavior, violence, spousal abuse, infidelity, drug experimentation and lewd nakedness, rancid pustules that insult humanity.

I would market Rohypnol and other date-rape drugs to be able to disseminate syphilis and AIDS throughout society with no regard for the trauma suffered by the victims.

I would get teenagers hooked on dangerous substances so they can race on highways and around curves in the dark of night, killing themselves, their passengers and unsuspecting drivers.

I would encourage parents to use television as the babysitter so children will develop as mindless automatons, subliminally manipulated toward the certainty of failure.

As a faceless opportunist on the internet I would tempt everyone to click on my website so that I would be able to enter their computers and utilize their impeccable credit for personal gain, even to the ruination of their financial future.

I would ban prayers from public schools and would dismiss administrator who failed to enforce my rule. I would demand that instructors falsify failing grades so students would be unprepared when entering the job market. For the unemployable I would teach vandalism; graffiti, mailbox destruction, cemetery despoliation, mugging, carjacking, home-invasion, bank robbing, and the advantages of gang affiliation.

I would delete American history from schoolbooks and libraries and replace truth with falsities. I would denigrate success and commend failure.

I would arrange millions of abortions so the individual murdering the fetus would always wonder if they aborted a future Chopin, Mother Theresa, Michelangelo or Johnny Carson.

I would encourage newly married couples to immediately start ogling the opposite sex so that the marriage is no longer a haven from stress or for the perpetuation of the species.

I would become a pornographer and feature graphic pictures of naked men and women to cause a plunge in social morality and an increase in violent attacks on women.

I would tell you anything you wanted to hear in order to be elected to Congress so I can become wealthy by consorting with those who pay for votes defined as political donations.

As a citizen I would inspire my proponents to protest, insisting on unaffordable entitlements that would lead to the ultimate insolvency of the system.

I would teach you and your children to be prolific shoplifters to deprive industrious merchants of their operating capitol, necessary to remain in business.

I would advocate having parties with the excessive consumption of intoxicants 24-7 so that rape, infidelity and crime would continue to spiral upward with accompanying social disintegrating.

I would unmercifully swindle senior citizens.

I would mangle your brain cells by promoting unceasing sporting events to hold you spellbound, while my cadre of supplicants defiled your culture.

I would demand the confiscation of firearms from the hands of hunters and sport-minded people, imposing my personal agenda of mandates on society.

I would inveigle my way into credit card companies and provide millions of solicitations for you to possess a prestigious credit card providing a low enough introductory rate to entice you to buy things you can't afford and do not need. Then I would hit you with fees that could bankrupt you. You would be paying unconscionable penalties and confiscatory interest rates for years.

I would mess with your morality until you began to solicit children for illicit contacts. By doing so, I would negate the moral standards on which this nation was built.

There are many ways I would harm you. But you should understand that I, Lucifer, am already here devising ways to assure finality for a nation floundering in a cesspool of superficiality. Sioux2222@gmail.com.

Excerpt from 2nd Timothy 3:1–7 NASB

But realize this, that in the last days difficult times will come. For men will be lovers of self, lovers of money, boastful, arrogant, revilers, disobedient to parents, ungrateful, unholy, unloving, irreconcilable, malicious gossips, without self control, brutal, haters of good, treacherous, reckless, conceited, lovers of pleasure rather than lovers of God, holding to a form of godliness although they have denied its power. Avoid such men as these. For among them are those who enter into households and captivate weak women weighed down with sins, led on by various impulses, always learning and never able to come to the knowledge of the truth.

Leech Lake, Minnesota

Wolverine River, Nunavut, Canada

Churchill River, Manitoba, Canada
Left to right-Tom Krautkramer-Ken Daniel-Bill York-Carl Hrechka-Darion
Seldes-Nate Haskell

To commemorate those stalwart Indian Chiefs who guided their people through three-hundred years of tribulation after the invasions by the Europeans.

Abbigadasset
(Pawtucket)
Abel Bosun (Cree)
Abis tos quos (Blood)
Addih-Hiddiseh
(Hidatsa)
Adoeette (Kiowa)
Aeneas (Okanogan)
Afraid of Bear (Sioux)
Afraid of Hawk
(Sioux)
Agate Arrow Point
(Warm Springs)
Ah Moose (Lac du
Flambeaux)
Ah-de-ak-too-ah
(Osette Village)
Ahlakat (Nez Perce)
Ahtahkakoop (Cree)
Ahyouwaighs (Six
Nations)
Alchesay (Apache)
Alexander
(Wampanoag)
Al-is-kah (Osette
Village)
Alligator (Seminole)
Alpheus Brass
(Chemahawin)
Always Riding
(Yampah Ute)
Amat-tan (Kashaya)
American Chief
(Kansa)
American Horse
(Sioux)
Amisquam
(Winnebago)
Anacamegishca
(Kenisteno)

Annawon
(Wampanoag
Antonio Buck (Ute)
Antonio Garra
(Cupeno)
Antonito (Pima)
Apaula Tustennuggee
(Creek)
Appachancano
(Appamattuck)
Apache John (Apache)
Appanoose (Sauk and
Fox)
Arkikita (Otoe)
Armijo (Apache)
Ash Kan Bah Wish
(Lac du Flambeaux)
Assonnonquah (Wea)
Atawang (Ottawa)
Aupumut (Mohican)
Autosse (Creek)
Awashonks (Sakonnet)
Baht-se-ditl (Neah
Village)
Baptiste Mongrain
(Osage)
Barboncito (Apache)
Bashaba (Penacook)
Batiste Good (Kiowa)
Bear Bird (Comanche)
Bear Claw (Lenape)
Bear Cut Ear (Crow)
Bear Ribs
(Hunkapapa)
Bear's Ear
(Comanche)
Bear Tooth (Crow)
Bedonkohe (Apache)
Bel Oiseau (Osage)
Bellrock (Crow)
Benito (Apache)

Berht Chasing Hawk
(Sioux)
Bich-took (Waatch
Village)
Big Bear (Cree)
Big Bill (Paiute)
Big Bow (Kiowa)
Big Eagle
(Mdewakanton Sioux)
Big Elk (Omaha)
Big Foot (Miniconjou)
Big Horse (Missouri)
Big Mouth (Arapaho)
Big Mouth (Brule'
Sioux)
Big Razor (Sioux)
Big Snake
(Winnebago)
Big Star (Comanche)
Big Star (Walla Walla)
Big Thunder (Sioux)
Big Thunder
(Wabanaki)
Big Thunder (Nez
Perce)
Big Tree (Kiowa)
Big Tree (Blackfeet)
Big Wolf (Comanche)
Billuk-whtl (Tsoo-
yess)
Billy Bowlegs
(Seminole)
Black Bear (Arapaho)
Black Beard
(Comanche)
Black Bird
(Potawatomi)
Blackbird (Omaha)
Black Bob (Shawnee)
Black Buffalo (Teton
Sioux)

Black Cat (Mandan)
Black Crow (Sioux)
Black Elk (Lakota)
Black Eye (Sioux)
Blackfish (Shawnee)
Blackfoot (Crow)
Black Fox (Cherokee)
Black Hawk (Sauk)
Black Hoof (Shawnee)
Black Horn (Sioux)
Black Horse (Seneca)
Black Kettle
(Cheyenne)
Black Mocassin
(Haida)
Black Moon
(Hunkpapa)
Black Rock (Teton
Sioux)
Blue Jacket (Shawnee)
Blue Tomahawk
(Kiowa)
Bone Necklace
(Yankton Sioux)
Bow and Quiver
(Comanche)
Brave Bear
(Cheyenne)
Bright Horn (Archaic)
Broken Arm
(Comanche)
Broken Hand
(Cheyenne)
Broken Arrow
(Coweta)
Buckskin Charley
(Ute)
Buffalo Eater
(Comanche)
Buffalo Horn
(Bannock)
Buffalo Hump
(Comanche)
Buffalo Medicine
(Teton Sioux)

Buffalo Piss
(Comanche)
Bull (Wea)
Bull Bear (Comanche)
Bull Chief (Cheyenne)
Bull Chief (Apsaroke)
Bull Elk (Comanche)
Bull Head (Pawnee)
Bull Snake (Crow)
Cadette (Mescalero
Apache)
Calero Rapala
(Comanche)
Callicum (Nootka)
Cameahwait
(Shoshone)
Canonchet
(Narragansett)
Canonicus
(Narragansett)
Cany Attle (Mouche)
Captain Elick (Creek)
Captain Jack (Modoc)
Captain Johnny
(Archaic)
Captain Logan
(Archaic)
Cashwahutyonah
(Onondago)
Cayangwarego
(Tuscorora)
Cayatania (Navajo)
Chacapma
(Potawatomi)
Chad Smith
(Cherokee)
Charger (Yankton
Sioux)
Charging Bear
(Sioux)
Charging Hawk
(Osage)
Charles Shakes
(Kwaguitl)

Charley Amathla
(Seminole)
Chato (Mescalero
Apache)
Chawookly (Coweta)
Checalk (Potawatomi}
Cheebass
(Potawatomi)
Cheeseekau
(Shawnee)
Cheetsamahoin
(Clallam)
Chetopah (Osage)
Chetzemoka (Clallam)
Chewago
(Potawatomi)
Chief Aslo
(Ashochimi)
Chief Beaver
(Delaware)
Chief Blinds
(Columbia)
Chief Bones (Palouse)
Chief-Comes-In-Sight
(Cheyenne)
Chief Egan (Paiute)
Chief Escumbuit
(Abenaki)
Chief Garfield
(Jicarilla)
Chief Grass
(Blackfoot Sioux)
Chief Horseback
(Comanche)
Chief Illiniwek
(Illinois)
Chief Michel
(Kootenay)
Chief Moses (Modoc)
Chief No Shirt (Walla
Walla)
Chief Oytes (Paiute)
Chief Pot Belly
(Palouse)

Chief Sagamore
(Sagamore)
Chief Sar-Sarp-Kin
(Salish)
Chief Timbo
(Comanche)
Chief Tonasket
(Salish)
Chief Yelkis (Mollala)
Chief White
(Chippewa)
Chihuahua
(Comanche)
Chihuahua (Apache)
Chilly MacIntosh
(Creek)
Chilliwack (Comox)
Chinnabie (Coweta)
Chittee-Yoholo
(Seminole)
Chochise
(Chiricahua)
Chomoparva
(Comanche)
Conge (Potawatomi)
Chono Ca Pe (Oto)
Chou-man-I-case
(Chickasaw)
Chu-gu-an (Kashaya)
Clam Fish (Warm
Springs)
Clermont (Osage)
Coast-no (Molalla)
Coboway (Clatsop)
Coloraw ((Ute)
Comcomly (Chinook)
Connessoa
(Onondago
Conquering Bear
(Lakota)
Cordero (Comanche)
Corn Planter (Seneca)
Cornstalk (Shawnee)
Cornstalk (Huron)
Counisnase (Molalla)

Crazy Bear (Oglala
Sioux)
Crazy Horse (Oglala
Sioux)
Crooked Finger
(Molalla)
Crooked Legs (Wea)
Crow (Cheyenne)
Crow Dog (Oglala
Sioux)
Crow Feathers
(Kiowa)
Crow Foot (Blackfoot)
Crow King
(Hunkpapa Sioux)
Crow's Breast (Gros
Ventres)
Cuampe (Ute)
Cuffey (Poosepatuck)
Curtis Zenigha
(Delaware)
Custologo (Delaware)
Cut Finger (Arapaho)
Cutshamekin
(Agawam)
Cyrenius Hall (Nez
Perce)
Daht-leek (Osette
Village)
Dan George (Salish)
David Vann
(Cherokee)
David Williams
(Nespelem)
Dead Eyes (Kiowa)
Decanisora
(Onondago)
Deer Ham (Ioway)
Deer Horn (Ponca)
Delgadito (Mouche
Apache)
Delshay (Tonto
Apache)
Diwali (Cherokee)

Does Everything
(Apsaroke)
Dohosan (Kiowa)
Donacoma (Huron)
Duggins (Molalla)
Dull Knife (Cheyenne)
Eagle (Nez Perce)
Eagle Chief (Pawnee)
Eagle Drink
(Comanche)
Eagle Elk (Oglala
Sioux)
Eagle Heart (Kiowa)
Eagle of Delight
(Cheyenne)
Eagle Ribs (Piegan
Blackfeet)
Edward Bullette
(Creek)
Egan (Paiute)
El Albo (Mouche
Apache))
El Sordo (Navajo)
Elizabeth Job
(Poosepatuck)
El Sordo (Comanche)
Encanaguane
(Comanche)
Enias (Entiat)
Esazat (Comanche)
Escumbuit (Penacook)
Eshcam (Potawatomi)
Esh-sta-ra-ba (Maha)
Eshtahumleah (Teton
Sioux)
Eskaminzin (Anaviapa
Apache)
Eskelteslan (Apache)
Essiminasqua
(Pawtucket)
Estrella (Mescalero
Apache)
E-TAA-NA-QUOT
(Chippewa)
Fast Bear (Kiowa)

Feeble One
(Comanche)
Fish Hawk (Umatilla)
Five Crows (Cayuse)
Five Wounds (Nez
Perce)
Flat Iron Mela Blaska
(Oglala) Foke
Luste Hajo (Seminole)
Fool Chief (Kansa)
Fool Dog (Kiowa)
Fools Crow (Crow)
Four Bears (Mandan)
Four Bears (Sioux)
Fragrant Eagle
(Comanche)
Frank Fools (Crow)
Fuskatche (Cusetah)
Gall (Hunkpapa
Sioux)
Garfield (Jacarilla)
Garry (Spokan)
Gatebo (Comanche)
Gem-le-le (Kashaya)
Georgia White Hair
(Osage)
Geronimo (Apache)
Good Heart (Crow)
Goose (Wea)
Gotokowhkaka (Wea)
Grande Corte
(Piankashaw)
Gray Iron
(Mdewakanton Sioux)
Gray Wolf (Piegan)
Great Bear
(Delaware)
Great Eagle (Caddo)
Great War Chief
(Navajo)
Green Horn
(Comanche)
Greenwood Laflore
(Choctaw)

Grey Beard
(Cheyenne)
Grey Eagle (Apache)
Grizzly Bear
(Menominee)
Guadalupe (Caddo)
Haatse (Makah)
Hah-yo-hwa (Waatch
Village)
Hiachenie (Cayuse)
Hairy Bear
(Winnebago)
Halletemalthle
(Cusetah)
Hamli (Walla Walla)
Handsome Lake
(Seneca)
Hatalakin (Palouse)
Hawk (Paugussett)
Heavy Runner
(Piegan)
He Bear (Comanche)
He Gnaws his Master
(Comanche)
He Who Saw Fire
(Comanche)
Head Carry
(Blackfoot)
He-dah-titl (Neah
Village)
He-Dog (Oglala
Sioux)
Herrero Grande
(Apache)
Hiachenie (Cayuse)
Hiawatha (Mohawk)
Hichonquash
(Tuscarora)
High Hawk (Sioux)
High Head Jim
(Creek)
High Horse (Omaha)
Hillis Hadjo
(Seminole)

Hoarse Bark
(Comanche)
Hobonah
(Wampanoag)
Hole-in-the-day
(Chippewa)
Hole-in-the-Forehead
(Pawnee)
Hollow Horn Bear
(Brule Sioux)
Homatah (Coweta)
Homily (Walla Walla)
Hoowanneka
(Winnebago)
Hopothe Mico
(Tallisee)
Hopoy (Coosade)
Horse Back
(Comanche)
Horse Chief (Pawnee)
Howeah (Comanche)
Hustul (Nez Perce)
Ignacio (Weeminuche)
Inkpadutah (Iowa)
Iron Bull (Crow)
Iron eye (Omaha)
Iron Hawk (Cheyenne)
Iron Mountain
(Comanche)
Iron Plume (Sioux)
Iron Shell (Brule'
Sioux)
Iron Shirt (Comanche)
Islander (Apache)
It-an-da-ha (Makah)
Itcho-Tustennuggee
(Seminole)
Jacco Tacekokah
Godfroy (Wea)
Jack House (Ute)
Jack-O-Pa
(Chippewa)
James Perry (Archaic)
Jason (Nez Perce)

Jim Henry
(Muscogee)
Jim James (Sinkiuse)
Jo Hutchins (Santiam)
Joc-O-Sot
(Mesquakie)
Joe Capilano
(Squamish)
Joe Moses (Sinkiuse)
John Grass (Sioux)
John Homo
(Chickasaw)
John Hoyle (Chowan)
John Ridge
(Cherokee)
John Ross (Cherokee)
John Wooden Legs
(Cheyenne)
Johnko' Skeanendon
(Oneida)
Johnson (Swinomish)
Johyellow Flower
(Ute)
Joseph (Nez Perce)
Joseph Brant
(Mohawk)
Joseph LaFlesche
(Omaha)
Joseph Perryman
(Creek)
Josua (Cowichan)
Juh (Apache)
Julcee Mathla
(Seminole)
Juleetaulematha
(Coweta)
Jumper (Seminole)
Kabay Nodem
(Chippewa)
Kah-bach-sat
(Makah)
Kah-ge-ga-bowh
(Ojibwa)
Kahlteen (Kalapuya)

Kai-kwt-lit-ha
(Waatch Village)
Kal-chote (Makah)
Kamiakin (Yakima)
Kanacamgus
(Agawam)
Kanagagota
(Cherokee)
Kanakuk (Kickapoo)
Kanapima (Ottawa)
Kanaretah
(Comanche)
Kan-hahti (Tejas)
Kape (Quinalt)
Katawabeda
(Chippewa)
Ka-ya-ten-nae
(Apache)
Ke Wish Te No (Lac
du Flambeaux)
Keesheswa (Fox)
Keesis (Potawatomi)
Keh-chook (Makah)
Kekequah (Wea)
Kemwoon
(Whuaquum)
Kennebis (Pawtucket)
Kennekuk (Ioway)
Keokuk (Sauk and
Fox)
Kets-kus-sum
(Makah)
Kicking Bear (Oglala
Sioux)
Kicking Bird (Kiowa)
Kientpoos (Modoc)
Kiesnut (Wishram)
Kilcaconen (Yeopim)
King of the Crows
(Crow)
King Philip)
Wampanoag)
Kinkananqua
(Tulalip)

Kishekosh (Sac and
Fox)
Kishkalwa (Shawnee)
Kitsap (Muckleshoot)
Kiwatchee
(Comanche)
Klah-ku-pihl (Tsoo-
yess)
Klah-pe-an-hie
(Makah)
Klaht-te-di-yuke
(Waatch Village)
Klakaghama (Siletz)
Klart-Reech (Kilikitat)
Klatts-ow-sehp (Neah
Village)
Kleht-li-quat-stl
(Waatch Village)
Koon-Kah-za-chy
Kiowa-Apache)
Konoohqung (Oneida)
Koomilus
(Tchulwhyook)
Koostata (Kootanai)
Kowa (Comanche)
Kwah-too-quahl
(Tsoo-yess)
Kyoti (Tsawatenok)
Lame Deer
(Minneconjou)
La Mouche Noire
(Wea)
La Peau Blanche
(Wea)
Lappawinsoe
(Delaware)
Lattchie (Molalla)
LA-WA-TU-CHEH
(Archaic)
Lawyer (Kwakiutl)
Lawyer (Nez Perce)
Le Soldat du Chene
(Osage)
Leahwiddikah
(Comanche)

Lean Bear (Cheyenne)
Lean Elk (Nez Perce)
Lean Wolf (Gros
Ventres)
Lechat (Ute)
Ledagie (Creek)
Leepahkia
(Peankashae)
Left Hand (Cheyenne)
Legus Perryman
(Creek)
Leschi (Nisqually)
Little (Oglala Sioux)
Little Big Man (Oglala
Lakota)
Little Carpenter
(Cherokee)
Little Charlie (Wea)
Little Crow
(Mdewkanton Sioux)
Little Edward
(Hunkpapa Sioux)
Little Face (Wea)
Little Hawk (Oglala
Sioux)
Little Horse
(Cheyenne)
Little Mountain
(Kiowa)
Little Pipe (Chippewa)
Little Pipe (Coyote)
Little Prince (Creek)
Little Raven
(Arapaho)
Little Robe (Arapaho)
Little Rose (Cheyenne)
Little Six (Kaposia
Sioux)
Little Thief (Oto)
Little Thunder (Brule'
Sioux)
Little Turtle (Miami/
Mohican)
Little Wolf (Cheyenne)
Little Wolf (Lakota)

Little Wound (Oglala
Sioux)
Locher Harjo (Creek)
Loco (Apache)
Logan (Huron)
Logan Fontenelle
(Omaha)
Lollway (Archaic)
Lone Man (Teton
Sioux)
Lone Wolf (Kiowa)
Long Jim (Nez Perce)
Long Mandan
(Kiowa)
Looking Glass (Nez
Perce)
Low-Dog (Lakota)
Luther Standing Bear
(Oglala Sioux)
Macasharrow
(Huron)
Macota (Potawatomi)
Mad Bear (Sioux)
Madokawando
(Drake)
Mahaskah (Iowa)
Mahtoree (Yankton
Sioux)
Majectla (Makah)
Major Ridge
(Cherokee)
Makhpiya-Luta
(Lakota)
Malatchee (Creek)
Mamanti (Kiowa)
Man Afraid of His
Horse (Sioux)
Man and Chief
(Pawnee)
Man-chap-che-mani
(Osage)
Mangas Colorados
(Membres)
Manhawgaw (Iowa)

Man-in-cloud
(Cheyenne)
Manitou (Umatilla)
Manitou (Spokane)
Mankato (Santee
Sioux)
Manteo (Croatoam)
Manuelito (Navajo)
Many Horns (Sioux)
Many Horses
(Apache)
Maple Tree
(Minneconjou)
Maquinna (Nuu-chah-
nulth)
Markomete
(Menominee)
Ma-sha-ke-ta (Maha)
Mashulatubbe
(Choctaw)
Massasoit
(Pokanchet)
Matoonas (Nipmuck)
Mato-Tope (Mandan)
McGillivray (Creek)
Mebea (Potawatomi)
Mecina (Apache)
Medicine Arrow
(Cheyenne)
Medicine Bottle
(Santee Sioux)
Medicine Crow
(Crow)
Medicine Horn
(Crow)
Medicine Horse
(Coyote)
Meetenwa
(Potawatomi)
Mehskehme
(Blackfeet)
Menawa
(Potawatomi)
Menomene
(Potawatomi)

*Mescotnome
(Potawatomi)
ME-SHIN-GO-ME-
SIA (Archaic)
Metacomet
(Wampanoag)
Metacoms
(Pokanchet)
Metea (Potawatomi)
Metchapagiss
(Potawatomi)
Miantonomi
(Narragansett)
Miconopi (Oconee)
Micanopy (Seminole)
Miitsisupukwuse
Pitun (Comanche)
Moanahonga (Iowa)
Moara (Ute)
Mo-Chu-No-Zhi
(Ponca)
Mocksa (Potawatomi)
Moise (Salish)
Mokohoko (Sauk)
Moless' (Sac & Fox)
Momee-shee (Maha)
Mon-Chonsia
(Kansas)
Monaco (Nipmuck)
Mona (Potawatomi)
Monkaushka (Sioux)
Moon Day
(Chippewa)
Mope-Chu-Cope
(Comanche)
Mo-pe-ma-nee
(Maha)
Moses (Sinkiuse)
Mougo (Teton Sioux)
Mougo (Miami)
Moukaushka (Yankton
Sioux)
Mountain Chief
(Blackfoot)
Mowa (Potawatomi)*

*Mow Way (Comanche)
Moxus (Abnaki)
Moytoy (Cherokee)
Much-kah-tah-moway
(Potawatomi
Mumagechee
(Oaksoy)
Mushalatubee
(Choctaw)
Muttaump (Nipmuck)
Muthtee (Coosade)
Nachite (Apache)
Nah-Et-Luc-Hopie
(Muskogee)
Naiche (Chiricahua)
Nana (Apache)
Nanawonggabe
(Chippewa)
Nanamocomuck
(Penacook)
Nanapashemet
(Nipmuc)
Nan-Nouce-Rush-Ee-
Toe (Sauk)
Nanouseka
(Potawatomi)
Nanotomenut
(Penacook)
Napikiteeta
(Piankashaw)
Natsowachehee
(Natchez)
Nautchegno
(Potawatomi)
Nawapamanda (Wea)
Nawat (Arapaho)
Nawkaw (Winnebago)
Neamathla (Seminole)
Neamico (Muscogee)
Neathlock (Cusetah)
Neebosh
(Potawatomi)
Necomah (Siletz)
Nehalam (Siletz)*

*Nehemantha
(Apalachicola)
Nelson (Muckleshoot)
Nemantha-Micco
(Creek)
Nenchoop (Neah
Village)
Neomonni (Iowa)
Nesourquoit (Sac &
Fox)
Nicaagat (Ute)
Nicameus (Kwantlens)
Ninigret
(Narragansett)
Ninusize (Cilan)
Nittakechi (Choctaw)
No Heart (Sioux)
No Shirt (Walla
Walla)
Nobah (Comanche)
Noon Day (Chippewa)
No-taw-kah
(Potawatomi)
Notchimine (Iowa)
No-Tin (Chippewa)
Numphow
(Pawtucket)
Nutackachie
(Choctaw)
Ocheehajou (Natchez)
Ohequanah (Wea)
Ohiyesa (Santee
Sioux)
Oh-Ma-Tai
(Comanche)
Oho-shin-ga (Maha)
O-Hya-Wa-Mince-Kee
(Chippewa)
Okee-Makee-Quid
(Chippewa)
Old Bear (Comanche)
Old Bear (Cheyenne)
Old Crow (Crow)
Old Grass (Blackfoot
Sioux)*

Old James (Nez
Perce)
Old Joseph (Nez
Perce)
Old Looking Glass
(Nez Perce)
Old Man Afraid of His
Horse(Sioux)
Old Tobacco
(Piankashaw)
Oliver Lot (Spokane)
Ollikut (Nez Perce)
Olyugma (Costonoan)
Onasakenrat
(Mohawk)
One Bull (Hunkpapa
Sioux)
One Eye (Comanche)
One Eyed John
(Simcoe)
One-Eyed Miguel
(Sierra Apache)
Oneka (Mohican)
Oneyana (Oneida)
On-Ge-Wae
(Chippewa)
Ohyawamincekee
 (Chippewa)
Ongpatonga (Omaha)
Onondakai (Seneca)
Onoxas (Potawatomi)
Oobick (Waatch
Village)
Ooduhtsait (Oneida)
Opa-lon-ga (Maha)
Opay Mico (Tallisee)
Opechancanough
(Powhatan)
Opotheyahola
(Tuckabatchee)
Opothle-Yoholo
(Creek)
Opototache (Tallisee)
Oquakabee (Natchez)
Orono (Penobscot)

Osceola (Seminole)
Oskanondonha
(Oneida)
Otsiquette (Oneida)
Otsinoghiyata
(Onondaga)
Otter Belt
(Comanche)
Ouray (Ute)
Over The Buttes
(Comanche)
Ow-hi (Yakama)
Oyeocker
(Appamattuck)
Paddy Welsh (Creek)
Pahayuca
(Comanche)
Pah-hat (Neah
Village)
Pahkah (Comanche)
Pai-yeh (Osette
Village)
Papakeecha (Miami)
Paranuarimuco-Jupe
(Comanche)
Pareiya (Comanche)
Paruaguita
(Comanche)
Paruaquipitsi
(Comanche)
Pa-she-Nine
(Chippewa)
Pashepahaw (Sac and
Fox)
Passaconaway
(Penacook)
Passaquo (Agawam)
Patkanim
(Snoqualmie)
Pawnawneahpahbe
(Yankton Sioux)
Pawnee Killer (Oglala
Sioux)
Paxinos (Shawnee)

Peamuska
(Musquakee)
Peaneesh
(Potawatomi)
Pebriska-Rubpa
(Hidatsa)
Pedro (Apache)
Pee-Che-Kin
(Chippewa)
Pee-pin-oh-waw
(Potawatomi)
Peo (Umatilla)
Peo-peo-thalekt
(Umatilla)
Perig (Potawatomi)
Perits-Shinakpas
(Crow)
Pernerney
(Comanche)
Peskelechaco
(Pawnee)
Pesotem (Potawatomi)
Pessacus
(Narraganset)
Peta Nocoma
(Comanche)
Petalesharo (Pawnee)
Peter Chafean
(Kalapuya)
Peter Cornstalk
(Archaic)
Peter Wapeto
(Chelan)
Peu-Peu-Mox-Mox
(Walla Walla)
Phil Peters (Saginaw
Chippewa)
Philip Martin
(Mississippi)
Pine Leaf (Gros
Ventre)
Pinnus (Nanimoos)
Pinto (Ute)
Pisumi Napu
(Comanche)

Pleasant Porter
(Creek)
Plenty Bear (Arapaho)
Plenty Coups (Crow)
Pocatello (Shoshone)
Poker Jim (Walla
Walla)
Po-lat-kin (Spokan)
Pomham
(Narraganset)
Pontiac (Ottowa)
Poor Coyote
(Comanche)
Pope (Tewa)
Poteokemia (Sac &
Fox)
Poundmaker
(Blackfoot)
Powasheek (Sauk and
Fox)
Powder Face
(Arapaho)
Powhatan (Powhatan)
Pretty Eagle (Crow)
Propio-Maks (Walla
Walla)
Pteh Skah (Assiniboin)
Puckeshinwa
(Shawnee)
Pushican (Shoshone)
Pushmataha
(Choctaw)
Pushmataha (Fox)
Putcheco
(Potawatomi)
Quai-eck-ete
(Molalla)
Quaiapen
(Wampanoag)
Qual-chan (Yakima)
Quanah Parker
(Comanche)
Quashquame (Sauk/
Foxes

Quatawapea
(Shawnee)
Quia-eck-ete
(Molalla)
Quick Bear (Sioux)
Quil-ten-e-nock
(Yakima)
Quiniapin
(Narraganset)
Quinkent (Ute)
Quiziachigiate
(Capote)
Qwatsinas (Nuxalk)
Rabbit's Skin Leggins
(Nez Perce)
Rainbow (Nez Perce)
Rain-in-the-Face
(Sioux)
Red Bird (Chippewa)
Red Bird (Winnebago)
Red Chief (Palouse)
Red Cloud (Lakota)
Red Dog (Sioux)
Red Eagle (Creek)
Red Echo (Nez Perce)
Red Fish (Oglala
Sioux)
Red Grizzly Bear (Nez
Perce)
Red Heart (Nez
Perce)
Red Horse (Sioux)
Red Indian (Ute)
Red Jacket (Seneca)
Red Leaf (Brule'
Red Nose (Fox)
Red Owl (Nez Perce)
Red Shirt (Sioux)
Red Thunder
(Yanklonai Sioux)
Red Whip (Gros
Ventres)
Red Wolf (Nez Perce)
Renville (Sisseton
Sioux)

Returning Wolf
(Comanche)
Richard Ward
(Poosepatuck)
Robbinhood
(Pawtucket)
Rolling Thunder
(Comanche)
Roman Nose
(Cheyenne)
Rouensa (Kaskaskia)
Rouls (Nuchawanack)
Roving Wolf
(Comanche)
Runaawitt
(Pawtucket)
Running Antelope
(Hunkpapa)
Running Bear (Sioux)
Running Bird (Kiowa)
Running Fisher (Gros
Ventres)
Running Rabbit
(Blackfoot)
Runs The Enemy
(Sioux)
Rushing Bear
(Pawnee)
Sa-da-ma-ne (Maha)
Sagamore John
(Nipmuck)
Saggakew (Agawam)
Saghwareesa
(Tuscarora)
Sah-dit-le-uad
(Waatch Village)
Sahhaka (Mandan)
Sakuma (Kiowa)
Salmon (Salishan)
Sam Jones (Seminole)
Samoset (Abknaki)
Samuel Chocote
(Creek)
Sanaco (Comanche)
Sanhyle (Sanpoil)

Sanilac (WyanPatte)
Santa Anna
(Comanche)
Santana (Kiowa)
Santank (Kiowa)
Santos (Aravipa
Apache)
Sapo-Noway (Yakima)
Sargerito (Comanche)
Sar-sarp-kin (Salish)
Sassaba (Chippewa)
Sassacus (Pequot)
Saturiwa (Timucua)
Scal-le-tush (Palouse)
Scarrowyady
(Oneida)
Scatchad (Neetlum)
Schonchin (Modoc)
Schwatka (Tulalip)
Scitteaygusset
(Pawtucket)
Scituate (Agawam)
Seattle (Suquamish)
See-non-ty-a (Iowa)
Selocta (Creek)
Sequoya (Cherokee)
Severo (Ute)
Shabbona (Ottawa)
Shabonee
(Potawatomi)
Shakopee (Santee
Sioux)
Shahaka (Mandan)
Sharitarish (Pawnee)
Shauhaunapotinia
(Iowa)
Shavehead
(Potawatomi)
Shaumonekusse (Oto)
Sheheke (Mandan)
Shenandoah (Onieda)
Shenkah (Paiute)
Shingaba W'Ossin
(Chippewa)
Shon-gis-cah (Maha)

Shooter (Teton Sioux)
Shoshanim (Nipmuck)
Short Bull (Brule
sioux)
Shot In The Eye
(Oglala Sioux)
Shot In The Hand
(Apsaroke)
Showaway (Cayuse)
Shustook (Tlingit)
Sianton (Kitchie)
SidpminaPata (Iowa)
Sinnahoom
(Waskalatchat)
Siskiyou (Siletz)
Sitting Bear (Kiowa)
Sitting Bull
(Hunkpapa Sioux)
Skemiah (Simcoe)
Skimia (Walla Walla)
Skowel (Skokomish)
Sky Chief (Pawnee)
Sleeping Wolf
(Comanche)
Sleeping Wolf (Kiowa)
Slockish (Walla
Walla)
Sluiskin (Skykomish)
Smoholly (Simcoe)
Smoke (Ponca)
Sobotar (Capote)
Soholessee (Natchez)
Soko (Comanche)
Sonikat (Snoqualmie)
Sopitchin (Teitton)
Sorrel Horse
(Arapaho)
Sparhecher (Creek)
Spencer (Cheyenne)
Spirit Talker
(Comanche)
Spotted Bear (Kiowa)
Spotted Crow (Sioux)
Spotted Eagle (Nez
Perce)

Spotted Leopard
(Comanche)
Spotted Tail (Brule
Sioux)
Spreckled Snake
(Snake)
Spring Frog
(Cherokee)
Squagis (Nanimoos)
Squanto (Pawhatan)
Standing Arrow
(Mohawk)
Standing Bear
(Lakota Sioux)
Standing Bear
(Ponca)
Standing Buffalo
(Kaposia Sioux)
Standing Elk (Brule')
Standing Turkey
(Cherokee)
Stan Waite (Cherokee)
Steencoggy (Molalla)
Steep Wind (Lakota)
Stic-cas (Cayuse)
Stilnaleeje (Coosade)
Stimafutchkee
(Coosade)
Stone Calf
(Comanche)
Stone Eater (Wea)
Storm (Arapaho)
Striker (Apache)
Struck By The Ree
(Yankton Sioux)
Stumbling Bear
(Kiowa)
Stumickosucks
(Blood)
Stwyre (Simcoe)
Sun Eagle
(Comanche)
Surrounded (Kiowa)
Swan (Wea)
Swell (Neah Village)

Swift Bear (Brule')
Tabbananica
(Comanche)
Tabbaccus
(Unkechaug)
Tack-en-su-a-tis (Nez
Perce)
Tah-a-howtl (Makah)
Tahalo (Neah Village)
Tah-Chee (Cherokee)
Tahrohon (Iowa)
Tahtahqueesa
(Oneida)
Tahts-kin (Neah
Village)
Talankamani
(Khemnichan)
Tall Bull (Cheyenne)
Tall Eagle Blackfoot
Sioux)
Tall Tree (Comanche)
Tallassee (Creek)
Tamahay (Sioux)
Tammany (Delaware)
Tamulston (Skam
Swatch)
Ta-noh-ga (Maha)
Tarantine (Penacook)
Ta-reet-tae (Maha)
Tarhe (Huron)
Tascalusa
(Mississippian)
Tasunkkakokipapi
(Oglala Lakota)
Tatubem (Pequot)
Tawny Bear
(Comanche)
Taza (Chiricahua)
Tcheenuk (Sanutch)
Tchoops (Pellault)
Tchoo-quut-lah (Neah
Village)
Tecumseh (Shawnee)
Ten Bears
(Comanche)

Ten Sticks
(Comanche)
Tenaya (Ah-wah-ne-
chee)
Tendoy (Lemhi
Shoshone)
Tennowikah
(Comanche)
Tenskwatawa
(Shawnee)
Te-sha-va-gran
(Maha)
Tet-li-mi-Chief
(Yakima)
The Brass Man
(Comanche)
The Crafty One
(Comanche)
The Crow
(Comanche)
The Dog (Comanche)
The Prophet
(Shawnee)
The Six (Ojibway)
Theyendanega
(Mohawk)
Thockoteehee
(Natchez)
Thomas (Walla Walla)
Thomas Hoyle
(Chowan)
Thomas LeFlore
(Choctaw)
Three Feathers (Nez
Perce)
Three White Crows
(Atsina)
Thunder Chief
(Blackfoot)
Thunder Cloud
(Blackfeet)
Tiamah (Fox)
Tiema Blanca
(Mouche)
Tilcoax (Palouse)

Timothy (Nez Perce)
Timpoochy Barnard
(Yuchi)
Tin-Tin-Meet-Sa
(Umatilla)
Tishcohan (Delaware)
Tlah-Co-Glass
(Tlakluit)
Tochoaca (Ute)
Tochoway
(Comanche)
Togulki (Creek)
Toion (Kashaya)
Tokacon (Yankton
Sioux)
Toke (Snoqualmie)
Tomasket (Colville)
Tomason (Nez Perce)
Tontileago (WyanPat)
Too-hool-hool-zote
(Nez Perce)
Too-whaai-tan
(Waatch Village)
Topinibe
(Potowatami)
Tortohonga (Yankton
Sioux)
Tortongawakw
(Yankton Sioux)
Tosa Pokoo
(Comanche)
Tosacowadi
(Comanche)
Tosawi (Comanche)
Toshaway
(Comanche)
Totkeshajou (Tallisee)
Touch-the-Clouds
(Minneconjou)
True Eagle
(Missouria)
Tsah-weh-sup (Neah
Village)
Tsal-ab-oos (Neah
Village)

Tsawatenok (Kwakiutl)

Tse-kauwtl (Makah)

Tuckabatchy (Natchez)

Tuekakas (Nez Perce)

Tuko-See-Mathla (Seminole)

Turkey Leg (Cheyenne)

Turning Hawk (Sioux)

Tushanaah (Coweta)

Tustennuggee Emathla (Creek)

Tuthinepee (Potawatomi)

Two Belly (Crow)

Two Guns White Calf (Blackfoot)

Two Hatchett (Kiowa)

Two Leggings (Northern Cheyenne)

Two Moons (Cheyenne)

Two Strike (Brule Sioux)

Ugly Game (Comanche)

Umapine (Cayuse-Umatilla)

Uinta (Umatilla)

Unanquoset (Penacook)

Uncas (Mohegan)

Unkompoin (Wampanoag)

Untongasahaw (Yankton Sioux)

Utina (Timucua)

Utsinmalikin (Nez Perce)

Victorio (Membres Apache)

Vincent (Coeur d' Alene)

Waapashaw (Sioux)

Waa-Top-E-Not (Chippewa)

Wabasha (Santee Sioux)

Wack-shie (Neah Village)

Waemboeshkaa (Chippewa)

Wahangnonawitt (Squomsquot)

Wahmeshemg (Potawatomi)

Wakaunhaka (Winnebago)

Wakawn (Winnebago)

Wakechai (Sauk)

Wak-kep-tup (Waatch Village)

Walamuitkin (Nez Perce)

Wallace Charging Shield (Sioux)

Wallachin (Cascade)

Wamditanka (Mdewakanton Sioux)

Wa-Na-Ta (Yankton Sioux)

Waneta (Iowa)

Wangewa (Iowa)

Wants To Be Chief (Sioux)

Wa-Pel-La (Musquake

Wapello (Sauk and Fox)

Wapowats (Cheyenne)

Warawasen (Setalcott)

War Bonnet (Cheyenne)

War Captain (Nambe)

War Cry (Kiowa)

War Eagle (Yankton Sioux)

War Eagle (Comanche)

War Shield (Crow)

Ward Coachman (Creek)

Washakie (Shoshone)

Wash-ca-ma-nee (Maha)

Wa-shing-ga-sabba (Maha)

Wasitasunke (Sioux)

Watchemonne (Iowa)

Waukesha (Ute)

WAY-WEL-EA-PY (Archaic)

Weasel Tail (Piegan)

We-du-gue-noh (Maha)

Weetamoo (Pocasset)

Wegaw (Potawatomi)

Wellamotkin (Nez Perce)

Weninock (Yakima)

Weshcubb (Chippewa)

Wetcunie (Otoe)

Wey-ti-mi-Chief (Yakima)

Weuche (Yankton Sioux)

White Bear (Kiowa)

White Bird (Nez Perce)

White Buffalo (Blackfeet)

White Bull (Minneconjou Sioux)

White Bull (Comanche

White Crane (Comanche)

White Eagle (Pawnee)

White Hair (Comanche)

White Hair (Kansa)

White Hawk (Minneconjou Sioux)

White Ghost (Kiowa)

White Horse (Kiowa)

White Horse (Yankton Sioux)
White Loon (Wea)
White Path (Cherokee)
White Shield (Comanche)
White Shield (Cheyenne)
White Swan (Yakama)
White Swan (Sioux)
White Thunder (Sioux)
White Wolf (Comanche)
Wickaninnish (Clayoquot)
Wicked Chief (Cheyenne)
Wild Cat (Seminole)
Wild Hog (Cheyenne)
Wild Horse (Comanche)
Wilford Taylor (Choctaw)
William (Neah Village)
William McIntosh (Creek)
William Weatherford (Creek)
Winamac (Potawatomi)
Winemakoos (Potawatomi)
Winriscah Dagenette (Wea)
Wishecomaque (Sac and Fox)
Witsitony (Comanche)
Wizikute (Sioux)
Wogam (Potawatomi)
Wogaw (Potawatomi)
Wohawa (Pawtucket)
Wolf Chief (Cheyenne)

Wolf Chief (Mandan)
Wolf King (Upper Creek)
Wolf Necklace (Palouse)
Wolf Road (Comanche)
Wolf Robe (Cheyenne)
Wolf tied with hair (Comanche)
Woman's Heart (Kiowa)
Wompatuck (Agawam)
Wonalancet (Penacook)
Wooden Leg (Cheyenne)
Woosamequin (Wampanoag)
Wopigwooit (Pequot)
Wovoka (Paiute)
Wyandanch (Montauk)
Xinesi (Tejas)
Yaha-Hajo (Seminole)
Yalukus (Molalla)
Yamparika-Povea (Comanche)
Yelleppit (Walla Walla)
Yellow Bear (Comanche)
Yellow Beaver (Wea)
Yellow Bird (Walla Walla)
Yellow Bull (Nez Perce)
Yellow Bull (Palouse)
Yellow Hair (Sioux)
Yellow Thunder (Ho-chunk)
Yellow Wolf (Nez Perce)
Ymipazo (Yakima)
Yonaguska (Cherokee)

Yoholo-Micco (Creek)
Yonipaw Camarake (Yakima)
Yooch-boott (Tsoo-yess)
Young Black Dog (Osage)
Young Chief (Cayuse)
Young Mahaskah (Iowa)
Young Tobacco (Piankashaw)
Young Whirlwind (Cheyenne)
Zele (Apache)

Dedicated to those millions of native people who nurtured this land for fourteen thousand years before the invasions by the Europeans.

Aamjiwnaang
A'aninin
Aasao
Aassateaque
Abchas
Abegweit
Abeka
Abenaki
Abihka
Abitibi
Abitibiwinni
Absarokee
Absentee-Shawnee
Acadian
Acadian Metis
Acahono
Acaxee
Accohannock
Accominta
Acho Dene Koe
Achumawi
Acjachemen
Acolapissa
Acoma
Aculhuas
Acuera
Adai
Adams Lake
Adawa
Adena
Adiisha Dena
Adirondack
Adnondeck
Afognak
Afton
Afton Mi'kmag
Agaiduka
Agawam
Agdaagux
Aginaa's
Agonnousioni
Aguacaleyquen

Agua Caliente
Ahantchuyuk
Ahopo
Ahousaht
Aht
Ahtahkakoop
Ahtena
Ah-wah-nee-chee
Ais
Aishihik
Aisious
Aivilivmiut
Ak Chin
Akainwa
Akhiok
Akiachak
Akiak
Aklauik
Akutan
Akwaala
Akwesasne
Alabama
Alabama-Coushatta
Alabamus-Koasati
Alachua
Alakanuk
Alamo
Alaska
Alatna
Alberta
Alcatraz
Alderville
Aleknagik
Alexandria
Alexis
Alexis Creek
Algaacig
Algonquian
Alibamu
Alibamous
Alickas
Alkah

Allakaket
Allalie's
Alleghan
Alleghenny
Alliklik
Alnombak
Alonas
Alpowai
Alsea
Altamahaguez
Altmautluak
Alturas
Aluet
Aluque
Aluste
Alutiig
Altamuskeet
Amacano
Amacapiras
Amah
Amahuaca
Amalecite
Ambler
American Indian
Americone
Amonsoquath
Anadaca
Anadahcoe
Anadariko
Anaktuvuk Pass
Anasaguntacook
Andastonez
Andato honato
Anderson Lake
Androscoggin
Angoon
Anhawas
Aniak
Anisazi
Anishinaabe
Anishinabek
Aniyunwiya

Annapolis Valley
Annette Island
An-stohin/Unami
Antelope Valley
Anvik
Aondironon
Aosamiajijij
Apache
Apalachicola
Apalachee
Apineus
Applegate
Aposkwayak
Appomattox
Appomatuck
Apsaaloke
Apsaroke
Aquelon
Aquidneck
Aquinnah
Aranama
Arapahoe
Arapaja
Arapooish
Arawak
Archaic
Arctic
Arikara
Arkansas
Arogisti
Aroland
Aroostook
Arosaguntacock
Arsenipoit
Asa'carsarmiut
Asapo
Ashaninka
Ashcroft
Ashepoos
Ashiapkawi
Asilanapi
Aslatakapa
Asnon
Assateaque
Assinais

Assiniboine
Atahun
Atakapa
Atakara
Atamauluak
Atasi
Ataxam
Atfalati
Atgasuk
Athabasca Chipewyan
Athapaskan
Atikamekw
Atka
Atlatls
Atlin
Atna
Atsina
Atsugewi
Attikamekew
Audusta
Augustine
Auk
Aunie
Avavares
Avoyel
Awaitlala
Awani
Awasis
Awatixa
Awatobi
Awaxawi
Ayotore
Ays
Aztec
Baada
Babine
Bad Faces
Bad River
Baffin Land
Bahwetig
Baisimete
Bannok
Barona
Barona Capitan
Barren Lands

Barriere Lake
Barrio Pascua
Batchewana
Battle Mountain
Bay King
Bay Mills
Bayagoulas
Bear Lake
Bear River
Beardy's & Okemasis
Bears Paw
Bearskin Lake
Beaver
Beecher Bay
Bejessi
Belkofski
Bella Bella
Bella Coola
Benton Paiute
Beothuk
Berengia
Berens River
Berry Creek
Betatakin
Betsiamites
Bidai
Big Bend
Big Cove
Big Cypress Seminole
Big Grassy
Big Island
Big Lagoon
Big Meadows Lodge
Big Pine
Big River
Big Sandy
Big Valley
Bigstone
Bigstone Cree
Biidaajimo
Biinjitwaabik
Biktasateetuse
Bill Moons Slough
Biloxi
Birch Creek

Birch Narrows
Birdtail Sioux
Bishop Paiute-
Shoshone
Bithani
Black Hill Sioux
Black Lake
Denesuline
Black River
Black Sturgeon
Blackfeet
Blackfoot
Blewmouths
Blood
Blood Tribe
Bloodvein
Blue Lake
Blueberry River
Boca Jhaon
Bodego Miwok
Bois Forte
Boise
Boneparte
Boothroyd
Boston Bar
Bow
Brandywine
Brevig Mission
Bridge River
Bridgeport
Brighton Seminole
Brokenhead Objibway
Broman Lake
Brotherton
Brule'
Brule Sioux
Bruneau
Buckland
Buctouche
Buena Vista
Buffalo Point
Buffalo River
Bull Head
Bungi
Burns Lake

Burns Paiute
Burnt Church
Burt Lake
Bussenmeus
Cabazon
Cabinoios
Cachil De He
Cachil Dette
Cachipile
Cacores
Cadboro Bay
Caddo
Caddo Adias
Caghnawaga
Cahinnio
Cahita
Cahokia
Cahto
Cahuilla
Cajuenche
Cajun
Calamwas
Calapooya
Calaveras County
Caldwell
Callipipas
Caloosa
Calusa
Cambas
Camin Lake
Camkuota
Camp Verde
Campo
Camuilla
Canabas
Canarsee
Cane Break
Canim
Canoe Creek
Canoe Lake
Canoncito
Canoyeas
Cantwell
Caouachas
Capachequi

Caparaz
Cape
Cape Fear
Capiga
Capinan
Capitan Grande
Capote
Carcross/Tagish
Cariboo
Carlin
Carmel
Carmel Mission
Carrier Sekani
Carrizo
Carry The Kettle
Carson
Carson Colony
Washoe
Cascade
Cascanque
Casco
Castachas
Castasue
Catabwa
Cathlacomatup
Cathlakaheckit
Cathlamet
Cathlanahquiah
Cathlapotle
Cathlathlalas
Catowbi
Cattaraugus
Caughnawaga
Cawittas
Cayoose Creek
Cayuga
Cayuse
Cedar City
Cedarville
Celillo
Chacci Oumas
Chachachouma
Chacchiuma
Chaco
Chaco Canyon

Chacato
Chadiere
Chaguaguas
Chahta
Chaiwa-Tewa
Chaloklowas
Chakankni
Chalkyitsik
Champagne
Chanchon's
Chanega
Chantorabin
Chapel Island
Chapen
Chapleau
Chappequiddick
Charah
Charew
Charley Creek
Chastacosta
Chatot
Chats
Chaushila
Chavi
Chawasha
Chayimanak
Chefornak
Chehalis
Chehaw
Chekalis
Chelan
Chelemela
Chemahawin
Chemainus
Chemakum
Chemapho
Chemehuevi
Chenakisses
Chenkus
Chepenala
Cher-Ae Heights
Cherokee
Cherow
Chesapeake
Cheslatta

Cheslatta Carrier
Chespiooc
Chesterfield
Chetco
Chevak
Cheveux on Port leue'
Cheveux relevez
Chewella
Cheyenne
Cheyenne River Sioux
Chiaha
Chi
Chichen
Chichimeco
Chickahominy
Chickaloon
Chickamauga
Chickasaw
Chickataubut
Chicken Ranch
Chico
Chicora-Siouan
Chictaghick
Chideh
Chignik
Chignik Lagoon
Chignik Lake
Chihokokis
Chilkat
Chilkoot
Chilliwack
Chilluckkittequaw
Chilocotin
Chilula
Chilucan
Chimakuan
Chimariko
Chimsean
Chine
Chinik
Chininoas
Chiniquay
Chinook
Chinookan
Chipewyan

Chippewa
Chiricahua
Chisasibi
Chistochina
Chitimacha
Chitina
Chilula
Chiwere
Chochiti
Chochnewwasroonaw
Choctaw
Choinumni
Chokonen
Chougaskabee
Choula
Choumaus
Choushatta
Chowan
Chowanoc
Chowwichan
Choya'ha
Christanna
Christian Pembina
Christiantown
Chuathbaluk
Chucalissa
Chukchansi
Chuloonawick
Chumash
Cibecue Apache
Ciboney
Cilan
Cicora
Circle
Citizen
Citizen Potawatomi
Clackamas
Clallam
Clark's Point
Clatskanie
Clatsop
Clayoquot
Clear Lake
Clearwater River
Dene

Clifton-Choctaw
Cloverdale
Clovis
Clowwewalla
Coahuilteco
Coaque
Coast
Coast Miwok
Coastal Band
Coastanoan
Cocatoonemaug
Cochimi
Cochiti Pueblo
Cocopah
Cocopu
Cofan
Cofubufu
Coharie
Coka
Cold Lake
Cold Springs
Colorado River
Columbia
Columbia Lake
Colusa
Colville
Comanche
Combahee
Comox
Conchakus
Concow
Conestoga
Congaree Eno
Connecedgas
Connewaugeroonas
Conohasset
Conoy
Conoyucksuchroona
Constance Lake
Cook's Ferry
Coos
Coosa River Creek
Coosan
Copalis
Copper

Coquille
Coranine
Corchaug
Coree
Cortina
Cosmit
Costa
Costano
Costonoan
Cote
Coticyini
Couchiching
Couer d'Alene
Council
Courte Oreilles
Coushaes
Coushatta
Covolo
Cow Creek
Cowasuck
Coweset
Cowessess
Cowetaw
Cowichan
Cowlitz
Coyote
Coyotero Apache
Craig
Cree
Creek
Crees of Quebec
Croatan
Crooked Creek
Cross Lake
Cross Lake Cree
Croton
Crow
Crow Creek Sioux
Culpala
Cultoa
Cumberland Creek
Cumberland House
Cumumbah
Cupeno
Curyung

Cusabo
Cusetah
Cussabee
Cussetaw
Cussobo
Cut Head
Cuttacochi
Cuyapaipe
Da'naxda'xw
Awaelatla
Dakota
Dakota Lake
Dakota Plains
Dakota Sioux
Dakota Tipi
Dakubetede
Dania
Darrington
Dassa Monpeake
Dauphin River
Day Star
Deadose
Dease River
Death Valley
Deeking
Deer Creek
Deer Lake
Dehcho
Delaware
Delaware-Muncee
Dena'ina
Denali
Dene
Dene Tha'
Deneh
Deschute
Devils Lake Sioux
Dewagamas
Dibaudjimoh
Diegueno
Digger
Dine'
Dineh
Diomede
Dionoudadie

Ditidaht
Dogue
Dog Creek
Dog River
Dogenga
Dogrib
Dogwood
Donnacona
Pat Lake
Douglas
Doustioni
Dresslerville
Dresslerville Washoe
Driftpile River
Dry Creek
Dubois
Duck Valley
Duckwater
Dudley
Dumanish
Duncan
Dunlap
Dwamishe Shingle
Springs
Eabametoong
Eagle
Eagle Bear
Eagle Lake
Eagle Village-Kipawa
Eano
East Cree
East Mesa
Eastern Cherokee
Eastern Shawnee
Eastman
Ebahamo
Ebb and Flow
Echota
Edisto
Eek
Eeyou
Eel Ground
Eel River
Eel River Bar
Egegig

Ehatteshaht
Eklutna
Ekok
Ekuk
Ekwok
Elasie
Elem
Elim
Elk
Elko
Elwha
Ely
Ely Shoshone
Embera
Emmonak
English River
Eno
Enoch Cree
Enterprise
Entiat
Epesengles
Epicerinis
Erie
Erie See
Ermineskin
Escaamba
Escamacu
Eskasoni
Esketemic
Eskimo
Esopus
Espogache
Esquimalt
Esselen
Essipit
Estotoe
Etchemin
Etiwa
Etocale
Etowah
Euchee
Eufaula
Eureka
Evansville
Eves

Exangue
Eyak
Eyeish
Faircloth
Fairford
Fall River
Fallon
Fallon Paiute-
Shoshone
False Pass
Faroan
Federated Coast
Miwok
Fernandeno
Fisher River
Fishing Lake
Flandreau Santee
Sioux
Flathead
Florence
Florida Creek
Flying Dust
Flying Post
Folsom
Fond du Lac
Fond du Lac
Denesuline
Foothills Yokuts
Forest County
Potawatomi
Fort Albany
Fort Alexander
Fort Ancient
Fort Belknap
Fort Bidwell
Fort Folly
Fort Hall
Fort Independence
Fort McDermitt
Fort McKay
Fort McMurray
Fort Mohave
Fort Nelson
Fort Peck Sioux
Fort Severn

Fort Sill
Fort Ware
Fort Williams
Fort Yukon
Four Hole
Four Winds
Fox
Fox Lake
Fraser Canyon
Fremont
Fresh Water
Frog Lake
Fuel
Fuloplata
Fushootseed
Gabrielino
Gaigwu
Gakona
Galena
Galice
Galisteo
Gambell
Gambler
Ganienkeh
Garden Hill
Gaspe
Gaspen River
Gaspesiens
Gayhead
Georgetown
Georgia
Georgia Cherokee
Gesgapegiag
Gila Bend Papago
Gila River Pima-
Maricopa
Ginoogaming
Gitanmaax
Gitanyow
Git-ga'at
Gitlakdamik
Gitsegukla
Gitwangat
Gitwinksihlkw
Gitxsan

Glen Vowell
God's Lake
God's River
Golden Hill
Good News Bay
Gordon
Goshute
Grand Portage
Grand Rapids
Grand River
Grand Ronde
Grand Traverse
Grand Village
Grassey Narrows
Grave Creek
Grayling
Great Serpent
Green River Snake
Greenville
Grigra
Grindstone
Grindstone Creek
Gros
Gros Ventre
Grouard
Guacata
Guadalquini
Guajiro
Guale
Guasco
Guidiville
Gulkana
Gull Bay
Gun Lake Village
Gwa'Sala-
'Nakwaxda'xw
Gwich'in
Hackensack
Ha'degaenage
Hadley
Hagwilget
Haida
Haihais
Hainai
Haish

Haisla
Halalt
Halchidhoma
Halfway River
Haliwa-Saponi
Halkomelem
Halq'meylem
Halyikwamai
Hamilton
Han
Hanis
Hannahville
Hanneton
Hano
Hanuanos
Hare
Hare Mountain
Hasinai
Hasinais Caddo
Haso
Hassanamisko
Hassenamesitts
Hatchet Lake
Denesuline
Hathawekela
Hattadare
Hattaras
Haudenosee
Havasupai
Hawoyazask
Hayfork
Haynoke
Haytian
Healy Lake
Heart Lake
Heiltsuk
Henya
Herring Pond
Hesquiat
Hidatsa
High Bar
Hihantick
Hilabia
Hileni
Hill Patwin

Hill Wintun
Hinonoeino
Hitchiti
Hocaesle
Hocak
Ho-Chunk
Hocomawananch
Hoh
Hohokam
Hohuana
Hois
Hokan
Holikachuk
Hollow Water
Holy Cross
Homalco
Honeches
Honellaque
Honniasont
Hoomus
Hoonah
Honniasonts
Hoopa
Hoopa Valley
Hooper Bay
Hootznahoo
Hopewell
Hopi
Hopland
Hornepayne
Horse Lake
Hostaqua
Horton
Hot Creek
Hothliwahali
Houeches
Houlton
Houlton Maliseet
Houma
Housetonic
Hownonquet
Hualapai
Huanchane
Huara
Huchnon

Hughes
Huichol
Hul'qumi'num
Humptulips
Hunkpapa
Hunkpatila
Hupa
Hupascath
Huron
Huron-Wendat
Huslia
Hutali
Huttlhunssen
Huu-Ay-Aht
Hwalya
Hydaburg
Ibihica
Icafui
Igiugig
Igiulivmiut
Igurmiut
Iichisi
I'isaw
Ima
Iliamna
Illiniwek
Illinois
Inaha-Cosmit
Inaja
Inde
Indian Birch
Indian Brook
Indian Canyon
Indian Island
Indian Knoll
Indian Township
Ingalik
Innocence
Innu
Innu-Aionun
In-shuck-ch/n'quatqua
Intielikum
Inuktitut
Inuit
Inuk

Inuna-ina
Inupaiq
Inutitut
Ione
Ioway
Iquluit
Iroquet
Iroquois
Isabella
Iskut
Iskutewizaagegan
Island
Island Lake
Islandlittle
Isleta
Iswa
Itaba
Itawan
Itazipco
Itivimiut
Ituan
Itza
Ivanoff Bay
Iviatim
Iwiktie
Jacal
Jackhead
Jackson Rancheria
James Smith
Jamestown
Jamestown S'Klallam
Jamul
Jatibonicu
Jeaga
Jemez Pueblo
Jena
Jhee-challs
Jicarilla
John Day
Joseph Bighead
Juamo
Juaneno
Jupe
K'omok
Kadohadacho

Kagita-Mikam
Kaguyak
Kah-Bay-Kah-Nong
Kahkewistahaw
Kahnawake
Kahon:wes's
Kahtonik
Kaibab
Kainai
Kake
Kaktovik
Kakumlutch
Kalapauga
Kalapooian
Kalapuya
Kalgani
Kalispel
Kalnawake
Kalskag
Kaltag
Kaluschian
Kamia
Kamloops
Kampa
Kanaka
Kanalak
Kanankawa
Kanatak
Kanesatake
Kaniagmiut
Kanien'kehaka
Kansa
Kaoutyas
Kapawe'no
Kaposia Sioux
Kappas
Karakwaw
Karankawa
Kareses
Karluk
Karok
Kasaan
Kasabonika Lake
Kashaya Pomo
Kashia

Kasigluk
Kasihta
Kaska
Kaska Dena
Kaskaskia
Kaskaya
Kaskinampo
Katlammet
Kato
Katzie
Kavelchadom
Kaviagmiut
Kaw
Kawacatoose
Kawaiisu
Kawchottine
Kaweah
Kawe'sqar
Kayapo
Kaytenta
Kealeychi
Keechi
Keeseekooenin
Keeseekoose
Kee-too-wah
Keewatin
Keewatinowi
Kee-Way-Win
Kehabous
Kehewin
Kenaitze
Kenisteno
Kenowun
Keres
Keresan
Kern Valley
Keroa
Ketchikan
Kettle Point
Keweenaw Bay
Key
Key Band
Keyauwee
Khotana
Khot-La-Cha

Kiabab
Kialegee
Kiana
Kiawa
Kichai
Kickapoo
Kigiktamiut
Kikiallus
Kilatak
Kilispel
Killisnoo
Kimsquit
Kina'matnewey
Kinbasket
Kincolith
King Island
Kingfisher Lake
Kingsclear
Kinistin
Kinuguit
Kinuhmiut
Kiowa
Kipnuk
Kiscakous
Kispoix
Kispoko
Kitamat
Kitanemuk
Kitasoo
Kitchie
Kitcisakik
Kite
Kitigan Zibi
Anishinabeg
Kititas
Kitkehahki
Kitlope
Kitsagh
Kitsai
Kitselas
Kitsumkalum
Kivalina
Kiwigapawa
Kiwistinok
Klahoose

Klallam
Klamath
Klanoh
Klasset
Klatklam
Klatsap
Klatskanie
Klatstonis
Klawock
Klickitat
Klodesseaottine
Kluskus
Kluti Kaah
Knik
Koasati
Koasota
Kobuk
Kobukmiut
Kodiak
Kogohue
Kolash
Kolchan
Kolomi
Kolomoki
Kolushan
K'omoks
Kongiganak
Konkonelp
Konkow
Konomihu
Kootenai
Kopagmiut
Koprino
Koroa
Koshare
Koskimo
Koso
Kotlik
Kot'sai
Kotsoteka
Kotzebue
Kouchiching
Koutani
Koutenay
Kowalitsk

Koyuk
Koyukon
Koyukuk
Ktunaxa
Ktunaxa/Kinbasket
Kuaua
Kugmiut
Kuitsh
Kuiu
Kullullucton
Kumeyaay
Kumiai
Kuskokwim
Kusso-Natchez
Kutchin
Kutenai
Kwadahi
Kwagiutl
Kwahada
Kwaiailk
Kwak'wala
Kwalhioqua
Kuitsh
Kwandahi
Kwantlen
Kwatna
Kwa-Wa-Aineuk
Kwayhquitlum
Kwethluk
Kwiakah
Kwicksutaneuk-
Ahhwaw-
Ah-Mish
Kwigillingok
Kwinhagak
Kyuquot
L'Ecureuil
La Conner
La Jolla
La Posta
La Romane
Lac Courte Oreilles
Lac Des Milles
Lac du Flambeau
Lac La Croix

Lac La Ronge
Lac View Desert
Lac-Saint-Jean
Lac-Simon
Lacumeros
Laguna
Laich-kwil-tach
Lakahahmen
Lakalzap
Lake Babine
Lake Helen
Lake Manitoba
Lake Miwok
Lake Nespelem
Lake Nipigon Ojibway
Lake St. Martin
Lake Superior
Lake Traverse Sioux
Lakes
Lakmut
Lakota
Lakota Wowapi
Lamale
Langley
Lansdowne House
L'Anse
Laplako
Lapwai
Larsen Bay
Las Vegas
Lassik
Latgawa
Laurentian
Lax-Kw'Alaams
Laytonville
Leech Lake
Lemhi
Lenape
Lenechas
Lenni-Lenape
Lennox Island
Lesnoi
Levelok
Lheidli
Lheidli Tenneh

Lheit-lit'en
Liano
Liard
Likely
Lillooet
Lime
Lipan
Listigui
Listuguj
Little Black Bear
Little Black River
Little Grand Rapids
Little Pine
Little Red River Cree
Little River
Little Saskatchewan
Little Shell
Little Shuswap
Little Traverse Bay
Lkumbsen
Llaneros
Loafer/Sioux
Lochapoka
Lohim
Lone Pine Paiute-
Shoshone
Long Island
Long Lake
Long Plain
Long Point
Lookout
Loon River Cree
Los Coyotes
Lost Ranier
Louis Bull Tribe
Luiseno
Louisiana
Loup
Lovelock
Lower Brule Sioux
Lower Elwha
Lower Kalskag
Lower Kootenay
Lower Nicola
Lower Similkameen

Lower Sioux
Lower Umpqua
Lower Yanklonai
Loyal Shawnee
Lubicon Lake
Luckiamute
Lucky Man
Luiseno
Lumbee
Lummi Nation
Lumni
Lushootseed
Lutainian
Lyackson
Lynch's
Lytton
M'chigeeng
Macah
Macapiras
Machapunga
Machia Lower Creek
Mackinac
Magaehnak
Maha
Mahapony
Mahekanande
Mahican
Maidu
Maihais
Makah
Maklak
Makoutepoeis
Makwasahgaiehcan
Malataute
Malecite
Malecites of Viger
Maliseet
Malmiut
Mamaceqtaw
Mamaleleqala-
qweqwa-sot-enox
Manahoac
Manakin
Manawan
Manchester

Mandan
Mangakekis
Mangas Apache
Manhattan
Manley Hot Springs
Manokotak
Manso
Manzanita
Marameg
Mariame
Maricopa
Marsapeague
Marshall
Marten Falls
Martha's Vinyard
Marti Gras
Mary's Igloo
Mascouten
Mashantucket-Pequot
Mashpee
Maskegon
Maskote Pwat
Maskutick
Maskwachee
Massachuset
Massapequa
Masset Haida
Massomuck
Match-e-be-nash-
shewish
Mathias Colomb
Matinecock
Mattabesic
Mattachee
Mattapoist
Mattaponi
Mattole
Maumee
Mapuche
Mawihl Nakoatok
Mawiomi
Maya
Mazipskiwik
McDowell Lake
McGrath

McLeod Lake
Mdewakanton Sioux
Mdewakantonwon
Meadow Lake
Mechoopda
Medaywakanoan
Meherrin
Meit
Mekoryuk
Melochundum
Melunglons
Membertou
Membrino Apache
Menasha
Mendocino
Menominee
Mentasta
Mentous
Merherrin
Merrick
Mesa Grande
Mescalero Apache
Meskwaki
Meso-Indians
Mesquacki
Metepenagiag
Methow
Metis
Metlakahtla
Metoac
Me-wuk
Michigamea
Mi'Kmag
Mi'Kmaw
Miami
Miao
Miawpukek
Mibinamik
Mical
Miccosucci
Michif
Michigamea
Michipicoten
Micmac
Middletown

Mikamawey
Mikisew
Mi'Kmag
Mi'Kmaw
Mikmawisimk
Millbrook
Mille Lacs
Miluk
Mimbre
Minatarre
Mingan
Mingo
Miniconjou Sioux
Minisink
Minnesota Chippewa
Minquas
Minto
Misawum
Misga
Mishikwutmetunne
Mission
Mississauga
Mississinewa
Mississippi
Missosukee
Missouri
Mistapnis
Mistassill
Mistassini
Mistawasis
Mitchell Bay
Mitchigamuas
Mitgan
Mitla
Miwok
Mixe
Moallalla
Moapa Nevada
Mobile
Mocama
Mocogo
Modoc
Mogollon
Mojave
Mohawk

Mohegan
Mohican
Moingwena
Molala
Monacan
Monache
Moneton
Mongontatchas
Monie
Mono
Monshackotoog
Montagnais
Montagne
Montana
Montauk
Montaukett
Montgomery Creek
Montreal Lake Cree
Moor
Mooretown
Moosomin
Moratoc
Moravian
Moricetown
Morongo
Mosa
Mosakahiken
Moses
Mosookee
Mosopelea
Mosquito Grizzly
Bear
Mouche
Mount Currie
Mountain
Mousonis
Mowa
Mowachaht
Muckleshoot
Mugulasha
Muh-he-ka-ne-ok
Muin Sipu Mi'kmag
Muklasa
Mukwema
Multnomah

Muache Utes
Munatagmiut
Munsee
Muscogee
Muscowpetung
Musgamagw
Mushagamiut
Muskeg Lake
Muskoday
Muskogean
Muskokee
Muskokeem
Muskowekwan
Muskwaki
Musqueam
Mussissakie
Mutsun
Muwekma
Mystic
N'laka'Pamux
Naausi
Nabari
Nabesna
Nacoochee
Nadako
Nadawaska Maliseet
Nadene
Nadoka
Nadouesteaus
Nahapassunkeck
Nahew
Nahua
Nahuatl
Nahyssan
Naicatchewenin
Naichoas
Nakhuston
Nakne
Nakoaktok
Nakota
Naltunnetunne
Nambe
Namgis
Nanasoho
Nanimoos

Nansemond
Nanticoke
Nanwalek
Napaimute
Napaskiak
Napgitache
Napochi
Narragansett
Nase-Gitksen
Nasharo
Naskapi
Naskapi of Quebec
Nassonis
Natchitoches
Natakmiut
Natashquan
Natchez
Natick
Nation Nueht
Nauser
Nauset
Navajo
Nawihl
Nazko
Neah Village
Nebedache
Neches
N'de
Nedhi
Neecoweegee
Nee-Tahi-Buhn
Neetlum
Nehkereages
Neketemeuk
Nekutameux
Nelson House
Nelson Lagoon
Nelson River
Nemaska
Nenana
Neo-Indians
Neosho
Nepissing
Nepnet
Nesaquake

Neskonlith
Nespelem
Netselia
Netsilik
Nettotalis
Neuse
Neusiok
Neutral
New Koliganek
New Stuyahok
New Westminster
Newark
Newhalen
Newtok
Nez Perce
Niagra
Niantic
Nicichousemenecaning
Nicola
Nicoleno
Nicomen
Nightmute
Niji Mahkwa
Nikolai
Nikolski
NI-MI-WIN
Ninilchik
Nio
Nipmuck
Nipewais
Nisenan
Nisga'a
Nishinan
Nishnabek
Niska
Nisqually
Nitinat
Noatak
No Bows
Noheum
Nohewee
Nokoni
Nomadic
Nome
Nomelaki

Nomtipom
Nondalton
Nongati
Nonowuss
Noohitch
Nooksack
Noorvik
Nooshalhlaht
Nootka
Noo-Wha-Ha
Noquet
Nor-el-muk
Norridgewalk
North Caribou Lake
North Spirit Lake
North Thompson
North West Angle
Northeast
Northern Cherokee
Northern Cheyenne
Northern Maidu
Northern Paiute
Northern Quebec
Northern Valley
Yokuts
Northfork
Northlands Dene
Northway
Northwest Coast
Northwest Shoshone
Northwestern
Norway House
Norwottock
Notchee
Nottawaseppi
Nottoway
Nowitna
Ntlakyapamuk
Nuchatlaht
Nuchawanack
Nuiqsut
Nulato
Numa
Numamiut
Nunapitchuk

Nunivagmiut
Nunivak
Nunivakhooper
Nuu-chah-nulth
Nuxalk
Nuxalko Two Kettles
Nuyaka
O'odham
Oagan Toyagungin
Oahatika
Oakfuskee
Oaksoy
Oak Lake
Oaktashippas
Obedjiwan
Objibway
Ocale
Occaneechi
Ocean Man
Ochapowace
Ochese Creek
Ochiapofa
O-Chi-Chak-ko-Sipi
O'Chiese
Ochiichagwebabigo
Ocita
Ockhoys
Ocoma
Oconee
Octotate
Ocute
Odanak
Odawa
Odsinachie
Offogoulas
Ofo
Oglala Sioux
Ogulmiut
Ohio
Ohlone
Ohogamiut
Oil Springs
Ojibway of
Onegaming
Ojibway of Pic River

Okelousa
Okanese
Okanogan
Okchai
Okfuskee
Okimakanak
Okinawan
Oklewaha
Okmulgee
Okwanuchu
Okwejagehke
Old Harbor
Old Masset Village
Omaha
Omaus
Onatheaqua
One Arrow
Oneida Nation of New
York
Oneida Nation of
Wisconsin
Ongmiaahranonon
Ongwanonsionni
Onieda
Onion Lake
Onodo
Onondaga
Ontonagon
Onyape
Oohenumpa
Oomaka Tokatakiya
Ooseooche
Oowekeeno
Opaskwayak Cree
Opatas
Opelousa
Opetchesaht
Oque Loussas
Oraibi
Ordovice
Oregon Jack Creek
Oriskany
Orista
Oromocto
Orutsararmiut

Osage
Oscarville
Osetto
Oshkaabewis
Osochi
Osoyoos
Ospogue
Osprey
Otapala
Otax
Otchagras
Otchentechakowin
Otesiskiwin
Otheuse
Oto
Otoe
Otoe-Missouri
Otomi
Ottowa
Oua
Ouabaches
Oufe Agoulas
Ouiagie
Ouje'Bougoumou
Oumamiouck
Oumas
Ounontcharonnous
Ouray
Ousita
Outachepas
Outaounones
Ouyslanous
Ouzinkie
Owanux
Oweekeno
Owenagungas
Owendats
Owens Valley
Oxford House
Oyale Lutapi
Oymut
Ozembogus
Ozette
Ozotheoa
Pabaksa

Pabineau
Pacaha
Pacheedaht
Pahrump
Pahvant
Paich-kwil-tach
Paimiut
Paiute
Pakana
Pakanii
Pakanoket
Pakit
Pakua Shipi
Pala
Pala Mission
Palaquessous
Paleanas
Palenque
Paleo-Indian
Palong
Palouse
Pamlico
Pampticough
Pamunkey
Pana
Panaloga
Panamaha
Panamint
Panana
Panara
Pani
Panimaha
Panis
Panivacha
Panka
Papago
Papenachois
Paquate
Parkeeaum
Parianuc
Pasca Oocolos
Pascsgoulas
Pascua Yaqui
Paskempa
Paskenta

Pasqua
Pass Cahuilla
Passamaquoddy
Patiri
Patofa
Patowomeck
Patuxet
Patwin
Paucatuck
Paugusett
Pauingassi
Pauloff Harbor
Pauma
Pauquachin
Pavioso
Pawhatan
Pawhuska
Pawnee
Pawokti
Pawtucket
Pays Flat
Payson
Peaurian
Peadea
Peauguicheas
Pechanga
Pecos
Pedro Bay
Peepeekisis
Peguis
Pehnahterkuh
Peigan
Pelican Lake
Pellault
Pemunkey
Penacook
Penatoka
Pend d'Orielles
Penelakut
Pennacook
Penobscott
Penotekas
Pensacola
Penticton
Penutian

Peoria
Peovis
Pepikokia
Pequawket
Pequot
Pera
Perfido Bay
Perryville
Person County
Peskadaneeoulkanti
Peter Ballantyne
Petersburg
Peticotras
Petun
Pheasant Rump
Nakota
Piachi
Pianguichias
Piankashaw
Piapot
Pia Yuman
Pic Mobert
Pic River
Picayune
Picts
Pictou Landing
Picuris
PideeKadapau
Piegan
Piekann
Pigwacket
Pikanii
Pilot Point
Pilot Station
Pilthlako
Pima
Pimaquid
Pima-Maricopa
Piman
Pinal Apache
Pinal Coyotera
Apache
Pine Creek
Pine Ridge Sioux
Pinkeshaw
Pinoleville

Pipestone Sioux
Piqua Sept
Piro
Piscataway
Piscataway-Conoy
Pit River
Pitaa
Pitahavret
Pitano
Pitka's Point
Piware
Pjobwe
Plano
Plat cotez de chiens
Plateau
Platinum
Pleasant Point
Plumas County
Poarch Creek
Pocasset
Pocomoke
Pocomtic
Pocumtuck
Pohoc
Pohogue
Pohoy
Point Barrow
Point Hope
Point Lay
Pojoaque
Pokagon
Pokanokut
Polar
Pomo
Ponca
Ponocock
Poosepatuck
Poplar Creek
Poplar Hill
Poplar River
Port Gamble
Port Graham
Port Heiden
Port Lions
Port Madison
Portage Point

Potano
Potawatomi
Potomac
Potter Valley
Poundmaker
Poverty Point
Povi-Tamu
Powhatan
Prairie
Prairie Island Sioux
Priest Rapids
Pribiloff Island
Principal Creek
Prophet River
Pshwanwapan
Pswanwapam
Pte Oyate
Puan
Pueblo
Pueblo Bonito
Puget Sound
Punhuni
Punka
Puntlach
Puturiba
Puyallup
Pyramid Lake
Qagam Toyagungin
Qagyuhl
Qahatika
Qawalangin
Quabache
Quachita
Quadichhe
Quahatika
Qualicum
Quanchas
Quanostino
Quapaw
Quara
Quartz Valley
Quassarte
Quatoghies
Quatsino
Quechan
Queet

Quiattanon
Quiattanous
Quigualtam
Quilcene
Quileute
Quimaieit
Quinaquous
Quinarbaug
Quinault
Quinipissa
Quinnepas
Quiripi
Quiripi-unquachog
Quohhada
Quonantino
Quon-di-ats
Quzinkie
Qwidicca-atx
Rainy River
Ramah
Ramapough
Ramona
Rampart
Rankokus
Rappahannock
Raritans
Red
Redding
Red Bank
Red Bluff
Red Clay
Red Cliff
Red Devil
Red Earth
Red Lake
Red Pheasant
Red Sticks
Red Sucker Lake
Redwood
Redwood Valley
Rees
Renais
Reno-Sparks
Resighini
Restigouche
Rincon

River
Roanoke
Roaring Creek
Robinson
Rockaway
Rock River
Rocky Bay
Rocky Boys
Rogue
Roherville
Rolling River
Rondaxe
Ronkokus
Roseau River
Rosebud Sioux
Round Valley
Ruby
Ruby Valley
Rumsey
S'Klallam
S'rntotchone
Saanich
Saboda
Sac
Sachdagughroonaw
Sacigo Lake
Saco
Saddle Lake
Sadlermiut
Sae
Saginaw
Sagkeeng
Sahap
Sahaptin
Sahohes
Saint George
Saint Johns
Saint Mary's
Saint Michael
Saint Paul
Sakonnet
Sakimay
Salamanco
Salamatoff
Salano
Salawik

Salchishe
Salina
Salinan
Salish
Salishan
Sallumiut
Salona
Salt River Pima-
  Maricapo
Salteaux
Saluda
Samahguam
Samish
Sammanish
Samson
San Carlos Apache
San Felipe
San Ildefonso
San Juan
San Manual
San Nicoleno
San Pasqual
San Poil
San Xavier
Sand Point
Sandia
Sandy Bay
Sandy Lacs
Sandy Lake
Sans Arc Sioux
Santa Ana
Santa Clara
Santa Rosa
Santa Ynez
Santa Ysabel
Santee Sioux
Santiam
Santo Domingo
Sanutch
Sanya
Sapala
Saponi
Sapotaweyak Cree
Sara
Sarcee

Sarsi
Saschutkenne
Satsop
Satuache
Satudene
Saturiwa
Saugeen
Sauk-Suiattle
Sault
Sault Ste. Marie
Saulteaux
Saura
Savannah
Savanois
Savoonga
Sawokli
Sawridge
Saxman
Sayisa Dene
Scammon Bay
Scaticook
Schaghticoke
Schahook
Schefferville
Scotts Valley
Secatogue
Secotan
Secwepemc-Shuswap
Sewee
Seine River
Seip
Sekanai
Selawik
Selchelt
Seldovia
Semiahmoo
Seminole
Seneca
Senijaxtee
Sequim
Seri
Serrano
Setalcott
Setauket
Seton Lake
Sewee

Shackan
Shageluk
Shagticoke
Shagtoolik
Shakopee Sioux
Shakori
Shamattawa
Shamokan
Shasta
Shawanoe
Shawonese
Shawendadie
Shawnee
Sheep Ranch
Sheldon's Point
Sherry-dika
Sherwood Valley
Shi'sha'lth
Shibogama
Shield
Shingle Springs
Shinnecock
Shipaulovi
Shi'sha'lth
Shishmaref
Shoal Lake
Shoal Lake Cree
Shoalwater Bay
Shoccaree
Shoshone
Shubenacadie
Shungnak
Shuswap
Shutaree
Sia
Siakaieth
Sicangu
Sigesh
SiHa SaPa
Siksika
Sikyakti
Siletz
Simcoe
Sinkaieth
Sinkakaius
Sinkiuse

Sinkquaius
Sinkyone
Sinodouwas
Sioux
Sioux Valley
Sishiatl
Siska
Siskiyou
Sisseton Sioux
Sisseton-Wahpeton
Sissipahaw
Sitka
Siuslaw
Skagit
Skagway
Skal vian
Skam Swatch
Skawahlook
Skeedee
Skeetchestn
Skidegate
Skidi
Skilloot
Skin
Skitwash
Skockuck
Skokomish
Skookumchuk
Skowkale
Skull Valley
Skuppah
Skway
Skykomish
Slave
Sleetmute
Sliammon
Smallon
Small Robes
Smith River
Smohallah
Snagua
Snake
Snoqualmoo
Snowqualmu
Snuneymuxw
Soacatino

Soboda
Socorro
Soda Creek
Sokaogan
Soke
Sokoki
So-kulk
Solomon
Songhee
Songish
Sonoma
Sooke
Soque
Sorcier
Sotequa
Sothoues
Souchitiomi
Souriquois
South Bentick
South Fork
Southeastern
Cherokee
Southern Paiute
Southern Ute
Southern Valley
Yokuts
Southhampton
Sovzhnaknek
Spallumcheen
Specum
Spirit Lake Sioux
Split Lake
Spokan
Spplam
Spuzzum
Squ'ay
Squam
Squamish
Squaxin
Squaxin Island
Squomsquot
St Croix
Stehtsasamish
St Francis/Skokoki
St Francois
St George

St Helena
St Johns
St Lawrence Island
St Michael
St Paul
St Regis
St Theresa Point
Staitan
Stalo
Standing Buffalo
Dakota
Standing Rock Sioux
Stanjikoming
Star
Star Blanket
Stebbins
Steilacoom
Stevens
Stewart Washoe
Stewarts Point
Stikeen
Stillaquamish
Sto:Lo
Stockbridge
Stockridge-Munsee
Stone
Stoney
Stoney Point
Stono
Stony River
Straits
Sturgeon Lake
Sucker Creek
Sugar Bowl
Sugeree
Suiattle
Suislawan
Sukininmiut
Sulpher Bank
Sumas
Summcamy's
Summerville
Summit Lake
Sunchild
Supai
Suquache

Suquamish
Susanville
Susquehanna
Susquehannock
Surruque
Sutaio
Sutslmc
Swallah
Swampy Creek
Swan Lake
Sweet Mouth
Sweetgrass
Swift Creek
Swinomish
Sycuan
Table Bluff
Table Mountain
Tabeguache
Tacatacura
Tache
Tacibaga
Tacusas
Taensa
Tafacanca
Tagish
Tahagmiut
Tahnuemuh
Tahitan
Tahtan
Tahupa
Taidnapam
Taino
Takamiut
Takelma
Takotna
Taku river
Talaje
Talakamish
Talapenches
Talapo
Talax
Taliyumc
Tall
Tallcree
Tallissee
Talmuchasi

Taltushluntude
Tamathli
Tamescameng
Tamoroa
Tanacross
Tanaina
Tanana
Tanawas
Taneks haya
Tangeboas
Tanoan
Taos
Tapala
Taposa
Tapoussas
Tarahas
Tarahunara
Tarascan
Taskarorahaka
Taskigi
Taskikis
Tasse
Tatasi
Tataviam
Tatitlek
Tawakomie
Tawakoni
Tawasa
Tawehash
Tazlina
Tchannus
Tchinook
Tchulhutt
Tchulwhyook
Tchunn
Tekesta
Tocopa
Te'mexw
Tee-Hit-Ton
Teet
Tegesta
Tehah Nahma
Tehatchapi
Tehoanoughroonaw
Tehome

Teitton
Tejas
Tekesta
Tekinago
Telida
Teller
Temagami
Te'mexw
Te-moak
Temuno
Tenawa Widyunuu
Tenino
Tennuth Ketchin
Tentoucha
Teoux
Tepa
Tepehuan
Tesgi Canyon
Teskesta-Tiamo
Teslin
Tesuque
Tete de Brule'
Tetlin
Teton
Teton Lakota
Tewa
Texas
Teyosta
The Wet'suwet'en
Thins
Thlingchadinne
Thlopthlocco
Thomez
Thompson
Three Affliated
Thunderchild
Tia
Tiakluit
Tiaoux
Tichenos
Tidewater
Tidu
Tierra del Sol
Tigua
Tillamook

Timba-Sha
Timiquan
Timiskaming
Timucua
Tinde
Tionontati
Tiowitsis
Tipai
Tipsoe Tyee
Tiwa
Tlalam
Tlatlasikwala
Tl'etinqox-t'in
Tlingit
Tloohoose
Tlo-o-qui-aht
Tlowitsis
Tlowitsis-Mumtagila
Toa
Toannois
Tobacco
Tobacco Plains
Tobique
Tocabago
Tocobagan
Tocoaya
Togagamiut
Togiak
Tohome
Tohono O'odham
Tolowa
Tokpafka
Toksook Bay
Tolomato
Tolowa
Tomeas
Tomez
Tomkas
Tompiro
Tongass
Tonguah
Tongva
Tonica
Tonkawa
Tonowanda

Tonto Apache
Tookabatchas
Toosey
Tootinaowaziibeeng
Topachula
Topingas
Toquaht
Torimas
Torres Martinez
Tortuga
Tosawi
Totonacs
Towa
Towiache
Towila
Tribe of the Sells
Trinidad
Trinity Wintun
Tsa Keh
Tsalagi
Tsanchifin
Tsankupi
Tsartlip
Tsawatenok
Tsawathineuk
Tsawout
Tsawwassen
Tsay Keh
Tsay-Keh-Dene
Tseil-wamuth
Tsekani
Tselona
Tseshaht
Tsetsaut
Tsetsehestehese
Tsetseu
Tseycum
Ts'ilhqot'in
Tsiljqot'in
Tsimshian
Tsitsistas
Tskwaylazw
Tsleil-Waututh
Tsnungwe
Tsoo-yess

Tsoya'ha
Tsqescen
Tsu T'ina
Tualatin
Tubatulabal
Tufulo
Tugalo
Tukabahchee
Tukaduka
Tukuarika
Tulal
Tulalip
Tulare
Tule
Tuluksak
Tunahe
Tunica
Tunica-Biloxi
Tuntutliak
Tununak
Tunxis
Tuolumme
Tupiqui
Turtle Mountain
Tusatulabal
Tuscarora
Tuscola
Tuskegee
Tutchone
Tutelo
Tutora
Tutuni
Twana
Twatna
Twenty-Nine Palms
Twightwee
Twin Hills
Two Kettles
Tyandega
Tyge Valley
Ty-hes
Tyone Martinez
Tyorek
Tyigh
Tza Tinne

U'mista
Uashat Mak Mani-
Utenam
Ucachile
Ucheam
Uchee
Uchusklesaht
Ucluelet
Uculegue
Ugashik
Uintah
Ukakhpakht
Ulibahali
Ulkatcho
Umatilla
U'mista
Umkumiute
Umpqua
Unalachtigo
Unalakleet
Unaligmiut
Unallapa
Unama'ki
Unami
Uncas
Uncompahgre
Unga
Union Bar
Unitah
United Auburn
United Houma
United Keetoowah
United Shawnee
Unkchaug
Upper Creek
Upper Kiskapo
Upper Lake
Upper Mataponi
Upper Nicola
Upper Similkameen
Upper Sioux
Upper Skagit
Upper Yanklonai
Urebures
Uscamu

Usheree
Utalapotoque
Utawawas
Utayne
Ute
Ute Mountain
Utina
Utinahica
Utu Utu Gwaitu
Utukokmiut
Utraca
Utsushuat
Uxmal
Uzita
Venetie
Vermillion Bay
Viejas
Village des Hurons
Waatch Village
Wabanaki
Wabash
Wabasseemoong
Wabauskang
Wabigoon
Waccamaw
Waccamaw-Souian
Waco
Wagmatcook
Wagmatcookewey
Wahkiakim
Wahnapitae
Wahpakoota
Wahpeton
Wahu
Wahunsonacock
Wailaki
Wainwright Native
Wakashan
Wakinyan
Wakokai
Wakpa
Walapai
Wales Native
Walhominies
Walker River

Walla Walla
Wallamotkin
Walpi
Walpole Island
Walua
Wamanus
Wampano
Wampanoag
Wanabaki
Wanapum
Wando
Wanniah
Wapekeka
Wapeton
Wapingeis
Wappinger
Wappo
War Lake
Warao
Warm Springs
Warroad Chippewa
Warraskoyak
Wasagamack
Wasco
Wascopum
Washa
Washagamis Bay
Washepoo
Washoah
Washoe
Washone
Waskagamish
Waskalatchat
Wasoco
Wasses
Waswanipi
Waterbee
Waterhen
Waterhen Lake
Watlala
WaukeshanWaxhaw
Wauyukma
Wauzhushk
Wawakapewin
Wawyachtonoc

Waxhaw
Wayanouk
Waycobah
Waywayseecappo
Wazhazhe
We Wai Hun
We Wai Kai
Wea
Weanoc
Weapemene
Weapememeoc
Weaponeiok
Webequie
Wecquaesgeek
Weeden Island
Weeminuche
Weenatouchee
Weetumkee
Wells
Wells Indian Colony
Wemindji
Wenachee
Wenatchi
Wendat-Huron
Wendover
Wenrohronon
Weott
Wesley
Wesort
West Main Cree
West Moberly
Westbank
Westbank First
Western Shoshone
Western Woods Cree
Westo
Wet'suwet'en
Wewenock
Weymontachie
Whapmagoostui
Whee Y Kum
Whilkut
Whispering Pines
White Bear
White Earth

White Mesa
White River Utes.
White Mountain
Apache
Whitecap Dakota/
Sioux
Whitefish Bay
Whitefish Lake
White River
Whitesand
Whitwater Lake
Whuaquum
Whymatmagh
Wichita
Wick-ram
Widdah
Wikwemikong
Williams Lake
Willopah
Wilono
Wiwohlka
Wimbee
Wimbre
Wind River Arapahoe
Wind River Shoshone
Wind
Winnebago
Winnefelly
Winnemucca
Wintoon
Wintu
Wiogufki
Wiscasset
Wisconsin
Wishmai
Wishram
Witchekekan Lake
Wichita
Wiwohka
Wiyok
Woccon
Wolaistoquyik
Wolf Lake
Wolinak
Wood Mountain

Woodbridge
Woodfords Washoe
Woodland
Woodstock
Wowapi Oti Kin
Wukchunmi
Wunnumin
Wusita
Wuskwi Sipihk
Wyam
WyanPatte
Wyiot
Wylackie
Wynochee
Wyogtami
Wyum
Xatalalano
Xatsu'll
Xeni Gwet'in
Yagua
Yaha
Yahi
Yahooskin
Yakama Cowlitz
Yakima
Yankton Sioux
Yanktonai
Yaminahua
Yamhill
Yampah
Yamparika
Yana
Yamhill
Yampah
Yankton Sioux
Yakonan
Yaminahu
Yanktonai
Yanomamo
Yaocomaco
Yanomamo
Yataches
Yatasi
Yaqui
Yellowquill

Yemassee
Yeopim
Yerington
Yewkaltas
Yfulo
Yaquina
Yavapai
Ybitoopas
Yea Patano
Yekooche
Yellowknife
Yoa
Yokayo
Yscanis
Yokotc
Yokut
Yomba
Yonkalla
York Factory
Youghiogheny
Young Chippewyan
Ysa
Yucanis
Yufera
Yui
Yuima
Yuki
Ysleta Del Sur Pueblo
Yuchi
Yuma
Yuman
Yumsai
Yuki
Yuohulo
Yupik
Yurok
Yustaga
Zaaging
Zapotec
Zia
Zia Pueblo
Zuni

EPILOGUE

Until your last day on earth
never quit wondering about a
new horizon
Never quit writing
Never quit dreaming
Never quit learning
Never quit thinking
Never quit exploring